D1644742

An author of more than nin[...]
adults, with more than seventy-five for Mills & Boon,
Janice Kay Johnson writes about love and family and
pens books of gripping romantic suspense. A *USA TODAY*
bestselling author and an eight-time finalist for the
Romance Writers of America *RITA*® Award, she won a
RITA® Award in 2008. A former librarian, Janice raised
two daughters in a small town north of Seattle, Washington.

Karen Whiddon started weaving fanciful tales for her
younger brothers at the age of eleven. Amid the gorgeous
Catskill Mountains, then the majestic Rocky Mountains,
she fuelled her imagination with the natural beauty
surrounding her. Karen now lives in north Texas, writes
full-time and volunteers for a boxer dog rescue. She shares
her life with her hero of a husband and four to five dogs,
depending on if she is fostering. You can email Karen at
kwhiddon1@aol.com. Fans can also check out her website,
karenwhiddon.com

CRIME SCENE CONNECTION

JANICE KAY JOHNSON

SAVED BY THE TEXAS COWBOY

KAREN WHIDDON

MILLS & BOON

First Published in Great Britain 2023
by Mills & Boon, an imprint of HarperCollins*Publishers* Ltd
1 London Bridge Street, London, SE1 9GF

www.harpercollins.co.uk

HarperCollins*Publishers*
Macken House, 39/40 Mayor Street Upper,
Dublin 1, D01 C9W8, Ireland

Crime Scene Connection © 2023 Janice Kay Johnson
Saved by the Texas Cowboy © 2023 Karen Whiddon

ISBN: 978-0-263-30723-8

0423

This book is produced from independently certified FSC™ paper
to ensure responsible forest management.

For more information visit: www.harpercollins.co.uk/green

Printed and Bound in the UK using 100% Renewable Electricity at
CPI Group (UK) Ltd, Croydon, CR0 4YY

CRIME SCENE
CONNECTION

JANICE KAY JOHNSON

Chapter One

Lieutenant Matthew Reinert sat behind the wheel of his department-issued SUV and frowned at an ordinary rambler halfway up the block from where he'd parked. In the past twenty minutes, the mild concern that had brought him here had morphed into alarm.

Illegal drugs were a chronic problem in his jurisdiction, just as they were in every decent-sized town in the country. Fentanyl had taken its toll, but most recently they'd been seeing overdoses from exceptionally pure, strong drugs. A new organization had moved into the northeast of Washington State, supplying meth, cocaine, oxycodone and heroin. What made these new traffickers different was the level of brutality they displayed toward competitors and used to punish dealers who had annoyed their employers. The gruesome deaths dealt as warnings weren't the norm in a city with a fairly low homicide rate.

Spokane PD had led the investigation until rumor had it that the traffickers had moved to the Spokane suburb that was Matthew's jurisdiction. Then came the tip from an occasional confidential informant, giving an address: the house Matthew was currently observing.

Matthew, as head of the major crimes division, wouldn't normally have been involved, but stories and excitement had flown. Hard *not* to hear the talk. Vice was pumped. SWAT was on the alert. Mike Kinney, deputy attorney general, had been nagging for Vice to get a move on. No doubt, he was ecstatic at what these arrests would do for his chance of promotion.

Just this morning, Matthew had been talking to the county deputy who'd led the combined city-county SWAT team. Their conversation had primarily centered on a separate joint investigation, but Brad Hargrave had complained about the pressure for him to request a warrant on the drug house.

"They aren't giving me anything!" he'd exclaimed. "And it's not my damn investigation. It's your Vice cops who should be on it."

"Not mine," Matthew had countered. "Tell you what, though. I'll see what I can find out."

Hargrave had thanked him fervently.

A quick stop by Vice detective Phil Banuelos's desk had left Matthew uneasy. Phil'd tried not to show it, but he hadn't been thrilled to see Matthew.

Phil had played the recording of the tip for him. "Guy's a low-level drug dealer," he'd said with a shrug. "Mostly reliable. He may have reason to resent this new act in town."

They'd been looking into the tip, but didn't have much yet except a couple of reports of sketchy-looking guys coming and going from the house in question, he'd admitted. "We don't really even have eyes on the house."

So how had the rumors and excitement blown up?

Impulse had brought Matthew here, detouring after another stop to look at the supposed drug house. Immediately incredulous, he'd done some online research and talked to a couple of neighbors. What he'd learned had made this mess potentially *his* business after all.

It was true that in your typical American city, drug traffickers didn't hole up in walled compounds. They hid in plain sight. He couldn't deny that this was the right kind of neighborhood, one that had slid downhill for years until recent signs of recovery. It still consisted mostly of rentals and a few vacant houses; from police reports, he knew it to be a hotbed of petty crime and domestic violence. Plenty of neighbors wouldn't complain even if they guessed traffickers did their business right next door.

That said…this particular house had been newly painted. The lawn had been mowed in the past day or two. There was a flower bed in front of the porch, for God's sake! Riotous flowering baskets hung from brackets to each side of the garage and from the beam supporting the roof of that front porch.

Matthew had yet to meet anyone even peripherally involved in the drug trade who hung flower baskets, far less fertilized them on a regular schedule.

He'd knocked on a few doors, even though he'd known he was stepping on toes. At this point, he didn't care.

The couple next door had looked astonished at his questions and insisted they hadn't seen any man there. Another less voluble neighbor across the street had appeared annoyed at being bothered but said, "She works for the newspaper. That's what someone told me."

Uh-huh.

Phil had said he'd been told it was "unclear" who owned the house, which had been a long-time rental. It hadn't taken Matthew more than a few minutes to learn that the house had sold a year ago to Alexa B. Adams, who held a mortgage on it from a local bank. There was no justification for confusion.

And Matthew knew that name.

Alexa Adams didn't just "work" for the *Tribune*. She was an investigative journalist, and a good one. A pit bull. Matthew had seen her byline in the newspaper often enough. Worse, he'd heard her name spat in disgust and even hate around the police station these past couple of months. Ms. Adams hadn't made any friends within the law enforcement community when she'd set out to identify problem officers, city and county, and to ask hard questions on why they hadn't been held accountable for questionable activities and outright breaking the law.

Wanting to believe this whole thing would die a natural death without him having to stick his nose in, Matthew decided he'd seen enough. He changed his mind when a car came around the corner and started in his direction. The sedan turned into the driveway of Ms. Adams's house. The driver parked and hopped out.

He lifted binoculars and watched as she took what was probably a laptop and file case out of her car and started for the porch, pausing to bend over and pick up the rubber-banded newspaper he'd seen being tossed onto her driveway earlier. Up to the porch and an instant later she disappeared inside. Presumably, she meant to go out again this afternoon or evening.

Lowering the binoculars, he rolled his shoulders to release tension. She was younger-looking than he'd expected, slight of build, and pretty, all of which was irrelevant. What she did took brains, determination and the kind of empathy that convinced reluctant people to open up to her. Not muscle.

And more power to her.

Knowing he needed to get back to the station and start figuring out who was responsible for stirring the pot, he still didn't reach for the ignition. He gave himself a minute to brood.

Given who the homeowner was and how deep the dislike for her went among a certain segment of police officers, he had to assume this whole thing had been aimed straight at the journalist, the goal to humiliate and frighten her. Even get her killed if the operation went south. Or maybe the instigator had never believed the raid would actually happen, just hoped word would reach her. The threat wasn't subtle.

If this fiasco turned out to have anything to do with that department-wide anger, those ruffled by her investigation could quit worrying about her and worry about *him* instead. Heads would roll. He should hand this to Internal Affairs, but he wasn't impressed with how easy they'd been on officers who *had* committed an offense. If an assault—even one disguised as an "oh oops SWAT raid"—was made on Ms. Adams, then he'd feel free to act, up to and including cuffing and charging members of his own department.

He had to ask himself how many officers had been involved in this setup. He'd absolve DA Kinney of any active role; ambition was Kinney's problem. But everyone else, including Vice detective Phil Banuelos who'd taken the tip and opened the investigation, had to be considered suspect.

Matthew grunted and started the engine.

Maybe he should leave Ms. Adams an anonymous tip, he thought with dark humor, but knew he couldn't.

UNEASINESS CRAWLED UP Alexa's spine as she slowed in approach to the park where she had promised to meet a man who'd called out of the blue. He'd claimed to be a confidential informant for the police department.

"I've given them some good tips," he'd said in a gravelly voice that made her think he was a long-time smoker.

"Thing is, I seen some of 'em doing shi—I mean stuff I don't like. There're cops who take what they want from girls who work the streets, if you know what I mean. That don't seem right to me."

It didn't seem right to Alexa, either. What's more, what he was apparently willing to talk about fit right in with her investigation of dirty cops right here in this small city.

The agreed meet was to happen at this downtown park that took up only a block but had a rose garden she admired, paths and some old maple and even cedar trees. Picnic tables were tucked in here and there, along with wrought-iron benches. Two sides were bounded by streets especially busy in the evenings since this was where bars, nightclubs and restaurants thrived.

Leaving home, she'd felt comfortable about the location, even with the approach of dusk. She couldn't be the investigator she was without taking calculated risks, which included sitting down with strangers who called because they'd read her articles and columns and decided to trust her with information. Plenty of them, from drug dealers to cops, didn't want to risk being seen with her.

Now, the streetlights starting to hum into life, Alexa was bothered to realize that the park itself looked awfully dark. She backed into a spot at the curb, got out and eyed the deeper darkness lurking between those big trees and behind dense rhododendron shrubs. For the first time, she wondered how many drug deals went down in the park, and especially how safe it was for a woman to stroll one of these paths at night.

Huh. Maybe tomorrow she'd do some research and find out.

People crowded the sidewalk on the opposite side of the street, enjoying the nightlife, greeting friends, going in and coming out of clubs and restaurants. Alexa eyed a couple of women, wearing especially skimpy attire, who stood at the far corner calling out to passing cars. Those almost had to be some of the "girls" her tipster had been talking about.

Her head turned. On this side of the street, what looked like a couple of older men sat in deep conversation on a bench at a bus stop. Otherwise…she was alone.

He'd promised, "I'll find you."

Well, she wasn't about to wander down one of those paths looking for him. *Circle the park*, she decided. *Stay on the sidewalk*. It was one block, that's all. *Keep an eye out*.

Her shoulders stiff, nerves prickling at the back of her neck, she started walking. Three-quarters of a block north, turn the corner. A couple who looked as if they'd had a few too many drinks was getting into a shiny, jacked-up pickup. They didn't even notice her. One restaurant halfway down the block was open, but otherwise traffic on this cross street had become close to nonexistent. Maybe she didn't want to circle the backside of the park. She'd just turn around when she got to the corner—

A vehicle door opened right behind her. She didn't have time to turn before a hand slapped over her face and a beefy arm wrapped around her middle. Alexa fought, kicking hard enough that her assailant swore and had to twist. He carried her only a couple of feet before slamming her down into the bed of a pickup. Her cheekbone hurt where it skidded on cold, ridged metal. The guy who'd grabbed her must have jumped up with her, because he drilled a painful amount of weight into her back with his knee.

Even as she tried to sink her teeth into a fleshy part of his hand, a bounce told her someone else had leaped into the truck bed with them. Two of them. Oh God, they were kidnapping her.

A voice said, "Do it."

Whatever hit her head *hurt* and she went limp.

ALEXA SURFACED WHEN the tailgate clanged. Hands dragged her out. Alexa grabbed for purchase with her fingers and found none. She couldn't scream; tape covered her mouth. Hands groped and ripped at her clothing.

They were stripping her, she realized in new panic. She saw her chinos fly upward.

Only a strangled sound escaped her before once again a big hand clamped over her face-. Her brief glimpse had revealed…not a face, no, only glittering eyes looking through holes in a fleece mask. He wore all black.

"Scrawny thing," one of them muttered. "Couldn't tell from—"

From? The photo above her column and on the website? If so, this wasn't random.

Somehow she freed an arm and got a handful of what felt like a windbreaker. *He* said a vicious word and tried to break her hold, twisting away. Black T-shirt beneath the windbreaker, Alexa saw that. Something fell out of his pocket and hit what had to be pavement with a tinny sound. One of the men backhanded her for her trouble and she fell to her knees. Just before that gloved hand snatched up the dropped object, she saw it from a watering eye. She *knew* that shape. It was a Wilden City PD officer's badge.

She kept fighting. Giving up wasn't in her nature. If they were determined to rape her, she probably couldn't stop them, but she wouldn't make it easy. She writhed, tried to scramble away, but got nowhere. Next thing she knew, she was facedown on asphalt as they tied her hands behind her back then her kicking feet at the ankles.

"Here," she heard one of them growl, but couldn't tell what was happening until one of the men bent over her.

"Think about what could have happened. This is your only warning," he snarled. "Back off, or you'll be sorry."

She hunched away from him, tried to stand but got only as far as her knees before she heard the powerful engine of the pickup rev to life and the crunch of gravel.

If not for the tape covering her mouth, her teeth might have been chattering.

Alexa found herself alone in darkness complete enough her eyes hadn't adjusted. When she tried to stand, she discovered she'd been tied to something. Her neck hurt so much, turning her head was hard, but she dimly saw a familiar shape. Her nose confirmed her guess. It was a dumpster. The men had left her in an alley, tied out like bait for a predator.

She blinked until she became aware of indistinct light coming from the end of the alley she could see. A couple of dim bulbs at what were probably back doors into businesses let her view the pale gleam of her own body.

Something primal rose in her until she realized she still wore a bra and panties. A sob trapped in her throat.

If she'd been able to scream, would anyone hear and come? Did she *want* anyone to come and see her like this?

She began frantically wrenching at the cords biting into her wrists.

MATTHEW HAD JUST backed out of the parking space behind the steak house where he'd met his brother for dinner when his phone rang.

"Lieutenant?" a terse male voice said. "This is Officer Gregory. There's something you need to see."

What he needed to see, apparently, was a nearly nude

woman, tied in an alley, with a piece of paper pinned to her bra that said, *Lieutenant Reinert, you should have been smart and stayed out of it.*

What in *hell*?

His mood wasn't fabulous after a day spent fruitlessly pursuing any lead at all to explain the push for a SWAT raid on Alexa Adams's house, eating up time he could ill afford from the rest of his job. Now, glad his brother had driven himself and had already left for home, Matthew rocketed out of the small lot and exceeded speed limits the five blocks to downtown. He saw lights flashing behind the busiest strip for nightlife the city of Wilden could boast. A quick jog and he turned into the alley, braking hard behind a squad car and jumping out. Another unit had responded, as well, having turned in from the other end of the alley so that it was completely blocked.

He was almost past the nearest squad car when he saw, pinned in two sets of headlights, a crouched woman, wearing only skimpy panties and bra, holding herself in a tight ball, her head lifted, her eyes both defiant and terrified.

He recognized her right away. This was the same woman who fertilized the hanging baskets and the flower bed in front of the porch of her home to coax those brilliant blooms to life.

A snicker from one of two uniformed officers, seemingly doing nothing but watching from near the front bumper of their car, had him stopping and turning. "Who was that?" he snapped.

"Ah…" He recognized them, took in the names on their chests. "You're laughing at a woman who has been brutalized?"

"They didn't tell you who she is?" one of them—Spiers—said. "It's that Adams woman. What goes around comes around."

"I'll be writing you up," Matthew said coldly before jogging the last few feet.

He took in the clothesline tied to a bar on the dumpster, one end cut, and noted pieces of more cut clothesline lying on the pavement. Seeing the inflamed strip of skin across her face where tape must have been ripped off, he swallowed his curses as he shrugged out of his leather bomber jacket and crouched in front of Alexa Adams. Why hadn't somebody already covered her?

He winced at her bruised, bloody wrists, not surprised that she'd fought to free herself.

"Let's get this on you," he said gently, wrapping the jacket around her. When her glassy gaze almost focused on him, he guided a hand into the arm of the sheepskin-lined coat then, a moment later, the second one.

He pretended to himself that he wasn't seeing her slender, even delicate, body, almost completely bared. Fury rose in him as he took in the swelling and discoloration already evident on her face. One eye was barely a slit. Had she been raped?

He called, "Do we have medics en route?"

"Can't be more than a minute away," said the officer holding a box cutter he'd just used to cut her free. Gregory, who'd called Matthew. His tone, at least, was calm and professional. "My partner is bringing something to cover her up."

Should have done that first, in Matthew's opinion, especially given the audience.

Chapter Two

Even as Matthew started to tug the zipper upward, his gaze caught on typed print on a torn sheet of white paper. Pinned to a bra as delicate as the subtle curves beneath.

Gregory'd had it word for word.

Lieutenant Reinert, you should have been smart and stayed out of it.

Had someone really believed that SWAT would swallow the tasty bait without questioning it? If so, that someone blamed him for ruining the plan. They'd found another way to scare Ms. Adams. Strip her of her dignity.

He zipped the bomber jacket closed right over the note. Less chance of messing up prints if they removed it at the hospital—although he knew quite well there wouldn't be any.

Aware another officer clutching a space blanket had come to a stop a few feet behind her, Matthew stayed where he was, crouched in front of Ms. Adams.

"I'm Lieutenant Matthew Reinert. I head our major crimes division. Can you tell me what happened?"

"I…" She tried to blink. A tear leaked from one eye. "Supposed to meet someone. Grabbed. Drove me here. Took off my clothes. Tied me up."

"Were you raped?" he asked bluntly.

She swallowed. "No."

That was a miracle, since she'd been left seminaked and trussed like a goose ready to go in the oven. Any kind of scum could have come upon her, and she wouldn't even have been able to scream.

"Who found you?" he asked.

She'd let her gaze drop, but now lifted it to his face again. "Nobody," she whispered. "There were two of them. One must have called 9-1-1. The siren and flashing lights and those headlights. Practically right away."

Matthew couldn't remember ever being angrier. Still, he fought to keep his voice gentle. "They took your clothes?"

"I think they might be in the dumpster."

Those sons of— It was all he could do not to say it out loud.

An ambulance was now backing into the alley.

"We need to take you to the hospital."

She grabbed his arm and started to stand. "Don't want to go. Not hurt that bad."

With firm hands, he settled her back on her butt. "You have to be checked out. You probably have a concussion. I'll bet your vision is blurry. There's a lot of swelling on your face."

"Ice—"

"Is in your near future," he agreed, "starting at the ER. This isn't negotiable."

A laugh that sounded scathing almost reassured him. "Got to cover your asses, I suppose."

"Maybe so," he admitted. "Do you know who these men were?"

Quite a crowd stood around them now, but as far as he was concerned, the two of them were alone in a bubble.

"Police officers," she said bitterly. Now her eyes were fixed on his belt. "Carrying the same badge *you* wear."

LYING IN THE ER cubicle, Alexa was embarrassed to realize that Lieutenant Reinert had held her hand in a warm clasp until the gurney had been pushed into the back of the ambulance. Worse yet, she'd clung to him. Apparently, his kindness had gotten to her.

No, it was more than that. He had…a strong face. A face she might have considered handsome under wildly different circumstances. Cheekbones were prominent, his jaw stubborn and shadowed by dark evening stubble, his eyes blue, or maybe gray. She couldn't tell, and was well aware a sexy face meant nothing about his character. Really, she'd been evaluating him in the hope of visible proof that he was trustworthy, because right at that moment she'd needed him.

He'd been grim, too, though. He'd said he would see her at the hospital, but had stayed behind when the ambulance pulled out.

It took time for a doctor to exam her, order a CT scan, decide she didn't need X-rays, and turn her over to a nurse to have her multiple abrasions cleaned. Yes, once the scan was done, she got to hold ice bags to some of the sorest places.

In the midst of all that, Alexa remembered that her phone and car keys had been in the pocket of her chinos. Would someone have retrieved her clothes, however disgusting they were? Think to bring them to her?

All she wanted was to go home, climb into bed and pull the covers over her head. She'd have a chance to quit shaking, to recover her inner, hard-assed self. The one that did battle every day with the forces of cowardice and bureaucracy determined to keep her from getting her hands on the records of the two dozen law enforcement officers she was hunting as if they were foxes and she wore a red coat.

Come morning, her temper would replace this sense of humiliation, even shame, the fear because she'd been so vulnerable. Then she'd make them all sorry. But *getting* home—

"Hey."

She turned her head to see who had slipped around the curtain, although she had no doubt from that deep, calm voice who it would be.

The lieutenant, tall and broad-shouldered, held a paper bag in his hand. His keen gaze met hers. Gray eyes, she realized. The color of sharp-edged steel.

"Your clothes," he said. "We need to hold onto them for the moment. Once you get them back, you'll want to add some bleach to the wash."

Probably, she'd made a face because he smiled crookedly. "I have your phone and keys, too. I did wipe those off. Is your car downtown?"

"Yes," she croaked. "Not that far from where I was dumped, I suspect."

"Ah." He pulled a chair up close to the narrow bed and sat down. "Do you feel well enough to tell me what happened in a little more detail?"

She'd already known that Matthew Reinert was in charge of the major crimes division in the city PD. Naturally suspicious, she'd researched him with extra care because of the authority he wielded, but she hadn't come up with so much as a hint that he was dirty or less than competent. In fact, the detectives who worked under him were clean, as far as she could tell.

"Was supposed to meet someone in the park," she said. Ugh. Her lips must be swollen, making enunciating difficult.

"Who?"

She wished she felt a little less rattled. Should she tell him? Why not? She'd been led into an ambush.

"He said his name is Jim Berkey."

Lieutenant Reinert's expression changed. He knew that name and didn't like hearing it in this context—but she knew he wouldn't tell her what he was thinking. Why would he when he was a cop, too?

After all, most cops were prepared to defend their colleagues to the death, whatever their personal integrity and sense of honor.

DAMN. MATTHEW COULDN'T possibly tell her about Berkey's original tip and the cascade of consequences that, thankfully, had been cut off. If he did, he'd be fired, no question. The time might come, but not yet. If he lost his job, she'd lose her protector, whether she saw him that way or not.

"Did you record the conversation?" he asked.

Her eyes narrowed. "That name means something to you."

"It does. I think I'd recognize his voice if this really was him. If so, we might be able to put our hands on him."

She thought that over but finally nodded. "I can let you hear it."

"Good. I'm told you aren't being admitted. The nurse I spoke to is going to rustle up a set of scrubs for you to wear home. I'll take you, unless you've already called a friend or family member to pick you up."

"No." She looked away again. "I...hadn't gotten so far as thinking about how I'd get home. I didn't even know if you'd find my keys and phone. What I'd appreciate is a ride to my car."

He frowned. "Didn't the doctor suggest you might have a concussion?"

She didn't want to answer. Her expression became mulish.

"Here's the deal. I'll drive you home. If you don't have someone you'd rather call, I'll take you back to pick up your car in the morning."

"Now that I have my phone, I can call someone right now—"

Matthew shook his head. "I'd have followed you home no matter what. I want to hear the recording as soon as possible, and do a security check on your house. This attack was very personal. We need to evaluate how safe you are at home."

Seeing the appalled look on her face, he was almost sorry he'd said that—but he couldn't leave her with any illusions. Apparently, she lived alone. That made her vulnerable. Maybe nothing more would happen—but if her reputation was accurate, this woman wasn't going to heed the warning. If she went on the attack again, as he fully expected, her enemies would up the ante.

"Yes. Okay," she said after a minute. "Thank you."

The nurse popped her head in just then and handed over what she cheerfully described as the latest style in scrubs. He kind of doubted the faded blue pants and top qualified, but Ms. Adams accepted them gratefully. The nurse added a pair of rubber flip-flops that she said were from the lost and found box, no need to return them.

Matthew stepped out to let Alexa get dressed. Once she was ready, he carried the bag with her clothes, letting her clutch her phone and keys. She looked kind of cute in the scrubs, but wouldn't want to hear that from him. The flip-flops were too big and slapped loudly with every step, but she seemed to be steady on her feet.

Fortunately, the walk was short, since he'd parked in one of the slots right outside the ER entrance saved for law enforcement. That she let him help her into the passenger seat of his SUV mildly surprised him. Her cheeks might have flushed under the bright lighting, but he suspected that was from frustration and anger rather than any shyness.

"My handbag is in my car," she said suddenly, just as he fired up the engine.

"We can swing by and grab it." If her assailants hadn't already done that. If so—he hoped she didn't carry a spare house key in her bag.

She directed him to her car, which he recognized from yesterday, and gave him her keys. The cloth bag was on the floor, not quite hidden but not obviously in sight, either. He checked both visors and found what had to be the remote to open her garage door, and took that, too. He locked the door again and took her bag to his SUV.

With the overhead light still on, she immediately spotted the remote. "Oh, thank goodness you thought of that!" She found her wallet and opened it. "Everything seems to be here."

"Extra house key?" he asked.

"I don't carry one."

Her place wasn't more than a fifteen-minute drive. They were halfway there when she spoke up. "How do you know where you're going?"

"Looked up your address." He wasn't about to admit having done surveillance on her house yesterday. If neighbors told her a cop had been asking questions, he'd hope they didn't remember his name or describe him too accurately.

"Oh." In the flickering light of streetlamps, he saw her visibly relax.

He had to wonder why she hadn't wanted a friend with her. Did she not have a man in her life she'd trust to hold her? If so, they hadn't progressed to living together, not if the neighbors were to be believed.

Well, it wasn't as if she'd let herself cry in front of *him*. He'd seen loathing when her gaze fixed on his badge. Chances were, she wasn't ready to distinguish between an honest cop and a dirty one. They all wore that same badge, after all.

And *that* got him speculating on whether she had a personal reason for her current crusade. An ugly experience with a cop pushing the boundaries to intimidate? A relative or former boyfriend who wore a uniform and had a short temper?

He couldn't ask her tonight, that was for sure.

She had been smart enough to leave on her front porch light and a living room light that spilled out the big window. Matthew parked in her driveway, got out and circled to the passenger side just in time to catch her as she started to topple out.

"Whoa!" he exclaimed, setting her on her feet. "You don't need any more scrapes or bruises tonight."

"It's these flip-flops," she mumbled, carefully separating herself from him.

He walked her up onto the porch with one hand hovering behind her. She carried herself stiffly but didn't tell him to back off.

He hadn't paid attention yesterday, but now shook his head as she unlocked the door. "We need to replace the front door."

She turned sharply. "What?"

"Better to have solid doors."

"I thought it was pretty when I bought the house."

"It is pretty," he conceded. "It's just—" He didn't have to finish.

She sighed. "One tap and an intruder could reach the dead bolt and knob."

"Exactly."

He hesitated. "I could replace it for you tomorrow. Pick up the door at whatever store in town you say, too."

Now she stared at him, suspicion in hazel eyes streaked with some gold. "Why would you do that?"

Guilt because he *should* have issued a warning yesterday when he'd realized someone in his own damn department was out to get her? Of course, he couldn't say that, and knew there was more to this impulse anyway.

"Call it an apology, just in case you're right about your assailants being cops."

She gave serious thought to that then nodded sharply. "Fine. Thank you."

Matthew felt uncomfortable during the walk-through of her house. It felt…intimate, probably because he was so aware of her as a woman. The worst was her bedroom, naturally.

He advised her to get bars to lay in the tracks of her windows and sliding door in back. The door to the garage was steel and, he was mildly surprised, had a dead bolt that she admitted to rarely employing.

"I mean, they'd have to get into the garage first."

The side door into the garage was wood, but not in great shape. Matthew would have been able to splinter it open with one kick.

"As long as you keep the door into the house securely locked, we can probably put off replacing this one," he said reluctantly.

He thought she was relieved. Journalists probably made even less money than cops.

When they returned to the living room, he asked to hear the conversation with Jim Berkey, the one that had obviously been a setup.

She played it for him on her phone, then replayed it twice while he frowned and listened, his head tilted.

"I've never met this Berkey, but that sounds like the one message I heard. Can you send me the recording?"

Alexa debated but couldn't come up with a good reason not to do as he asked. A crime had been committed. Lieutenant Reinert *should* be investigating. However begrudging she felt, he seemed to be taking what had happened to her seriously.

He gave her his phone number, waited until a ding told him he'd received the phone recording, then said, "I'll pick you up in the morning and we can stop at the lumberyard on the way back."

"Can you really afford the time?" she asked doubtfully.

Matthew smiled. "I can." He hoped he could talk his brother into helping. The job would go a lot faster with two.

They set a time, she locked up behind him, and he walked to his SUV, noting those glorious flower baskets in the porch light.

THE HOT SHOWER felt fabulous, but she made it record-short, unhappy that, with the bathroom door closed, she couldn't hear anything beyond it…like breaking glass. She was painfully aware of being naked, remembering when they'd torn her clothes off and she'd feared rape. She had no doubt they'd gaped at her lying on the pavement wearing only bikini panties and a bra that was as skimpy. Her skin crawled even more at the idea of the responding police officers doing the same.

Had Matthew Reinert gaped, too?

What if those men weren't satisfied with their stunt and came back for her? Might they be mad that Lieutenant Reinert had driven her home himself?

Yes, she'd seen the note pinned to her bra. She'd waited to see if he'd volunteer an explanation for it. The grimness she'd seen on his face hadn't been all about her; some of it had had to do with the pointed message to him.

What should he have been smart enough to stay out of? Did it have anything to do with Jim Berkey?

She was exhausted and aching despite a hefty dose of ibuprofen, but decided she had to eat. Feeling exposed in the kitchen, she let down all the blinds first thing, although was then uneasily conscious she couldn't see if someone was slinking through her yard.

If she had her car, she thought she'd have driven straight to the nearest hardware store and bought the window bars the lieutenant had recommended.

Of course, they wouldn't come after her so soon, she told herself. They'd need to plan. She was probably safer tonight than she would be tomorrow night or the next or—

How comforting.

She made and gobbled a sandwich, left on her porch lights, front and back, as well as the light in the hall bathroom, and finally made her way to bed. After thinking for a minute, she grabbed a dining room chair and took it to her room, wedging it beneath the doorknob once the door was closed. Doing that was probably useless, but she felt slightly better when she actually climbed into bed, pulled the covers up…and didn't sleep.

Oh, they'd pay for this, Alexa vowed.

There'd been a recent rule change she knew damn well had been put into effect to frustrate her to the point she'd give up on her quest. Obviously, they thought they *could* make her give up. Thus tonight. Well, they'd soon find out how wrong they were.

The new rule, apparently borrowed from the cities of

Seattle and Everett in western Washington, said that if the same person or organization requested multiple records, the department would only work on one of those requests at a time. That meant the month to three months she'd wait for the first tranche of information she'd asked for turned into *years* when they were all lumped together. Especially when she demanded body or squad car camera footage, the delays were already unbelievable. And given that she was focusing on multiple officers, somebody, somewhere, thought they'd managed to tie up the process in knots she'd never untangle.

They were wrong about that, too, but—

Wait.

She rolled onto her back and looked up at the ceiling.

The city would expect her to sue. When she did, it would be a gimme. No, she couldn't prove she'd seen that badge, but the note addressed to Reinert had been a big mistake on their part. The threats they'd whispered to her made it clear it had been a targeted hit on a journalist who was investigating the police department. Oh yes, the you-know-what would hit the fan.

That meant she had them over a barrel.

What if she held the possibility of a lawsuit over the city and police department as a ruthless bargaining tool to compel them to hand over the records she'd requested? *All* the records? Now.

Oh yeah.

For the first time since those hands had grabbed her, Alexa felt herself…well, not relax, she never did that, but her tension transformed into energy with a purpose.

Alexa sat up in bed, turned on the lamp and looked around for her laptop. Her mind was working too feverishly for there to be any chance of sleep, so she'd make notes. Lay out her campaign now that she had a serious weapon in her hands.

She'd do some online research on local attorneys who might be willing to take on such a formidable opponent. Then, attorney at her side, she could lay her cards on the table.

They were all going to be deeply sorry when they realized they'd dealt her four aces.

Chapter Three

After she'd researched attorneys and had secured a midafternoon appointment with the one who struck her as the best bet, Alexa got dressed in expectation of Matthew's arrival. No, Lieutenant Reinert's. He had his own agenda. They weren't friends. She felt sure he wouldn't like her asking about the note that chided him for an unknown offense that clearly involved *her.*

When she heard his truck in the driveway, she hurried out, almost immediately shivering. March in eastern Washington was more winter than spring. She wouldn't be outside long enough to bother going back for a coat, though.

The guy who lived on one side of her seemed to spend an awful lot of time doing something to the engine of an old car sitting on cinder blocks instead of wheels. Today, a group of his buddies hung over the engine with him, beer cans in hand despite the early hour. A couple of them nodded when they eyed her. That was about as friendly as this neighborhood got.

On the other hand, she wasn't the most popular woman in town, so maybe she was the lone pariah on the block.

The lieutenant got out to greet her, but another man sat in the back seat of the extended cab pickup. Alexa decided her dismay was because the presence of someone else might keep her from confronting Reinert about what he knew.

But, damn it, if she got the labor to install a new door out of this, she wouldn't complain.

"Morning," the lieutenant said in that distinctive voice. "I brought my brother along."

Today he wore khaki cargo pants and a long-sleeved black T-shirt. He was missing only the badge and holstered gun at his belt, which were probably locked in the glove compartment.

"Dragged his brother along," the much younger guy in the back called out.

Alexa laughed, hearing how cheerful he sounded.

"Meet Nate," the older brother said with good humor, opening Alexa's door for her.

She climbed up into the cab, remembering how he'd boosted her last night in the hospital parking lot. His hand had been right on her butt, if she was remembering right.

Putting on the seat belt, she swiveled to see Nate. The resemblance between the two men was obvious, from the strong bone structure to the gray eyes, although Nate was thinner, less…finished. And there had to be a big gap in age between the brothers—at least ten years, and likely more.

"Yeah, I was an oops baby," Nate supplied, likely having read her expression. He sounded undisturbed by what might be fact or might be supposition, but she had to wonder.

"Oh," was her intelligent response.

The affection between the brothers was obvious as they maintained an easy banter during the drive downtown, where the lieutenant was able to pull up right behind her car.

"Hasn't been stripped," he observed.

"In Wilden?"

He grinned. "You never know."

Nate hopped out to join his brother in the front seat as she unlocked her own car and said, "Home Depot seems to have the best selection in doors, if that's okay."

"We'll be right behind you."

Her car started fine, although she found it unnerving if also comforting to have a huge black pickup hugging her bumper all the way across town.

They parked next to each other and walked in together. Matthew broke off to collect the locking devices for her windows and patio door. He hadn't actually pulled out a measuring tape last night, but claimed to have a good idea of dimensions. She and his brother headed for the area where doors were displayed, Alexa very conscious of the sidelong looks her bruised face attracted.

"I suppose any glass is verboten," Nate remarked as she gazed wistfully at a gorgeous, solid walnut door with beautiful inset beveled glass.

"I'm afraid so." Oh, well—she couldn't afford the price anyway.

"He's big on security."

She glanced sideways. "Always?"

"Pretty much."

"I suppose that makes sense, given what he must see every day."

Nate grinned at her. "So I tell myself."

"I hope you didn't have anything important planned today."

"Nah. He has an old place he's working on. I'm his apprentice. We usually have a good time."

This felt awkward. "I don't know why he's doing this, but you really don't have to. So…thank you."

He gave her an odd look but said only, "No problem. Hey, what about this one?"

The door was solid wood rather than steel, but had beautiful detailing on the panels and was stained a rich cherry color she liked. When Matthew reappeared, he conceded that it would do. "It could be broken in, but—"

She rolled her eyes. "Why would anyone bother when they could just tap a windowpane?"

His grin reminded her of his brother's, but her reaction was quite different. It was as if her heart did a somersault. Alarmed, she thought, *Oh no. He's conning you. You* know *he is.* She absolutely couldn't afford to become susceptible to his smiles or gritty voice or powerful shoulders.

She paid and then drove home while the two men collected the door at the back of the hardware store and followed. There, they unloaded the door, the new hardware she'd also picked out, and tools. After hovering for a minute, she decided she couldn't do a single thing to help and was just in the way. She'd pretend they were hired workmen. Be as impersonal as possible.

Sitting at her dining room table, she checked messages on her laptop and phone, responded to a few emails, and pretended she didn't hear the crack of wood giving way, the thud of a hammer, the thump as they presumably set the new door in place. Never mind their voices somewhere in the same register, Nate's less gritty.

And why am I staring into space?

At one point, she offered them iced tea, which both guzzled. She could offer to make them sandwiches—

No, she couldn't. None of this was Nate Reinert's fault, and it *was* nice of him to help, but she had no reason to be more than pleasant to a law enforcement officer high in the hierarchy of the department she was investigating. The department that was fighting back, tooth and nail, to keep her from learning anything about officers who should have been long since fired or never hired. She had trouble believing Lieutenant Reinert didn't know about the history of some of those officers.

When he appeared in the kitchen to hand her the keys to her new door, she hopped to her feet, as if that could alleviate her awareness of her average height and slender, less-than-formidable body versus his sheer size.

"I hope you know this doesn't mean I'm going to back down."

A first hint of a smile deepened a crease in his cheek. "Never crossed my mind. I've read your columns, Ms. Adams. I'm not an idiot."

"Oh. Well, then, thank you." She transferred her gaze to the younger Reinert, who'd appeared behind his brother. "Both of you."

She walked them to the door, admired it and repeated her thanks. Nate bounded down the porch steps and headed for the pickup. Matthew hesitated, giving her the chance she'd been waiting for.

"I need to know what that note meant." That came out more belligerently than she'd intended. "You already knew something before I was kidnapped."

His hesitation went on long enough to heat her temper, but she managed to keep her mouth shut until he said, "Can this be off the record?"

"No!"

"Then I'm afraid at this point I can't tell you what I suspect motivated the message to me, except to say that you've stirred up some serious anger within the department."

"As if I didn't know that. What I didn't expect was a physical attack."

"I didn't, either. I was thinking it would be more along the lines of a dead rat on your doorstep." His shoulders moved.

"A warning. If I'd guessed—" He shook his head. "I promise you that I'll do my best to find out who attacked you. This was completely unacceptable."

"While employing and promoting officers who provide cover for drug dealers, bully prostitutes and rough up people whose only crime is looking different from them *is* acceptable?"

His eyes turned cold and his expression hardened. "I didn't say that, and don't believe it. I'll be putting my best detective on this." He nodded and turned away.

Alexa stepped back. Just before she closed the new door, he paused. "Watch your back, Ms. Adams. Call if you need me."

Then he walked away, and she locked the dead bolt and bent to rest her forehead against the door. She needed a moment before her knees quit quaking.

"SHE THANKED YOU. She can't be that mad," Nate said.

Scowling ahead at the jackass who'd been so determined to make a left turn, he'd brought the busy intersection to a tangled halt, Matthew only grunted in response to his kid brother's determined optimism. Nate always had been unnaturally sunny.

If Alexa Adams really appreciated his gesture, she'd forgotten it by the time she demanded answers at the end. He couldn't even blame her. She had a right to know—but Matthew knew damn well that he'd be expected to keep his mouth shut. That hadn't changed.

"How come we're just sitting here?" his brother asked. "You could blast the siren, and even give that guy a ticket."

"I'm not a patrol officer." His truck did have a siren and flashing lights he could use in an emergency, but this didn't qualify as that.

The light changed and traffic resumed a normal flow.

"Let's grab a burger," he suggested.

"Yeah! You owe me!"

Matthew grinned, although it required an effort on his part. What happened last night didn't sit well with him. The way Alexa had shrank from him today the one time he'd passed close to her was worse.

Not "Alexa," he corrected himself. Ms. Adams.

His phone rang. Recognizing the number, he answered with a "Reinert."

"You know I've been hunting for that damn CI all morning," his sometime detective partner told him. "Far as I can tell, Berkey's done a bunk. Why would he do that if he was straight with his information or really meant to meet up with the reporter last night?"

"Because he's afraid one of the traffickers would have guessed where the tip came from? Because he set her up *a second time*?"

Art Dwyer growled something wordless.

"Oh, by the way, I'll be sending you the recording from Ms. Adams. I'd swear it's the same voice."

"Okay. I'll keep on it. You done with your good deed?"

"I am. I was just about to feed my brother as recompense."

"You *like* construction."

Matthew couldn't deny it. In his limited spare time, he was currently restoring a 1910 house that had caught his eye even if it was three or four times too big for a single man, and he'd dragged Art in as assistant more than a few times. Nate even more often, of course.

Dwyer gusted a breath. "You taking the afternoon off?"

"I wish." He didn't hold back although Nate was eavesdropping. He could trust his brother's discretion. "Panic has been spreading. I'm to join a meeting to discuss Ms. Adams's allegations. The current hope is that we can get away with insisting she made up the details that point to cops as her assailants."

"We both know she's telling the truth. The note to you is a giveaway if nothing else."

"You and I aren't in denial." He sighed. "If there's any afternoon left when the meeting lets out, I'll work from home. Unless something comes up." He'd cast his bread on the waters and mostly could only wait until he saw who nibbled. He didn't have to be at his desk to do that.

"Something always comes up," his fellow detective said morosely before ending the call. No goodbye necessary.

"OF COURSE SHE'LL SUE!" Matthew snapped. Was the county executive really that naïve? He didn't say that but could tell from her expression that she knew what he was thinking.

A babble of voices broke out that made his eardrums quiver, and not for the first time since he'd taken a seat at the long table in the conference room to discuss the debacle. Did these people even listen to each other?

He didn't fully understand what this meeting was supposed to accomplish. Representatives from county government, city hall, both law enforcement agencies, all gathered to point fingers and try to pretend *they* had no responsibility for last night's disaster.

And no, the bad intel about the drug traffickers hadn't come from the county commissioner or city mayor. Nobody in this room had snatched a journalist, banged her up and done their best to humiliate her. What he hated was finding out that the prevailing opinion was exactly what he'd anticipated—everyone wanted to frame Alexa Adams as a liar.

Matthew wished like hell he hadn't been compelled to

attend this meeting. He'd much rather get back to tracking down every single person who had any connection to Jim Berkey, or who'd done either shoddy surveillance or flat-out lied about the house Berkey had identified as belonging to the traffickers. Matthew didn't believe for a minute that it had just been an error, as he'd been told several times already this morning. Wrong address. Too bad, but that kind of thing happened.

Really? It was chance the home belonged to a reporter investigating bad cops? The same reporter who had been attacked the next day?

He wasn't impressed with the self-congratulatory tone, either.

See, the raid didn't happen.

Our precautions are solid.

So solid, nobody had made a serious attempt to determine whether the tip was valid until Hargrave had questioned it, and Matthew's curiosity had been awakened.

They all knew full well that a couple of the most notorious police shootings in the country had supposedly been the result of a wrong apartment number or address. In his opinion, there was no excuse for that kind of screwup. Ever. Or being so offhanded about an attempt to manipulate SWAT.

His gaze drifted to Mike Kinney, who wouldn't admit for a minute that his ambition had led to a push to jump the gun.

But what roused Matthew's temper the most was the repeated insistence that Ms. Adams had no proof whatsoever that she'd seen a police badge.

"Even if she saw one," the police chief snapped, "what's to say it was ours? Badges look a lot alike. It could even have been a prop if someone wanted to mislead her."

"And the threat they made?" Matthew felt compelled to ask.

"Who knows what investigations she's involved in? Even she doesn't claim it was specific. And that's if the threat was ever really made."

The undersheriff's eyes met Matthew's. A steady man in his forties with a solid career in law enforcement, he'd mostly stayed quiet so far, but now he spoke up. "The note—" a copy of which lay in front of the Wilden police chief "—certainly implicates local officers. What could it refer to besides the attempt to justify a raid on Ms. Adams's home, which was squelched by Lieutenant Reinert's research?"

People started talking over each other.

"It could mean anything!"

"Offer this woman a settlement right away," the city attorney declared.

Matthew pushed back his chair and stood, momentarily silencing the room. "Maybe before you try to pay her off, you might consider offering the respect of letting her know if the assault was committed by local officers, they'll be appropriately punished. Rushing to discredit her will do nothing but make her believe she's right that both our departments are tolerating dirty cops and that we'll go to the wall to defend them."

"She's a damned journalist!" the police chief snapped. "We admit any culpability, she'll be on us like—" Belatedly cautious, he cast a glance around.

"I think it's safe to say she won't take this lying down anyway," Matthew pointed out.

"Unless she signs a nondisclosure agreement." That was the city attorney again.

"I never knew how much of an optimist you are."

Her face tightened.

Matthew shook his head. "I doubt you could come up

with enough money to silence Alexa Adams. What she wants is the truth. I suggest we think about giving that to her." Even knowing he wasn't doing his career any favor, he shoved the chair back up to the table and walked out.

His job was to investigate, and that's exactly what he was going to do. That, and worry about the second strike—or was it the third?—that he fully anticipated.

Chapter Four

"They're going to fight this thing in every way possible," Alexa's new attorney told her.

Diana Troxell was maybe midforties, her sleek dark hair cut in a bob, her makeup always flawless. She had a steel magnolia reputation—a smile that was downright sweet, and a way of slicing and dicing her opponents with surgical precision. Alexa had seen her in action in court several times and admired her refusal to back down. There'd been a couple of times Alexa had had to blink and think, *Wait. Did she really just say that?*

She'd already thanked Diana for getting her in so soon. Now she queried, "They?"

Diana waved a hand. "City, county, cops. All of them."

Alexa said, "You do know they'll try to deny the two men who set up a fake meeting and jumped me were cops?"

The attorney made a couple of quick notes. "Of course they will. Too often, politicians can claim gravity has ceased to exist and make people believe them, as we both know. In this case, that's not what I meant, though. Sure, they'll claim you misunderstood the threat, but from what you've told me, *something* happened earlier that they didn't share with you. Something that could have been really bad. I expect them to tell me what that was.

"The note left with you letting Lieutenant Reinert know his intercession wasn't appreciated is the clincher for us. They won't want to have to explain whatever went on to a jury.

"What I anticipate is an offer to pay you off, preferably right this minute, before you have a chance to get greedy or think you can add an another zero or two to that number. But when you turn down the payment and demand they open the door to their records? Let you rummage around so you can publicly excoriate officers in their own police departments, thereby shaming the higher-ups for not even trying to make those same officers walk the straight-and-narrow? For hiring officers who've been fired from other departments for unethical, racist or even illegal acts?"

"You think this is hopeless."

Diana's grin had a sharklike quality she rarely displayed. "No, I'm just saying they're not going to leap at the opportunity to save themselves some money and say, 'Sure. We have nothing to hide.' Even if we achieve an agreement, I'm going to guess a lot of the records you're seeking will turn out to have been misfiled or lost. There'll be apologies, promises to find whatever it is, and time will drag by."

"No different than what I've experienced this past six months."

"Exactly. That said, once we have the right signatures on a dotted line, we'll have recourse to legal actions when they don't fulfill their agreement. I'll *enjoy* taking those legal actions." The grin widened. "So much, I'll happily take on your case pro bono. I respect what you're trying to do. Citizens should be able to trust their police officers. I was taught when I was a kid that I could. Nobody mentioned those cops that use their guns and authority to threaten people because of a personal beef or lie on their reports and in court about how a violent incident escalated, or bullied teenage girls into sexually servicing them."

"And that's just skimming the surface," Alexa agreed. "There are at least twenty complaints on file about a county deputy who clearly profiles the people he pulls over, or which side in a dispute he comes down on. And then there are the ones who have really friendly relationships with a few prostitutes. Why arrest when you can enjoy?"

The attorney leaned forward. "I do have an obligation to remind you that you're taking a hard road when you could be cashing a good-sized check instead. That said, I can hardly wait to read your articles when you blow the lid off that kettle."

"If I wanted good-sized checks, I'd have gone to law school."

The two women smiled at each other.

With a brisk nod, Diana said, "I'll call to set up a first meeting. I can hardly wait to sit down with them. They won't have a clue what you want, or a game plan to stop you."

"We can only hope."

HITTING NOTHING BUT dead ends wherever he turned, Matthew hardly tasted a bite of the sandwich and bakery cookies he'd brought for lunch on Monday. He ate mechanically, despite a churning gut, wishing he'd felt he could have taken the day off. Any day.

He'd ignored a few calls from people he didn't really want to talk to, but had barely finished lunch when his phone rang and he saw Art Dwyer's number.

"Nothing on Berkey. A dead woman was found in a dumpster in an alley backing our favorite stretch of bars," Art said. "First responder recognized her, says she's a prostitute who worked that area. Garbage truck already did a number on the scene, but it sounds like she was killed a day or two ago. Garbage worker didn't like the smell and was smart enough to stop the mechanism before he dumped the load into his truck. He took a look."

"Those guys should have strong stomachs."

"Not strong enough."

"Were you up for this one?" Matthew asked. Dwyer had been concentrating on picking up any trace of Jim Berkey, and he was dogged on that kind of trail.

"Everyone knew I've been working the other murders of prostitutes."

Three, to date, within the past year, as well as a couple of previous ones. Yes, prostitutes were vulnerable members of the population, but Wilden wasn't a big enough city to expect so many murders that were so similar.

"I wanted to get in on this one from the beginning," Art added. They all had their crusades.

"I'm sorry." And he was, but Art, like him, couldn't resist dedication to the job when it kicked in.

Matthew made the drive in just over ten minutes, parking on the street. The uniform guarding the end of the alley recognized him and waved him by. He edged past the garbage truck and was hit hard by the stench. Harder than usual; he wasn't sure it was possible to become accustomed to the smell of a decomposing body, human or other mammal, but the myriad foul smells made for a horrific medley.

Art was deep in conversation with a couple of uniformed officers and two guys in dark green uniforms indicating they were probably the garbage collectors. Seeing Matthew, he grimaced in greeting, and jerked his head toward the dumpster, back on its wheels on one side of the alley.

Matthew donned latex gloves he almost always carried and hoisted himself up to look inside. He couldn't see much of the body, maybe because the contents had been stirred during the gathering process, but enough. A bare breast and shoulder, bleached-blond hair sticking to what was left of a face seen in profile, a spike-heeled black boot slimed by some unknown substance, and a swarm of black flies.

His favorite kind of crime scene.

He and Dwyer left the dumpster and its contents to the CSI duo who had pulled up to the other end of the alley. Matthew spoke briefly to the middle-aged garbage collector who'd spotted the body and then let him and his partner go on with their route. Apparently, his boss hadn't been compassionate enough to suggest they take the day off. Then the two detectives divided the businesses that backed onto this alley to canvass them.

Question number one. Why hadn't anyone tossing the past day or two's refuse into the dumpster given a thought to the stench?

Matthew was grateful that Art was there, even if he did feel guilty since poor Art had been more than due a weekend off.

Matthew's first interview was with the manager of the bar that had a back door opening ten or twelve feet from the dumpster in question.

The guy shrugged at the question. "Alley always reeks. We get some homeless sleeping there sometimes. It was bad enough yesterday, I glanced behind both dumpsters to be sure one of them hadn't died, and figured it was an animal." He sighed. "You identified the victim?"

"We think it's one of the girls who work the neighborhood. Can't be sure yet. You get to know them at all?"

"Yeah, they duck in here sometimes when the weather is especially bad. Never stay more than a short while to warm up or wait out a squall. You know they'd be in trouble if they did. I shouldn't let them, but…" He shrugged. "I don't let their pimps cross my doorstep." His voice had hardened. "Far as I'm concerned, they can sit in their damn cars. I've tried talking to girls when I can see they're kids, but—" Another shrug.

Matthew nodded. Siccing social services on teenagers who'd already swallowed the hook rarely did any good, either. He hoped this victim wasn't a kid, although he didn't deceive himself that any of them would live long, happy lives.

He was becoming something of an expert on the lifestyle, since the city had seen the string of murders of prostitutes this past year. Statistically, more than usual, although investigators hadn't been able to positively declare that one perpetrator was responsible. Matthew and Art had their suspicions, but these were some of the toughest homicide cases to solve. Getting away with killing a hooker was all too easy.

Art and he met on the sidewalk half an hour later, neither having learned anything useful. Nobody had seen a thing. Heard a thing. Most bartenders didn't remember what girls they'd seen walking the sidewalk the past few nights, or whether they'd noticed a familiar one missing.

Of course they didn't.

Maybe they were just being honest. It wasn't their business; that kind of activity wasn't any different from passing traffic except when there was a fender-bender.

"We need to come back tonight," Art grumbled. "Michelle isn't going to be happy."

Wives were rarely happy about a detective's erratic hours, but Art Dwyer's marriage was an exception to what Matthew had come to think was the rule. Art had been a cop for almost twenty years, having hit the big four-oh in July. Today, when he told her he had to go out again, his wife would scold him, kiss him and send him out with an insulated mug of hot coffee.

Occasionally, she did or said something that gave Matthew a pang of… Not jealousy, exactly. Yearning for a relationship like that? Maybe.

Strangely, Alexa Adams's face appeared before his mind's eye, and he almost smiled. Now, *there* was a tough woman who'd be so busy hunting down evil, she wouldn't think a thing of her husband doing the same, even if he carried a gun doing it and risked his life in a way she didn't.

Even the impulse to smile died as Matthew remembered last night and how easily a half-naked woman tied out like bait in an alley could have met a worse fate—one that might have left her dead.

STANDING UNDER THE streetlamp so he could see the two women's faces, Matthew scribbled in his small spiral notebook. He kept a wary eye on the sidewalk traffic, even though bar hopping was less popular on a weeknight. Still, this was a nice evening.

"Color?" he asked.

Both hookers were sure the last time they'd seen Tansy, she was getting into a pickup.

"I don't know," one said.

She was so young, he was tempted to haul her in to find out her real age and whether she had family looking for her, but knew he wouldn't tonight. He needed cooperation.

"It was dark," said the other prostitute, who looked more like she was pushing forty years old, which probably meant she was twenty-five or so. "And I didn't pay that much attention. Why would I?"

"Even at night, you'd have been able to tell if it was

white," he argued. "If you can picture a pickup, you must have an idea of color."

They looked at each other.

"It wasn't white," the girl offered. "It was more, like, dark. Black. But it could've been red or blue or, I don't know, gray?"

He did know, but had hoped one of them might have seen the truck passing under a streetlight as it drove away.

"No glimpse of the driver?"

The glance at each other looked shiftier. To this point, he thought they'd told him the truth, but knew there was something they didn't want to say.

Two heads shook.

"You're sure you haven't seen her since?" he asked.

This time, the headshakes seemed straight up, even though they were getting antsy, aware their handler was nearby and irritated because they weren't working.

"Okay," he said. "Thanks. Here's my card—" he handed one to each "—in case you think of something."

They were so eager to get away, they stumbled over their own feet. Nodding, he strode off, scanning the pedestrian traffic for any other working girls.

He found a few more women to talk to, finally rejoining Art Dwyer a couple of blocks down.

Art said, "Nada. You?"

"Pickup truck. Probably not white or any other light color."

Art's snort said it all. This was eastern Washington. Any man who didn't drive a brawny pickup would have to expect to defend his masculinity in another way.

Matthew had an excuse; he owned one because he needed it to haul lumber and other supplies for the never-ending renovation of his house. If not for that, he actually would have preferred to drive something that handled better in snow and ice.

Somehow, he'd bet the ninety percent of other cops in his department who drove pickups would have their own excuses.

Looking around, Matthew said, "Call it a night. I can watch the camera footage of the alley then knock off, too." *He* didn't have anyone waiting at home for him.

"Appreciate it," Art said. They walked together until he veered off toward his truck—charcoal gray—and Matthew continued to the one and only bar that bothered with a security camera. Not one in front, unfortunately, but the owner had gotten tired of the hookups and drug deals taking place behind his business and had hung a big sign on the inside of the back door saying, You Go Out, You'll Be On Camera.

As it happened, Matthew had already watched the segment taped that he had hoped would show traffic in the time frame of the assault on Alexa. Not a single vehicle had traversed this block of the alley during that stretch of time. He hadn't been surprised, since most Wilden PD officers would know to avoid the camera.

The bar wasn't on the block where the body had been dumped, but Matthew could live in hope that, unlike local police officers, the killer didn't know about the camera and had driven several blocks down the alley rather than risk being seen turning at the corner and then into the alley where the body would be found.

Except, of course, he'd hoped it wouldn't be discovered until the garbage truck dumped its load at the transfer station—or, better yet, at all. Nobody would likely have gone to the police just to report a prostitute was missing. If they had, any action taken would have been minimal, given that it was reasonable to assume she'd simply fled her pimp and/ or maybe even the lifestyle.

At the bar, Matthew was showed into an office and, allowed to close the door, he shut out the live music and voices in front while he pored over the usual grainy, black-and-white film. There was just enough action in the alley that he couldn't fast-forward as much as he'd like—an occasional car or truck moving slowly, a few drunks probably taking a shortcut to their vehicles, the easy-to-spot homeless wearing multiple layers of clothing or carrying all their possessions, one pushing a heavily laden shopping cart. Given the harsh winters, the numbers of homeless were well below what was common on the western side of the state, but there were always a few who couldn't deal even with nights in a shelter.

Nothing stood out to Matthew, but he made particular note of all pickups since he didn't yet have an approximate time of death to better pinpoint realistic possibilities. In a few cases, he could make out license plate numbers. For all he strained his eyes, sometimes he failed. One black pickup appeared to have something covering the plate. Unfortunately, that one had been traveling east-west, which meant the driver was on the far side of the vehicle. Matthew couldn't even tell if he was looking at a man or woman.

Eventually, frustrated, he thanked the bar owner, who agreed to copy three days of footage and get it to Matthew. An expert could probably enlarge details.

Then he went home, reminded too well why his investigators had yet to so much as identify a suspect in any of the murders of the prostitutes who worked the streets within a ten or twelve block area of his city. Art Dwyer in particular had been giving it his all.

Back when Matthew had been in uniform, he'd arrested enough johns during stings to develop a serious disgust for the business. Too many of the men who thought nothing of using some fourteen-year-old girl were respected business-men, contractors, accountants, plumbers, real estate agents. Even an occasional reverend and one city councilman. As much as the murders and other crimes Matthew had seen, it was those johns, embarrassed because they'd been caught but not ashamed of their abuse of vulnerable women, who'd turned him into a cynic.

And most of all, he despised the cops who were supposed to be policing an illegal activity but instead blackmailed women with no good alternative into offering sex.

Them, he wanted to bring down.

Chapter Five

Alexa parted the blinds in the guest bedroom and watched a car passing on the street. Had it slowed down in front of her house? No, she was being paranoid. After a moment, she yanked at the window to make sure the lock was secure then went to her home office to do the same.

Beyond the reach of the light over the patio, her backyard was dark and shadowy. She'd liked the mature shrubs surrounding the house when she'd bought it, but now those deep shadows made her uneasy. She'd never see someone lurking beside that big lilac or the butterfly bush. Maybe she could cut the bushes back—

Oh, for Pete's sake. She'd never had a break-in before, not here and not at the apartments she'd rented in the years before buying the house. The attack had been committed by cops, and she'd been lured out of her home. No break-in required. As it turned out, they hadn't wanted to steal anything or rape her.

Just humiliate her, she reminded herself, stomach tightening before she shoved at the memory. Or if she didn't back off from her investigation would another assault escalate?

Go to bed.

Since she'd now checked every window and door, a few twice, just as she had last night, she'd run out of excuses.

Alexa seriously thought about finding a weapon to tuck under her pillow—a butcher knife? a hammer?—but talked herself out of it again. Would she have gotten anywhere trying to fight back with that kind of weapon against two brawny men with police training? Plus, neither a hammer nor a knife was of much use when facing an opponent carrying a semiautomatic gun.

She brushed her teeth then braided her hair. The night was warm, but she wore flannel pajama pants and a baggy T-shirt instead of skimpier attire. Normally, she'd open the window to cool her room, but not tonight. Instead, she went back out to the hall to nudge up the air-conditioning.

Finally, she crawled into bed, where she lay rigid, listening to every sound, categorizing each, trying to remember if it was normal or out of the usual. An hour later, she was no closer to sleep than she'd been when she turned out the bedside light.

Surely, sleep would come.

It did, but not until well after midnight. Fortunately, she had no grand plans tomorrow. She planned to work on an article her editor was not so patiently waiting for. Unrelated to her more intense focus on dirty cops, this article was about some money the county public works department had either misplaced or misspent—it wasn't yet clear. They'd been dodging questions, and the county executive had asked for patience before the newspaper went public with something that might just be an honest mistake.

Most people came clean about honest mistakes, in Alexa's experience. Since the attack on her couldn't be called an honest mistake—and the county and city attorneys had made a lot of excuses to put off meeting with Diana—Alexa had written a colorful story about it. Her editor had strategically held it for the Tuesday morning paper—right before Diana met with the city and county powers that be.

Barely out of her shower come morning, Alexa heard her phone ringing. She expected multiple calls in response to the article and planned to give interviews rife with emotion and bewilderment for the benefit of the viewers of local TV news.

By midmorning, all those city, county and law enforcement higher-ups would see the writing on the wall. And, by God, she'd keep the pressure on as long as she needed to. Yeah, she could issue not-so-subtle threats as well as they could.

She cracked her front door, looked both ways and crept out onto her porch to snatch up her newspaper before rushing back inside and locking the dead bolt.

MATTHEW WAS DETERMINED to push for this murder to be worked as hard as every other one, even though public interest tended to be anemic when the victim was someone with a police record. Tired of being stuck behind the desk too much of the time, he was glad to take an active role in the investigation, partnering with Dwyer.

Tansy Gould's fingerprints were on record, confirming her identity. Full name: Tansy Elizabeth Gould. Age: twenty-two. Height: five foot three. Weight: one hundred and four, confirmed by the ME's office. She was currently blond, but her now-expired driver's license listed her as having brown hair and hazel eyes.

The autopsy produced no surprises. Her cause of death was straightforward: a bullet had ripped out her carotid artery. Some lucky crime scene investigators were giving that alley another once-over and digging through the dumpster in search of a bullet. Of course, nobody had heard a gunshot, which might mean the murderer had used a suppressor. But she also could have been killed elsewhere and then transported back to her own neighborhood. It did appear her body had been wrapped in a sheet of plastic that had torn as garbage was dumped on top of her and then partially twisted off when the dumpster was lifted and upended before the process was halted and reversed after the garbage collector with the sensitive nose took action.

Starting his day, Matthew read his morning newspaper while he ate a bowl of cereal. Alexa Adams hadn't held back either the details of the assault, or the fear she'd experienced. The anger was there, too, plenty powerful, as was her certainty she'd been attacked by cops fearing her investigation into their wrongdoing. To his surprise, she hadn't mentioned the note directed at him.

He left the paper on the table and grabbed his keys, anticipating another day of fingerpointing.

Matthew's first task once he reached the station was to call the victim's mother in Bellingham, on the other side of the state, to tell her not only that her daughter was dead but that she'd been murdered. He'd heard that same scream before, but never got over the painful empathy.

Mrs. Gould's story didn't surprise him. Tansy and her father had never gotten along. She'd run away several times, starting when she was thirteen, become involved in the drug scene, and finally, at seventeen years old, completely disappeared.

Weeping, Mrs. Gould said, "I tried to convince myself she'd come home someday. If she looked, she'd have seen on Facebook that her daddy died. I guess mostly I suspected someone like you would call me eventually with this kind of news."

He promised to keep her informed. He'd be in touch as soon as the body was released.

Tansy's mother was crying hard when he ended the call, feeling like he'd been kicked in the chest. Even if they made an arrest, what would that mean to a mother who not only had to live without her child, but also knew how wretched that life had been and how horrific her death?

Having already taken a few calls from other people in the department who'd read Alexa's article this morning, he was able to easily switch mental gears when his boss paused by his desk to let him know of the recriminations flying between city and county. A lot of people who rarely showed their faces at the station were probably working today.

"Nobody will admit publicly that they believe her, but they know damn well it was cops who set up that scene. Sheriff's office insists it happened in town. Couldn't have been *their* deputies. Chief wants to find a way to dump responsibility on them. What *I* want is to find out who those two men are, and whether they're behind the tip that was supposed to mushroom into a SWAT raid."

If anybody working with Art had located Berkey, Matthew felt sure he'd have been updated. Undercover Vice detectives were supposedly looking, too, but, for all he knew they'd taken the d, ay off.

"Guy's probably running for his life," Matthew reported now in disgust, "but he'll surface. If talking will save him from a prison term, I have to believe he'll name names."

The deputy chief grimaced and nodded. "Keep on it," he said unnecessarily, rapping his knuckles on Matthew's desk and walking away.

Somebody had kindly left the morning *Tribune* smack in the middle of the blotter on his desk where he couldn't miss it. He read it again, and noted that the murder of the prostitute hadn't made it into the paper yet. It wouldn't hit the front page, anyway, he thought cynically.

Walking out to his vehicle in the early afternoon, he brooded. The attack had been aimed at him as well as Ms. Adams, albeit not as directly.

There were people who didn't like him, including some in the police department. He was known for his unbending sense of right and wrong., which wasn't to say that he didn't understand why some cops ventured into the gray— he got as frustrated as anyone when he knew some piece of slime was walking because of a technicality, say, but vigilantism was as bad, in his opinion. He'd back an officer who'd momentarily lost his temper and said something impolitic, say, but had no patience when an act revealed arrogance or a bias.

In this case, if the original effort had actually resulted in a raid, it had been solely pointed at Alexa Adams. How serious the warning to him to butt out was…well, he'd find out.

This morning's newspaper article had made it clear that she wasn't backing down.

Getting into his police SUV, he couldn't help wondering when, not if, they'd go after her again, and whether she'd be seriously hurt or worse this time.

ALEXA'S PHONE VIBRATED, startling her. She was working at a secluded table in the branch library, one she was tempted to make a permanent claim on with a reserved sign. It was usually available anyway during hours when not many kids were around.

Although she'd hoped to hear from Diana Troxell, this caller was a fellow reporter at the *Tribune*. They had been consulting each other fairly often lately, since he worked the crime beat. Curious, she answered, keeping her voice low.

"Hey, there's a cop here looking for you," Greg Wells said. "Didn't know what to tell him."

She'd put in requests to interview half a dozen of the cops she was investigating, but they hadn't exactly yet leaped to volunteer for a chat, even with a union rep present. But to make their way into the *Tribune* building in search of her?

"Who is he?"

"Lieutenant Reinert." Gary's carefully neutral tone told her he knew very well who Reinert was.

Was this more of the nice guy who deeply regretted what had been done to her? Or had he been sent bearing a less friendly message? She gave a huff.

"I'm at the Madison branch library, working. If he wants to trek over, I should be here for another couple of hours."

After a murmur of voices, Gary said, "He says he's on his way unless he gets a callout."

Of course, her ability to concentrate was shot after that. She'd been reading everything she could uncover about a longtime scandal: the disappearance of drugs from the evidence locker at the county sheriff's office headquarters. Given that deputies had to check out any evidence borrowed—say, for court—and were theoretically on camera even when they wanted to look at a piece of evidence, the fact that someone had walked out unobserved with enough illegal drugs to sell for a nice side income should have triggered a bigger to-do than it so far had, in Alexa's opinion. To date, the sheriff and his spokespeople talked about inventory problems, how probably nothing had really disappeared.

Uh-huh. Alexa wondered what they'd say if, in a spirit of civic high-mindedness, she offered to help with an inventory.

She managed to take a few notes, but wondering why Reinert wanted to talk to her again was a distraction. She'd have guessed that orders would have come down from on high for him *not* to talk to her.

Her view of the front blocked by tall shelving units packed with books, she didn't so much as hear a footstep before he appeared around one of those bookcases, expression quizzical.

"Hiding back here?" he asked.

And, blast it, his voice had enough texture to make goose bumps skitter down her spine.

He was dressed for the job in chinos, a dark green T-shirt and boots, the holstered handgun and badge at his waist making a real statement.

"That's the idea," she said, closing out her program before he could oh-so-casually circle the table to see what she was working on. "I concentrate best here. No interruptions."

His dark brows arched. "Is that a hint?"

"Oh." She was afraid her cheeks had flushed. "No, actually it wasn't."

"Good." He pulled out a chair and sat facing her, as relaxed as if he were lounging at his desk.

She decided to go for blunt. "What do you want?"

"Thought you'd like to be updated on my investigation."

"You'd really tell me if you find out which of your peers attacked me?"

Those dark eyebrows twitched.

Okay, she'd sounded as incredulous as she felt.

She went on. "Your chief and the city attorney haven't ordered a lockdown on communications yet?"

"Not to my knowledge," he said easily, his gaze never wavering from her face. "I think you're entitled."

She was, but hearing him say so blew her away. "So? What have you learned?"

His expression darkened. "Nothing. Nothing at all. We still can't find Jim Berkey, which makes me uneasy."

"You think…?"

"Probably he's just gone to ground. But, uh, he left an earlier tip that was aimed at you, too, although it took us a while to realize that."

"What?" Even having him share this much information stunned her. "Are you going to give me the details?"

"I can't. I shouldn't have said that much. I will say I was the one who shut down any consequences of the false tip."

What kind of consequences was he talking about? Had she been accused of a crime?

"Thus the message to you.".

"And the much stronger one to you."

"'Back off or else'?"

"Hard to read it any other way."

She could tell there was something he seemed reluctant to say, but she only nodded.

"Well, thank you for the report."

"Nice spread in the newspaper."

Alexa smiled. "Thank you. I was pleased with it."

That had to be amusement glinting in those gray eyes now. "Don't suppose you're backing off?"

Was that really what he wanted to know? Chilled, she said, "Not a chance."

Reinert nodded but didn't say anything for a minute. Something in the way he surveyed her felt personal—male-female—instead of having anything to do with the topic of conversation. Finally, confirming her suspicion, he said, "I'd suggest we go get a cup of coffee, but if I'm seen consorting with you, that might cause a problem."

"I'll bet it would," she agreed. Weirdly, she felt an unfamiliar buzz of excitement. He was unnervingly good-looking; how could she not admire his broad shoulders and long, muscular body? If his independence in coming to talk to her was honest, that attracted her, too. And she liked the hint of laughter she'd seen in his eyes and quirking one corner of his mouth.

"I'll let you get back to work." He pushed back the chair and rose to his feet. So big, she felt a momentary cramp of fear until she remembered the careful way he'd crouched in front of her in that alley to wrap her in his coat, shielding her from other eyes.

Expression troubled, he said, "As I said last time we talked, I encourage you to be cautious, Ms. Adams. Paranoia is an occupational hazard in my profession, but I don't think it's unreasonable to wonder if there'll be another salvo fired at you."

Her throat tightened. "Wouldn't that be taking a big chance, for whoever is behind this?"

"Yeah, they have to feel you snapping at their heels. They might be getting a little desperate if they know you're likely to come across something that will bring them down."

He took a business card out of a pocket and tossed it on top of her laptop, even though he'd already given her one as well as his phone number. "In case you tore the first one up," he said, his lips twitching. "Call me if anything makes you nervous." Then he nodded without waiting for her response and walked away, vanishing around the bookcase.

Alexa picked up the card and studied it. Would she dare call a cop to rescue her from another cop? She didn't know... but this time she'd go so far as to put him on speed dial.

MATTHEW LOOKED UP at the rap on his door. Vice detective Phil Banuelos stuck his head in without waiting for a response. "Got a minute?"

"If you have answers, I want to hear them."

It was Banuelos who should have thoroughly investigated Berkey's original tip. Obviously feeling defensive still, the first thing he said was, "You know that damn tip didn't come through me."

A patrol officer had passed on the message, unusual in that his few dealings with Jim Berkey, the CI, had been casual. Why would Berkey have chosen a cop he barely knew to pass on important information?

"You did vouch for the sleazeball," Matthew pointed out.

"The information he gives us is usually good." He hesitated. "Can I hear the call to the journalist again?"

Matthew pulled it up on his laptop and let it play, not liking the mumble or the street noise—traffic, voices that rose and fell, shouts—that made words indistinct.

The dark-haired detective leaned forward, absolutely intent. Then he slouched back in the chair. "Almost has to be him. That he's gone under now makes me nervous." He paused. "I wish I'd tried to reach him after the drug house tip."

Matthew gritted his teeth. Banuelos should have done a lot more than that, like some basic research or set up surveillance that would have immediately nipped the whole thing in the bud.

"Thing is, I'd been talking to him about this particular crowd. Pushing a little, you know. When I'm dogged enough, he comes through sometimes."

The hint of apology in the other detective's voice had Matthew rolling his shoulders to try to loosen the tension that would crawl up his neck and give him a headache if he let it. As ticked as he was at Banuelos, he knew how overworked he was.

"You didn't stop by for this," he said abruptly. "You have something else on your mind?"

"One of my detectives says he's been told that the drug gang was never in Wilden. He's trying to trace the original rumor on the street, but so far with no luck."

Yeah, there was a surprise.

Chapter Six

"The reaction was about what you'd expect," Diana told Alexa. Both had assumed they'd get some kind of response today from city and county entities. "Every single one of 'em is shocked by the suggestion that this 'incident'—that's the word of the day—is in any way their responsibility," the attorney continued. "Nobody in either department would consider *threatening* a journalist. That the thought even crossed your mind is absurd. Still, they deeply regretted that your assailants tried to convince you they were cops."

Alexa snorted. "As Detective Reinert put it, I'm obviously paranoid."

Still working from the library, Alexa had packed up her laptop and files and gone outside for this conversation. A few people had passed by since she'd settled on the handsome bench under a maple tree, but nobody was within earshot now.

"He's been in touch with you?" The attorney sounded horrified. "And he said something like that? I'm going to fry his ass—"

"No, no," Alexa hastened to say. "He did stop by to talk this afternoon, supposedly to update me on his attempt to figure out how things went so wrong. Without being willing to give me details, he told me there'd been an earlier shot fired at me that he'd shut down. Thus the annoyed note aimed at him. I do think his real intent was to warn me to be cautious. That's when he said he's probably paranoid, but it's an occupational hazard. And maybe that's true, but he made it clear that he doesn't believe the company line you're describing, or that whoever is threatening me is finished."

There was a moment of silence. "It's…unusual he'd communicate with you the way he has."

"I think he may be sincere," Alexa heard herself say. And she was the original skeptic.

"Don't get too trusting," her lawyer warned.

"Me?"

Diana laughed then went on to tell her that she'd informed them she was preparing to file a lawsuit, and felt sure the details Alexa had described in her article would be persuasive to a jury.

"They tiptoed around a concession that a payout might be possible as long as they didn't have to admit to any culpability for your unpleasant experience. They just want this to go away, of course. That discussion might have gone further, say, to specific numbers, if I hadn't said that what you were asking for was open access to public records for the purpose of researching police officers suspected of conduct the public should know about."

She sounded exceptionally cheerful. "I said there's no reason the staff should be so overwhelmed that it can take months to a year to supply information they are legally obligated to make public. That we suspect the recent rule change limiting requests is aimed at *you*, because they know they have an embarrassing number of officers in their departments who should never have been hired or who should have been fired for behavior on the job here in our own city."

Alexa laughed. "And?"

"They're outraged. Almost every police officer ends up being the subject of an occasional complaint from the public. There are people who dislike them, who don't understand how difficult the job they do is, who misunderstand what was happening in front of them although it's understandable that it appeared disturbing."

"Uh-huh."

"Don't worry. I won't let up. Your ears should be burning right now. I'll bet you're the subject of whole lot of conversations among the upper echelon in both police departments as well as the city and county. We'll see what they offer in response to my demands."

"Nothing we'll want to accept," Alexa said dryly.

"Not a chance. I'll keep you informed."

Alexa sat enjoying the sunlight for a few minutes. She had a bad tendency to hole up inside when she got obsessed with a particular investigation. She'd read about work/life balance, but didn't give it a thought most of the time. Maybe if she had a partner...

Yeah, her average was three or four dates before the guy realized that she was a modern-day, female Don Quixote, so determined to tilt at windmills she wasn't about to let anything or anyone get in the way.

This wasn't the first time it had occurred to her that she might have a lot in common with cops in general, and especially detectives. They might get her, and her them.

Too bad she'd met so many who were supercharged and macho with a tendency to swagger. They came with their own problems, the kinds that led to substance abuse and or troubled relationships.

Wouldn't you know, a picture of Lieutenant Matthew Reinert appeared in her head, as it had too often this week. Looking too good to be believable.

She walked to her car, thinking about dinner. She hadn't defrosted anything this morning, but she could cook something simple like black bean quesadillas.

A couple of turns and she reached the main drag. Temptation momentarily called to her when she passed her favorite pizza restaurant, but she resolutely continued, braking when traffic slowed ahead of her.

A siren *whooped* right behind her, making her levitate. What the heck?

The marked city police car crowded her bumper, the rack of roof lights flashing.

Had she forgotten to signal or—

She heard Detective Reinert saying, *I don't think it's unreasonable to wonder if there'll be another salvo fired at you.* Was that what this was?

Alexa turned into the parking lot for an auto parts store and came to a stop. The police car rolled right up behind her.

Hands shaking, she shifted into Park and put on the emergency brake. For what seemed like forever, the officer behind the wheel just sat there. Trying to scare her?

No, probably looking her up for any priors, she reminded herself. Didn't squad cars have a computer now so he didn't have to call in for information?

In her side mirror, she saw that at last the officer was climbing out of his car. His hand rested on the butt of his gun as he walked forward. Wait—she should've gotten out her license and registration. She hastily took the folder from the glove compartment that held the registration.

A knock on her window made her jump.

Alexa rolled it down. "I don't understand why you stopped me, but—" She reached for her purse on the passenger seat.

His voice whipped out. "Hands on the steering wheel! Now! Do it!"

Completely rattled, she let the wallet drop back into the purse and started to comply. Before she could, the barrel of a gun was inches from her face.

"What are you *doing*?"

"Out of the car!" He wrenched open the door and grabbed her shoulder, which hurt on top of her recent injuries. Of course, her seat belt kept her in place. Next thing she knew, he was leaning over her, his breath bad, that gun pressed into her cheek. With the seat belt unfastened, he pulled her out of the car. She fell to her still-tender hands and knees on the gritty asphalt. People were staring, she knew that, but she didn't have room for humiliation right now, only now-too-familiar fear.

"I don't understand," she tried to say.

"On your feet!"

His hands were so rough as he wrenched her to her feet, she was going to have new bruises to go with the old. He planted her against her car, face pressing the back seat window.

"Hands against the car! Keep 'em there!"

Oh God. What was happening? Why?

He held a gun on her. She might have a print in her cheek from the barrel. If his finger tightened...

Was he one of the cops she was investigating? In this position, she couldn't possibly see his name.

"Why did you stop me?" she cried. "Why are you treating me like this?"

A handcuff snapped closed around her wrist and, before she knew it, he'd yanked both arms behind her and fully cuffed her.

Terrified and mad, she yelled, "You have no reason to arrest me! None!"

"I pulled you over because your brake light is out," the cop said. "When I looked you up, your vehicle is highlighted with a warning that you're armed and dangerous."

"I'm dangerous, all right," she managed to rasp through gritted teeth. "I know my rights."

"I'm doing my job," he growled.

"My name is Alexa Adams. Call Lieutenant Matthew Reinert." Were those tears burning hotly in her eyes? She surely did hope not. "He said he'd come if something like this happened again."

"How do you know Reinert?"

The ridge along the top of the window had to be etching a line in her face. "You heard about the woman who was stripped and left tied up in an alley Friday night? That was me."

Silence.

"Give me a minute."

Would he really call? Apparently so, because over the noise of passing traffic on the street, she thought she heard the scuff of his feet as he walked a short distance away. *Please don't let the lieutenant be too busy to answer his phone.* But she heard the murmur of one side of a conversation. Eyes closed, she tried to eavesdrop but couldn't distinguish any words.

A minute later, he returned and said, "I'm going to let you sit down on the back seat of your car. If you'll straighten up…"

She did. He opened the door.

"You won't take the cuffs off?"

"Not until the lieutenant says it's okay."

He maneuvered her so that she could sit sideways on the

seat, her feet on the pavement. Her shoulders had already begun to ache. She stared at the officer, who'd backed up a couple of steps. So she couldn't tackle him with one lunge? This was the first time she'd really been able to see him.

He had to be early thirties. His head was shaved. He had a square face, a short, thick neck, and the shoulders of someone who spent a lot of time beefing up. There was nothing friendly or sympathetic in his eyes as he stared back at her.

The name pin on his pocket said…something Jackman. She thought. Not a name she'd come across before, although that didn't mean he didn't support his fellow officers who, say, felt justified in roughing up suspects. And, she'd surely be doing some research on him.

"You that reporter?" he said after a minute.

"Yes, I am."

"Why would you want to blacken the names of a lot of good men?" He sounded genuinely puzzled.

"Aren't there any good women in the police department?" she asked.

He obviously didn't get her point. Alexa let her head sag forward.

Please, Lieutenant, please don't be too far away. Please hurry.

MATTHEW DID A lot of swearing as he steered around stopped cars and hit his lights when he needed to cross an intersection. He was still grappling with the implications of that call. Ms. Adams's automobile license had been tagged to ensure the next cop who set eyes on it would pull her over, and not be polite after they did so.

How in *hell*—

Yeah, stupid question. Something told him getting an answer wouldn't be any easier than finding out how she'd been targeted for the raid that hadn't happened or the assault that had. But, man, whoever this was hadn't wasted any time. Maybe because they'd found out that she didn't want money in recompense for their mistake, she wanted access to any personnel records she asked to see.

That, of course, she was entitled to request and read. Hardly anybody who worked for the government—local or statewide—really grasped the concept of public records. Of what it meant to be an employee of the taxpayers.

He hit his siren again and maneuvered through a tangle of vehicles until he worked his way free enough to accelerate. The auto parts store was three blocks away. He covered the distance in a minute or less, turning in and pulling up right next to Alexa's car. The lights on the squad car still flashed, with the result that anyone in the parking lot or passing was sure to gape.

Matthew stopped abruptly enough that his SUV rocked. He hardly noticed as he leaped out and stalked around the front bumper of her vehicle until he saw Officer Jackman looking a little uneasy as he guarded the open door of her car.

Her head came up. The dark hair she usually wore in a smooth knot at her nape had come undone. He'd seen the turmoil in her eyes before. Relief might be mixed with the anger and fear this time. He'd like to think so.

"You cuffed her?" he said incredulously.

"It said 'armed and dangerous,'" Jackman mumbled.

Matthew let loose with an expletive and bent over Alexa. "Damn, I'm sorry. Here, let me—" He used his key to free one of her wrists, then the other when it fell to her side.

"You came." This expression was almost naked. She hadn't believed him when he'd said he would.

"I keep promises," he said tersely. "I didn't expect to have to this soon."

"Me, neither." She actually tried to smile, although it was so shaky he couldn't be positive what she'd intended.

He crouched inside the V of the door to be at her level. "Did he hurt you? Do anything I need to know about?"

Her gaze flickered past him to Jackman then back to his face. "I...think I'll have bruises, but only because he yanked me out of the car, and I fell to my hands and knees." She held out her hands, skinned and with some grit clinging. "And..." This time she bit her lip. "He pulled his gun on me. Put it right in my face." Deep breath. "But I guess he had reason to think I was a threat."

He mumbled a word under his breath he hoped she didn't make out. "Where were you going?"

"Home." She made a sound.

Damn, he hoped she was safe there, at least. "Can you drive?"

She obviously gave his question some thought, finally nodding. "It's not that far."

"I'll follow you."

"I warn you, I'm calling my attorney."

Matthew met her eyes straight-on. "You should."

Her head bobbed. "Can I go now?"

"Give me just a minute, okay?"

He rose and walked around behind her car. After a moment, he gestured the other cop over. Jackman joined him in studying the brake light, which wasn't just "out." It had been smashed.

"Looks like someone used a boot," Jackman said uneasily. "Or a rock."

"This wasn't chance. She was set up," Matthew said grimly. "Again."

Jackman cleared his throat. "Yeah, it, uh, kind of looks like it."

Matthew took out his phone and snapped several photos of the damage; a couple that included her license plate. Then, shaking his head, he returned to Alexa, holding out a hand. She gaped at it for a minute as if not understanding why it was hovering there in front of her. Then, tentatively, she laid her hand in his and he tugged her to her feet, being careful not to put any stress on her shoulders or hurt her sore palm.

"Thank you," she mumbled.

He closed the back door of her car and opened the driver's door. Yeah, her keys were still in the ignition, her purse on the seat. A piece of paper had fallen to the floorboard. He picked it up to see that it was the registration for the car. He laid it beside her purse and backed away, letting her get in before closing the door. No question she already knew this wasn't an honest mistake, but he'd wait until they reached her house before he showed her the smashed light.

She put on her seat belt and started the car, but when he turned away to have more words with Jackman, Alexa just sat there. Collecting herself, he guessed.

As he walked to his vehicle, she finally started forward, aiming for an exit from the parking lot. Within minutes, he'd snugged up right behind her on the four-lane road. He always stayed aware when he was driving—and most of the rest of the time, too, but now his gaze flicked nonstop: rearview mirror, in front of him, one side-view mirror then the other. Businesses fronting the road, every other damn car on it. He felt like he did before closing in for an arrest with the expectation that things would go south. Tense, trying to figure out what might go wrong, seeing things that weren't there.

Only this time, the adrenaline didn't translate into excitement. Dread might be a better word.

As he'd expected, whoever had masterminded the campaign to scare off Ms. Adams wasn't done. As ugly and humiliating as the original assault had been, this had had the potential to be as dangerous. Jumpy enough to pull his gun, Jackson had been a hair from actually pulling the trigger. If Alexa had taken something from her purse that he'd even momentarily thought might be a weapon—say, her phone—he could have tightened his finger. Fired.

Killed her.

Somebody had a real hate on, and this episode made it a certainty that he was a cop. Matthew wished he were making any progress whatsoever in figuring out who that faceless piece of garbage was.

He was going down, but Matthew had to keep Alexa alive and unscathed until that happened. Something told him she wouldn't be willing to take a nice long vacation, or back off on her investigations for now.

No, once the fear receded, she'd be madder than ever. He'd feel the same—but he was more afraid for her than he'd have been for himself.

Chapter Seven

Alexa sat on a stool at her breakfast bar, fingers knotted together as she listened for the occasional sound as a cop did a walk-through of her house. A cop who *seemed* sincere, but…how was she to know?

Would her executive editor agree to run an article insisting that she was just one reporter, that if she was deterred or killed, ten others would take her place, swarming the two law enforcement agencies? Would whoever felt threatened by her believe that if he read it?

And…was it even true? Sure, she had the full support of her editors, but this was her crusade. Her idea to write a series of articles on problem officers and the consequences of letting them stay on the job. If the public couldn't trust the men in uniform, they needed to know that.

A door down the hall opened then a moment later softly closed. Closet doors slid on their tracks in what had to be her bedroom. She hadn't left anything out in her home office that she shouldn't, had she?

Damn. Why was she just sitting there? She should have already called her attorney.

When Matthew walked quietly back into the kitchen a minute later, Alexa was explaining the latest to Diana, who was furious.

"I can clear my schedule at nine tomorrow if that isn't too early for you. We need to strategize again. There's no way they can deny this traffic stop happened, is there?"

"No." Alexa discovered she had a lump in her throat. "At least…"

Matthew had his phone in his hands, and hers pinged.

"I sent you a few photos," he said.

"Just a minute," she said to Diana, and went to texts to see the pictures he'd forwarded. A couple of close-ups of her broken taillight, but also a photo that showed the squad car behind her, rack of lights still flashing, and Officer Jackman hovering near her bumper. Not really recognizable unless the photo was enlarged, and then she felt sure he would be.

"Thank you," she murmured, and explained to the attorney that she had pictures.

Once she set her phone down, she looked at Matthew, who was leaning against the kitchen counter, seemingly relaxed and even feeling at home. Of course, he had a holstered gun and badge on his belt, which made her wonder how fast he could move from that casual pose if he felt the need.

"Why are you helping?" she asked bluntly. "Can't you get in trouble for aiding and abetting the enemy?"

His eyes rose. "You're not the enemy. You aren't attacking law enforcement officers. If I understand right, your goal is to root out the ones who shouldn't be wearing a badge. Sometimes there's a fine line between an action that a civilian would jump on and the way a particular situation should ideally have been handled. We make mistakes, but that's not what we're talking about. If it was, I'd support my peers. The ones who enjoy beating up suspects, or blackmail women into servicing them sexually or violate the rules to punish an ex-wife's new boyfriend…" He shook his head.

"When they're caught, they should be fired and, when appropriate, arrested. No hesitation. The complaints shouldn't disappear into the files, and we sure as hell shouldn't hire officers with serious complaints on their records from other departments. If you can persuade the public to press for change, I'm all for it."

She tipped her head and studied him. Heaven help her, she *liked* the deepened lines in his face that made him look like he shouldered a great deal in life. She would never have imagined being attracted to a cop, not given their usual image, but if this one was really being honest, that meant he cared. Physically...tall, rangy, with a strong-boned face and penetrating gray eyes, he pushed her buttons.

And he'd come racing, siren blaring and lights flashing, when she'd needed him.

"I should have thought to take these pictures." She nodded at her phone. "I let myself get rattled."

"Most people get a little shaken up when they've had to look down the barrel of a gun." He wasn't amused; his tone was grim. "Plenty of cops carry Glocks that don't have a safety. The triggers are...sensitive. I don't think you're the only one who's rattled, by the way.

"Jackman is a good cop, as far as I know, and you can be damn sure he's seeing nightmare scenarios flashing before his eyes now. He was set up, in a different way than you were, and realizing how easily it happened—and could happen again—has to shake his confidence. That could make him hesitate when he shouldn't, but it'll also make him think twice when that's smart to do."

"I should hope so!" Alexa hesitated. "Do you, um, have time for a cup of coffee?"

"Tell you the truth, I'm getting hungry." He eyed her with

what she thought might be wariness. "What I should do is wish you a good evening and leave."

Her heartbeat picked up speed.

"But I'm wondering whether you might like to go out together and get some dinner."

Just ask, she told herself. "Are you thinking we can keep talking about who might be behind these attacks on me and what we can do to flush him out? Or—"

He smiled, a little ruefully. "Or. Definitely or…"

SHE'D BEEN THE one to call in an order for a pizza and salads so they didn't have to go out. Matthew didn't comment, but Alexa figured he'd be relieved. Associating with a cop wouldn't make her automatically suspect among her peers, but a cop dating a journalist who was investigating his department? Really, she didn't understand why he wasn't politic enough to be avoiding her like the plague.

Except, she could guess. If she asked, he'd be arrogant enough to say that he didn't give a damn if he got called in by his chief for a butt-chewing. Well, he might be able to shrug that off, but she hated the idea of him getting fired. She'd be left hanging out there with no backup.

And, yes, being trusting enough to think of him that way came as a surprise to her, but how could she not?

He'd darned well better not have any vision of ending the evening in her bed, though. Her trust didn't stretch that far.

As it was, she was torn between wishing she'd just said no about dinner and being glad to have company. If they were really going to talk, at least this was better. No background music, he wouldn't have to stay hyperaware of his surroundings the way she'd heard cops tended to be. Nobody could eavesdrop, either. Still…part of her edginess had to do with the possibility he might kiss her goodnight. Or try, anyway. He'd expressed his interest bluntly.

They made stiff conversation until the doorbell rang. He insisted on answering the door, in case of an unpleasant surprise, and on signing the credit slip. Alexa didn't love his insistence on paying for the dinner, but all he did was raise his eyebrows and say, "Call me old-fashioned. I did the asking, I foot the bill."

By the time he returned to the kitchen with the pizza and a bag presumably holding their salads, she'd already gotten out plates and napkins and poured herself some water.

"Would you like a beer?"

"Sure, but…what about you?" he asked.

She wrinkled her nose. "I don't like beer. Lucky for you, some friends left a couple in my fridge."

"Ah. Wine?"

"To tell you the truth, I'm not much of a drinker. I had a stepfather who was a raging alcoholic. It kind of left me with some scars, if you know what I mean."

"Yeah. I know."

His terse response ramped up her curiosity about him. Since she'd met one part of his family… "So, your brother— Nate, right?—is here in town. Does that mean your family is, too?"

"No. My parents split up a few years ago and Nate came to live with me. He graduated from high school here and is just finishing his AA degree at the community college."

"He didn't stay home until he finished high school?" None of her business, but the question just popped out.

"Home? Where was that? Anyway, it seemed as if Mom and Dad pretty much ditched Nate—" He grimaced.

"It must be almost as weird having your parents split up

when you're an adult as when you're still home and in the middle of it."

Matthew seemed to be really good at suppressing what she thought of as physical tells, but the way he rolled his shoulders gave away some discomfiture.

"In general, it's not as traumatic, I imagine," he said after a minute. "But my parents turned into strangers. I kept thinking, Wait! But no, Mom really said that, and yeah, he'd been screwing—" He stopped abruptly.

It was obvious he hadn't meant to say that much. Alexa lowered her guard enough to reach across the table and touch the back of his hand lightly. "You don't have to tell me about it."

His gaze dropped to her hand. "It's okay. That was only part of it. The worst was that neither of them saw what they were doing to Nate. They became unbelievably self-centered. I'm left wondering whether I was deceiving myself all those years. Did they really change that drastically, or did I just imagine my family was solid?"

"If you'd been younger, too—"

His expression closed. "I was glad I had the resources to take Nate in."

Wow. This felt unnervingly like a real date; one that had moved on with pedal-to-the-floor speed, too. Forget what movies or hobbies they liked—they'd gone right for the gut. Alexa couldn't seem to pull herself back, though.

Heck, she'd always been nosy. Why else become an investigative journalist? Supposedly, curiosity killed the cat, but she hadn't died yet.

Although, this past week, she'd come perilously close—*twice*—and that had to be because of her nosiness.

This was innocuous, though. "Nate still lives with you?" she asked.

Matthew laughed. "No, he has an apartment with some friends. He's already been accepted to Washington State University and is thinking of going into chemical engineering."

"Not criminology?"

"When I suggested it, he laughed at me."

"Doesn't want to walk in his big brother's footsteps, huh?"

He sobered. "The honor, justice and public service police are supposed to embody hasn't been on the best display lately."

Perturbed, she said, "You don't take pride in what you do?"

Matthew released a long breath. "I do, but I'm finding myself looking around real uneasily of late."

It felt weird to be talking like this. Actually, it felt strange having Matthew—forget distancing him by calling him "lieutenant"—here in her house, sitting at her table in the small nook off the kitchen. He filled more space than should be possible, probably through sheer force of personality.

Although she couldn't discount the breadth of his shoulders, or his muscles, either.

Her cheeks felt warm. Hoping he hadn't noticed, she said, "You seem like a confident guy."

He set a half-eaten piece of pizza onto his plate. "I am. Not being able to get answers about who is targeting you isn't bolstering my confidence, though."

Wiping her fingers on a napkin, she nodded. The things he'd said earlier, about how problem police officers should be handled, fit with this man's character, as she was beginning to see it. His expectations for himself would be high, and she bet he tried to hold the people around him to standards just as high. Was frustration the real reason he was sitting here, close enough that his knees were bumping hers? Not attraction. But his needing to earn her...what? Faith that he could keep her safe? Or did he want to hear her say, *None of this was your fault. Go in peace.*

Maybe.

He shook his head slightly, as if shaking off a disturbing subject.

"What about you? Are you a local?"

"Not even close. Can't you hear the accent?"

Wheels visibly turned. "Boston?"

"Close enough. I came out to the west coast for school. Speaking of confidence, I was filled with it until I had that degree in journalism and started looking for a job. In one way, I knew that newspapers were biting the dust right and left, but, naturally, some executive editor would recognize brilliance when he saw it and snap me up." Alexa made a face at her naïveté. Honestly, she couldn't have picked a worse time to launch her career.

Well, except for every one of the intervening years, when more and more newspapers went under.

"I didn't want some online gig, and television news wasn't for me. I was incredibly lucky to be taken on here by the *Tribune*. Even luckier to have an editorial staff that eventually saw enough promise in me to turn me loose to pursue in-depth investigations. This kind of stuff can be expensive, in terms of the time it takes to produce results and—" she grinned "—the risk of lawsuits."

Matthew laughed. "Yet here you are, threatening to file your own lawsuits."

"Sometimes, it's the only way to get results."

"Can't argue."

They ate for a minute without either saying anything. She kept wondering about him.

"You must have worked construction at some point," she remarked.

"Nope. Don't I wish." He smiled at her expression. "I bought a house a couple of years ago. Built in 1910. Big-time fixer upper. I thought it might be fun."

Her turn to laugh. "I've had friends who bought old houses that had, in theory, already been renovated. They say there's still one headache after another."

"I can only hope to get to that stage. Right now, it's more like backaches, bruises, a broken collarbone when a wall collapsed on me, and constant bewilderment. Before I start any project, I have to teach myself how to do it first."

Alexa enjoyed the humor in his voice and on his face. Not everybody could laugh at themselves. "I take it you've replaced some doors."

"No, no, no. I took the doors down, stripped them, re-painted or refinished them, replaced hardware and rehung them. Doors, I have down pat. I'm feeling good about plumbing. Spackling, I'm a champ." He shook his head. "The only thing I've hired out is replacing the wiring. Electricity scares me."

She nodded. "For good reason. I've written about some house fires. Remember the one where the baby was killed?"

"Yeah. I know the mother. She works in the DA's office. She and her husband haven't tried for another child. It's been—what?—three years."

"Something like that." She frowned. "I'm surprised I haven't run into you before."

"We might have been in the same courtroom or some-place like that before. I've read your stuff, and you're now famous in the police department."

"Don't you mean infamous?"

He laughed again, his eyes glinting. "I was being polite."

"It's a little late for that."

Every trace of humor left his face. After a moment, he asked, "Am I tarred with the same brush? Are you trying to tell me this isn't happening?" His gesture encompassed the two of them.

MATTHEW WAS STILL brooding about her answer Wednesday while he pretended to be absorbed in the test results that would determine promotions within the department. His division was below strength, so he should be jumping on this. Instead, he kept seeing that moment yesterday evening.

Alexa had stared at him for longer than he'd liked, then taken a deep breath and said with what felt like painful honesty, "I don't know. I'm…a little off cops right now. And… not very good at trust at the best of times."

Which this wasn't. He got that. Now, he regretted having laid his feelings on the table. He felt sure the undercurrent of sexual attraction had been going both ways, that her interest in his family and background had been a good sign. The sense of intimacy had taken him by surprise, but some instinct had pushed him to open up to her more than he usually would on a first date. Not "some instinct." He'd seen her at some seriously low moments. The only hope of achieving any balance had been in baring his vulnerable underside.

A rap on his door yanked him back to the present.

"Come in."

Art Dwyer walked in. "Got a few minutes?"

"Of course I do." He waved at the chairs on the other side of his desk.

Art took a seat. "Did you hear about that stop Ward and O'Brien made last week? They claimed to think the guy was going for a gun?"

Damn, this wasn't about Berkey. Since Dwyer was working a dozen active cases, that wasn't a surprise.

"I heard. I can't say I know either of them, except—" He looked at the list of names and test scores displayed on his monitor. "Jim Ward?"

"Yeah."

"He took the exam for a promotion."

Dwyer grimaced.

"Don't worry. He scored near the bottom of this bunch."

"Good, because I have a lot of concerns about him. Yesterday, I surprised him and a couple of his friends when I came out a door right by their huddle in the hall. They were smirking and laughing about roughing up a guy they'd hoped was an illegal."

Matthew shook his head, not in disbelief but in disgust. He'd already heard at least some of the follow-up. "The witnesses with their cell phones tripped them up."

"And the fact that their victim was a US citizen born in this country."

Matthew grunted. "How is he? Do you know?"

"Released from the hospital. They kept him overnight because of the concussion. He has multiple broken ribs, broken cheekbone, forearm—from the clip I saw, he was trying to protect his face—and his nose is a mess."

Matthew swore pungently. "Tell me Ward and O'Brien are on suspension." That, he hadn't heard.

"Initially, no. Once the *Tribune* and our local TV news channels got some of the cell phone footage and raised a stink, the two were pulled off the street while an investigation is conducted."

"But from what you overheard, they still don't think there'll be any consequences."

"Can you blame them?" Dwyer ran a hand over the thinning hair on top of his head. "King County fired O'Brien four years ago for a seemingly unprovoked assault on a homeless man. The complaints since we snapped him up are legion. Ward less so, but he was on a prostitute sting—"

Matthew's phone rang. He'd have let the caller go if it had been almost anyone else. "It's Carrera," he told Art. "Detective in the sheriff's department. Do you know him? He heard about our interest in Berkey and thought he had a lead." The only hint of a lead so far.

Art stretched out his legs and waited, head cocked in interest.

Matthew answered his phone. "News?"

"One of our informants says he knows where Berkey is right now. The house is outside the city limits. You free to join me?"

Matthew opened his mouth to give eager agreement, but had to close it. He was supposed to accompany one of his rookie detectives to interview several persons of interest in a murder. Teaching, overseeing, had become increasingly big parts of his job with each promotion.

Yeah, but this was that SOB Berkey. And Art had worked harder than Matthew had to get his hands on the tipster. He deserved in on this.

"Hold on a sec," Matthew said into the phone, then explained quickly to Art.

"Hell, yes, I want to be there!" Matthew's friend and fellow detective jumped to his feet as Matthew told Carrera he was sending Dwyer instead. Art took Matthew's phone long enough for the two men to arrange where to meet up.

Returning the phone, Art said, "I need to run. Laying our hands on Berkey has to be a priority right now. The rest of what I stopped by to say can wait. It's the prostitute angle—" He shook his head. "I'll let you know what we find."

Left alone again, Matthew sank reluctantly back into his desk chair and did battle with the desire to run after his fellow detective and say, *Forget about it. I'm on this.*

If there was anyone in the department he trusted, bone deep, it was Art Dwyer.

And what had he meant by "the prostitute angle"?

Murders, yes, but "angle"?

Chapter Eight

Alexa had spent her day so far diving eagerly into the spate of records and—yes!—even some body camera footage that both the city and county had released in a not-so surprising burst of compliance. It had taken her a couple of hours to realize that she'd been given the least damaging material she'd requested. Yeah, she didn't like some of the conduct she was seeing, but most of it wouldn't make it into her article. Or series. She didn't yet know which.

Matthew hadn't had to tell her that cops were human; they panicked and made a bad decision, or suddenly cracked when someone pushed the right button, and kept pushing. That was to be expected. Handled in-house, preferably resulting in more training or counseling. A suspension at worst.

She watched again as a woman rose on tiptoe so she could get into a cop's face to scream at him in a voice that made Alexa think of fingernails on a good, old-fashioned blackboard. He stayed patient, giving the admittedly vague answer that was also the only one he could offer, six or seven times before his impassive face gave way to anger and he said some regrettable things.

No, he shouldn't have. But what he'd done wasn't close to the ugly behavior that Alexa was digging deep to find.

Sighing, she moved to the next file then decided to pour herself a cup of coffee first.

Her phone rang while she was in the kitchen, so she had to backtrack. Matthew Reinert was calling, she saw. With mixed feelings, she answered. "Hey. Did you learn something?"

There was a pause. "About who set you up? No, although it looks like we may put our hands on Jim Berkey. I'm tied up and couldn't go, but I sent Detective Dwyer. I have faith in him. Right now, I'm just waiting."

"This Berkey might not be willing to talk." The side of right and order was unlikely to be nearly as frightening as her two assailants. Alexa could speak to that.

"We'll see." He paused. "I have someone digging into the origin of the 'armed and dangerous' designation on your car, too, but she's not getting anywhere, either. At the moment, I'm just…checking in. Making sure you're okay," he said in the voice that might as well have been a touch.

Thank goodness, he wasn't there to *see* her bare toes curl. "I'm working from home today. I've got to tell you, I'm tempted to rent a car for a while, so I'm not such an obvious target."

"That's actually not a bad idea."

"You're serious?" she said incredulously.

"Given that traffic stop? Damn straight I am." He sounded affronted. "That's assuming, of course, that nobody is actually keeping an eye on your house."

Because if someone was, driving a different car would do her no good. That's what he was saying.

"Surely nobody in Dispatch would buy another sudden tip saying I'm armed and dangerous."

"Probably not, but word doesn't always get to everyone it should."

"Did I mention that print journalists don't make big salaries?"

He laughed. "Have I mentioned that cops don't, either?"

"My point," she said with dignity, "is that renting a car for what might turn out to be weeks isn't in my budget. I'd rather spend that money on a midwinter vacation. Sunshine, turquoise waters, golden sand beach…"

"Which you can't enjoy if you're dead," he said bluntly.

"Was this call meant to cheer me up?"

"I did mean to be supportive," he admitted. "Mostly… I wanted to hear your voice."

She went very still. That wasn't the cop speaking. It was the man. He sounded as if he was on edge, maybe because he really believed Berkey would give them some answers. He had to know that she wouldn't be able to consider having any kind of relationship with him—and he'd been upfront about having that in mind—as long as a good part of his department was made up of her antagonists.

Or…he was facing some kind of danger? But how likely was that? From what she could gather, the average detective spent as much time as she did on the phone and computer rather than pull out his or her gun and chase down suspects. Matthew had administrative responsibilities besides.

Maybe not being able to go after Berkey himself was rubbing him the wrong way.

Still… "You're being careful, too, aren't you?" she said as an alternative to all the other things that had crossed her mind. "I'm not the only person those guys are mad at."

"I'm looking at that as a positive. I might never have met you if not for the note left with you."

Did she hear a smile? Her heart threw in an extra uncomfortable beat.

Given all her doubts, she sidestepped the implication. "Will you let me know what you find out?"

"I will. But you keep being careful, Alexa." And then he was gone.

SEEING THE NAME on the screen, Matthew snatched up his phone and pushed back from the desk. "Carrera?"

"It's Art!" The unfailingly even-tempered detective sounded distraught. "He was shot. He...doesn't look good."

"*What?*"

"He went to the back door, I knocked on the front. Heard firing out back, ran around. Art was down. It was a headshot, Reinert. He's alive, but— Just a minute." Carrera talked to someone else then came back. "We think the shooter was in the alley, close enough to use a handgun. An ambulance is on the way. Do you have his wife's number?"

"Yes. I'll call her. Art isn't conscious?" He knew better, but had to ask.

"No." Carrera's swallow was audible. "I hope that siren is the ambulance. Listen, I gotta go. More units have responded. Shooter is probably long gone, but—"

"Berkey?"

"House appears to be vacant. This was a setup."

"Another setup," Matthew said grimly.

"Yeah." Carrera ended the call.

Feeling sick, Matthew scrolled to Art's home number and hit Call.

Michelle answered on the second ring. Matthew knew she always kept her phone close. Maybe she'd spent twenty years expecting this call.

"Matthew?"

"Art's been shot. He's on his way to the hospital."

"He's alive?" Her voice shook.

"I wasn't with him. I'm told he was shot in the head and is unconscious."

"Oh God." She was quiet for a bare instant then exclaimed, "I have to go. I have to be there!"

"I'm on my way, too—" But he realized he was talking to dead air.

He beat her to the hospital, for what good that did. The ambulance had arrived just ahead of him. Nobody with any real information had time to talk to him. Five minutes later, Michelle ran in, gaze frantically searching until it locked on him.

He gripped her arms when she reached him. "I don't know any more yet. They're too busy working on him to come out and talk."

She whimpered and he wrapped his arms around her. About Art's age, she'd fed Matthew a few hundred meals, even plied a paintbrush a few times at his house, and they'd become good friends. He wasn't surprised when she didn't let herself lean on him for long, though.

"I should call Steph. She'd want to be here."

Their fifteen-year-old daughter.

"Why don't we wait?" he suggested gently. "Until we get some word?"

If Art was dead—Matthew didn't even want to think about it. Art's family would be devastated. It would take time for his boy to get home from college. Stephanie wasn't at a good age to handle this kind of devastation. Finances— No, he had to believe Art would have made sure they were okay.

As if that worry was at the top of anybody's mind.

He walked her up to the counter, where she gave the receptionist info including health insurance number, allergies, et cetera. Then all they could do was wait.

After what felt like an eternity, Carrera called.

Glancing at Michelle, who was staring straight ahead and probably seeing nothing, Matthew walked away before answering.

Voice flat, Carrera said, "We didn't find anything. An old man at the corner heard a car start close by not long after the gunshot, but he's slow on his feet and by the time he got to the window, the car was gone. Assuming he'd have been able to see it from his front window anyway."

"The house?"

"No indication anyone has been living there, or even just squatting. Neighbors say it's been empty for a while. They know the landlord and think he's short of cash. Can't afford to fix the house up, no one will rent it in such lousy condition."

Matthew didn't care about the house, but the questions had had to be asked. You never knew what passing tidbit would provide the all-important lead.

"I don't know if it's occurred to you yet," the other detective said, "but I can't help wondering if *you* weren't supposed to be the victim. Everyone in both our departments knows who's the driving force behind the investigation into what happened with the reporter woman, and that you're determined to get your hands on Berkey. They'd have had good reason to think you'd walk right into their ambush."

The thought had crossed Matthew's mind, but he found himself shaking his head. "They also have to know that I spend most of my time behind the desk these days, that delegating is my job."

"Everyone is saying you've been taking this stuff personally."

Oh good. Nice to know he was the subject of intense gossip—and that he'd been transparent despite his usual impassive demeanor.

"I have taken offense, you're right about that," he admitted. "But anyone watching for me couldn't have mistaken Art for me. If they were after me, why shoot him?"

Noticeably dropping his voice, Carrera said, "If the shooter was a cop? Sure. Everyone knows Dwyer. *And* what good friends you are. This could have been another message for you."

That note flashed before Matthew's inner eye, chilling him. *Lieutenant Reinert, you should have been smart and stayed out of it.*

He'd ignored instructions. In doing so, had he killed his best friend?

Or had Art been the real target because *he* was the one heading the hunt for Jim Berkey? Something else every cop within the city and county would know.

After ending the call, he walked back to Michelle, who was watching him. As he dropped into the seat beside her, she asked, "How did this happen?"

She was a cop's wife, and he wasn't going to lie to her.

She looked almost numb as he told her as much as he felt he could.

"Mrs. Art Dwyer…?" a voice called.

"Heard someone talking at the courthouse," Diana Troxell said. "I'm still there, in the ladies' room right now."

It hadn't surprised Alexa to hear from Diana; they had been talking regularly. This was different, though. Something about the hushed voice told her that whatever the attorney had overheard, Alexa wouldn't like it.

Clutching her cell phone, she asked, "What did you hear?"

"A cop's been shot. It doesn't sound good."

Alexa felt as if she'd just stepped off the edge of a cliff. She'd start falling any second. "Wilden PD?"

"Yes, but when I tried to find out who, nobody would say." There was a murmur of voices in the background. Presumably, Diana was no longer alone in the restroom. "I've got to go," she said hurriedly. "I'll let you know if I hear more, and if it has anything to do with you."

All Alexa could think was, What if Matthew was dead?

No, that was surely unlikely. But there'd been that unsettling *something* in his voice when he'd called. The death of a detective working under him would impact him, which meant it mattered to Alexa. Realizing how true that was came as a shock. Her feelings for him should be a lot more mixed than they were.

I could fall in love with him, she thought, looking down at the cell phone she still held.

Oh, dear God, what if he'd been killed? Nobody would tell *her*, even if he had been shot pursuing a lead that had to do with the attacks on her. She could track down his brother, but the obvious step was just to call Matthew. Since she'd entered his number in her phone, she didn't even have to hunt for it.

If he didn't answer… Well, there were lots of reasons he might not, especially in the aftermath of such a disaster. She couldn't assume anything. But she knew she wouldn't be able to concentrate on anything else until he called back.

Which he'd do. Of course he would.

ONCE ART HAD been moved to ICU, first his wife then Matthew had been allowed in to see him.

Standing beside the bed, Matthew swore under his breath as he gazed down at the stocky man who looked dead except for the fact that his chest rose and fell with each breath. He was breathing on his own; that was good news, the doctor had said. His head was heavily bandaged. Matthew had asked where the bullet struck and noted that it had been low enough, it might have been aimed at his neck. A few inches lower, that bullet would have torn through Art's neck and throat, probably opening the carotid artery.

Just as it had Tansy Gould's.

Coincidence? Or not? Good shot? Or a miss? Matthew asked himself. The shooter would have assumed Art was wearing a vest.

As it was, the bullet had ricocheted off Art's head, but had shattered his skull where it struck. He was officially in a coma; they'd drained fluid from his brain and were monitoring him closely.

"At this point," the doctor had said, after clearing his throat, "we can't tell you what to expect. He could open his eyes a few hours from now, or remain in a coma for an unknown length of time."

He didn't say, *Or slip away*, but Michelle and Matthew both heard the unspoken words.

Michelle would be allowed to sit with her husband for intervals. She made the decision to update her daughter with calls but not let her see her father like this.

Looking shell-shocked, Michelle called the mother of a friend of Stephanie's, who would pick her up at school, and then phoned their son, Brian, at the University of Washington.

She'd intended to tell him to stay at school until they knew more, but Brian wouldn't have it. Matthew was to pick him up at the airport. He was glad; Michelle was forgetting that *she'd* need support, too.

He couldn't kid himself. A fellow cop had shot Art. Had

to be. This felt like a nightmare, so many things going wrong in his department. He'd trusted most of the men and women with whom he served. That trust was quaking under his feet now, and he had to wonder whether the chief would have his back. He, his minions, and the city officials all seemed to want to sweep anything troublesome under the rug. What happened when he let them all know, from Internal Affairs to the police chief himself, that he felt certain someone wearing a badge had fired that bullet? Had set a trap and laid in patient wait to kill a long-serving member of the department—a good, kind, smart man?

Matthew had a feeling he was going to become a thorn digging into their bare flesh. He'd already resolved to uncover the truth of the lowlife dogging Alexa. He wouldn't relent in his pursuit of the piece of scum who'd shot Art, no matter who it turned out to be. If he was ordered to defend the department's reputation above all, his superiors were about to receive a shock.

And he was for damn sure going to give Art's wife both truth and justice, however cold the comfort that either offered.

A COUPLE OF hours later, Matthew sat at his desk, the door to his office closed. He felt paralyzed. Brian had let him know he wouldn't be able to fly in until morning and said he'd get an Uber to the hospital, which let Matthew concentrate on an investigation that had no obvious strings to pull.

They had no witness, no shell left at the scene. Fingerprints taken from the front and back doors of the house led nowhere. Why would the shooter have approached the house? He hadn't needed to.

Matthew called to check in with Michelle again. No change.

His job was to take a look at everything Art had been

working on, not make assumptions despite the Berkey connection. Jim Berkey's name had been thrown around a lot lately. Someone who wanted Art dead for an unrelated reason might have heard the name, used it as a lure.

That meant, gut feeling aside, he couldn't rule out the possibility the shooter *wasn't* a cop.

So. Proceed on the assumption that Art had been targeted because of something he knew or suspected. Start by examining all his recent investigations, which Matthew would have to take over or reassign anyway. Temporarily, he wanted to believe, but he had no choice.

The last conversation they'd had right here in this office nibbled at Matthew. If only they hadn't been interrupted. Art had seemed worried. What was it he'd started to say?

They'd been talking about the traffic stop Ward and O'Brien had made, Matthew remembered, and the conversation Art had overheard. Those two officers were in serious trouble now, which they must know even if they'd been smirking for their buddies. What if one of them had said something that would increase their legal peril, and knew Art had overheard it?

Matthew shook his head. The traffic stop was already being scrutinized, body camera and cell phone footage available. Would anything said carelessly really make matters worse?

No, Art had been working his way up to a point. He'd said something about how Ward had been in on a prostitute sting—but Art hadn't had a chance to tell Matthew what had happened.

Matthew's jaw tightened. Dirty cops and prostitutes. That was the connection. And it so happened Art had been primary on the series of murders of local prostitutes—and his recent focus had been the latest murder: Tansy Elizabeth Gould's. What had he learned?

Suddenly energized, Matthew had just pushed back from his desk when his cell phone rang. Alexa.

He answered. "Hey."

"You're all right."

"You heard about the shooting," he said slowly.

"Only that…that a police officer was injured or killed. Diana—my attorney—heard talk at the courthouse."

He paused. "She heard right. I'm…dealing with the fall-out," he said. "And trying to figure out what the hell happened."

"Was it…a patrol officer? Or someone you work closely with?"

He pinched the bridge of his nose. "He's a good friend. A detective, too, so we worked—work—together daily. He's in a coma. Right now, we just don't know…" His throat closed.

Damn. Surely, he'd piqued the journalist's interest.

But all she said was a soft, "I'm sorry."

"Thanks. I can't give you his name until the department is ready to release it."

"I wasn't trying to butter you up. I'm not on the crime beat."

"I know you're not." He hesitated. "Can I stop by this evening?"

She was quiet. "I was afraid it was you."

He waited.

"Yes. Yes, of course. If you want, I can make dinner."

"I'd like that," he said simply.

Chapter Nine

Knowing he'd see her this evening centered him in some way, helped him face his task of going through Art's desk, computer, phone—if he could figure out the password—and probably even his car.

Matthew was immediately reminded about Art's habit of scribbling notes to himself on random pieces of paper and scattering them behind him like confetti. He also filled notebooks of several sizes. Not all those notes made it into his computer files or reports. Art still preferred pen and paper. Sometimes even pencil and paper, which made for eye strain. The result was slow going for Matthew, who had to start by sorting out which note went with which investigation and in what order.

It didn't take him long to discover that his fellow detective had been digging into the histories of several officers within the department, including the two he'd mentioned to Matthew. His interest hadn't started with them, though; apparently, he'd already become uneasy, pursuing what Matthew guessed were several of the same threads as Alexa's.

What had interested Art most, though, were ones who'd been caught using the services of prostitutes when they were supposed to be arresting them. He was sure one had given warnings a couple of times right before operations, meaning the run-down motels that were supposed to be the hot spots had proved astonishingly peaceful and crime-free when the cops showed up to hammer on doors.

Sergeant Newsome called Peters on it, Art had noted. Matthew had to squint to read his handwriting. *Peters admitting having a relationship with*—this name was illegible—*and he's afraid he let the plans slip. Says he's not seeing her anymore. Knows it was stupid (ya think???), groveled. Newsome chewed him out and let it go with a warning.*

Matthew sat back to mull over the incident. Was Vice sergeant Newsome really that naïve? Did he have complete faith in his officers? As Art had probably done, Matthew grunted in disbelief.

What Art was looking for, it appeared, was any connection between the cops who'd gotten too friendly with hookers and the murders of several of the local ones.

Stunned by where this trail seemed to be heading, Matthew found himself queasily agreeing with the logic. No arrests had been made for a reason; the pimps that might otherwise be suspected had unshakable alibis, and witnesses were either nonexistent or too intimidated to come forward. What's more, the killings had looked damned cold-blooded, not displaying the kind of rage they'd see if a john had lost it.

A man threatened with the possibility of losing his job now, especially a man who routinely carried a gun and had a good idea how to avoid leaving any trace of his presence at a crime scene… Yeah, that made sense.

Matthew blew out an unhappy breath. Then he went back to sifting through notes that were too often nonsensical, in hope of finding the open spots in the puzzle where they belonged.

INVITING LIEUTENANT MATTHEW REINERT to dinner a second night, and in a row, wasn't the smartest thing Alexa had ever done. She and her voice of common sense needed to talk before she got too carried away. As in, asking him to stay the night.

Just say no.

She wrinkled her nose. The fact that she was worrying at all about whether she'd do that meant she was seriously considering it.

The doorbell rang in the middle of her attempt to squelch any enthusiasm for having sex with a man she hardly knew, one who'd rushed to her rescue, sure, but also represented a police department riddled with corruption. She wasn't yet ready to forget that.

Besides, she had some serious doubts about why *he* was interested in her. Journalist? Cop? Not exactly an obvious pairing.

When she let him in, her heart took a little hop despite everything. When he wasn't right in front of her, she forgot the impact his sheer physical presence had on her. His height, breadth, all those muscles that she felt sure weren't cultivated for show, never mind the glint in his steely eyes and the quirk of his mouth, definitely pushed her buttons.

"Smells good," he said.

"What?" She backed up. "Oh, I'm stir-frying. Ginger beef. I don't eat much meat, but I love this recipe."

He followed her toward the kitchen. "When Nate lived with me, I did a lot of stir-fries, too. I made more effort when I wasn't cooking just for myself."

Having plugged in the wok, she really studied him. Deeper than usual lines scored his face, aging him. "You look…" Alexa hesitated.

Matthew grimaced. "Lousy day."

"Detective Dwyer?" The police chief had held a press conference, looking outraged and determined. She'd wondered how much was sincere.

"No change in Art's condition." He leaned a hip against the edge of the countertop. "Is there anything I can do?"

"Give the rice a quick stir?"

He complied. "Art's wife is going through hell. Telling her was—" He rubbed his forehead with the back of his hand.

Art Dwyer had been with the local department for fifteen years, Alexa now knew, having started his career with a few years in Portland, Oregon. He had to be older than Matthew, who outranked him, but not everyone wanted to take on administrative responsibilities. Truthfully, she was surprised that Matthew did. Or maybe she shouldn't be; he did have what seemed like an effortless air of command. Probably, he couldn't help himself.

Dumping strips of beef into the sizzling oil to join the green onions and ginger that smelled so good, she said, "There's no way to ease into it, is there? Being the one to deliver the news..." She shivered. That would be bad enough, but loving the man who lay in a coma because someone had tried to *kill* him—*that* would be worse. The fact that she could so easily imagine being in that position scared her.

He lifted the lid of the pan on the stovetop. "I think the rice is done."

Think about this later, Alexa warned herself.

"Set it aside and put that other pan on the burner. Asparagus," she told him.

They kept talking. Matthew gradually worked the subject back to his friend and the friend's family. Alexa winced. One kid in his first year of college, the other a sophomore in high school. If their father died, neither was at a good age to be hit with such a hammer blow—although, really, was there such a thing as a good age? Babies, toddlers, wouldn't feel the devastation, but then they'd be fated to grow up with no memory of their father, which was hard in a different way.

He asked about her family, not her favorite subject, but he'd said enough about his own, she answered.

"No father. I love my mother, and I know she loves me, but she absolutely refused to talk about him. If she'd gone the sperm bank route, wouldn't you think she'd have said?" Alexa shrugged, as if lacking any knowledge at all of her father wasn't still as sore to the touch as the worst bruise. "I can't imagine her sleeping around to the point she didn't know which man was the father when she got pregnant. It was a shock having her marry when I was eight, but that only lasted a few years."

Matthew watched her with interest. "She's still alive?"

"Oh, sure, and as stubborn as ever." Alexa grimaced. "When I was a teenager, I descended so far as to search her closet and the boxes stashed in the attic for evidence. How could there not be something?"

"Is she still in the house where you grew up?"

"Yep. My grandparents gave her a great deal on it when they retired to Florida, which means Mom *also* grew up in that house."

"You picture yourself moving back there when she's gone?"

She gave a slight shrug. "I really don't think so. It's hard enough to separate myself from Mom's stern voice. If she were a ghost and I were living there, she'd never quit lecturing me."

Matthew laughed. "So does this big mystery in your life explain why you've been hunting for answers to other questions ever since?"

She grimaced. "Probably?"

That earned her another laugh.

He looked so tired, once they finished their meal she refused his help cleaning up, letting him relax over a cup of coffee. Not until she'd closed the dishwasher and joined him again at the table did she say, "Did this happen when your friend was looking for Berkey?" She felt selfish, but almost hoped not; that the shooting had nothing to do with her problems.

Creases deepened on Matthew's forehead. He moved his shoulders as if to release tension. "I'm asking you not to put this in print. But... Art and a detective from the county sheriff's office went to what turned out to be a vacant house because Jim Berkey was supposedly squatting there."

"His name was used *again* to set someone up, only this time it was Detective Dwyer?"

"Yes. Except Berkey's name has been bandied around enough lately, every scumbag in town may have known that Art was hunting for the guy. Cops make enemies. He had a lot of open investigations."

"But..." Yet again, Alexa found herself deeply disturbed for reasons she didn't understand. Because this man could, despite his air of confidence and solid competence, as easily be a target? Could have *been* a target?

"What if you'd gone instead?" she rushed to say.

His face closed, but the hand that lay on the table fisted. She expected him to shrug her off but, after a moment, he said, "I almost did."

"Then you—" Even the possibility stole her breath.

"I didn't." He reached for her hand.

She squeezed it back and held on tight.

"I'd asked Art—" his voice was hoarse "—to find Berkey. He was the public face of the investigation. I think that bullet had his name on it."

And Matthew felt guilty, she realized.

"You assign investigations. That's what you do. It could have been any detective during any investigation."

Emotion flickered through his gray eyes, darker than usual, but eventually he nodded. "You're right. But, you know, patrol officers are killed more often than detectives. It's not something that I usually worry about."

She nodded.

"I want to believe Art will wake up anytime. He started to tell me something right before he left, but—" He clamped his lips shut.

She opened her mouth to ask him what that was, but stopped herself. "I'm being nosy, aren't I? You have no reason to tell me all. Especially given that I'm a journalist."

"No, I can't tell you everything. I do want to remind you to keep being careful." Now he sounded grimmer than she liked.

"As if I'd forgotten," she mumbled. "I will, but…"

He raised dark eyebrows.

"Given what I do for a living, I'm kind of used to acquiring enemies. Cops aren't the only ones that happens to."

"No." He sighed, swallowed the last of what had to be cold coffee by now, and said, "I'd better get out of here."

"You look exhausted." Worried, too, but she didn't say that.

When he pushed back his chair, she rose to walk him to the front door. He wouldn't be asking to stay, she could tell, which was both a relief and…a slight letdown.

This was not the right time for anything like that, she told herself firmly. She still had plenty of questions about why he was here at all, anyway. He could be visiting her conspicuously to make a statement. *Don't mess with her. I'm watching.* Or maybe he was playing good cop to soften her antagonism toward the department and city.

Only, she knew that whatever his underlying motivation, he was physically attracted to her. That would be hard to fake.

At the front door, he stopped short of reaching for the knob.

"Alexa." Just that. He held out a hand.

She hesitated, but couldn't resist so much temptation and laid her hand in his. He drew her to him, and she went. When he first bent to her height, he gently bumped his forehead against hers and nuzzled her. Only then did he seek her mouth.

The electricity was immediate. There was none of the usual awkwardness. He explored and tempted instead of demanded, and by the time he stroked his tongue along the seam of her lips, she was already parting them. He tasted of dinner and coffee and something indefinable. *Him*, she thought hazily. By this time, she'd risen on tiptoe and flung one arm around his neck while her other hand gripped his shirt as if to make sure he couldn't get away.

He pulled her in tight to his big, solid body. And, oh, it was all she could do not to rub herself against him, but she had that much self-control. She kneaded his neck, though, and savored that thigh-to-chest contact—and the evidence that he definitely did want her.

Matthew was the one to gentle the kiss, nibble on her lower lip and then her earlobe, go back to nuzzling before finally sighing. One of his hands gripped a hip, half lifting her, while the other cupped the back of her head. All ten fingers flexed before he deliberately released her. Alexa was slower to follow suit.

She blinked a few times before seeing his wry expression.

"I hope we can…take this up another time," he said in a voice that was a little rougher than usual.

"I… I hadn't—" She stopped short of an outright lie.

Now he looked sardonic. "This can't be a surprise to you."

"No." She made a face at him.

He smiled crookedly. "Good night, Alexa." Once he'd opened the door, he pressed another brief kiss on her lips, said, "Lock up tight," and loped toward his big pickup.

She did flip the dead bolt and then all but collapsed against the door.

THE NEXT DAY, Alexa stepped into warmth, the good smell of grilled burgers and deep-fat-fried potatoes, the clatter of cutlery on dishes and the voices of diners chatting while they ate. The man who'd reluctantly agreed to talk to her had chosen this out-of-the-way diner, presumably in the hope none of his fellow cops would see them together.

"I'm meeting someone here," she told the hostess, and scanned the booths that ran around the outside of the dining room. She was sure he'd prefer a booth to a more open table or the stools at the counter. In fact… "Oh, I think that's him."

In his forties, Scott Travers was still a uniformed patrol officer. A thin man whose hair was receding, his eyes never left her as she walked the length of the room to the back corner booth. When she reached it, she said, "Officer Travers?"

He flicked a glance toward the nearest table and she realized her mistake. He was out of uniform today and didn't want to be identified as a cop. But all he said was, "Scott."

She nodded and slid in to face him. "Alexa."

"Yeah, I met you just to ask—" He broke off at the appearance of a waitress.

Both ordered, Alexa having barely glanced at the menu. She might as well squeeze in lunch, however high fat. She did love cheeseburgers and fries.

Only when they were alone again did she say, "Ask me what?"

"I don't want to be in the newspaper." He sounded desperate. "I don't know how you found out about the one thing—"

"I have my own confidential informants."

He swore and let his head fall.

Their drinks arrived, giving him a reprieve. After a sip of her soda, she said, "I won't make a promise until I hear your side."

The word that escaped him sounded more despairing than angry, which was an improvement on most of her interactions with the cops on her list.

Scott Travers was the first to agree to sit down with her. Her calls hadn't otherwise gotten her far, most recipients cutting her off before she even had the chance to give her spiel—the one about how she was open to all sides in any contentious situation, that she wasn't trying to trap anyone into incriminating himself. No "herself," as she'd told Matthew, since every cop on her list was male.

Of course, that might have to do with how few women deputies and officers served in this eastern Washington county outside Spokane.

Alexa had expected to batter her head against the blue wall of silence that famously prevented law enforcement officers from condemning each other's mistakes, crimes or misconduct. What disturbed her was her certainty that many officers weren't refusing to talk to her out of any deep loyalty to the fraternity. Nope, they were running scared.

She was still tempted to pop into one of the city's three precincts this afternoon and go face-to-face with her targets, but that wasn't compatible with being careful, per Matthew's advice. As it was, she had taken a circuitous route on quiet residential streets to get here.

Still, she couldn't let herself surrender to nerves. Especially not since the brief flurry of records released to her had passed, just like unexpected snow that wasn't sticking. The two law enforcement agencies as well as city and county governments were digging in their heels.

"Will you tell me why you accepted a bribe?" she asked, seeing no reason to whitewash the choice he'd made.

His throat worked. His gaze fastened on her again. "I was getting slammed. My ex kept needing money beyond childcare for our boy. He's really smart, being offered chances at special summer programs. One at the UW. She's working, too, but in an office. I just… I should have said no, but how could I?"

Call her skeptical but… "These drug traffickers just happened to know the right moment to hit you up?"

He heaved a sigh. "No. I pulled this guy over. Ran him, figured out who he worked for, and had reason to make him pop his trunk. He was transporting a load of coke. I'd taken him out of the car and was starting to cuff him when he said if I let him go, he could do something for me. I hate drugs!" He swallowed again. "But—"

"The temptation was too great."

He swallowed. "I guess so."

"Nobody in the department ever found out?"

Travers shook his head. "As far as I know. I claimed the license plate I gave when I first called in the stop was wrong."

"And then falsified your report."

The desperation seeped from him like the stink when someone ate too much garlic. She was afraid he was about to cry. But what if he was playing her? "I don't even know how you found out."

Nor would she tell him. She especially wouldn't tell him that all *she'd* known was that he'd been seen accepting a packet in a surreptitious manner, and that by "a citizen" hoping she'd look into it. She'd gone with her best guess and hit a bull's-eye.

"Have they approached you again?" she asked.

"Sure. They've threatened to rat on me, but I told them I wasn't going to help. If I lose my job, so be it. That's been… I don't know, seven or eight months? Nothing's happened."

The waitress showed up to put their meals in front of them, and neither said anything until she'd bustled away. Picking up a french fry, Alexa asked then, "And your son attended the summer program at UW?"

"Yeah." Pride flashed on his face. He reached behind him for his wallet and flipped it open, finding a photo and pushing it in front of her. "That's him, getting the certificate."

The resemblance was clear between the thin, gawky boy and his father. The kid was grinning in the picture.

"He's a senior now. He applied to Stanford and got their early acceptance. We're hoping for a good financial aid offer. They seem to really want him."

Alexa opened her mouth to ask what he'd do if that offer didn't measure up, but he kept talking.

"He'll be applying to the University of Washington, too, and even Eastern, just in case. He knows we're not loaded."

She smiled and pushed the wallet back across the table.

They ate, talking generalities at first then about the department. He was more open than she had expected, not willing to name names, but acknowledging some of the issues she was investigating.

Alexa quirked her eyebrow. "Taking bribes to allow

criminal acts to pass unnoticed is another category altogether, though."

Alarm flashed. "I'd never do it again!"

"I…actually believe you," she said slowly. "Me, I'm after the officers who take payoffs on a regular basis. Who work hand-in-hand with drug traffickers, say, or maybe a pimp. And the ones with a history of excessive use of force."

He pushed his empty plate away. "You know, most of us hope you scare the department into doing some housecleaning. That doesn't mean I can afford to help you."

Sad that individual cops all had to be afraid of what would happen to them, or even to their families, if they spoke out openly about the bad apples they had to work with.

She assured Scott Travers, who'd at least had the guts to meet with her, that unless she learned he'd lied to her, his name wouldn't appear in print. Her instinct said he was a good cop who'd stumbled only the once.

Unfortunately, her investigation into his more corrupt co-workers was going nowhere despite the pressure Diana was applying. She kept getting told the same old lines. Alexa wasn't the only individual making requests. Budget cuts meant the public records personnel were dealing with a backlog of a thousand or more requests. They were working as fast as they could, but individuals like her who insisted on making multiple requests even in a single day weren't helping.

A thousand requests? Really? Alexa would believe it of a city the size of Seattle or even Portland. Maybe. The city of Wilden employed a hundred and fifty officers, though, the county less than a hundred. Were that many members of the public demanding records from that police department? Not a chance. And no, the county in the form of the sheriff's office wasn't showing any more willingness to cooperate.

Of course she had other investigations ongoing, but backing off wasn't in her nature. She wasn't about to buckle to the campaign of terror. All it told her was that somebody was desperate to prevent her from zeroing in on his record, and that couldn't be because he'd accepted a few bribes or used his access to information for personal reasons.

No, the man who was so determined to stall her, if not eliminate her altogether, was hiding something that would cost him his job at the very least, and probably put him away in the state correctional institute. *He* was afraid she was too good at her job.

That meant her focus had to have turned his way, however glancingly.

Now, she had to figure out when and how.

And was he one of the men she'd called today?

Chapter Ten

Still immersed in Art Dwyer's records that afternoon, Matthew would have preferred not to take a call from Dispatch, but assigning detectives was part of his job. Damn it, he'd barely gotten off the phone with Michelle only to learn that there'd been no change in Art's condition.

"Reinert here," he said, recognizing the woman's voice.

"The manager of the solid waste transfer station says a garbage truck just dumped a body. They've stopped the machinery and kept the driver from leaving. I've dispatched an officer, but assume you'll want a detective there as soon as possible."

"I will." He jotted down names and additional information, thanked her, and ended the call. Kurt Gannon was next up in the rotation, followed by Bonnie Mendoza. Instead of picking up his phone again, he stood and looked out at the bullpen. Both detectives were working at their desks. Kurt could have handled this alone...but Bonnie could still use some seasoning.

He called them into his office, gave them what he had and sent them on their way. "Let me know as soon as you have an ID."

Kurt, nearing retirement, was the "one foot in front of the other" kind of guy—no intuitive leaps there—but he knew how to do the job. Bonnie, barely thirty, had impressed Matthew, although she didn't have quite a year as a detective under her belt.

He tried to put the death they were investigating out of his mind, but he knew why he couldn't. The most recent murder he'd worked himself—along with Art Dwyer—was the prostitute whose body had been found in a garbage container. People rarely climbed into a dumpster on their own to die. This latest victim was male, though, so they weren't looking at another prostitute.

His distraction didn't keep him from flipping open yet another notebook and seeing the date at the top of the first page: the morning of the day Art had been gunned down. Chilled, he started reading.

Art had gone back the previous night to talk to all the girls working the part of town where Tansy Gould's body had been found. He'd met with more uneasiness, more headshakes, but he'd handed out cards again and, come morning, had received a call.

Kept her voice low so no one could overhear her, he'd written, *but she says she's not the only one who saw Tansy get in the pickup truck. Didn't see her again. Word is a cop was one of her regulars. She was scared to say no even though he didn't pay, and Johnny wouldn't have let her anyway. Amber is sure that was the cop. Of course, none of them saw the license plate.* The nib of Art's pen had dug deep into the lined paper on that last sentence. He knew the women were observant enough to be able to identify a regular who frightened one of them.

A cop.

That's what Art had wanted to talk about before the interruption that day. Not just about dirty cops, but about the likelihood one of them was also killing women he didn't trust to keep their mouths shut.

Or maybe just because he enjoyed killing. He could do so almost at will given how vulnerable these particular victims had been.

Matthew flipped back through the pages he'd separated out where Art had speculated on who in the department might be capable of being a monster even as he carried a badge.

Half a dozen names jumped out at Matthew. He knew all of the men.

Don Rommel. Mike Swartz. Rick Shanahan. Ken Kasperson. Brian Danner. John Blykowski.

Seeing Kasperson's name in this context surprised Matthew. Blykowski was a sheriff's deputy, and their paths had barely passed. The other four, he'd never liked.

Art had a B list, too, that included Jim Ward, one of the two cops he'd overheard talking about the brutal traffic stop. Wonder of wonders, both Ward and O'Brien had been fired yesterday. From what Matthew heard, even the union reps hadn't fought the decision hard. What Matthew suspected was that the chief knew Alexa was watching and had deluded himself that this might head her off.

Now, he scrabbled for his own notes, where he'd written down additional names of officers who'd done something that caught Art's attention. The six, though, were the ones Art knew or suspected had been caught at one time or another because they'd gotten involved with a prostitute or compelled one to service him. It happened. Matthew read about officers in other cities arrested because they ran an escort service on the side or were in the employ of the owner of a topless bar whose girls were available for additional hire.

There were some real pieces of scum out there, but Matthew hadn't wanted to believe Wilden PD harbored anyone that crooked.

Speaking of delusion, he thought ruefully. Art had had good instincts, and he wasn't making any bones about his belief that a cop was the killer they were looking for.

Come to think of it, Art and Alexa would have had a lot to talk about if they'd had the chance to sit down together. *Please, God, they did have that chance.*

Question was how many of the names Art had highlighted were also on Alexa's list?

A visit to the records department was one way of getting answers. She'd have requested camera footage or reports on particular incidents, but he had no doubt she'd also sought discipline records for a number of individual officers.

His phone rang, Kurt Gannon's name popping up.

"No ID on the guy," the detective said, "and he looks like he might have been living on the street. Skin and teeth, you know how it is."

Matthew knew.

"Thing is, Bonnie recognized him from when she was in uniform. Called himself Jim Berkey. Supposedly gave us occasional tips." That last was wary; Gannon had heard the rumors.

"Not all good ones," Matthew said grimly. "He originated that debacle involving Alexa Adams. His name was used to lure Art to the location where he was shot, too."

"It wasn't Berkey who set up Art. He was already dead. The medical examiner isn't here yet, but I'd say two or three days, tops."

"He almost has to have been in hiding." If the CI had had any brains left at all, he'd have started wondering if whoever talked him into passing on false information might be afraid that under pressure Berkey'd give up the name.

"Keep me informed," Matthew told his detective and ended the call.

This murder cemented his fear that Alexa was indeed at the center of a lot of unsettling events. She was just as much a threat to a killer cop as Art had been—before he'd been gunned down.

Matthew frowned into space. He wanted to put an around-the-clock bodyguard on her. No, he wanted to *be* her around-the-clock bodyguard, but he couldn't imagine she'd agree to that. After all, the woman was investigating multiple officers in this department. How was she supposed to do that if the lieutenant in charge of the major crimes division was watching everything she did and eavesdropping on every conversation?

And just who *had* she talked to? he wondered.

Better question: if he was open with her about his suspicions, was there any chance at all that she'd share and share alike?

Uh-uh. Why did he feel sure trust didn't come easily to Alexa Adams?

SHE *REALLY* HAD to learn to say no.

The only good reason to encourage Matthew Reinert to hang around was if she believed for even a teeny, tiny second that he could be coaxed into an indiscretion about his fellow officers.

Alexa scrunched up her nose. That was extremely unlikely, and not true anyway. He'd come rushing to rescue her when she called. That was worth something. Still, when he'd called offering to bring a pizza, she could have said, "Oh, gosh, I have plans. Can we do that another night?"

But no. She'd hesitated, credit to her first healthy instinct for self-preservation, then succumbed without listening to the inner voice saying, *Whoa! Think about this.*

So now she was listening for the sound of his deep-throated truck in her driveway, to be followed by a door-bell or firm knock on the door *he'd* installed for her.

Why hadn't she realized how sneaky his generous effort had been?

And there was the engine, quickly cut off, followed by the doorbell.

She was dumb enough to feel anticipation lurking beneath all the common sense warnings she'd been giving herself.

Letting him in, she said, "This isn't a good idea. Why are you here?"

He smiled, kissed her lightly and said, "Why else?"

"I can think of a bunch of underhanded reasons," she mumbled to his back as she locked up before trailing him to the kitchen.

He surveyed the table, where she'd already set out two placemats, napkins, plates and a beer for him and a rare glass of wine for her. If there was a glint of amusement in his eyes when he glanced at her, she could hardly blame him.

Not until they sat down did she get a good look at his face. Oh, he might have been smiling, but tonight that was just surface. Lines too deep, eyes too dark, tension chang-ing the set of his shoulders.

"Your friend?" Surely, she'd have heard if Art Dwyer had died, but— It could have just happened.

"No change. I stopped by the hospital on my way here."

"Oh." She plopped down in her chair. This had to be get-ting to him. "There's nothing else wrong?"

He sighed and sat, too, placing the pizza box in the middle of the table and opening it. "I have some worries," he admitted. "But can we eat before we talk about it?"

"*I'll* just worry."

He muttered something, dished up a couple of slices of the pizza and pushed the box closer to her. "Yeah, okay."

She took a slice, but didn't start eating.

"Jim Berkey? His body was found today."

She absorbed that. "Oh. You said you hadn't been able to find him."

"He wasn't dead the whole while, but someone got to him before we did." The dark undertone was unmistakable.

"You think…" Alexa hesitated.

"I do think."

Once again, he'd managed to scare her.

Matthew started to eat, making her realize he really was hungry. She wasn't so much, after her greasy lunchtime indulgence. She nibbled, though, watching him devour half the large pizza with the kind of mechanical hunger that made her wonder if he was even tasting his food.

Finally, he sighed and met her eyes. "Can we talk off the record?"

The last time he'd asked that same question, she'd almost laughed at him. Now…a shocking amount had changed.

ALEXA'S EYES NARROWED.

Talking to her about an open investigation shouldn't be an option, even if she hadn't been a journalist. But, damn it, she was in the middle of every problem on his desk, and Matthew didn't think that was by chance. She might as well have had a bull's-eye painted on her front door. No, Matthew thought immediately, make that right in the middle of her back, and that's what scared him. What if he had to sit at her side in the cubicle next to Art's, praying for a flicker of her eyelashes?

When Jackman had pulled her car over and found out it came tagged with an "armed and dangerous" designation, they were all lucky that simple traffic stop hadn't turned into a tragedy. Alexa had done the logical thing in pulling her registration out of the glove box; under the circumstances, any cop would have been jumpy enough to wonder what she was really going for.

Matthew had no doubt that her focused investigation into problem officers was the reason both incidents had happened, just as Art's similar investigation provided the motive for his attempted murder. That meant, if she wouldn't step out on the limb, he just about had to.

"I hope you'll keep this to yourself, but I think I have to tell you. Art Dwyer had come up with a list of rotten cops," he said bluntly. "With my attention pulled too many ways, he's been the primary looking into the killing of a prostitute whose body was found shortly after the raid on your house. Not the first one killed, either, as you probably know. He came to me to talk about what he suspected, but we were interrupted. He was in a coma before we could finish that conversation."

"I read about it. But…you're saying…" Her mouth opened, closed, opened again. "That you believe he was shot by a fellow *cop*?" Her voice had risen toward the end. "Maybe the same one—"

He said stiffly, "I have to consider it a real possibility now that I've had time to dig through his notes."

Even as she still stared in apparent shock, he saw that she'd started thinking. "But…why me?" Alexa shook her head. "Dumb question. I already know the answer. He has to be someone whose background I'm digging into. We'd already guessed as much. Did he not know Detective Dwyer was asking the same questions?"

"Maybe not, initially. But at some point, he found out. That's why I'm hoping to compare notes. There may be a lot of commonality between your list and Art's, but there might not be, too."

"If there are only a couple of officers he and I were both investigating…"

Matthew bent his head. "I'd have a really good place to start."

They stared at each other until his eyes burned and he had to blink first.

"I can't reveal sources. You know that," Alexa almost whispered.

"I'm not asking for sources. Only for a list of who you're investigating. I shouldn't be telling you any of this," he said roughly, "but if what I'm suspecting is true, this son of a bitch has already killed several women and tried to kill a good cop to protect his secrets. He won't hesitate to go after you again."

Thus the creepy-crawly feeling she had every time she stepped out her front door lately, even if she was only walking out to the street to get her mail or newspaper. Art Dwyer hadn't been gunned down on his own porch, but from the killer's point of view, why not repeat something that had worked so well the first time?

She shivered just thinking that.

"My editor—oh, and the executive editor—would fire me if they knew I was even *thinking* of cooperating with you."

"Packing up and taking a leave of absence right now would be smart," Matthew said, those sharp gray eyes drilling into her. "That would be a good alternative to cooperating with my investigation."

"He—whoever he is—would have to know I could keep looking for answers long distance. What if he sets out to find me? And…what? Do I disappear for a week? Two weeks? Months?"

Matthew didn't know what to tell her. He could dig deeper into the reasons Art had put each man on his list, but what were the odds he'd be able to actually place one of them in the alley behind the vacant house at the right time? Hell, that would take a miracle.

Crinkles between her eyebrows let him know she was holding a serious internal debate.

He held his breath, awaiting the outcome.

Finally, Alexa huffed, her eyes drawn to his. "Can I see your list, instead of the other way around?"

"Will you promise me that you won't start an investigation on anyone I name unless you stumble across information on your own?"

Indignation had her gaping at him. "How can I not—" She mumbled a few words under her breath. "Fine. I won't forget those names, though."

He suppressed a smile. "I wouldn't expect you to."

"Let me put the pizza in the fridge before we start. Unless you want more?"

"No, I'm done." He started to rise. "I can do that—"

"That's okay." She already had the box closed. "Don't forget it when you go. I can't imagine I'd eat much of it, and what's left would probably be barely enough for your lunch tomorrow."

He'd relaxed enough to laugh. "You're right."

A moment later, they settled down again, him cracking open a second beer. He had a written list folded in his pocket, but those six names that had lit up like neon signs, he knew without refreshing his memory. He was reluctant to include the two that had surprised him—especially Kasperson, who seemed like an okay guy—but he needed to find out whether she knew anything about them, too.

"John Blykowski."

Alexa blinked a couple of times. "Sheriff's deputy."

"Yeah."

"I'm looking into his background. He's not at the top of my list, but I heard something about him."

Matthew gave a clipped nod. "Ken Kasperson."

"Never heard of him."

But she was tucking that name into a safe place for future reference, he felt sure.

"Don Rommel."

"Oh yeah."

Ditto for the last three names. Her lip curled at two of the names: Brian Danner and Rick Shanahan.

"Can you tell me what you've heard about these men?"

She had to mull it over some more before she decided to answer his question.

"Their involvement with hookers," she said finally. "All of them, except the guy I'd never heard of."

Matthew scraped a hand over his face. "That's why they interested Art, too. What I don't know is whether he'd learned anything to make him think one of them had committed acts of violence toward the women to protect his reputation and job."

"Versus just breaking the law and even keeping it from being enforced?"

"Yeah," he said with new weariness. He didn't mention two other possibilities: that the list should be longer, cops who'd committed the same infractions not having been caught yet, and that the officer inciting the assaults on Alexa was one she was investigating for behavior that had nothing to do with hookers.

Then Alexa really did shock him.

Chapter Eleven

"You remember the cop who was killed two years ago?" she asked, sounding unusually tentative.

That was enough to make him stiffen.

No, he hadn't forgotten the first law enforcement officer killed in the line of duty in this county in fifty-two years. If Art didn't survive, he'd be the second. Matthew swore. "Do you have any reason to believe there's a connection?"

Alexa squirmed a little. "He wanted to talk to me. Said he'd gone to his commanding officer and been told, in essence, to shut his mouth. I agreed to see him, but he dragged his feet." She shrugged. "I think he had mixed feelings about talking to a journalist. He was killed before we could set up a meeting."

"I had no idea. What did you do?"

"I talked to his wife, just tiptoeing around, you know, but I didn't get any vibe that he'd told her about what he'd seen on the job that was disturbing enough he'd take it to an outsider. Especially a journalist. He was proud to wear the badge, she'd said. I called a few of his friends for statements." Her mouth twisted. "His commanding officer, too."

"I remember the article," he said slowly. "You didn't even hint. I wondered about it, though, mostly because your name doesn't usually appear on straightforward news items."

"It got assigned to me because he'd wanted to tell me something. I did what digging I could, but got nowhere. Now I can't help wishing…"

He couldn't help doing the same. He'd try to keep it quiet, but Matthew had every intention of finding out what patrol officer Alan Sharpe had done in the weeks immediately preceding his death.

"There was an intense investigation, of course," he said, "but the detectives came up empty. We all make enemies over the course of our careers, so there were too many places to look."

She nodded. "So, now what?"

Without being really specific, he told her what he intended, and she didn't question his vagueness. He'd already given her more than he should have, and she knew it. If Chief Paulson learned about this conversation, Matthew's head would roll.

Face it, having a relationship with a journalist wouldn't be easy. They'd be dodging land mines constantly.

What did you do at work today, dear?

Uh, sorry, I can't tell you.

And yet, Matthew tried not to lie to himself. He wanted Alexa Adams, prickly as she could be. He liked her brains, her courage, and the empathy that had driven her to do what she did for a living. He liked the occasional vulnerability she'd let him see, and the knowledge that her pride refused to let her make a habit of that.

In fact, he felt way more for a woman he'd known for only a week than he should.

Damn, he didn't want to go, but she was the one who had to do the asking before he could stay, and he suspected the idea hadn't even crossed her mind this evening. She'd be as eager to start her research as he was, given new strings to pull.

When he pushed back his chair, she did look surprised but glanced at the clock. "I didn't realize it was getting so late."

Eight o'clock.

"Pizza," she reminded him and then walked him to the door as she did every time he came over.

This time, he didn't reach for the knob. Instead, he stood gazing down at her face, seeing so many shifting emotions and thoughts, he couldn't read any of them. She didn't retreat from him, though, and when he set down the pizza box on the chest by the door and slipped a hand around the back of her neck, she lifted her own hand to rest it on his chest.

Her voice soft, husky, she murmured, "Good night."

Matthew made some sound in his throat, definitely nonverbal, and bent his head. Tonight, he aimed for gentle. He had to build trust. Something about the quiver of her lips, the way her pupils contracted, the bite of her fingers when they flexed on his pectoral muscle, challenged his determination. When his tongue slid into her mouth, the tastes were as complex as she was. He wanted more.

She rose on tiptoe, fists closed on his shirt as he deepened the kiss and gripped her taut butt to lift her. Twice he had to pull back so they could both breathe; twice, he dove back in for more.

But, damn, he knew better. She responded to him with all the heat he could hope for, but that wasn't the same as her inviting him into her bed when she was in her right mind. The last thing he wanted was her to regret their love making.

So, finally, he lifted his head, said in an unrecognizable voice, "I need to go," and waited for her to blink repeatedly until her brain kicked into gear.

When she dropped back to her heels, nodded and released

his shirt, Matthew wasn't surprised. He couldn't deny disappointment; he was so aroused, the idea of going home and booting up his laptop to browse what records he could access was unimaginable.

As was getting a good night's sleep.

He kissed her again, lightly, grabbed the pizza and said, "Good night." Alexa behind him, he opened the door, scanned the front yard and stepped out onto the porch.

"I'm sorry."

He turned back, his smile rueful. "I understand, you know. We're not an obvious pair, are we?"

An answering tremulous smile made his heart give an odd thump.

"I don't know about that. I'm beginning to think—" Her eyes widened as she cut that thought off.

He'd already been hit by how much they had in common. Still, this was too soon. He wasn't even a hundred percent sure *he* could trust her not to run with what he'd told her tonight.

"We have time," he told her. "In the meantime, you be careful."

"And once again, we end an evening on an upbeat note."

Descending the porch steps, he was amused by her effort to convince him that she could take care of herself, thank you very much. At the same time…her gutsy attitude scared him. So much so that when he slid in behind the wheel of his pickup, he gave serious thought to circling the block and coming back to park where he could see her house and watch over her.

But a direct attack… No, that seemed unlikely after the elaborate efforts to get to her using other members of the police department. He expected more of the same. But when and how?

"I THINK I need to quit threatening and actually file a suit," Alexa's attorney announced the next morning. "All this foot-dragging and the excuses are starting to really tick me off."

Alexa put her phone on speaker and poured herself her second cup of coffee for the morning. "Really? It took you this long?"

Diana laughed. "You've had longer to work up a temper."

"Oh, come on! You must deal with government officials all the time."

"True." She sighed. "Okay, anything new I need to know?"

"No. I really want to interview these guys, but I don't have enough ammunition to apply serious pressure until I see the information in the records I've requested. Catch-22."

"No new releases?"

"No. After that little spurt of not very interesting stuff, I'm getting a resounding lack of action."

"So what *are* you doing?"

"Oh, mostly working from home. Finishing up another series, pursuing what leads I can with this one. You know, calling victims."

"Who give you an earful."

"Yep. It's really maddening when I *know* there's body or squad car camera footage that will give me a lot better idea what really happened."

"Will the newspaper help us lean on the city?"

"Oh, they've already put some weight behind my requests, but we hadn't quite reached the point of filing suit when all this intimidation started happening. I know they'll join us in a suit, and probably foot the bill. In fact, let me give you the name of the head of their legal department."

Turned out that Diana already knew who that was. She promised to call then asked, "What about your cop?"

"*My* cop?"

Diana snorted.

"He's still holding back some things. I guess he has to," Alexa said grudgingly. "I think more stuff has been happening that links back to me than the department is willing to admit."

"What about the detective who was just shot?"

Alexa didn't say a word. The silence spoke for itself.

Her attorney said crisply, "I assume your car plates are up to date, the sticker hasn't happened to fall off, and you're driving like a little old lady. You don't even *think* about rolling through a stop sign even if there's no other car visible for blocks?"

Alexa hated to admit it, but who else could she be honest with? Well, her editor, up to a point, and Matthew. But since he wasn't a hundred percent up-front with her, she was left in an emotional tangle where he was concerned.

"Um, I'm not driving any more than I can help, and then not out on busier roads where someone might spot me." She hesitated. "Lieutenant Reinert would prefer I stay on lockdown at home until he gets to the bottom of this."

The lengthy pause held a significance Alexa recognized. "You're sure he isn't impeding your investigation by pretending to be your buddy?"

"I…really think he's sincere. But I'm suspicious by nature, so naturally I've considered the possibility." Was that true? she had to ask herself. Or had her attraction to him made her foolishly credulous?

She couldn't honestly answer that question.

OFFICER ALAN SHARPE had worked a couple of prostitute stings in the weeks before his death.

Matthew sat back in his desk chair. Damn, he'd been hop-

ing there'd be no link to the problems Art Dwyer had seen…
but deluding himself never did work very well.

And yeah, Jim Ward had been dinged for "inappropriate" actions on a similar sting.

Why, Matthew couldn't help wondering, did the department waste so much time and manpower on trying to control or eliminate prostitution in their small city when all the efforts to date had achieved absolutely nothing? Except, maybe, corrupt some law enforcement officers.

He had to remind himself that whoever had killed Tansy Gould would have been using and discarding troubled young women no matter what, though. In fact, he'd have been less likely to draw attention to himself if he hadn't been forced to be part of a law enforcement action.

Thinking about the case, he called Kurt Gannon, the detective assigned to investigate Jim Berkey's murder.

"Wish I could tell you more," Gannon said. "We think we've found out where he went to ground, but people who knew he was there have no idea when he left. Or more likely, was grabbed."

"Okay. Short of a witness who saw him the few days before his death, we've probably reached a dead end."

Two hours later, Matthew was called into the chief's office. His temper stirred, but he told the PA he was on his way. Taking the stairs two at a time instead of the elevator, he wanted to believe Chief Paulson had summoned him for an update on the several threads of investigation, and particularly into the attempted murder of a long-time officer in his own department. Leaving that unsolved would be a blot on Paulson's reputation.

Unfortunately, Matthew had never much liked the chief, who was more politician than cop. Listening to him talk to the media, you'd think he had personally broken every case, rescued that choking child, thrown himself in the path of a bullet to save the life of an innocent woman. Hell, stopped traffic for the mama duck and her ducklings to cross the road.

The truth was, Matthew couldn't recall the last time Paulson had actually asked for updates on an investigation. He became irritated when, in his opinion, matters didn't move fast enough, but he'd convey his impatience through the several layers of authority that lay between him and his lieutenant leading the major crimes.

Paulson occupied the corner office on the third—top floor—of the police station. The door was open—nice, since he often claimed to have an open-door policy for the men and women who served—but really this was an outer door that led to his PA's desk and a waiting room. As usual, the door to the inner office was closed.

Matthew nodded to the woman behind the desk. "Ms. Yunker."

She smiled. "Lieutenant. The chief is anxious to talk to you. Go on in."

Paulson didn't rise from behind his desk after Matthew rapped lightly and walked in. He wore a crisp uniform, the hat set carefully on the corner of his remarkably pristine desk. Presumably, he'd been studying something on his computer monitor, or at least pretending to. Simmering anger already showed on a face that was developing jowls.

"Chief," Matthew said mildly. "You wanted to see me?"

"I did, and I'm sure you know why."

Because he'd gone to Records asking for everything they had on several officers within the department?

Apparently, the chief couldn't be bothered to ask for an update on Art's condition. Matthew certainly wasn't going to volunteer the latest from Michelle, who'd said there was increased activity behind Art's eyelids and his muscles and nerves had been jerking.

Now, he said, "I'm afraid not." Since he hadn't been told to take a seat, he remained standing in a relaxed parade stance.

Face turning red, Paulson roared, "What the hell do you think you're doing, investigating your fellow officers as if they were criminals!"

Keep your temper. "Sir, I have to follow where the evidence takes me. You know that. I've become convinced that an officer in this department has gone rogue and killed several people as well as shooting Detective Dwyer."

"I was told that there's no hit on the bullet recovered from the house wall," the chief snapped.

"That's correct." And news he'd received only that morning. It was interesting that the report had also gone to the police chief, and that he'd bothered to read it. "It didn't come from the gun of a career criminal, or we'd likely have at least a forensic hit."

Paulson snorted. "So you leaped to thinking one of your colleagues tried to kill your detective."

Matthew didn't like telling anyone what he was thinking—except, apparently, Alexa Adams, investigative reporter, he thought with chagrin. He didn't see that he had a choice now.

Still on his feet—too tense to sit even if he'd been offered the option—he laid it out. Dwyer had good reason to believe Tansy Gould had been obliging a local cop. He let some irony creep into his voice on the one word. *Obliging.* Witnesses felt sure the pickup truck she'd climbed into before vanishing belonged to that cop, one of her regulars.

Paulson shook his head. "Some hooker who was probably

high tells you she last saw another hooker get into a police officer's personal vehicle, and you take that as gospel?"

Matthew ground his teeth. "Detective Dwyer was primary on this investigation, which included the deaths of at least three other women we believe worked as prostitutes. There were clear similarities in how they were killed, and in how their bodies were disposed of. Until now, there'd never been any witnesses, which suggests the other women were scared to speak out. Art had been asking questions within the department. I believe he alarmed the wrong person, who was afraid Art was closing in on him."

Before the chief could erupt again, Matthew added, "I also believe that same person is responsible for the false tip about the drug house that could have sent us astray, as well as tagging Ms. Adams's vehicle with a BOLO that resulted in a frightening traffic stop for her.

"We've also confirmed that the man who set up a supposed meeting with her so she could be snatched was a longtime confidential informant. The voices match. Who else but a cop could have managed all that? Who else would have known Detective Dwyer would jump at a possible chance to lay his hands on that CI?"

The chief's color had worsened, looking like a heart attack waiting to happen.

"That sounds like a fantasy you've cooked up! Is there one solid piece of evidence backing up any of this absurd story?"

Matthew opened his mouth but Paulson talked right over him.

"A hooker who *thinks* she saw. A CI who is a known crook. That seems to be the sum of it."

Somehow he kept his voice in control, but he started to

lean forward, stopping himself with an effort from flattening his hands on this idiot's desktop.

"You are aware that the CI who gave the tip that meant to trigger a SWAT raid, and who also set her up to be assaulted, has now been found dead? His body left in a garbage dumpster, just as the prostitutes' bodies all have been? After all, it's pretty obvious he was only doing favors for someone. Someone who has it in for Ms. Adams, a journalist who also happens to be investigating a number of the same bad apples in this police department that Detective Dwyer also suspected?"

Paulson stood. "Be careful, Lieutenant. You sound as if you're in league with a reporter who has targeted this department to boost her career. I'll assume you intend to take a harder look for *solid* evidence that might lead you to the real perpetrator, or perpetrators. Even you have to see how ridiculous it is to tie Detective Dwyer's death to some pranks played on a journalist trying to dig up nonexistent dirt. I've told the head of records to deny your requests. You will not join that woman in trying to blacken our reputation. Is that clear?"

"It's clear," Matthew said stiffly. He bent his head slightly. "Sir." He had to get out of there before he told this useless sack of you-know-what exactly what he could do with himself.

And then he had to figure out how to bypass Chief Paulson's efforts to cut him off at the pass.

Chapter Twelve

When her phone rang, Alexa didn't recognize the number or the area code, but that wasn't unusual these days.

When she answered, a male voice said curtly, "This is Brian Danner. I've gotten your messages. I'll sit down with you if you can meet me at the Chatter Box in the next hour."

Wariness almost edged out excitement. "I can be there, but I'm curious why you've changed your mind about talking to me."

"You want to meet or not?"

"I do want."

Dead air.

Well, it wasn't as if she'd expected the guy to be friendly, or even considerate. Among his other problems, he had a reputation for a hot temper.

Within an hour. Did that mean he was already there, waiting for her? Alexa glanced down at herself, wrinkled her nose and hustled to her bedroom to change clothes and do something to her hair.

She yanked her ratty T-shirt over her head then paused in front of her closet. Should she let Matthew know she was going out, and why?

No, of course not. The day she had to ask permission

from anyone but her editor to do her job was the day she had to change careers.

A minute later, Alexa was backing her car out of the garage. She stopped in the driveway while she calculated the best way to get to the western edge of town. Of course, Danner wouldn't have suggested meeting her anywhere near the police station or either of the satellite precincts. She studied her GPS before deciding to ignore it except for the last few blocks, where she pretty much would have to join a major road.

Oh, how she hated the way her heart was pounding when she backed into the street and accelerated cautiously forward. She'd always operated with common sense, but that wasn't the same thing as the apprehension that dogged her nonstop these days. *I'll get past it*, she told herself while wondering whether she should have asked someone from the newspaper to accompany her. Or Diana Troxell maybe would have—for a sky-high, by-the-hour charge, but a cop afraid of losing his job for malfeasance wouldn't be frank in front of an attorney. And certainly not in front of a lieutenant in his own department.

At sudden movement in front of her, she braked sharply. A kid on a bike, not paying attention to traffic. She breathed deeply a few times, ordered herself to pay attention, and set off again.

At last, she reached the four-lane road that passed in front of the Chatter Box. Because of railroad tracks behind it and a giant warehouse to one side, she could only turn into the parking lot from this street.

Three blocks.

She looked longingly at her phone, lying on the seat beside her.

One block later, a squad car burst from a parking lot to

her right and the flashing lights came on, followed by a blast of the siren. Both terrified and mad at herself—she'd *known* this would happen—she put on a turn signal and pulled into the next lot, this time in front of a Mexican restaurant where she'd never eaten.

Within seconds, a uniformed officer appeared outside her window and yanked on the door handle. "Unlock! Unlock!" he yelled.

Shaking, she did as he asked.

He wrenched open the door. "Keep your hands on the wheel!"

Alexa hadn't even thought of moving them. Except, she could so easily reach over and pick up her phone...

The cop's gaze lowered to something on the front passenger-side floor. Suddenly, just as had happened the last time, he drew his big black gun.

"What are you—"

"Do you have a permit to carry a concealed weapon?"

" I don't own a gun at all!"

"Then why is there one not quite hidden on the floor?" He nodded past her.

Her head turned and her stomach rolled queasily. Oh God, he was right. Only the grip showed, but that was undeniably a handgun, probably a semiautomatic like his.

She recoiled. "It's not mine. I swear it's not. Somebody planted it there!"

His grin was ugly. "Now, who would want to do something like that to you?"

Boy, that wasn't subtle. He was all but telling her he knew damn well how the gun had appeared in her car—but not in a way that anyone listening to a recording would recognize as gloating.

How was he going to explain pulling her over in the first

place? Her gaze fell on the nametag above the pocket on his dark blue uniform shirt.

R. Shanahan.

No wonder he looked vaguely familiar. She'd studied photos of him. Late thirties, handsome if not for that sneer and the shaved head, bulky in the way of men who spent a lot of time lifting weights.

"Out of the car!" he commanded. She'd barely pushed the seat belt release when he hauled her out and shoved her roughly down on her face on the pavement. Grit ground into her cheek. His knee pressed the middle of her back. Déjà vu.

He started talking on his radio, but she couldn't quite make out what he was saying. Backup—she heard that.

Within an impossibly short period of time, two more police units pulled in, blocking her car, and two more officers stood over her, one also pointing his ugly handgun at her. Moments later, yet a third arrived. She couldn't see his face, only his legs.

Shanahan produced plastic cuffs. He wasn't gentle wrenching her arms behind her back to put them on.

"You planted that gun!" she cried. "This whole thing was a setup. You won't get away with it."

Rick Shanahan leaned forward until she could feel the heat of his breath on her cheek and whispered, "Sure we will."

None of them was pretending. She'd seen the smirks as they manhandled her.

"I'm entitled to a phone call."

"And you'll get one. Once you're at the station."

But first, he officially placed her under arrest and recited her rights. Meanwhile, a second officer also shackled her ankles.

Two of them lifted her. One hand groped her right breast.

She tried to twist away, but the only result was the careless-ness—or was it viciousness?—of how they tossed her into the back of Shanahan's car behind the prisoner partition.

The door slammed.

Alexa hadn't quite landed on the seat. They were prob-ably pleased to make her as miserable as possible. Her lower body was there, but she was nose-down on the floor. She tried desperately to free a hand from the cuffs that bit into her wrists, but failed. With her arms behind her, she couldn't even use her elbows for leverage. Now, blood rushed to her head, and she was bitterly afraid she was crying.

She'd known better than to allow herself to be grabbed again like this. If she hadn't let the attorney awaken her fears where Matthew was concerned, she'd have called him before she'd set off to a meeting like this. He wouldn't have had to drive her, or go in with her, just follow her until he saw her walking in.

The horrible position with the edge of the seat digging into her stomach brought bile to her throat. One pothole or speed bump and she'd be puking. If only she thought any of the cops would actually be responsible for cleaning it up, she might not have minded.

Struggling for calm, Alexa made herself picture the faces of the other officers. At least one other was familiar, too. Brian Danner, her caller. Oh, he'd wanted to meet up with her all right.

The other… No, she didn't know.

Which one had proposed setting up this ambush? He'd obviously found enthusiastic coconspirators.

They're afraid of me, she reminded herself. *She* had the power, and they hated that.

Keep thinking that.

She didn't quite throw up on the drive to the station, but

it was a close call and the taste in her mouth was vile by the time Shanahan hauled her out and set her on her feet.

"This time she had a concealed weapon," he told someone. "You know damn well it was under the seat the last time she got pulled over. After Reinert jumped in to protect her—" his tone had become ugly "—nobody searched her car."

Forgetting her ankles, too, were restrained, she tried to take a step and fell hard. First—painfully—to her knees then onto her side. None of the several uniformed cops had so much as put out a hand to stop the tumble.

One did bend over and cut the plastic cuffs off her ankles so she could be yanked to her feet once again, hustled through a heavy steel door, down a hall and into a small bare room. A holding cell.

She only had one thing to say. "I'm entitled to a phone call."

"You'll get one. Eventually."

The door closed with a substantial clunk, leaving her to shuffle, wincing from the pain in her knees, to the bench bolted to the floor and wall. She sat, hating the knowledge that her face was smeared with tears and snot, and that she couldn't wipe off either. At least the room didn't have a window. There was a camera mounted up in one corner, though, so somebody was probably still watching her. She wouldn't give them the satisfaction of showing any more discomfort than she could help.

Was humiliating her their endgame? Somehow, they'd planted that gun in her car, but they wouldn't find her fingerprints on it because she'd never touched it. Had they considered forcing her to pick it up? But how could they, if they were playing this for the benefit of their superiors? Turning off a vest camera wouldn't look good, not when she'd put in records requests on at least two of the officers. And there would have been the risk of being seen by a passerby on the road or a diner peering out the window of the restaurant.

If not, she strongly suspected that they'd have cooked up an excuse for having had to shoot and kill her.

As for the gun, likely they'd insist she had worn gloves when handling it. Any kindergartener knew to do that much. And what was that saying? Possession was nine-tenths of the law? She had indubitably been caught possessing that awful thing.

She had no way of checking the time, which crawled. Her nose wrinkled at the taste in her mouth, but then she realized the room stank, too. Bleach and probably vomit and maybe even blood.

Fortunately, anger stretched and replaced the humiliation. It gave her the strength to ignore her increasingly painful shoulder and plot how she'd see Rick Shanahan and all his buddies behind bars.

A scraping sound preceded the appearance of an unfamiliar officer, who had something in his hand. A phone. Her phone?

"I'll remove those cuffs now," he said. No sympathy there, but no hostility, either. "You can make a call. Only one."

Jaw clenched, Alexa didn't say anything, only shifted to give him space to free her from the handcuffs. Even so, a sound escaped her when her shoulders screamed after being released from the unnatural position.

The cop set the phone beside her. "Make the call." He crossed his arms and stayed where he was.

It wasn't easy picking up the phone, but she did. The time flashed on the screen. Roughly two and a half hours since she'd been pulled over.

She desperately wanted to call Matthew, but she most

needed an attorney. *Please don't let this call go to voice mail*, she prayed.

The number was Diana's mobile phone and she answered.

"This is Alexa. I...seem to have been arrested. I was pulled over and they found a gun that had been planted in my car. Can you come?"

The response was a growl before Diana said, "Are you at the Broadway Ave. station?"

"Yes."

"I'm on my way. I assume you haven't answered questions of any kind."

"All I've done is insist on making a phone call."

"Good. See you in—"

"Can you call Matthew?" Alexa asked. "Tell him what happened?"

"Yeah." Diana sounded gentle. "He may be a lot closer than I am."

Alexa's eyes burned, but let them see her cry again? No.

EVEN FROM THE BACK, Matthew recognized Rick Shanahan's swagger. It couldn't be an accident he'd just appeared from an office right by the holding rooms.

"Shanahan," Matthew snapped.

The guy turned. His surprise was so obviously faked, Matthew had to curl his fingers into a fist to keep from grabbing the SOB's shirt collar and twisting until he confessed what part he'd played in this latest stage set.

"Did you bring in Ms. Adams?"

"Yeah, who told you?"

"Her attorney called me. I did some checking. What in the *hell*?"

"Hey, the woman saw me parked by the road and flipped me off. Took offense from that, you know. So I pulled her over. Unfortunately for her, the gun she'd hidden under her passenger seat had slid out enough for me to see it. What else was I supposed to do but bring her in? Let her shoot me?"

Matthew lowered his voice. "If I find out you set this up, you'll be answering to me. Do you understand?"

Shanahan widened his eyes. "Are you threatening me, Lieutenant?"

"Yeah. I am."

Matthew brushed past him. He didn't bother to look over his shoulder. If Shanahan grabbed him and took a swing, it would be a positive pleasure to take him down.

When he let himself into the holding room and saw Alexa's face, the coal of fury he'd been carrying burst into flame. He let some really nasty words rip.

"I cannot believe—"

She tried to smile. "Me, either. I mean, who reruns a show that sucked the first time around?"

He chuckled, although the flicker of humor did nothing to quell the raging blaze in his chest. Tear tracks had dried on her face. One cheek had been scraped almost raw.

Sitting next to her, he asked, "Are you hurt? Besides this?" Making sure his back was to the camera, he gently touched her cheek.

She winced. "I…fell onto my knees. And…then onto my left shoulder. I'm sick to my stomach. Actually, not much of me feels good. Did I mention this was a rerun?"

He bit back an obscenity. "Tell me what happened."

"I was on my way—"

"No, from the beginning. Where were you going?"

So she told him. Brian Danner—or somebody pretending to be him—had called, claiming he wanted to talk to her. Of course, he'd set the meeting place. She'd taken a roundabout route— "I've been trying to be really careful," she said, as if he'd accused her of carelessness.

He nodded reassurance.

She'd had barely a few blocks to go on one of the main drags that ran through Wilden and out to the highway.

"Now I wish I'd thought to circle way around and approach from the other direction." She made a face. "Although I suppose I'd have waited for Danner for a while, and when I gave up and started for home they'd have pulled me over."

"Danner could have been waiting for you inside the restaurant."

Her eyes widened at his noncommittal remark before she saw the tiny jerk of his head toward the camera. He could tell exactly what she was thinking: *he* might have to be careful but she didn't.

"Not a chance. He appeared way too fast and pointed a gun at me." She huffed out a breath. "It was déjà vu. Lights flashing, siren deafening me."

"Shanahan claims you flipped him off and that's why he pulled you over."

Her mouth dropped open. "What? I'm not stupid enough to do something like that even if I had recognized him. Which I didn't until we'd…well, interacted for a while."

"'Interacted'?"

She told him what Shanahan had whispered in her ear, as well as his original gibe when she'd insisted the gun was a plant.

Now, who would want to do something like that to you?

Matthew had to unclench his jaw to say, "Has your car been parked in the driveway at your house at all? Even for a few minutes, while you carried groceries in, say?"

"No!"

Knowing the camera wouldn't show his face, he grinned at her indignation. "We'll check to see whether anyone broke into your garage."

"I don't suppose I can go home."

Wishing he could pull a miracle out of the hat he never wore, Matthew said, "I'm afraid not yet. Your attorney should be here any minute. She'll get things moving." What Matthew knew was that Alexa wouldn't be going home alone, although he decided not to tell her that yet.

Alexa's nod was stout enough, but for a fleeting instant, her expression betrayed that vulnerability she was so determined to hide. "I've never been arrested before."

A little grimly, he said, "This will make one hell of an article in the *Tribune*."

Her chin came up. "Yes, it will."

There was the Alexa he knew and— Loved? Even the thought stole his breath. This was way too soon. It had to be.

He wished he believed himself.

Chapter Thirteen

The gun, it developed, was remarkably lacking in any fingerprints at all.

As Diana suggested sharply, "Consistent with it having been planted in my client's car, as seems obvious happened."

Better yet, Matthew had taken another detective—Joe Agostini—along with him to inspect the side door into Alexa's garage. The dead bolt wasn't closed—in fact, the door was unlocked entirely—but he saw and photographed marks on the hinges. The door had been removed from the frame, it appeared, presumably because that would have made less noise than bashing it in. However, the perpetrator had had trouble putting it back into place.

The indisputable evidence that someone had, in fact, broken into Ms. Adams's garage, along with the lack of fingerprints on the weapon itself, and the previous incidents involving her, had convinced Judge Sutton to nullify any charges. She'd eyed Shanahan and Danner, appearing as the arresting officers, over the top of her readers long enough to unnerve anyone, then nodded curtly.

"Dismissed."

Alexa walked out of the conference room with her attorney, Matthew following.

Behind him, a voice said, "Lieutenant."

He turned, eyebrows raised.

Brian Danner had separated himself from his coconspirator. "What's she got that would make you back her when she's out to get any cop she can catch who might've made a mistake? Who hasn't made their share?"

"There is nothing between Ms. Adams and me that affects my stance on this campaign to terrorize her." Matthew looked the other man in the eye. He hoped—no, he believed—he was telling the truth. "I'm doing my job. Yes, everyone makes mistakes, including people in law enforcement, but that's not the same thing as willfully breaking the law we were hired—and are morally obligated—to enforce.

"Ms. Adams is focused on officers who have used the cover provided by a badge, a uniform and a gun to steal drugs from the evidence locker, to use unacceptable levels of force because they enjoy it or because they're biased against their victims, or to blackmail women into relationships they can't say no to. Anyone involved in setting her up repeatedly needs to be fired. Do you hear me?"

Danner's lip curled. "The average citizen doesn't get what this job is like. *You* should know better." He walked away.

Matthew let him go.

FEELING AS IF she had to try to declare independence, Alexa said, "Thanks for the offer, but Diana can drive me to my car."

Looking as immovable as a huge block of granite, Matthew shook his head. "We need to talk."

Diana glanced at her phone. "I do have an appointment at three."

Alexa's shoulders sagged. "Fine." She hugged her attorney. "Thanks for running to my rescue."

Diana grinned at her. "Does he get a hug, too?"

Matthew wore a matching grin. "Yeah, do I?"

Alexa rolled her eyes, feeling very teenaged but justified. "Can we go?"

They parted in front of the police station, Diana's heels clicking on the pavement as she hurried away.

"You know you can't have your car back yet, anyway," Matthew said.

Alexa turned. "What?"

"Crime scene people are going over it." He lifted a hand to prevent her from speaking up. "At this point, that's to your advantage. Being that it was likely a cop who planted that gun, there probably won't be any fingerprints. But someone could have been careless opening the car door. The rubber floor mat could hold a print."

"*Likely* a cop?"

"Jim Berkey wasn't a cop." The set of his jaw was hard, the determination dark in his eyes. "Any of the cops you're investigating could have hired or coerced somebody into doing a little dirty work."

She had to nod. Of course, he was right, although she had a suspicion either Danner or Shanahan would have enjoyed placing that gun in her car, positioning it just so. If only she'd *really* had to slam on her brakes when that kid on the bike had ridden out in front of her. The gun would have come flying from under the seat.

Walking stiffly beside him to his pickup—did that mean he was taking the rest of the day off?—Alexa glanced down at the torn knee of her chinos, barely exposing the gauze covering her scrapes, and the other dirty, gritty knee. Gauze wrapped her hands, too. The medic had cleaned her cheek and dabbed on a disinfectant that stung, but not seen the need to cover the scrape. She hadn't been near a mirror, but she still had a good idea how awful she looked.

"When do you think I'll get my car back?" she asked as she fastened her seat belt.

"A day or two." He started the engine but didn't shift into Reverse. Instead, he turned his head to meet her eyes. "I don't want you driving."

"But… I have to keep doing my job or they win."

"Would the newspaper provide a car and driver for you?"

"I—" She thought about that. "Maybe." Actually, there was a good chance that, after hearing about today's events, they'd suggest it even without her asking. Or they could reimburse Uber or Lyft charges…except then she'd be accepting rides from strangers, and right now she didn't dare do that.

"I'm going to stay with you," Matthew said, no give at all in his voice. "In fact, let's go by my place now so I can pack a bag."

She blinked a couple of times as she tried to wrap her mind around the fact that this man was planning to move in with her and clearly had no intention of accepting anything resembling a "no." And she'd only met him…a week ago?

Did she want to say no? A little unnerved, she realized how much she wanted to take him home with her. If he was within earshot, she might be able to sleep without constantly jerking awake at any noise. He wouldn't be able to play bodyguard during the day, of course, but the sight of his pickup parked in her driveway during the night might be enough to serve as a 24/7 deterrent. She could hope.

The worrisome part was that she liked the idea of him spending the night for other reasons. Shutting her bedroom door in his face wouldn't be easy.

She found herself sneaking looks sidelong as he drove. He seemed pensive, although she had no doubt he was alert. Her gaze dropped to his strong hands, wrists and forearms.

Those powerful hands wrapped the steering wheel in a relaxed grip. She flashed back again to the man who'd already been stripping off his leather jacket as he'd walked toward her in that awful alley, his first thought to shield her. Had he known how comforting that coat was, too, with the warm sheepskin lining that she realized in retrospect smelled faintly of him?

Once he pulled into a driveway leading to a shabby detached garage beside a stately, two-story home decorated with obviously restored gingerbread and a broad front porch, Alexa gave way to temptation in another way and accompanied him into the house for what he described as the basic tour.

The staircase rose from a central hall. The living room lay to one side, irresistible with gleaming wood floors and moldings, creamy walls and a fireplace mantel carved from solid oak. A lion's head was frozen midroar at each end of the mantel.

She had to be gaping. "Did you do all this work by yourself?" she asked.

"A lot of it." He gazed around, as if appraising the result anew. Although a slight curl at the corner of his mouth suggested that he liked her reaction. "I've recruited a few minions."

Smiling, she said, "Your brother."

Matthew grinned. "Yeah, there's a reason he can hardly wait to get away to college."

"Friends, too, I suppose."

His expression closed so quickly, she knew she'd taken a misstep.

"Not…" She couldn't finish.

"Art? Yeah. We're good friends. I'm hoping…"

"Has there been any more news?"

"I'd dropped by the hospital when your attorney called. Art hasn't regained consciousness yet, but he's getting restless. I wish I were as convinced as his wife is—" He grimaced, turned abruptly and walked back into the hall.

Alexa followed, seeing a dining room with a built-in buffet that was still waiting for the kind of intensive stripping and refinishing that had awed her in the living room, then a half-complete kitchen.

"I mostly had to take this room down to the studs," Matthew said, having regained his composure. "Unfortunately, it had been remodeled a couple of times before. The last was in the seventies. Ugliest vinyl flooring you've ever seen, and the countertop was pretty bad, too. Whatever had been here originally was long gone."

"There probably *wasn't* much here," she pointed out. "The pantry and a wood-burning stove might have been it."

"Yeah, the pantry is good."

He left her to wander around to her heart's content while he went upstairs to throw a few things into a bag, as he put it. She did admire and envy a sizable pantry, peek at a half-bath under the stairs that had been beautifully restored, and a home office, also done. It seemed he'd started with the downstairs. His complaints about plumbing made her wonder if he hadn't also tackled an upstairs bathroom, but it was just as well he hadn't invited her up with him.

Except, of course, that he was coming home with her, instead.

When he came downstairs, his face was stern. All cop, he said, "The gun found in your car is being sent to the state lab. There was talk about test shooting it here, but I shut that down. I want it examined by outsiders."

He hated saying that, and Alexa understood why. He was admitting to her that he couldn't entirely trust anyone in his own department. Without that trust, how could he do his job?

"Was there any objection to using the state lab?" she asked.

He locked his front door and they started toward his truck. "Some pushback from above." There was deep reserve in his voice. "No reason to think the gun had been used in any major crime, I was told. I said there was plenty of reason."

Alexa climbed into the truck, dropped her handbag and stared at him. "You think that was the gun used…" She couldn't quite bring herself to finish.

Matthew did it for her. "To shoot Art. Yes, I do. They had to be setting you up for something bigger than a concealed weapons charge. If we're right that all of this is tied together, putting you in possession of a gun used to kill a cop makes for a harder hit. Right now, that's my best guess."

Feeling sick, Alexa stared straight ahead through the windshield while Matthew drove. If what he feared was true, that meant one of those men had set out to cold-bloodedly shoot a fellow officer. How else had he acquired that particular handgun?

Which one of the four who'd mocked and mistreated her was the killer? They'd obviously joined together to set her up.

"If that's true," she said slowly, "were they all in on trying to go after Detective Dwyer?"

His sideways glance let Alexa see eyes that looked more like molten metal, burning hot, than hardened steel.

"Hard to say." His hands tightened on the steering wheel until it creaked and his knuckles showed white. "But they seem to have all been in on the plan to eliminate *you*."

A little sick turned into a lot sick. If in fact that gun had been used by a killer, she wasn't off the hook yet. How could investigators *not* look at her?

Given that Lieutenant Matthew Reinert headed major crime investigations for the Wilden City Police Department, she had to ask herself how solid his support for her really was—and how she could have the faith in him that she did.

MATTHEW LAY ON his back in the guest bedroom, too occupied brooding to so much as think about sleeping.

Learning that Mike Swartz had been one of the four officers in on Alexa's arrest had disturbed Matthew. That meant three of the four were on both Alexa's and Art's list of problem officers who'd had relations with prostitutes. The name of the fourth guy, Josh Barry, hadn't pinged any alarms for Alexa. Matthew hadn't seen it in Art's notes, either. It was conceivable Barry had simply been patrolling in the area and responded to a request for backup. Matthew intended to talk to him first thing in the morning. He'd already checked to be sure the guy was working. If Barry hadn't wondered at all about the way Alexa was treated, the corruption in the department went deeper than even Matthew had begun to suspect.

He'd be sitting down with the other three, as well, even if they weren't under his direct command. If he had to stalk them in the parking lot, he'd do that.

He had a hard time believing the three—leaving Josh Barry aside for the moment—had conspired to murder a fellow cop. More likely, they'd come together to take Alexa down a notch because they were like-minded SOBs. Or they knew they were all on her radar and couldn't afford for her to trumpet their sins to the entire city.

They wouldn't have even needed to learn specifics about her records requests; she'd presumably called each officer with a request to sit down with her and discuss the problematic conduct that had been alleged to her. That, of course, had made it easy to set her up the way they had today.

A powerful sense of urgency had been driving Matthew since he'd gotten the call today from Alexa's attorney. Setting that kind of trap was a careless move. Reckless, even, and not so smart. Less so if Matthew was wrong about the gun and it hadn't fired the bullet that intended to kill Art, of course. Otherwise, those three men had turned the spotlight on themselves.

What he couldn't dismiss was the possibility that someone else entirely had given them a nudge, expressing the wish into a willing ear that there was a way to keep up the pressure on that nosy journalist. *How dare she go after us, when she has no clue what it takes to do our jobs?*

Yeah, it could have happened that way. With a groan, Matthew sat up, thinking he'd turn on the light and make some notes, but stopping himself before he reached for the switch on the lamp.

He had to get some sleep. His thoughts had begun to spin in circles, which wasn't helpful. Unfortunately, his acute state of wakefulness had as much to do with the real, live Alexa as it did with the investigation that involved her.

To start with, he didn't like leaving her alone tomorrow, or any day. So far, her enemy had tried to avoid murder. Shooting a cop had been brazen; if Alexa was killed right afterward, along with the tipster responsible for several incidents, even Chief Paulson would be forced to connect the dots.

At least, Matthew would like to think so.

Knowing she was too smart to take unnecessary risks should be more reassuring than it was. And, yes, he understood why she refused to give up her quest, but she'd spoken to the *Tribune* publisher late this afternoon, and he had readily agreed to provide a car and driver for business and personal errands.

Matthew had heard him say, "If you need groceries, have a doctor appointment, anything, don't try to get yourself there. I'll insist on a single driver, so you won't have any doubts when he shows up."

Matthew intended to protect her during any personal errands, but he'd been glad to hear her employers weren't stinting with their backup.

It really wasn't her arrangements for tomorrow keeping him awake, though. Their evening together had been unexpectedly comfortable, spiced with the physical attraction he could never entirely shut down when he was with her. In occasional furtive glances, he'd read wariness, but that was understandable given how he had bulled his way into staying nights at her house.

Now she lay in bed one wall away from the guest bedroom where he was supposed to be sleeping. It didn't help that he knew exactly how enticing she looked beneath her practical everyday garb.

He groaned and slapped the pillow down on his face. He had a ways to go before there was any hope of being invited into her bed.

He growled under the pillow and forced himself also to remember the bruises and swelling, the torn flesh on her wrists and the shock and fear on her face.

He concentrated instead on the relief and welcome that had lit her face at the sight of him when he'd walked into the holding cell.

Chapter Fourteen

Late morning, Diana called to announce that she'd quit with the foot-dragging and officially notified everyone concerned that Monday morning she was filing a lawsuit that lumped together the ambush and assault as well as the two traffic stops and the planted gun. She'd be requesting damages, too.

"Unless the department mounts a serious attempt to identify any individual officers behind this campaign of terror," she declared, "it will become apparent that, in fact, WPD as a whole is responsible for it. And, given their failure to promptly respond when it comes to your records requests, an unbiased observer—say, a juror—won't be able to help concluding that this has all come about because they're afraid to have anyone shine a light on the conduct of many of their officers. Which includes several, at the very least, who should never have been hired in the first place."

Phone to her ear, Alexa exclaimed, "How beautifully put. Thank you."

"You're welcome." A smile could be heard in the attorney's voice.

"How much money are we asking for in damages?"

The answer was so staggering, her mouth dropped open. "Well," she finally croaked.

"Naturally, we're sticking to our initial goal of oiling

the gates leading to the records that are being withheld. But this has gone way beyond that now. I'm trying to scare the you-know-what out of Reggie Paulson, not to mention the mayor and city council members who either think racist, brutal and corrupt policing is the way to go, or else are sticking their collective heads in the sand."

Alexa blinked. "I'm so glad I picked *you* out during my search."

Her attorney laughed. "If we actually win that full settlement…"

"I'll throw the pro bono thing out the window. Promise."

After having such a good night's sleep, courtesy of the comfort of Matthew's presence only a wall away, and now this conversation, Alexa found herself in an astonishingly good mood.

JOSH BARRY SAT stiffly in front of Matthew's desk, but he hadn't seemed reluctant when Matthew caught him on the way in the door and asked for a few minutes before he set out on his usual patrol shift.

"The stop yesterday?" Barry sounded a little puzzled but also uneasy.

"Yes."

"I didn't know the driver was Alexa Adams until I got back to the station after my shift was over. I mean, I wasn't the arresting officer, so once Officer Shanahan loaded her to bring her back here, I took up my patrol where I'd left off."

Matthew nodded. "Did anything that happened once you arrived at the scene appear out of the norm?"

A short, solid guy in his late twenties, Barry squirmed. "Ah…well, I almost pulled my sidearm because two of the other three already had, but then I saw a petite woman, alone, who appeared to already have been subdued. In fact,

I don't know why they needed me, but Shanahan asked for my continued backup." He fell silent but a nerve in his cheek twitched.

Matthew gave him some time.

"Unless she really fought before I arrived, I thought they were rough with her," he blurted out. "Once she was out of the car, there was no need to throw her down or cuff her ankles."

"Now that you know who she is, do you have any thoughts on why the stop occurred, and why they were so hard on her?"

Barry surged almost to his feet before sinking back down. "Everyone knows she's investigating people in our department. She wants to dump on our reputation."

Matthew raised his eyebrows. "*Our*?"

Holding a hint of desperation, brown eyes met his. "That's…what they're all saying."

"All? Or only the officers guilty of misconduct the public wouldn't condone? Misconduct that's been swept under the rug?" He let his voice harden. "I'd argue those are the officer who actually *are* blackening our reputation, shaming the men and women who do this job honorably."

Barry grimaced. "Maybe most of us keep our heads down more than we should, but I agree with you, and I think the majority of the guys do, too. I hear and see things…"

"Brian Danner was your FTO." Field training officers had an outsize influence on rookies.

"Yeah, uh, I think things went on he didn't let me see. I mean mostly he was okay, you know?"

They both knew what he was saying. Reporting your FTO for conduct unbefitting a law enforcement officer wasn't the way to find acceptance and guidance when joining a police force.

"Are you usually on the same shift as Danner? Or either of the others, for that matter."

He nodded. "Since I came off nights six weeks ago. But—" another hesitation "—Shanahan and Danner were both on my turf. Unless they were on break, meeting someone for lunch or coffee. Shanahan was supposed to be downtown, and Danner... I'm not sure." His expression eased. "It was lunchtime, though, so probably he and the others *were* meeting up, and that's why they were all so close by when he put out the call."

Yep. They'd arranged to meet up, all right, but not at a coffee shop or café. Matthew saw Josh Barry's face tighten again as he, too, saw the unwelcome possibility.

"What do you want, Lieutenant?" he demanded suddenly.

"Honesty. I needed to know if you were part of what they were up to—and I need you to keep your mouth shut about what I'm suspecting."

"I heard the call for backup. That's all."

"That's what I needed to know," Matthew said, rising to his feet. "Thank you for your honesty."

Barry nodded and stood, too. He appeared to have aged since he'd walked into the office. Getting your eyes opened to the evil hiding in plain sight had a way of doing that to you, Matthew thought.

THE CRIME SCENE report concluded that the gunman who'd shot Art Dwyer had stood by the detached garage off the alley. Making a shot from that distance—one that missed by only a hair—suggested unusual capability. Reality was, too many cops didn't keep their skills up. Matthew had an interesting conversation with the police range master.

Of the original list of five WPD officers who interested both Alexa and Art—and leaving aside, for the moment,

John Blykowski, the sheriff's deputy, Rick Shanahan and Don Rommel were the most diligent at keeping their skills sharp at the shooting range. Brian Danner trailed them, but was, in the words of the range master, "Okay."

"I wouldn't mind having him back me up." Ed Lee was a retired cop. "But he's not on the level of Shanahan and Rommel. They have some kind of competition going. They can both empty the magazine and gut the bull's-eye without a single wandering shot. Steady hands." He shook his head. "I worry that they're too cocky."

The description didn't surprise Matthew. The attitude was one of the things he didn't like about several of those officers. Sure, confidence was a requisite for this job, but you also had to believe in the rule of law, understand that you were employed by the citizens of your city. A decent man never let himself forget that the lowest dirtbag you arrested was a human being.

Ed Lee went on to say that Ken Kasperson came in often enough to maintain his middling skill and certification. Mike Swartz showed rarely, usually in company with a friend.

That could mean he went to another range, or, if he lived out of town, even had one set up on his own property.

Instinct had Matthew wanting to corner Shanahan and the others without warning, and without sending any signals up the command structure. That would mean cutting out Sergeant Estevez, who supervised patrol officers on the day shift. Matthew knew how he'd feel if the tables were turned. Sergeant Enrico Estevez's solid reputation helped with his decision.

Taking the risk, Matthew went to Estevez's office mid-morning. He already knew the patrol sergeant's workweek was Tuesday through Saturday, so he should be in.

Enrico Estevez had a thin build, a face sculpted like a Mayan frieze, and a booming voice that never required any help from a bullhorn. That voice could make the biggest, toughest guy freeze.

He frowned when he saw who his visitor was. Matthew explained bluntly that he'd like to interview Swartz, Shanahan and Danner.

The sergeant's eyes narrowed. "This have to do with that traffic stop yesterday?" he finally said.

"In part. Their names keep popping up in an investigation of mine."

Eyebrows climbed.

"Art Dwyer's shooting," Matthew said reluctantly. "Plus the…attempts to scare off Ms. Adams, the journalist." He'd never gotten even a whiff of anything off in Estevez's past, but their paths hadn't crossed much to date.

The sergeant leaned forward. "You're suggesting—?"

"I'm having to consider the possibility that Art was targeted by a fellow cop. Yes." Matthew told him why.

The lines on Estevez's forehead deepened, if anything, as he visibly checked for flaws in the logic of Matthew's argument. His next words suggested he hadn't found any.

Estevez gave a brusque nod. "Yeah, I'm okay with you talking to those guys. I hope like hell you're wrong, but I can't argue with your reasoning. I was already unhappy about yesterday's stop. Don't know if you've heard that Ms. Adams's attorney is filing a lawsuit that would damn near bankrupt this county. Yesterday was apparently the kicker after the load of garbage she's already been handed."

"Ms. Adams is investigating three of the four officers involved yesterday."

"Is she."

The flat, unsurprised response told Matthew that Sergeant Estevez knew about conduct that justified a journalist's investigation. Matthew guessed that the conduct had either occurred before Estevez had been transferred to command of the men in question, or that he'd been overruled when he tried to rein in Danner, Shanahan and Swartz.

Matthew had no trouble envisioning Chief Paulson deciding that boys would be boys and shouldn't be held accountable.

"Good," he said, pushing himself to his feet.

"They're all coming in early from their shifts. I'd intended to sit them down. You can have them instead." Estevez gave a tight smile. "I'll separate them to be sure they don't have a chance to coordinate their version of events." The smile turned into a grimace. "At least, any more than they already have."

Matthew felt good about the sergeant as he took the stairs up a level to the major crimes unit. He wasn't thrilled to have to wait until nearly the end of the day for those interviews, but it wasn't as if he didn't have plenty to do today to keep him occupied—there were alibis to pursue, not to mention scheduling a talk with Officer Alan Sharpe's widow.

ALEXA LIKED HER assigned driver right away.

"Don't worry," he said when he got out to meet her in her driveway. He held open the back door of the large SUV for her. "I can't move fast on my feet, but I'm a hell of a driver."

She evaluated him briefly, liking what she saw. Tall and lanky, he looked to be in his forties and wore a wedding ring.

"Can I sit in front with you?" she asked.

He grinned. "Sure thing." He held out a hand. "Vince Rowan."

"Alexa Adams." They shook.

"I already knew that."

She laughed, buckled her seat belt and said, "Can you make sure we're not followed?"

His eyes sharpened. "Absolutely."

"Give me a minute, then."

Olivia Sharpe answered the phone promptly. She sounded surprised at Alexa's request but agreed that she was free now. "Come right over."

Alexa had intended to go to her home-away-from-home at the library, where she had privacy, quiet, and the comforting awareness that she wasn't quite alone, saving the conversation with the killed officer's widow until a phone call this evening. But now that she had a second pair of watchful eyes, she thought it might be safe to visit instead of rely on a phone call. She'd been afraid that, if her nemesis knew she'd tied Sharpe's death to the attack on Art Dwyer, he'd redouble his effort to shut her up.

Not that Danner and Shanahan and company could afford to have her house watched 24/7...but she couldn't poke her nose outside without wondering.

She gave the address to her new driver, watched as he entered it in the GPS, then sat back for the ride across town.

The house wasn't hard to find. A rambler, it reminded her of her own, except the homeowner had not just a green thumb, but time for serious gardening. Roses rioted over porch railings. Fragrant masses of lavender and a lot of other perennials Alexa didn't recognize filled deep flower beds between rose stems.

"I doubt I'll be here long," Alexa said as she opened her door.

"Wait," Vince told her. "Why don't you let me take a look around before you get out?"

Bemused, she hovered inside her open door until he got

out, strolled as far as the street and stuck his head around the corner of the garage, so he knew what was between houses, before he finally came around to escort her to the walkway leading to the front door.

Alexa eyed him. "So, you're not just a driver, you're a bodyguard?"

Humor gone, he said, "I'm unarmed, but you're not the first client I've chauffeured who fears being followed."

Sure enough, at the deep-throated sound of an approaching vehicle, he stepped in front of her.

They both watched a black pickup pull into the driveway right behind the hired SUV. With a sense of inevitability, Alexa saw Lieutenant Matthew Reinert exit his vehicle, cast a quick glance at her and walk toward them with a now-hard gaze fixed on her escort.

"WE SHARED THE desktop computer," Olivia said nervously, her eyes flicking between Alexa and Matthew. "He had a work laptop, of course, but they took that. And the phone."

Alexa had trouble believing that a man as alarmed as Sharpe had been, ordered by his supervisors to forget what he'd seen, wouldn't have left notes somewhere. After all, this was a guy desperate enough to consider confiding in someone outside his department. No, not just someone specifically, a journalist, who would certainly not have kept quiet about whatever he'd told her.

If he kept notes…well, in times past, she thought ruefully, he'd have hidden them beneath the false bottom of a drawer, or the like. Now, however, they almost had to be digital.

If he'd said anything incendiary to friends, wouldn't you think one of them would have come forward after he was murdered?

And would he have told a friend something he *hadn't* told his wife?

Or *had* he talked to Olivia?

If the friend was also a cop, though, could he have been involved in whatever wrongdoings Sharpe had observed, or, at least, been stubbornly blind to them?

Blind enough not to wonder given Sharpe was murdered so soon after, though?

Alexa had considered the possibility that Olivia did know why her husband had been killed and kept quiet because of threats. Although, you'd think she'd have moved away if that were the case.

After meeting the woman, Alexa just couldn't see it.

"Did he spend much time on the computer here at home?" Matthew asked. He'd been a rather quiet presence thus far, although a man with his size and commanding air was hard to ignore. Now, it went without saying that he'd seen right away where Alexa was going with her questions.

"Well...yes," the pretty blonde said. "But when he was working, it was always with the laptop." She seemed to have trouble pulling her gaze from the enormous, framed portrait of her husband hanging over the fireplace, or maybe it was from the half dozen other photos displayed on the mantel.

"Was he into computer games? Or did he mostly email?" Alexa asked.

"Not games. But emails, sure. I mean, sometimes, but we both grew up locally and saw our friends and family often. That's why I decided to stay here in town after. It's hard, because everywhere I look, there's a memory of us together, but—" She broke off.

"This is where your support network is," Alexa said softly.

Olivia's smile seemed grateful. "Yes."

"So?" Matthew was undoubtedly trying for patience but beginning to fall short.

"So...? Oh! The computer. He was writing a book," she explained. "He loved Joseph Wambaugh. That kind of mystery."

Hiding her tension and excitement, Alexa said, "How far along was he?"

"Halfway, maybe? He kept getting ideas and going back, so he wasn't progressing very fast."

Matthew's eyes met Alexa's. It was a little alarming that she could read his message. *She'll respond better to you than me.* He must have sensed that from the beginning.

"Have you read the manuscript?" she asked as gently as she could.

"Some of it when he first started writing," Olivia said. "But that's not the kind of stuff I read, so I couldn't do much but be encouraging."

"Since he died?"

Her lips compressed. "Even thinking about it makes me sad."

"Would you permit us to do so?" Seeing instant wariness on Olivia's face, Alexa reminded her, "You're aware that he called me before his death because he'd seen something he'd thought was wrong and nobody within the department would pay attention to him. It's conceivable that while he had his manuscript open, he played with ideas about what to do about the problem that was worrying him. Made pro and con lists. Things like that."

Increasingly distressed, Sharpe's wife cried, "But he never dreamed anyone would kill him over what he saw!"

Matthew spoke up. "All I can tell you is that we're revisiting the investigation into his death because there are definite parallels with how and why Art Dwyer was shot. I need to pursue any possibility. I'd be grateful if you can help. Bad enough that someone thinks he got away with killing an officer of the law. But now…if he's tried to do it again?"

Let's not forget Tansy Gould and the other young women, Alexa thought. Although she didn't believe for a minute that Matthew had forgotten them. His goal was maximum emotional punch on this widow, who now stared at him in shock.

Chapter Fifteen

"I don't—didn't—really know Art," Olivia said hesitantly, "but when my son was born, Art's wife called out of the blue. She gave us a stroller, crib bedding and a ton of clothes because she said they'd decided not to try for a third baby. It was such a blessing. I'd had to quit my job." Blue eyes wet, she looked at Matthew. "I should call her. Do you have her number?"

"I do." He swallowed. "I think Michelle would be really grateful to hear from you. She's hanging on to hope, but it's hard."

Olivia's hands curled into fists. "I'll do anything I can to help you catch the monster who killed Alan. I can email you the manuscript. Would that do?"

"Yes. Thank you."

Alexa didn't say anything, but she was thinking it: he'd darned well better share a copy with her. What she did say was, "While you're at it, you might take another look at any other documents created in the month or so before his death, read emails he sent out, hunt for unexpected activity. You may have done that at the time, but with some distance, you have a fresh eye now."

Olivia nodded firmly. "I will."

Thank God, she hadn't replaced the computer yet, Alexa couldn't help thinking.

"Did the detectives who spoke to you at the time ask to look at your home computer?" Matthew asked.

Olivia frowned a little. "No. No, they seemed to think someone he'd arrested had killed him in revenge."

"That's still possible," Matthew conceded, "but I'm no longer convinced."

Teary-eyed again, she walked them to the door and, accepting Matthew's card, promised to email the manuscript immediately. Matthew entered Michelle Dwyer's number in Olivia's phone before thanking her again for her time and cooperation.

Vince waited outside, leaning against the SUV. Apparently, her driver had passed Matthew's test once they'd exchanged a few words.

"How'd it go?" he asked, straightening.

"Fingers crossed," Alexa said. "I think I'll head to the library next."

Matthew frowned. "I don't like you being isolated in back the way you were the day I stopped by."

She rolled her eyes. "I'm not isolated. People wander in and out through the stacks. The back door is kept locked, and Vince will be waiting out front."

Matthew frowned but gave a short nod. "Okay. Want me to bring something home for dinner?"

Home? Really? Heat tinged her cheeks at Vince's interested expression.

"I'll find something. But I'd better have a copy of that manuscript in my inbox by the time I open my email account."

He had the nerve to hesitate. "This is part of a homicide

investigation, only indirectly linked to your research into problem officers."

Alexa took a step forward to get right in his face. "I got here first. In fact—" she scowled "—how'd you know I was going to see Olivia?"

Matthew's mouth quirked. "Maybe great minds think alike."

She didn't so much as blink.

"I called to make an appointment to see her today. She told me you were coming. I figured it would be easier for her to get it all out once."

He could be thoughtful, but call her cynical. He just hadn't wanted her learning something he hadn't.

Her stare was evidently getting to him because he snapped, "Fine!" *He* stepped forward until only inches separated them and she had to tip her head back to keep glowering at him. "But you keep anything you see to yourself, is that clear? Arresting this piece of scum for murder is the priority, not your front-page headline."

Alexa would have liked to see heat blisters popping out on Matthew's lean cheeks, but a woman couldn't get everything she wanted. Without another word to him, she swung around and stalked to the passenger side of the SUV.

Vince was behind the wheel before she managed to close her door. Reading her mood, he gave her a sidelong glance. "We'll have to wait for the lieutenant to back out."

She snorted.

"Don't know that I've ever heard of a reporter and a homicide detective working a case together."

"We're not. Exactly."

"Kind of sounded like you are."

"He—and I—think the person out to get me also murdered one cop and tried to kill another."

"Ah." Vince closed his hands around the wheel and gazed out the windshield for a minute, even though Matthew had already backed into the street. "Art Dwyer and Alan Sharpe."

"Yes." She turned her head to look at him. "You knew?"

"I follow the news," Vince said simply. His eyes met hers. "Maybe I shouldn't say this, but it seems to me he has a point."

She huffed out a breath. "About our priority? Of course he does. What irritates me is that he'd think for a minute I'd rather get a spectacular headline than see that…that *monster* behind bars."

Vince looked over his shoulder and accelerated out of the driveway. "I imagine cops get cautious for a reason."

Unwilling to trust that people will act from their better natures?

Alexa bumped her head a couple of times on the seat back. "I get that."

That was only one of many reasons why Matthew shouldn't be making himself *at home* with her.

And why she shouldn't get used to having him there.

MATTHEW WAS STILL seething when he let himself in Alexa's front door with the key she'd given him that morning in case their schedules didn't coordinate. The key he'd added to his chain with great satisfaction.

"It's me," he called and followed the sound of a pan banging onto a stove into the kitchen.

He caught a flash of emotion in her eyes when she glanced at him, but couldn't decipher it. He did drink in the sight of her slim, utterly feminine body and fine-boned, stubborn face.

She didn't greet him with any great enthusiasm but asked, "Black bean quesadillas okay?"

"Yeah." Despite his dark mood, he kissed her on the cheek, enjoying the soft give, before backing away. "Last thing today, I talked to those sons of bitches who arrested you. Got nowhere, and I'd swear they were all smirking on their way out of my office."

Just as Art had described Jim Ward, O'Brien and their buddies, come to think of it. He might have narrowed his list too soon—except those two had been fired. He'd like to think they were frantically job hunting with no success.

Still, someone who hadn't risen to his attention could have incited Shanahan and company, he had to remind himself.

Alexa made a scoffing noise. "Why aren't I shocked?"

He scraped a hand over his jaw. "The better question is why am I?"

She summoned a crooked smile for him. "Because you're an optimist?"

Matthew's anger relented, leaving him able to laugh. "That's me." He nodded toward the cutting board she'd set out on the counter. "Can I do anything?"

"No, this is really simple. My go-to dinner when I don't have a lot of time."

He sipped a beer and they talked as she dumped two cans of beans along with salsa and corn into a saucepan and set it to simmering. A minute later, she added diced bell peppers and some spices. It seemed neither of them was eager to talk about the frustration engendered by reading what messages had been left to them from beyond the grave by Officer Alan Sharpe, because neither raised the subject. Alexa told him she hadn't stayed long at the library because she'd felt guilty leaving the driver sitting in the parking lot.

She shrugged. "I mean there's no reason to think I'm not safe here."

Matthew wished he believed that. The brutality of the first attack made it clear that Alexa having been set up repeatedly wasn't only the actions of some dirty cops afraid they'd lose their jobs if she pursued her investigation and their names appeared in the *Tribune*. Those cops had gone way beyond nasty tricks. They must know how quickly any of those incidents could have turned tragic and either hadn't cared or had hoped for her death.

He came right out with it. "I got results on the ballistics today. They put a rush on it because we suspected the gun had been used in the attempted murder of a cop and the shooting of another one."

She went very still. The green in her hazel eyes had darkened. "It was used to shoot Art?"

Matthew bent his head. "Art and Alan Sharpe as well as Jim Berkey." He reminded her that Berkey had been responsible for the tip leading to the raid on her house. "Tansy Gould and the others, we don't know."

They hadn't recovered bullets from the bodies or the garbage dumpsters.

The results from the state lab tied in a neat knot the parallels between her investigation and Art's, and the not-so-coincidental fact that Jim Berkey had been murdered, his body disposed of in the same way several prostitutes had met their ends.

Alexa nodded and seemed to withdraw. He couldn't blame her.

"Michelle thinks Art is going to open his eyes any minute," he reported, voice rough from the hope he tried to keep in check. "Doctor is optimistic. Nobody is talking about whether he could have suffered brain damage."

Alexa only nodded again, looking even more somber. She served the melted cheese and black bean quesadillas at the table, along with asparagus and a tub of sour cream.

He'd already taken a bite when she picked up then set down her fork and looked at him, all her frustration in her expression.

"Did you read it?"

"Yeah."

"Why didn't he name names?" she exclaimed. Or maybe she was begging for an explanation.

Matthew had immediately known why Sharpe hadn't identified fellow officers even as he'd read the shocked paragraph describing the three of them ushering hookers away from a hotel just before an operation was sprung. Seeing some groping, and fright more than gratitude on the faces of the women. And then the one cop who had been assigned to participate in the sting had melted back into his place, confident nobody had seen.

Until Alan Sharpe had started telling his tale and getting shut down. Even so, the three officers had had to ask themselves…what if someone eventually *did* listen?

Sharpe was dead less than a week later.

Murder was a damned extreme reaction in the circumstances. Getting caught being involved with prostitutes would likely not have resulted in more than a slap on the hand, which was apparently the norm these days for WPD. Maybe a reprimand. Unfortunately, one of those three men, at the very least, had to be protecting darker secrets. If anybody had seriously started looking into the guy's history with prostitutes, he might have been connected to the series of murders.

"Sharpe was still struggling with his loyalties," Matthew said. "We stand up for each other. Keep our mouths shut. What he saw wasn't so terrible. Yeah, he disapproved of law enforcement officers getting involved with women who broke the law every day, and especially of the married guys. But he didn't see anyone get hurt."

"Except, he wondered," Alexa said tautly. "The women were being saved from an arrest—"

"Probably not their first."

"And he thought they were every bit as afraid of the men 'helping them' as they would have been of spending a night in jail and adding a charge to their records."

"To his credit, that's why Sharpe decided to speak out. He just never imagined…" Matthew shook his head.

"No." Alexa looked down at her plate for a long moment then started to eat.

She'd cleared her plate before she stormed, "It's maddening! Having our suspicions confirmed, but with the creeps still anonymous. And I can't help thinking those three may be just the tip of the iceberg. There could be half a dozen more officers doing the same thing. I mean I've gotten tips about at least a couple more."

"Art had others on his list, too," Matthew agreed. "But we know that one of the three officers Sharpe saw was our target and the man out to shut you up." *No matter what.*

Alexa had to be thinking the same, but she responded as if this were an intellectual problem, not a personal one. "Because why would he have murdered a fellow officer if *his* name wasn't one of those Sharpe would have shared with his sergeant or whoever he went to?"

"Exactly. And I know for a fact that Sharpe spoke both to his sergeant and to the lieutenant above him, even though jumping above the sergeant's head must have caused some tension. My best guess is that they both told him more might have been going on than he realized, and the men and women he worked with needed to be able to trust him. If they couldn't, maybe he should quit his job."

Alexa's chin came up. She vibrated with sudden aggression. "What if one of your detectives came to you with suspicions about a coworker? Would you say the same thing?"

Stunned, Matthew stared at her. Damn. That was what she still thought about him? He'd been an idiot to be falling for her, to love sharing breakfast and dinner with her even if he hadn't made it into her bed yet—

Her face convulsed. "I'm sorry! I don't know why I even said that! No, I do. I keep trying to—"

When she didn't finish, he prodded, "To what?"

Cheeks glowing hot, she was too gutsy to avoid meeting his gaze. "Protect myself, I guess. Not like I know what you have in mind, I mean about—" she flapped a hand in a gesture meant to encompass the two of them "—but since it wouldn't work anyway…"

"You're afraid," he said slowly.

"No! I'm just…"

"Afraid." He shook his head when she opened her mouth to keep arguing. "*I've* been afraid you'd never be able to trust me. What you just said tells me that maybe you can't."

"No." It was almost a whisper. "I do. What happened wasn't your fault. You haven't let me down. I don't believe you will."

"Every time I have to leave you, I'm afraid he—they—will get to you." That anguish roughened his voice.

"But our only chance is to keep digging," Alexa protested. "You *have* to go to work."

He wanted to ask her again to go into hiding. To let *him* do the digging. He didn't waste his breath. She wasn't the "running away" kind—and if she were, he wouldn't feel the way about her that he did.

Matthew pushed back his chair and stood. "Alexa."

She rose more slowly, her gaze never leaving his. "This… this still isn't smart."

"I don't care." He held out a hand. "I want you."

He saw her deep breath, her lashes flutter down. And then she walked around the table and laid her small hand in his.

With a gentle pull, he drew her to him. This kiss felt as if it would mean something in a way the others hadn't, but he didn't let himself overthink it. Not when he so desperately wanted her in his arms.

Go easy.

That concept crashed when she threw herself the last short distance to press against him, when she rose on tiptoe and fiercely gripped his shirt as *she* went for his mouth.

Matthew gripped her butt to lift her high enough to wrap her legs around his waist and backed her into the closest wall.

The kiss was openmouthed, sizzling hot, and urgent.

ALEXA HELD OUT as long as she could but finally had to wrench her mouth away to snatch a breath. Nobody had ever kissed her like this, as if her taste was ambrosia. She'd be glad if he never quit, except he was also using his strong hands on her butt to move her up and down, rubbing the most sensitive part of her body against his erection. Increasingly desperate, she tightened her thighs to ride him as if they didn't have several layers of clothing between them.

"*God.*" Matthew lifted his head. Dark color ran across his lean cheeks and his eyes were wild. "Alexa. I can't take much more. If this isn't a yes…"

She was too far gone to consult that voice of common sense. She'd wanted this man since the first time she had really let herself see him. But even before, in the alley, his hands had been so gentle when he wrapped his coat around her. The same hands had been strong and competent when he worked on her front door.

She loved those hands.

In fact— No, no, too soon!

She nipped his neck, tasting salt and man. "This is a yes."

Matthew made a strangled sound and hoisted her a little higher. "Hold on tight."

Whether she was being smart or dumb, she needed him. To occupy herself to ensure sure she didn't have time for second thoughts, Alexa tormented him as he carried her out of the kitchen and down the hall. She licked his throat, nibbled his scratchy jaw, and squirmed. Had she ever felt this *needy*?

Panting, he returned the favor by squeezing her butt cheeks and allowing his long fingers to slip lower, to tease and retreat. Given the ridiculously short length of time they'd known each other, she felt as if she'd been waiting for this man forever. If only she was reacting entirely to his big, solid body and the penetrating gray eyes, to the strength and certainty he exuded, but Alexa knew it was more.

The more that still frightened her.

She didn't notice when they went through the doorway into her bedroom. The first she knew was when those strong hands shifted to her hips so that he could peel her off him and set her on her feet. She had to release her clasp around his neck. He hadn't changed his mind, had he?

He yanked her shirt over her head and tossed it. Question answered. Seconds later, her bra slid down her arms and dropped to the floor. Matthew said a few things that sounded almost prayerful as he enclosed her breasts in his hands then rubbed gently. Even as she arched into his touch, she grabbed the hem of his shirt and tried to lift it.

A momentary struggle ensued; he didn't want to let go of her, but she won. And, oh, his chest, hard belly and powerful shoulders were as beautiful as she'd imagined. The vee of nut-brown hair only emphasized the defined muscles beneath.

They both explored, stroked, squeezed, until he groaned and she let out something like a whimper. He broke, lifting her again to lay her across the bed. He unbuttoned her pants, and with a few wriggles on her part and tugs on his, she was naked. Sprawled, waiting for him.

She'd never seen a man undress that fast. Especially one who had to untie laces, kick off boots and socks and stow a holstered gun, phone and badge on the bedside stand.

Oh, and drop a few packets beside them. Not strictly necessary, but she'd never made love with a man without insisting he use condoms. This time, reaching out to squeeze his impressive erection, she was tempted to tell him to forget sheathing himself. Of course, she wouldn't; she might be bold on the job, but she'd always protected herself personally—both physically and emotionally.

Matthew didn't even ask, though. He put on a condom and came down on top of her. The next thing she knew, they were kissing again as deeply and hungrily as when they'd started. When he took his mouth from hers, she cried, "No!" but he went for her breast instead, licking, suckling, before switching to the other breast. His fingers slid between her folds until she lost it and climbed on top of him.

"Now!"

He laughed up at her, eyes molten, and helped her fit herself to him. And then she rode him, and he rode her, and for the first time in her life, she screamed when her body imploded.

He made a harsh sound and she felt every second of his long, shuddering release.

Chapter Sixteen

"If I thought this would go on long enough, I'd install an alarm system on this house," Matthew said grimly the next morning as he pushed away his empty plate after finishing breakfast.

Alexa looked surprised. Maybe because he'd become a cop instead of her lover a little too abruptly. But what she said was, "You'd install one yourself?"

He hesitated. "Probably not now. I can't afford to get distracted."

"And I'm sure an alarm involves the dreaded electricity," she pointed out.

He grimaced, but playfully, able to relax. "Caught me making an excuse."

Better yet, he'd install a security system on *his* house, and she could move in with him. Not something he could suggest in the near future. He felt more positive than he had in a while this morning, though, thanks to their lovemaking. But also more apprehensive. He hated knowing he wasn't any closer to identifying his man than he'd been two weeks ago.

"What are you doing today?" she asked. Sort of casually, as a girlfriend or even roommate might ask over the breakfast table, but with a serious undertone he couldn't mistake. "Can you take it off?"

He did take a lot of full weekends off, but under the circumstances? Matthew hesitated. "Unless you need me, I thought I'd put in a few hours and sit with Art to give Michelle and the kids a break. What about you?"

She paused long enough to make him wary. "I have an interview with a cop who I've been browbeating. Not anyone relevant to what's been happening, I'm pretty sure. Vince is driving me, the guy is going to get in the car to talk while Vince sits on a park bench right nearby."

"That should be okay," Matthew conceded grudgingly.

"Then—" She didn't quite meet his eyes. "Late this afternoon, early evening, I'm going to flash some pictures around downtown once the nightlife starts up. I know Sunday night isn't the best, but…"

"You're going to show photos of *cops*?" He'd been wanting to do the same, but knew full well he'd lose his job if he did.

"Sure," Alexa said breezily. "Not ones of them in uniform or anything like that. I've found some on social media sites. You know."

"I'll shadow you."

She shook her head. "You stand out." Now she did survey him, boots to face. "All cop, plus alpha male. You'd scare anyone away who is on the fence about whether to talk or not."

He couldn't afford to be seen canvassing with her, but he was better at staying out of sight than she guessed. All he said was, "Your driver?"

"He has to stay in the car, but he'll change parking spots to stay close."

"Is he armed?"

"I…doubt it. Would you want him to be?"

Busy as the streets and sidewalks were downtown even

on a Sunday when the dinner hour approached and activity in the bars picked up, no. Especially not a guy who was extremely unlikely to put in the number of hours needed to maintain any level of skill with his weapon.

"No. You'll tell me anything you learn?"

"Unless it's unrelated to your investigation." Her eyes narrowed at whatever she saw on his face. "You know I may be investigating cops for a long time to come. I won't let you stop me."

He stood and went around the table, giving her a lopsided grin. As annoyed as she undoubtedly was, when he held out a hand, she laid hers in it and let him pull her to her feet.

"I get that. But you and I both know this is different. We're looking for a killer who thinks *you're* his personal bull's-eye."

Her shoulders sagged. "I haven't forgotten. Why else did I agree to let you stay here?"

He raised his eyebrows. "Is that the only reason?"

She eyed him cautiously. "Well…maybe not."

Not as reassured as he'd like to be, he nodded.

"I just can't let myself be so intimidated I don't fight back," she said in a rush.

And there it was, damn it—one of the reasons she'd drawn him so powerfully from the beginning. Her stubborn refusal to back down, and the will that allowed her to bounce back and defy whoever and whatever had tried to mow her down.

Beneath it all, he'd recognized from the beginning that they had something major in common, too: the need to stand up for right, goodness, justice. And no, he wouldn't put his own motivation in such soppy terms, but it served.

He bent to kiss her. He'd intended to make a point, but he loved the feel of her lips, the hot rush of her breath, her taste, and he got carried away. It wasn't easy to rein himself in, but finally he raised his head and looked down into her dazed eyes.

"Last night was amazing."

Alexa blinked until her gaze was as sharp as usual. Then she smiled. "Yes, it was."

"Good." He kissed her again but didn't linger. "Text me. I want to hear from you regularly today, and especially tonight."

Even if he trailed her, chances were good he'd lose sight of her some of the time.

"Yes, sir!" She saluted.

He grinned and left.

DARRELL WALKER OPENED the back door of Alexa's hired SUV and hopped in. His head turned all the while, something close to panic on his face.

"We should have met somewhere farther out of town."

"What are the odds anyone who knows you will go by? If they did, all they'll see is the back of my head. You could be meeting anyone."

He wasn't that distinctive-looking, she thought. He was handsome in a generic way, stubble darkening his jaw, his head shaved to a stubble, too, like so many other cops around here. At least he didn't have that overmuscled look.

When she reminded him that he'd agreed to her recording the conversation, he said curtly, "Yeah, don't care."

Even though she eased into her questions, Darrell remained tense and defensive. Yeah, he might have been a little rougher with the guy she mentioned than he should have been, but he'd been refusing to get out of the car and Darrell couldn't be sure he didn't have a gun under the seat, say.

"In the body camera footage, it's clear his hands were both on the steering wheel, in compliance with your order."

"But you heard me order him to get out of the car, too, didn't you?"

"I also heard him ask why he'd been pulled over. That seemed like a reasonable question to me."

"He was speeding."

"You didn't use a radar gun."

"I didn't have to. He rocketed by me."

The doctor who'd had to spend the night in the hospital after Darrell Walker threw him to the pavement and kicked him a few times had been positive he hadn't exceeded the speed limit.

"Why didn't you answer his question?"

Darrell glared at her. "I didn't pull him over to chat. He was challenging me."

She kept her expression calm. "You have three other complaints on your record for hurting motorists who either insist they did nothing to justify being pulled over or were pulled over for a minor infraction, such as rolling past a stop sign."

His face set. "My word against theirs."

"As it happens, all four injured complainants are non-white. Can you comment on that?"

"Every one of them refused to follow my clear directions!"

And so it went. Alexa couldn't help wondering why he'd agreed to meet with her, and agreed to allow her to record their conversation.

Eventually, she thanked him for his time and he said, "You know these are all old complaints, right?"

The most recent had been eight months ago—unless there were others that hadn't been included in the file to which she'd been given access.

"I *do* follow orders."

"I'm glad to hear that," she couldn't resist saying.

Hand on the door handle, he said, "Maybe you should write about what *cops* have to put up with every day, turn the spotlight around for once." He leaped out, slammed the door and, with his shoulders hunched and his head down, walked toward his car.

For all that he'd disgusted her, Alexa found herself pondering his suggestion as she moved to the front passenger seat to wait for Vince to get in behind the wheel.

It might *be* interesting to listen to the rank and file's stories of abuse they'd accepted with stoicism and unfailing civility. Write an article reminding readers that there were plenty of good cops out there.

ALEXA KNEW HERSELF to be conspicuous although she tried really hard to appear to be ambling along, checking out different bars, even stopping to read the menus a couple of restaurants posted in their front windows. The growing darkness helped in one way, but not in another. Sometimes enough light fell through the windows of a restaurant or tavern to allow the few women who even pretended to look at the pictures to see them. Otherwise, she had to aim for corners, where the streetlights stood.

So far, she was striking a big fat zero, except for the giveaway twitches that told her the women were lying. Vince wasn't very happy now that it was getting dark and he was having trouble tracking her.

For the second time in about two minutes, her phone dinged.

Yep, him again. Time to quit?

Not yet, she responded.

Up ahead, she spotted two girls at the corner, both wearing skirts that barely covered their butts—butts they made the most of when they took a few steps to flaunt themselves at passersby while smiling an invitation at single, male drivers.

Alexa glanced back just as the light down the street changed, causing a lull in traffic. Only during those brief breaks could she get any of the women she approached to so much as hear her beginning spiel.

That, by the way, had changed.

Alexa approached these two with a "Hey. Do you have a second?"

Both swung around to appraise her, and obviously concluded she wasn't any competition. She hid her instinctive horror at seeing how young they were, especially the blond girl. For all the makeup and posturing, she couldn't be more than fifteen or sixteen, and maybe even younger than that.

"My name's Alexa," she told them. "I'm looking for a guy who killed my sister." She'd given up on being honest about being a reporter for the *Spokane Valley Tribune* early on. "I'm hoping you can tell me if you've seen any of these men."

"You know BJ wouldn't like it," the older of the two said.

"I just want to know if you've seen them picking up girls. And no, I won't even ask for your names. It won't take a minute."

Out of the corner of her eye, Alexa saw that the light over the cross street had turned yellow. Her window of opportunity was shrinking here.

Both had their backs to the street now, so she hastily whipped out the eight photos she'd chosen. Somebody would have to be really close to see that the three women were doing anything but talking.

Neither of the young women could resist letting their gazes drop to the photos Alexa displayed one at a time. Three were faces she'd plucked off the internet, men who weren't even local. This wasn't exactly a blind test, but she tried to convince herself she was coming close.

The older was the first to touch one photograph.

"I think he was seeing a girl who works a few blocks down for a while. I don't know if he does anymore."

Jim Ward.

Alexa nodded. Traffic had started up and, taking a side-long look, she became aware of a thin, tattooed man getting out of a car parked across the street. BJ, she guessed. *Hurry, hurry.*

"Him." The pitifully young blonde poked a photo. "He, um, has a regular." She frowned. "Or he did."

Rick Shanahan.

"I've heard—"

The older girl shushed her and grabbed the pile, flipping quickly through the rest. "Him, too," she said.

Brian Danner. Alexa felt the tiny hairs on the back of her neck prickle.

"He never pays, and BJ doesn't say anything."

Alexa met a blistering stare from the creep across the street and she stepped back. "Thanks, you've been a big help."

She hadn't retreated ten feet when a car pulled to the curb and the blonde sauntered over and bent to talk to the driver through the open window. Now her skirt didn't alto-gether cover her butt.

If Alexa hadn't been so mad, she might have cried for a girl who wasn't even old enough to attend a high school prom.

One more block, she decided.

The crossing light changed to green but she looked both ways anyway before stepping into the street. Partway across, some instinct made her turn her head. Her gaze caught on the tall man with tousled nut-brown hair who had just stepped out of a door alcove.

MATTHEW WALKED IN the door to find Alexa standing only a few feet away, arms crossed. "Really?"

He grinned at her. "Surprised you, didn't I?"

She snorted. "I knew you wouldn't be able to resist trailing me. You did stay out of sight better than I expected," she admitted with clear reluctance.

"You didn't know I was there until you saw me," he countered.

"Vince had already spotted you."

"I don't believe you."

She smirked, an expression he found he liked on her face. Her phone appeared in her hand and she opened a string of texts for him.

Looking down, he saw that she had told the truth. It reassured him, in a way, knowing that her driver was that observant.

"You win." He handed her back her phone. "You have any ideas for dinner?"

"I ordered Thai."

He grinned again at the take-it-or-leave-it tone. "Sounds good to me."

Instead of going straight to the kitchen, she led him to the living room where she plopped down at one end of the sofa. He sat right beside her and wrapped an arm around her. Nuzzling the top of her head, he asked, "Mad at me?"

She sighed. "No. Knowing you were there was...comforting. Every time I crossed a street, I expected a car to come out of nowhere and flatten me."

He shook his head. "Too much foot and vehicular traffic. Nobody would get away with a hit-and-run."

"I guess so."

He let the silence go for the moment, content to be holding her, inhaling the mint smell of her shampoo. Finally, he asked, "Learn anything?"

She tipped her chin up so she could see his face. "Not as much as I'd hoped. One picked out Brian Danner. She told me that he never pays, and her pimp is okay with that. I think a couple of others recognized him, too."

Matthew grimaced. How did these guys live with themselves?

"Only one said she recognized Rick Shanahan, although I could tell the other woman—girl—with her did, too."

"Was that the really young one?"

"You saw?" She shivered. "Can't you arrest a girl like that and get in touch with her family?"

"I tried a few times, early on." He shook his head. "If it's possible to identify family at all, it usually turns out to be toxic. Kids run away for a reason. Sending them back doesn't really work, and they don't tend to be receptive to anything social services offers."

Alexa ducked her head so he couldn't see her face. "I know that. It's just…"

He rubbed his cheek on her head again, until his evening stubble caught strands of her hair. "I know," he murmured.

After a moment, Alexa continued. "She started to say something about Shanahan. That he had a regular. Then she said, 'Or he did.' Past tense. Her partner shut her up."

Because the regular was dead? Body found tossed in a dumpster?

When Alexa asked, Matthew told her about his day. He concluded by saying, "Feel like we're going in circles?"

"Yeah, but we always end up in the same place. Crooked cops."

"I have Danner and Shanahan at the top of my list," Matthew admitted. "I've been able to eliminate a couple of the others for Dwyer's shooting."

She pulled back and raised her eyebrows.

"Mike Swartz and Don Rommel. Swartz's sister got married last weekend. He flew out Thursday to be in Texas for the wedding. Rommel plays bass in what's mostly a garage band. They had a gig Thursday through Sunday night at a local tavern."

She nodded.

"But I keep reminding myself that there could be someone in the background nudging these guys who are running scared because of your investigation."

"And Detective Dwyer's."

"Yeah." He cleared his throat. "Whoever he is, he didn't kid himself that he could steer Art in a new direction or scare him."

Fortunately, security at the hospital was pretty tight in the ICU.

Alexa asked how Art was doing and, for the first time, Matthew was able to sound—and feel—positive. "I'd swear he was trying to respond when I talked to him. He looked grumpy that he couldn't manage it."

She laughed. "I…keep thinking about him."

A moment later, the conversation reverted to where they'd left off, though, when she asked, "Wouldn't anyone expect *you* to take up where Art left off? Or assign another detective to it?"

"Except for me, Art's the most experienced and capable

detective in the department. And everyone knows I can't put as much into any investigation because of my administrative responsibilities. Or he could think he's smarter than I am."

Alexa made a rude sound that had him smiling ruefully. Nonetheless, any stir of humor didn't derail him.

"You, though…" He made sure she was paying attention. "They've tried everything, and your response? You're still at it, putting pressure on the city and county, interviewing cops who've been in trouble. You filed suit against the county, and everyone knows what you're really demanding is unlimited access to camera footage and disciplinary records. You're not backing off."

She didn't say a word, but her pupils had dilated. "You think…"

"I do think. He's gotten away with killing one cop. The other is in a coma. He'll think he can kill you, too, and go on his merry way."

Chapter Seventeen

Monday proved to be an astonishingly relaxed day. There wasn't much he could have accomplished if he'd chosen to go in, and he wanted to spend time with Alexa when they weren't discussing killers.

As it was, they slept late and made love a third time upon awakening. She put him to work cleaning house while she did the same, and seemed pleased when he did a few simple repairs that she probably could have accomplished but had put off. The closest they came to talking about the danger to her was when she warned him about the one outing she'd already scheduled for the week: an hour she committed once a month to talking to kids in the alternative school. He thought about trying to dissuade her but didn't want to ruin the mood.

Together, they cooked a fancier than usual dinner that would feed them both for at least three days, then watched TV. He insulted her taste, she insulted his, and they found a middle ground they both enjoyed. As he enjoyed going to bed with her again.

Back in his office Tuesday morning, muscles looser than they'd been in ten days or more, Matthew got sucked into his job supervising half a dozen current investigations and a request for a warrant that the detective knew was on shaky ground. Matthew sent the detective away to shore up his arguments.

Then, first chance he had, he arranged to meet a dispatcher for coffee. He'd had an idea, which might not turn out to be doable, but he was desperate enough to try anything that might help him be proactive where Alexa's safety was concerned.

Maria Jernberg was the wife of a state trooper, a good friend of Matthew's. Max and he had gone through the police academy together and connected again when Max had been transferred to this region.

Maria was a short, dark-haired, dark-eyed woman who'd worked for Child Protective Services before deciding she needed something less stress-inducing. To everyone's amazement, she apparently missed the word "stress" in the job description and hired on to Dispatch. If Max was to be believed, Maria was thriving.

She jumped up to hug Matthew when he appeared in the break room. She waited until he'd poured himself a cup of coffee and, after a glance around at the half dozen people circling tables, said, "Why don't we sit outside?"

He agreed even though the sky was overcast and the day cool. He let her pick out a picnic table, but before he even swung his leg over the bench, she said, "You want something."

Since they didn't make a habit of taking breaks together, he guessed he wasn't surprised that she'd read him.

"Yeah, and I don't even know if it's possible."

"What?"

"You need to keep what I'm going to tell you to yourself."

Her eyebrows arched. "Even from Max?"

"Not from Max, but he has to keep his mouth shut, too."

After a frown, she agreed.

He gave her the bare bones, explaining his belief that a cop within the department had killed Alan Sharpe, shot Art Dwyer and was threatening Alexa.

"So what is it you think I can do?" Maria said slowly.

"I'd like to know if either of two men I have my eye on go off the grid. Do they report breaks? Maybe one won't respond to a call because he's not where he's supposed to be? If you find out either has gone AWOL, I want to hear about it."

She thought about his request. "You know I get tied up for twenty minutes or longer when I take a call from someone in real distress."

He set down the disposable coffee cup. "I do."

"That said, I'll try. Can I hint to others on my shift that I've been asked to monitor the activity of a couple of patrol officers?"

He winced. "If this gets out, I could lose my job and so could you."

Her mouth firmed. "Then about all I can do is keep an ear out."

"That's better than nothing."

They talked about other things, but he could tell he'd disturbed her.

On parting, he initiated the hug after he thanked her. "You tell Max to give me a call if he's developed a new-found interest in stripping woodwork."

Maria giggled. "Don't hold your breath. I'm lucky if I can get him to mow the lawn. Now me, I like painting."

"Hey. Why didn't I think to ask sooner?"

"Your loss," she said airily, and they split up.

HE'D BEEN TELLING Alexa more than he should, but he didn't mention that conversation to her. End of the day, he hadn't heard from Maria anyway, which made him realize what a long shot it would be for her to happen to hear another dispatcher trying in vain to reach Shanahan or Danner.

Matthew's tension was winding tighter again, and probably Alexa felt the same, however hard she worked to maintain her "I'm fine. I can handle anything" front. While they ate the dinner of leftovers that evening, they steered clear again of their intersecting investigations or her frustration at being mostly grounded. They watched a couple more episodes from the limited series they'd started last night. He was maybe too distracted to be engaged, but sitting on the couch cuddling Alexa made him happy.

Not so happy that their lovemaking was as tender as he'd intended it to be. Instead, with her willing participation, he took her hard and fast, but even that didn't unwind his gut-deep fear that he'd fail her.

And, damn it, the better the nights with her were, the more Matthew hated leaving her for the day. Yesterday, at least she'd agreed to stay home. When he'd left for work, he'd been glad to see her neighbors hanging over the engine block of a junker in their driveway. He'd waved. They'd looked wary, but he'd believed they'd respond to a screaming woman.

Over breakfast, Alexa had reminded him about her visit to the alternative school.

"I love doing it, and they've been surprisingly engaged. Several of the teachers are doing the same thing—bringing in outsiders to talk about their jobs. Like, a nurse practitioner in a bio class, an IRS agent, believe it or not, in an advanced math class. It's fun." Her expression changed. "I'll bet you'd be welcome—"

Matthew laughed, but actually liked the idea once his focus wasn't so intensely on keeping her safe.

"Can you reschedule?" he asked without a lot of hope.

She just looked at him. "For a week from now? Two weeks? A month?"

Recognizing that he couldn't answer that question, acid ate at his stomach lining. Unless and until there was another attack— Not something he wanted to think about.

"Vince has already agreed to pick me up, wait for me outside and drive me home," she said.

Matthew swore. "Middle of the afternoon?"

"I'm booked for an hour, starting at two thirty. The school day ends at three thirty, so I won't be alone coming out."

He made a mental note of the time she'd be out, and she promised to text when she made it into the building and then safely home afterward. He was actually a little surprised that a woman as independent as Alexa, as cautious as he sensed she still was with him, was indulging him so readily.

Matthew couldn't let himself think about the longer term, when she *couldn't* do her job without getting out and talking to people.

ALEXA KEPT STEALING looks into the passenger-side mirror. She had a lot of faith in Vince, but couldn't relax the way she would if she were going somewhere with Matthew.

They were moving steadily, and she hadn't seen any particular vehicle making every turn with them. Once, she spotted a squad car stopped at a red light on a cross street as Vince and she went through the intersection, part of a river—well, more like a small stream—of traffic. If the police car turned to follow them, she couldn't see it.

"We're okay," Vince said, making her realize he'd seen her nerves. "In fact, here we are." The turn signal blinked and a familiar Wilden District Alternative School sign appeared on the right. The drive curved through a pretty acre or thereabouts of woods, bright green with the promise of spring that the temperature didn't quite match.

Probably dating to the fifties or sixties, the prosaic, yellow-brick building wasn't huge. Mostly, she could tell which of the couple of dozen cars in the lot belonged to teachers and administrators, and which to students. Vince eased up to the red-painted curb right in front of the double glass doors and braked.

"When you're ready to come out, call me. I'll pull up right here."

She agreed, and he stayed put as she climbed out, closed her door and hustled into the building. Once inside, she stepped to one side and peeked out, watching as the SUV moved to an open slot in the parking lot. She had no idea why she felt so antsy; this was a really unlikely place for someone to launch an attack on her.

Class sizes were nowhere near as big as in the high school. Numbers varied as kids decided to enroll or drop out. The class she'd joined had stayed pretty stable, probably due to the teacher. Alexa really liked Sheila Taft, a plump woman of about her age, possessing what seemed to be unlimited energy and patience both.

The minute Alexa walked into the classroom, a kid named Jeremy Scoleri said, "Hey, you're famous!"

Alexa made a face at him. "And what a pain it is."

She let herself be more up-front with the nine students than she probably should, but she excused herself because part of her role here was to let them into her world. She'd talked before about the ups and downs in journalism, from layoffs to front-page headlines and getting an article picked up by a wire service. Reality was, foreign correspondents risked danger on a daily basis.

She half sat on Sheila's desk at the front of the room.

"Some of what's been happening to me might have been coincidental. I mean stuff happens."

With one voice, they corrected her choice of words, and she laughed. "Remember, growing your vocabulary is important."

"Stuff?" a cheeky girl named Tia said.

"Just pointing out that obscenities are too often used in place of more descriptive words. Don't be lazy, think about stronger words. Used to be, you'd swear and that *was* strong. Now it's commonplace."

She had them rework some sentences until more questions drew her back into her harrowing past few weeks.

"What was it like?" a usually quiet girl asked. "Being kidnapped and tied up and…you know?"

"Terrifying," she said simply. "Afterward…well, the lieutenant who showed up was pretty nice."

"I was in the car once with my dad when we got pulled over and he was arrested," an often sullen boy said. "*Nobody* was *nice*."

"As you know, I had later experiences where that was the case for me, too—" She stopped abruptly. "Hey, you've all been reading the newspaper!"

That caused laughter, some embarrassment, and a warm glow in her chest. They had been. Her visits really were making a difference in their behavior and interests.

MATTHEW STOOD IN his office door and watched Brian Danner walk away down the hall. This interview had been different. Danner was plenty cocky until Matthew had come right out and said harshly, "Your name keeps coming up. You were patrolling in the neighborhood where Detective Art Dwyer was shot. Did you pull that trigger?"

Danner had gaped at him. His mouth opened and closed

a few times before he'd managed to talk. "You're nuts! Why are you even asking?"

Matthew let his teeth show. "What about Officer Alan Sharpe. Remember him? Dead because he raised suspicions about his coworkers? Alexa Adams wasn't the only one investigating you and your buddies. Funny that the same gun was used to shoot Sharpe *and* Dwyer—and it was the same one planted under Ms. Adams's car seat. Detective Dwyer had his eye on several of you, too, because he believed one of you didn't just abuse your authority to compel hookers to service you. He knew one of you murdered several of them." Matthew had let contempt infuse his voice. "Does Tansy Elizabeth Gould's name ring any bells, Officer Danner?"

"I— No. Wait. Was she the one found…?"

Had that been shock on his usual smug face?

"Discarded in the dumpster? Carotid artery ripped through by a bullet?"

Danner shot to his feet. "I'm a good cop!"

Matthew sat back in his chair. "Then you might want to tell me where you got that gun. Or which of your friends had it."

Danner had fled. There was no other way to describe it.

And as he now watched the guy's strides get longer and longer until he was almost running, Matthew had to listen to his instincts.

Brian Danner was scum, but he wasn't the killer cop— even though he now had to know who was.

The big question that rose to mind was whether he had enough conscience to come back and answer that last question.

Unsettled, Matthew returned to his desk and picked up his phone. He read again the text from Alexa that had arrived forty minutes ago.

Delivered by Vince, safe. Nobody followed us.

Matthew kept staring at the message. He'd thought he was so smart, scheduling this meeting in the middle of the hour when Alexa would be out and vulnerable. But if Danner *wasn't* guilty of anything but harassment where she was concerned…

He reached for his phone and called Maria Gannon.

"Can you try to locate Rick Shanahan?" he asked, not even attempting to hide his urgency.

"I can try. Did something happen?"

"Not yet. I have a gut feeling. I'm heading out. Call me."

What if he'd misread Danner, who had broken into a run because he was afraid he'd miss Alexa's exit from the school?

Matthew took the stairs two at a time and burst out at the bottom into the lobby. He didn't slow until he hit the parking lot.

MATTHEW MADE HIMSELF stay within the speed limit and resisted the temptation to use lights to clear his way. He'd calmed down a little, helped when he'd seen Danner just sitting in his truck in the parking lot outside the police station.

This was probably stupid. Alexa was still in that classroom along with a bunch of students and a teacher. Neither she nor the hired driver had seen a tail. He could see her rolled eyes when she saw him parked in front of the school.

He didn't even pretend to pray often, but he knew that's what he was doing. His panic made no real sense, but it was real. He kept seeing the moment when Danner had understood he was an accessory to something a whole lot worse than he'd imagined.

Would he call Shanahan? Or conceivably a different dirty

cop, the one he knew had supplied that handgun to slip under Alexa's car seat?

Ugly thought.

And if it wasn't Shanahan, Matthew knew he was at an impasse. Brooding, Matthew wondered whether he should have looked harder at John Blykowski, the sheriff's deputy, or Ken Kasperson. Both had apparently had some involvement with prostitutes. Either could conceivably be pulling the strings.

Right now, he had to go with his gut. Either Shanahan or Danner had seemed to be the driver of that last incident leading to the arrest. Alexa might not like having a guard driving home, but she could live with it.

SHEILA BROKE IN. "I'm afraid it's three thirty. You have your assignment for tomorrow. Let's thank Alexa for her time today."

Hoots and applause heightened her good feeling. Kids shoved their textbook and notebooks or tablets in their packs and crowded for the door, sweeping Alexa along with them.

Vince, she thought suddenly, and pulled out her phone.

Other classroom doors hadn't yet opened, so their group was the first to spill out into the hall. When Alexa looked out the glass doors to the parking lot, she saw that Vince was just backing out of the slot toward the back, but he'd be here any minute. She went outside with several of the students clustered around her, Sheila smiling and accompanying them.

Probably making sure no one said anything too outrageous, Alexa in amusement.

Jeremy and another boy asked her what she thought about police officers now, and she stopped where she was, only a few steps from the curb.

"I think most get into it for the right reasons and are trustworthy," she said honestly. "If you looked at people in any profession, I feel sure you'd find bad apples. Keep reading the newspaper and you'll find out about businessmen or women who can't resist the temptation to embezzle more money than they make. Politicians who abuse their position."

"Stinks." Jeremy said.

The SUV had circled the lot and was approaching from her left. She took a step that direction.

Crack.

For one foolish moment, she looked around in bewilderment, not understanding what that sound had been. But then it was followed by more.

Crack, crack, crack.

Gunshots, Alexa realized, shocked as red blossomed on Sheila's chest and she crumpled.

Chapter Eighteen

His phone rang, bouncing on the seat beside him where he'd tossed it. Maria Gannon's number.

"Reinert."

"Shanahan isn't responding on his radio," she said tersely. "He might just be blowing me off, but—"

If she said any more, Matthew didn't hear her. Ending the call, Matthew gain, was unsure whether he'd so much as thanked Maria.

Knowing he had close to half a mile to go, he turned on the flashing lights and accelerated. Once, an idiot driver didn't see him starting into an intersection and came right at him. Matthew gave one blast of the siren and swerved to avoid a collision.

He wasn't far from the turn into the alternative school when his radio crackled to life.

Gunfire at the alternative school. There were people down, the initial callers not sure how many. The school was going into lockdown.

Various units responded, all farther away than Matthew, but he stayed silent, knowing the shooter was listening. Surprise had to be his best tactic.

Driving like a madman now, Matthew still looked for any parked vehicles. A dense stand of deciduous woods separated the road from the school, leaving him blind as he made the turn. Nothing. If Shanahan had parked out here, it wasn't near the entrance. Would he have just driven in? Matthew didn't think so. The guy still thought he could get rid of that journalist and go on in his vicious, corrupt way.

Maybe not Rick Shanahan.

At this moment, it didn't matter who the shooter was. Matthew had to bring him down.

ALEXA SAW THE shock on the face of the boy closest to her. She tackled him and they both went down hard on the concrete. He started to struggle.

"I should be on top. I bet someone is shooting at *you*."

Jeremy. It was Jeremy she'd taken down. She started to lift her head to see what had happened to the others, but the boy rolled her.

"Keep down."

He was trying to protect her with this body. Guilt struck, but that was something she'd have to deal with later. She couldn't live with it if he died in her place. And Sheila...

Jeremy was right. Those shots had been intended for *her*.

Another shot rang out, then another. There was a strange metallic sound, and she knew. Vince had accelerated to use his SUV to try to block those shots. She turned her head, scraping her cheek on the rough surface. The SUV—there it was, a tire up on the curb, the fender connected to a bike rack. She couldn't see Vince at all, and prayed he had thrown himself out of sight. If he was injured...

Sickened, she thought, *I won't make it to him.* But...

"Sheila," she gasped. "I have to—"

Jeremy ignored that. "I dropped my pack. You got your phone?"

Oh. Good thing somebody was using his head. Except

people inside would probably already have called 9-1-1 to report gunfire outside. Was anybody in a position to see that one of the teachers had been shot? And what about... oh God, what was his name?

It came to her in a flash. "Brody?" He'd been right here, too.

"He ran back in." The boy sounded as scared as she felt. "I think."

"Are *you* hurt?"

He didn't say anything.

MATTHEW HEARD A blast of gunfire. Had to be from a rifle. Unfortunately, those damn woods provided plenty of cover.

His tires screeched as Matthew rocketed into the parking lot. The rows of cars blocked him from seeing what was directly in front of the school.

Where Alexa might have just come out.

He saw a boy crouched behind one of the nearest cars. The boy's face was blanched white.

Matthew's tires screeched again as he wrenched the wheel into a sharp left turn that brought him toward the front. He first recognized the SUV hired for Alexa, canted onto the sidewalk, but no sign of the driver. Could Alexa have made it behind the SUV, or even into it to hunker down?

Then he saw the half dozen people out front of the school. All flat on the pavement, unmoving. He didn't let himself try to determine whether they were injured, dead, or just being smart. Glints betrayed the shattered glass of windows and doors at the front of the school. There could be dead or injured inside.

A bullet punched a hole in his windshield and exited at an angle, giving him a good idea where to find the shooter. He had a rifle; he could park and try to take the guy out from a distance. Small movements told him that at least a couple of the people lying in front of the school were alive. He calculated in the way he did when under pressure even as he took in the blood pooling to the side of the woman who lay awkwardly and utterly still. Dark-haired, but… He couldn't be sure, but he didn't think that was Alexa.

He might be able to block them all from the gunfire by pulling up right in front of the cluster, though if he did that, the shooter would escape. And Vince's vehicle was already serving some of the same purpose.

Matthew made a decision to keep going, to accelerate straight for the killer.

WAS THAT MATTHEW? Alexa couldn't be certain.

"Sheila needs help. We can—" Her voice broke. "We can keep down and wriggle over there."

"That was a cop. He's going to get shot!"

The possibility terrified Alexa. Jeremy was afraid they'd be left completely vulnerable again. *She* was afraid the strong man who'd been asking for her trust, and maybe even more, would die. The thought made her feel as if she was looking into an abyss. There was just…nothing.

Sheila.

"You can stay where you are. Let me—"

"No."

He pushed himself up a few inches. When she squirmed sideways, Jeremy did the same. Alexa was stunned at this boy's courage.

Sheila *looked* dead. Alexa had taken some first-aid classes, but that was all. Pressure on the wound. That was about all she knew.

A fusillade of shots rang out. She tried to flatten herself

against the pavement as much as possible, and knew Jeremy was doing the same.

Jeremy jerked, and she cried out. Something stung her cheek. What if this brave boy was killed?

MATTHEW ZIGZAGGED TOWARD the woods, sure now he could see the glint of a scope and the fire of each shot. He hunched as low as he could and still see where he was going. Bullets kept punching holes in the window glass and probably the metal. He'd swear he felt the breeze as one missed his head by a fraction of an inch, but at least now those shots were being aimed at *him*.

That's it, you bastard. I'm coming for you.

It felt as if his swing through the parking lot had taken forever—minutes, at least, but he knew better. Seconds had a way of stretching during combat.

He wanted to drive straight into the woods and have the satisfaction of seeing the shooter's body slammed by the grille of the SUV, fly into the air, maybe smack the windshield. The trees were too mature, though, so at the back of the lot, he slammed on his brakes, opened his door and threw himself out, crouching behind the door, SIG Sauer in hand.

He took a chance and dropped flat to open fire where leaves fluttered.

Were those running footsteps? Oh yeah. The guy still thought he'd get away.

Glad he was wearing a vest, Matthew launched himself in pursuit.

BLOOD WAS STILL flowing from an awful hole in the teacher's back. That was a good sign, wasn't it? If someone was dead, their heart would quit pumping blood. This was only the exit wound, Alexa reminded herself.

Someone pushed open the glass door.

Alexa yelled, "Stay inside! It's not safe yet!"

The next shots sounded different. A handgun instead of a rifle, maybe? They were a little farther away, too. She risked rising to her knees and tearing off the shirt she wore over a camisole, wadding it up and pressing it to Sheila's back.

"Jeremy?" She looked over her shoulder, realizing for the first time that he, too, had taken a bullet. He was clutching his upper arm, but he wasn't mortally wounded, at least. "I need…"

He pulled his T-shirt over his head and handed it to her. There was blood on the sleeve, which made it less than ideal but still better than nothing. Crouched, like her, he helped her turn Sheila over. The entry wound was higher than Alexa had thought, although it had taken a downward path through her body. Her face was slack; she didn't react at all to being moved. Alexa pressed the cotton fabric to the wound and prayed.

She could hear sirens, several of them. Help was on its way. With her free hand, she fumbled for her phone and pulled it from her pocket.

9-1-1.

"Wilden City Emergency Services," a man's voice said.

"I'm at the alternative school." She heard herself panting. "We have injured people here. I hear sirens. We need ambulances."

"They are en route, ma'am. Are you all right?"

"I'm fine." No, she wasn't fine at all, but he was talking about physical injuries.

"Is the shooter still active?"

"I…don't know. He was a minute ago, but a police unit

arrived and I think that officer may be in pursuit." Unless he was dead. From here, she couldn't see the black-and-silver vehicle.

"There's already a law enforcement presence?" He sounded startled.

"Yes. I think he might be Lieutenant Matthew Reinert. Tell anyone coming to watch out for him."

"I will. Please stay on the line—"

She ended the call and dropped her phone.

All she could think was, *Matthew. Please be all right.*

HE CAREENED OFF a tree trunk and spun to one side, not letting himself slow down.

Shaking leaves and the crackle of breaking sticks and branches wasn't twenty feet ahead of him.

"Police!" he yelled. "Stop and lay down your gun."

Pop.

A bullet chipped a nearby tree. At least Shanahan—maybe Shanahan—was firing wildly now, aware he had less than a minute to escape. Matthew had been trying to keep count of shots taken and thought his target must be close to emptying his magazine. Odds were he'd be too shaken to make a change on the run like this. No matter what, his skin must be shredded, as Matthew knew his was, too. Had it occurred to the guy that he couldn't just leap into his vehicle, then drive in as if he, too, were responding to the radio distress call?

Through the foliage, Matthew caught sight of the road and the shine of black metal. If it was Shanahan, had he switched to his own vehicle for this little outing? Damn, Matthew hoped so. That would be the pickup seen in the vicinity of a couple of the murders. However he'd scrubbed out the truck bed, it was hard to eradicate every trace of blood or skin.

The dark shape ahead of him ran right into the truck, bounced off it and circled around the front.

Matthew put everything he had into a last burst of speed, choosing to go around the back. "Drop your weapon!" Matthew ordered one last time.

Shanahan lifted it instead, aiming at point-blank range.

Matthew fired, and kept firing. Shanahan stumbled back into the V formed by the open door, his face changing. Matthew didn't see blood—*vest*, he thought with surprising clarity—and he aimed high, for the throat. He pulled the trigger one last time and saw Shanahan's gun fall to the dirt.

ALEXA SAT ON the pavement as an EMT dabbed at the cut on her cheek with something that stung.

"Are you sure you're not dizzy?" the young woman asked. "You might have hit your head when you went down."

"No, I'm fine," she kept repeating, although that's the last thing she was. She couldn't quit shaking. If only someone would *tell* her what was happening.

Police were everywhere. A while ago, the tense atmosphere and state of readiness had suddenly relaxed, telling her the shooter had either escaped or was down. But which? And what about Matthew? That *had* to have been him, coming to the rescue. Otherwise, he'd have showed up by now. She knew he would have.

Seeing an officer approaching, she said, "Lieutenant Reinert? Do you know—"

His gaze went past her. "He's here."

"Oh, thank God!" She tried to turn, prevented by the EMT.

And there he was, striding toward her, his gaze intense, his stride never deviating. He seemed oblivious to the bus-

tle of activity, just as he had in the alley the first time she'd
seen him.

He looked awful, a dark red splotch on his forehead already swelling, scratches dotted with blood everywhere on
his face, neck and forearms. But he was alive. Essentially
uninjured.

If there hadn't been so many onlookers, she would have
burst into tears. As it was, she took a few deep breaths.

He reached her, taking in her incredibly minor wounds
from above before crouching in front of her.

"I was so afraid," she whispered.

His gray eyes burned into hers. "You and me both. I
couldn't be sure—" He swallowed.

"It was Sheila. The teacher who invited me out here. She
got shot instead of me. Have you heard…?"

Two ambulances had screamed away at least fifteen minutes ago. One carrying Sheila. The other, Vince, who, although bleeding, had been able to crawl out to check on
Alexa, as well as Jeremy and another student unlucky
enough to be grazed by a shot through a window where
he'd probably stood to stare out.

"The teacher is alive," Matthew said, his voice gravelly
but also…tender. "I'm told they took her right into surgery.
Nobody else is hurt badly. It could have been worse."

"If he'd shot me right away, no one else would have been
hurt."

Matthew grimaced his empathy. "He must have realized
he'd taken down the wrong woman. He'd taken a huge risk,
and didn't want to quit without killing you."

Her fault.

No. The man had already been killing women. She
couldn't forget that.

As the EMT loaded her supplies in the back of the ambulance and slammed the doors, Matthew said, "I think I used up a couple of my lives."

Alexa's eyes burned but she laughed, too, if with an edge of hysteria. "You and me both. If you'd died—" She couldn't make herself finish.

In that same voice, he laid himself on the line. "I've been falling in love with you. You have to know that."

Damn. Now she *was* crying. "I kept thinking, I never said anything. I'm such a coward."

Not until his expression changed did she realize he'd braced himself. He hadn't been sure of her.

He wrapped her nape with one of his big, strong hands and gave a gentle squeeze. "Not you. You're the bravest woman I've ever known. You…had good reason to distrust me."

"Only at first."

Somebody in a uniform backed into Matthew, momentarily rocking him.

"Who was it?" she asked.

"The man who wanted to kill you? Rick Shanahan."

He'd shielded his expression.

"Did you have to kill him?"

"Yes. He made his choice." Matthew shook his head. "He really thought he could pick you off and drive away, nobody the wiser."

Her teeth chattered. "If he'd had even a couple more minutes to get off a few more shots…" She looked at him in bewilderment. "How did you know to come?"

He told her his reasoning then drew her to her feet and pulled her snugly into his arms. "Your friend'll be okay. Have faith."

She searched his eyes. "The boy who got shot in his arm? He put himself in front of me. Jeremy might have saved my life. He's a hero."

"And we'll make damn sure everyone knows he is."

Alexa sighed and stirred against him. "You're not in trouble, are you?"

"For shooting a fellow officer?" His jaw tightened. "No. But a good portion of the Wilden PD is once this all comes out. I predict a bunch of resignations, suspensions and outright firings. As far as I'm concerned, the firing should start at the top."

Alexa rose on tiptoe and kissed him. Then she said, "Leave it to me."

Matthew laughed. "I have full confidence in you."

Amazingly, he always had.

Equally amazingly, her shakes were gone. "So, can we go home?" she asked.

One side of his mouth lifted. "I'm afraid there'll be a few hours of interviews first. After that, the only question is which house will be home?"

This was too soon to go *that* far, and he had to know it. But…she had complete faith the question would come up again, and probably soon. Fortunately, the answer was easy. She'd enjoy working on restoring his historic home. And really, where they lived didn't matter that much, did it?

"But we have to go to the hospital first," she said urgently.

He smiled, kissed her again, and said, "Of course we will."

* * * * *

SAVED BY THE TEXAS COWBOY

KAREN WHIDDON

To all those friends—you know who you are—who are always there for me. Whether in person, by phone or virtually, I appreciate your kindness, wisdom and logic.

Chapter One

Despite the blazing sunshine and the bright blue, cloudless West Texas sky, Marissa Noll couldn't quite manage to quiet the aching thrum inside her. Though not often, she sometimes had days like this. While she knew the cause, she'd never been a big believer in living in the past. And honestly, she had everything she could possibly need right here in Getaway, Texas, even if it sometimes felt like she didn't.

"Mornin', Miz Noll!" Several masculine voices chimed in to greet her as she walked into the Tumbleweed Café. Smiling, she waved at the round table full of elderly ranchers, men too stubborn to ever retire, their weathered faces creased and permanently tanned from the relentless West Texas sun. Some of them had been her patients, coming in for physical therapy after a stroke or a broken bone. Others were just men she'd grown up knowing. This sense of camaraderie, of family, was one of the things she loved about living in a small West Texas town. She'd never been able to even imagine living anywhere else.

Marissa treated herself to breakfast at the Tumbleweed once a week. She always ate at the counter, since she didn't like taking up an entire booth all by herself. As she made her way toward the counter, she caught sight of Serenity

Rune, the town psychic, getting up from a stool. As usual, the older woman wore a colorful caftan and an armful of jangling bracelets.

"Marissa!" Serenity exclaimed as she turned and caught sight of her. "How are you?"

But before Marissa could respond, Serenity froze and held up one hand. Her gaze sharpened as she stared, looking Marissa up and down. "Oh, my!" Serenity exclaimed, her lined face breaking out into a broad smile. "Your life is certainly about to change."

Then, while Marissa gaped at her, trying to process what the older woman meant, Serenity sailed off, disappearing out the front door.

Change was actually one of Marissa's least favorite things. She supposed some might call her a stick-in-the-mud, but she preferred to think of herself as steadfast and reliable. Salt of the earth, one of her elderly patients had called her. She'd considered that high praise indeed.

Change. Huh.

Taking her seat and waving at Clara, the waitress working the counter today, Marissa considered Serenity's prediction. Not that she entirely believed in psychics, but Serenity did have a reputation as being right. She'd been predicting things for years, most often with uncanny accuracy. The town sheriff had even been known to consult with her. So when she told Marissa that her life was about to change, Marissa felt inclined to believe her.

Dang it.

"Coffee?" Clara asked, setting down a sturdy white cup and pouring before Marissa even answered. "Do you know what you want today?"

Since Marissa usually ordered the same thing every week,

she decided to try something different this time. Maybe such a small thing would be enough to fulfill Serenity's prophecy for change. "I'll have the blueberry pancakes," she said, impulsively choosing the first item on the breakfast menu.

Clara's brows rose, registering her surprise, but she only nodded. "Coming right up."

While waiting for her food, Marissa sipped her coffee—two creamers, one sugar—and looked around at the crowded restaurant. She'd been coming to eat here for her entire life. Her parents had taken her as a child, she'd come after Friday-night high school football games and her very first date had been in one of those red leatherette booths over by the huge front window.

Jared Miller. She'd managed to avoid thinking about him for weeks, a new record for her. He'd been not only her first date, but her boyfriend all through high school and part of college. When she'd imagined the future, she'd always pictured herself by his side.

Things hadn't worked out that way. It had taken a while, but she'd gotten past it and moved on. After graduating from Texas Tech University, she'd left the area for a few years, choosing Texas Woman's University for her master's in physical therapy. Attending school in the Dallas area had only made her long for home and as soon as she'd graduated, she'd returned to Getaway. It was back there that Jared's absence had felt even stronger.

Even though they'd helped pay for some of her college, her proud parents had assisted her, helping to pay off some of her college debt so she could finance her dream of opening her own physical therapy studio—the first one ever in Getaway. After making sure she'd gotten a good start, they'd sold their house and purchased a luxurious motor home and decided to tour the country. As for Marissa, business had been good and she couldn't be happier.

Breakfast arrived. The short stack of fluffy blueberry pancakes smelled delicious. Clara refilled Marissa's coffee, smiling as she slid the check across the counter. "No hurry, hon. Enjoy your meal."

Smiling back, Marissa picked up her fork, prepared to do exactly that. She'd just taken her first bite when her cell phone rang. Briefly, she considered ignoring it, but decided she'd better check the caller ID just in case one of her patients had run into trouble.

The name showing on her screen had her choking on her food. Somehow, she managed to swallow, all the while staring at her phone and wondering if she wanted to answer it.

Jared Miller.

Nope, nope, nope. Not going to touch that one. Declining the call, she shoved it into her purse and tried to go back to her delicious breakfast, which now tasted like sawdust.

"Are you okay?" Clara asked, pausing on her way to refill everyone's coffee cups. "You went a little pale."

Blinking, Marissa managed to nod. She picked up her coffee cup and took a drink, before attacking her pancakes with the same steadfast determination she'd used back in the day to study for her exams.

Jared. Every pulse of her heartbeat sounded out his name. She hadn't heard from him since he'd left college to try his hand at making a living riding bulls in the rodeo. Why now? She didn't want to think about any of this.

But her meal had been ruined. Pushing away the now-empty plate, she grabbed the check, left a couple of dollars on the counter for Clara and headed for the cashier to pay.

Outside, she strode briskly toward her SUV. As she

stowed her purse on the passenger seat, her phone began ringing again. Hands shaking, she took several deep breaths before digging it out from her purse. Jared again. This time, at least she'd had some warning. She inhaled once more before answering.

"Marissa." The familiar husky voice still sent a shiver down her spine, despite the fact that she hadn't talked to him in nearly five years. "I'm glad I caught you."

"Who is this?" she asked, just to give herself time to get her act together. Though she'd never deleted his number, she could have, that's for sure.

"It's Jared," he replied, sounding surprised. "I can't believe you don't recognize me."

Tempted to ask *Jared who?* she knew that would be going too far and he'd see right through her, so she didn't. "What do you want?" she asked, aware she sounded rude and not caring.

"Wow." Clearly taken aback, he paused. She could picture him running his fingers through his thick, dark hair. "You sound like you aren't exactly happy to hear from me."

She wasn't. But suddenly realizing that if she continued to act this way, he'd think she'd never gotten over him, she took a deep breath and attempted to put a little normalcy in her voice.

"I'm sorry," she apologized. "You just surprised me. It's been a long time. How have you been?"

He rumbled a reply that both was and wasn't an answer. She—despite the huge amount of time that had passed since she'd seen him—still knew him well enough to understand this meant he wasn't good.

Not her problem, she reminded herself. In fact, Jared hadn't been her problem for a long, long time. He'd made sure of that. Even though he'd attended Texas Tech before her and then with her, he'd left midway through his third year and her first. He'd not only quit school, but he'd left her. He'd left *them* and the future they'd planned together. Throwing herself into her studies had been the only thing that saved her.

Realizing dimly that he'd continued speaking, she tried to focus. Clearly making small talk now, he talked about the rodeo, which she'd expected, since chasing after buckles had always been the love of his life. While she listened, she checked her fitness tracker, which doubled as a watch, and realized if she didn't get moving, she'd be late for her first client of the day.

As she started the Tahoe, wondering if she could drive with her phone pressed against her ear, part of her marveled that this man could still affect her so strongly. She'd moved on. She had a rich life with a job she loved, her own home and even a new boyfriend. All of which meant that Jared deciding to call her meant absolutely nothing.

Finally, he stopped talking, apparently waiting for her to comment.

"What's up?" she asked instead, deciding to cut directly to the chase. "Why are you calling me?"

"I'm back in town," he said. The simple statement sent her heart rate into overdrive.

"I heard you're a physical therapist now," he continued. "And I wanted to book an appointment with you."

Though she had a thousand questions, none of which she wanted to ask right now, she took a deep breath. Aware she needed to get off the phone and collect herself so she could drive the few blocks to her office, she said the only thing she could think of, which also happened to be the truth.

"I'm driving now and don't have my appointment log in front of me. Let me call you back once I get to the office." She ended the call without waiting for his response.

Wow. Serenity had been right again. Change. Definitely that.

The short drive down Main Street passed in a blur. Left on Pinyon Avenue and there was her place, a white frame house where she both lived and worked. The elegant sign reading Getaway Physical Therapy that she'd had made usually made her smile, but not today.

Today, her entire world had been turned upside down. *Change* didn't even adequately describe it.

This thought made her grimace. Too dramatic, she decided, getting out of her vehicle and using her key fob to lock the doors. She had thirty minutes to pull herself together before her first client of the day arrived.

Once inside, she made a pot of coffee and booted up her computer while waiting for it to brew. She had a full schedule today, which was a good thing. The earliest she could fit Jared in would be tomorrow and only because Mr. Clements had canceled. Otherwise, Jared would have to wait an entire week.

Did she really want to treat the man who'd broken her heart in a million little pieces? As the only physical therapist in town, did she even have a choice? After all, she was a professional. She'd opened her place to help people and shouldn't discriminate just because of something that had happened in the past.

Plus, she didn't really want Jared to think he still affected her after all this time. And he wouldn't, she vowed. She'd find out what his therapy needs were and get him scheduled.

Just not yet.

Her first patient arrived. Mrs. Davenport, her short white haircut still stylish as usual, was accompanied by her grown son, Leonard, since she couldn't see well enough to drive. The elderly woman had broken her ankle a few months ago and now that it had healed, she came twice a week for physical therapy so she could continue walking. Leonard had insisted his mother start using a cane and Marissa had agreed.

For the next three hours, back-to-back clients kept her too busy to think about anything else. Finally, noon arrived, and she turned the open sign to closed and went back to the kitchen to heat up her lunch. Maybe once she ate, she'd summon up enough strength to call Jared back and see if he wanted the appointment tomorrow.

"There you are," an achingly familiar voice drawled from behind her.

She jumped, nearly dropping her can of sparkling water as she spun around. "Jared," she gasped. "I didn't hear you come in."

He looked the same, she thought. And different. The handsome boy had become a sexy-as-hell man. Tall and lean, with even broader shoulders and narrow hips, he still wore his trademark Wrangler jeans and Tony Lama boots. He carried his trademark Stetson in one hand. He'd let his dark hair grow out, and the shaggy scruffiness of it became him. Though she knew he'd scoff at the thought, she'd always considered him the epitome of masculine beauty. Even now, her mouth went dry as she stared at him.

Dangerous, she thought, as a shiver snaked down her spine. The microwave pinged, which meant her frozen dinner had finished cooking. Glad for the distraction, she turned away from him and reached blindly for her food. And narrowly avoided burning her hand.

"Is this a bad time?" he asked, sounding both puzzled and slightly amused, which aggravated her.

"It's my lunch hour." Avoiding looking at him, she managed to keep her tone mild as she carried her meal to the small table. "But if you came by to see about making an appointment, I had a cancellation and I've already put you in the schedule for tomorrow afternoon."

Forcing her gaze up to meet his, she gave what she hoped looked like a professional smile. "Two o'clock. Will that work for you?"

"Sure." Without being invited, he limped closer. He pulled out the chair opposite from hers and took a seat. "I know you saw my limp. Don't you need to know the reason I need therapy?"

Yes, she did. She also wondered why he'd even come back to Getaway. But that part wasn't any of her business. Whatever he'd been in the past, now he was her client, nothing more. "Rodeo injury, likely hip or knee?" she guessed. Then, before he could answer, she continued. "I treated your pal Custer Black for his knee and he was able to go right back to bull riding."

Jared nodded. "I heard."

"I'll have some forms for you to fill out before your visit," she continued. "You can list everything on there. I can grab them for you to take home with you if you'd like."

"Sure," he drawled, leaning back in his chair. "Whatever works for you."

Since she couldn't eat with him staring at her, she pushed up out of her seat and went to get the paperwork. She could feel his gaze burning on her back as she walked away.

"Here you go." Practically shoving the forms at him, she looked pointedly from him toward the door. "If there's nothing else, I really need to get back to my lunch. I've got another client coming in right after one."

He didn't budge. She swore she saw bewilderment in his expressive brown eyes. "Listen, Marissa," he began. "I was hoping we could actually catch up. It's been a long time since we even talked. Do you really have to act like this?"

"Like what?" Anger flashed through her, an emotion she didn't bother to hide. "I'm your physical therapist, Jared. Nothing more. If you're not okay with that, then you'll have to drive to Lubbock or Midland for your therapy."

Never taking his gaze from her, he slowly nodded. "I can handle that, though I don't understand why we can't be old friends."

"Old friends?" She shook her head. "We might have been a lot of things to each other, Jared, but we were never, ever just friends." With that, she marched over to the door and held it open. "Now, I'm going to have to ask you to leave. I'm currently closed and I really need to have my lunch."

Expression inscrutable, he jerked his head in a nod and pushed to his feet. Then he crammed his black Stetson on top of his head and strode past her, limping as he went. "See you tomorrow," he said, right before she closed the door on him.

Damn. Inexplicably, tears stung the backs of her eyes. She hated that this man could still affect her so strongly. Worse, she didn't understand why.

Back in the kitchen, she sat and managed to choke down the rest of her meal. Five years had passed since the last time she'd set eyes on Jared Miller and that had been the day he'd broken her heart.

Pushing the melancholy away, she tossed her plastic container in the trash, wiped down the table and got ready for her next client. The sun would continue to shine, birds would sing and life would go on exactly as it had before Jared Miller had appeared on her doorstep. Just like it had five years earlier when he'd chosen the rodeo over her and the life they'd planned with each other.

DAMN. JARED CALLED himself all kinds of names as he drove away from downtown Getaway. How could he have possibly believed that he and Marissa could be *friends*? One look at her beautiful, heart-shaped face and desire had punched him hard in the gut. She looked the same—still lovely, still sexy in an innocent, untouched way. Despite trying, he'd never been able to entirely erase the memory of her and the way they'd pledged undying love to each other. Which turned out to have been a lie.

With one year remaining in his degree program, he'd been so unhappy he could no longer hide it. He'd gone to her, shared his hopes and plans, looking for her to understand, to approve. Fool that he was, he'd honestly believed she loved him enough to go with him as he followed his dreams.

Instead, she'd refused. She'd had no idea how badly she'd hurt him by choosing a life without him. There'd been a lot of women since then, though he'd taken care to always keep things casual. No way did he ever intend to risk that kind of heartache again.

It had taken him a while and a bit of hard-earned maturity to understand that maybe part of the reason Marissa hadn't been willing to live the vagabond life of a rodeo bum might have been because she had dreams of her own. He'd been too young and full of himself to understand that and now that he did, he couldn't blame her. He couldn't blame either of them. They'd been each other's first loves, and nothing could take that away from them, but he figured enough time had passed that they'd be able to move past all of that. Become friends. Instead, she acted as if he'd insulted her. In retrospect, maybe he had. Neither had made any attempt to contact the other after the day he'd left. While he couldn't speak for her reasons, for his part he'd been too broken, too bitter. He'd thrown himself into his new life, fully embracing the constant traveling, the parties and the dangerous animals that could make or break his career.

All of that was over now, thanks to a mean-spirited bull named Demonslayer. When Jared had woken up in the hospital, his buddies had told him he was lucky to be alive.

He'd taken that as truth. And when the doctors had suggested his bull riding days were over, he'd actually felt a sense of relief. He'd given five years of his life to this sport, and while he'd gotten close to making pro status, he'd had enough. Time to go back home and lick his wounds. Maybe he'd even give some thought to finishing up his degree in order to better run the family ranch.

Truthfully, when he'd made the decision to return to Getaway, he'd figured he could handle occasionally running into Marissa around town. And when his doctors ordered physical therapy, he'd been prepared to make the long drive into Lubbock a couple of times a week.

Then one of his buddies had casually mentioned Marissa's physical therapy business. Jared hadn't been surprised to learn she'd followed through on her own dreams. In fact, he'd been kind of proud of her. Maybe, he'd thought, just maybe, they could be friends. Surely, after all this time, the spark of attraction would have died.

Except it hadn't. One look at her, and he craved her again,

just as if no time at all had passed since he'd held her in his arms.

Maybe he should just drive to Lubbock. Marissa made it abundantly clear that she hadn't been happy to see him. While he…he'd had to freaking battle back the urge to pull her into his arms and kiss her until neither of them could think straight.

Which made things way too complicated, at least as far as he was concerned. Taking care of his father and the family ranch would be overwhelming enough. He should probably stay far, far away from Marissa Noll.

Except for one thing. Jared Miller might be a lot of things, but he wasn't a coward. Backing out now would have Marissa thinking not only that she'd won, succeeding in driving him away, but that she scared him. He couldn't have that, no sir. Especially since he planned to be in Getaway awhile now that his rodeo career had ended.

Back at the family ranch, Jared parked and then went looking for his father, J.J. The senior Miller hadn't been doing well and had been too proud to admit it, especially to his vagabond son. Jared had been in for a hell of a shock when he'd first arrived. He'd gone too long between visits and his father had taken a few falls and appeared to be having difficulty with his memory.

Jared might have been bruised and battered in both ego as well as body, but the bewildered way his father had looked at him had just about broken his heart.

He'd known right then and there what he'd be doing from now on. Years ago, his father had wanted him to continue running the family ranch and Jared had refused. Rodeo had been all he wanted. Determined to make a name for himself, as well as money, he'd left town and hadn't looked back. He'd given up everything and everyone to chase his dream. And if that bull hadn't stomped him in Vegas, he'd probably still be doing it.

Full circle, he thought. And no regrets, not really. The traveling, the partying, the buckle bunnies, hell, the entire lifestyle had started to get old. The competition aspect, the thrill of climbing on a bull's back and feeling in his bones that he'd hang on long enough to be the best, was the only part he missed.

He'd accomplished enough to be able to say he'd done what he wanted, sown his wild oats, gotten it out of his system and now he was ready to settle down. Truth be told, there was only one woman he could imagine spending the rest of his life with, and she clearly wanted nothing to do with him.

He'd simply have to change that. He *would* change that. After all, there was nothing he liked better than a challenge.

His father wasn't in the house. Pushing back a little niggle of worry, Jared searched each room a second time. Concerned, he walked out to the now-empty horse barn. Nope, not there. Turning, he thought he saw movement in the overgrown vegetable garden in the back corner of the yard. He set out for it at a jog.

There. His father. Sitting under a large live oak tree, wearing a battered straw cowboy hat. The older man looked up as Jared approached. This time, instead of a blank stare, Jared saw relief and recognition in the older man's eyes.

When he reached him, Jared squatted down in front of him. "What are you doing, Dad?"

"I thought I'd see if we had anything ready to pick out here," his father replied. His sad smile broke Jared's heart.

"You know how your mother likes to make fried green to-matoes."

"I remember," Jared said, keeping his voice gentle. His mother had been gone for over fifteen years. Sometimes his dad remembered that. Other times, he seemed to believe she was still alive. Clearly, this was one of those times.

"But there aren't any tomatoes," his father continued, his voice rising. "There's nothing out here at all. Looks like the rabbits or the deer ate it all. Nothing's left but weeds."

Since no one had planted anything in the garden—at least that he knew of—Jared wasn't surprised. He only knew he needed to convince the older man to come back to the house before he got overheated. Right now, in the middle of June, the sun was hot, especially for someone his age. The last time Jared had checked, the temperature had reached the low nineties.

"How about we go on back to the house and I'll make us some lunch?" Jared suggested, holding out his hand to help his dad up. To his relief, the older man took it and al-lowed himself to be hauled to his feet. Jared put one arm around his dad's stooped shoulders and gently guided him back toward the house.

When Jared had first arrived back home a couple of days ago, he'd been shocked at how badly the house, the barn, the fields—heck, the entire ranch—had deteriorated. Luckily, his father had hired someone to keep up with the few re-maining cattle and horses. Otherwise, Jared suspected the poor animals might have been left in the pasture to fend for themselves.

"Why didn't you tell me?" Jared had asked, kicking him-self for not making time to stop by and visit his father. "I could have done something about the condition of this place." And he would have, even if he'd had to reach out to some of his old buddies in town and hire them.

His father had looked at him with a blank expression. "Tell you what?" had been his response. "What do you mean? The ranch is fine."

And that's when Jared realized his father truly didn't comprehend. In fact, he seemed to spend a lot of time living in the past. Over the last several days, Jared had come to see that the elder Jared Miller was not doing very well at all.

Yesterday, he'd called Doc Shepherd, the family doctor. And, after his father had given the physician permission to speak with his son, Jared had learned his father was in the beginning stage of early-onset dementia. It would, Doc Shepherd had told him gently, only get worse. His father was only sixty-two years old.

Right then and there, Jared had known how his future would look. Even if physical therapy helped heal him, the retirement from rodeo he'd only been considering until now had just become real. He wouldn't be going back out on the road. His dad needed him, the family ranch did, too, and he'd realized with a sense of relief that this was where he would stay. He'd come full circle, landing back in Getaway. He'd returned home.

And, of course, he'd thought of Marissa. Truth be told, he'd never stopped thinking of her. All through the five years of traveling from rodeo to rodeo, town to town, Marissa had been constantly on his mind. He wasn't sure how or even if he could stop thinking about her.

One thing at a time, he reminded himself. He had plenty of work to do around here at the ranch, though his bum knee hampered him somewhat. After surgery, during which they'd replaced most of his knee, he had high hopes that physical therapy might get him, if not as good as new, at least pretty damn close.

Jared fried some bacon and made a couple of BLTs. His father's eyes lit up when he saw them. "My favorite!" he said, clapping his hands like a small child. "Thank you!"

Setting the plates down on the table, Jared felt both sorrow and a rush of love as he looked at his father. Like most of the local ranchers, he had a tanned, weathered look from years spent working outside in the brutal Texas sun. That much hadn't changed.

His father had always been a man of few words, a quiet thinker who planned out every move he made. He'd long been a shrewd businessman, running his small ranch by himself, doing what he had to do in order to keep it running. He'd been dedicated to his breeding program of his beloved Angus cattle. The small herd that remained were the descendants of years of careful breeding.

When Jared's mother had been alive, she'd tried to get him to introduce a few Texas longhorn cattle instead of only the coal black Angus, but his father had steadfastly refused. After losing his wife to lung cancer when Jared had been twelve, his father had gone out and purchased a magnificent longhorn steer and two cows, lamenting that he hadn't done so earlier. That bull had lived out his days on the ranch, siring perfect longhorn calves, which had sold for a pretty penny.

Away for so long, Jared hadn't realized how much his father had deteriorated until he'd returned home. Now the older man's blue eyes were often cloudy, his mind fuzzy. Seeing him struggle to remember small things broke Jared's heart. He hadn't known, or he wouldn't have stayed away so long. Rodeo career or no rodeo career, his father had been there for him through thick and thin. Jared could do no less for him now.

Chapter Two

Change. The simple word kept running through Marissa's head. Serenity had been right again. Marissa didn't like change. She never had, for as long as she could remember. She'd always been a fan of the familiar, of keeping to the same routine.

Damned if she'd let the reappearance of one tall, dark and gorgeous cowboy mess things up. Never again.

One of the things Marissa liked the most about her physical therapy location was the way she'd been able to convert the place into part office, part residence. She'd had some renovations done, making two entrances, each on opposite sides of the house. She'd had the contractors build a clear separation between work and home, even going so far as to make sure the two spaces shared no inside connection. When she left work for the day, she actually went outside, and then walked around to the relocated front door on the far side of the house.

With her routine to keep her steady, until recently, she'd always felt safe and secure in both her home and her business. Her clients respected her privacy and, as of yet, no one had ever come to her residence and tried to get her to open up her therapy office for them.

Lately though, she hadn't been able to shake the feeling that someone was watching her. She'd never actually seen anyone, not even a quick glimpse from the corner of her eye, but still. The back of her neck sometimes prickled and she swore she could feel someone's gaze on her, though when she spun around trying to catch them, she saw no one. Imagination? Maybe. Most likely, since she didn't have a single enemy that she could recall. Rayna, the local sheriff, ran a tight ship and Marissa knew if she went to her and told her about her feeling, Rayna would take her seriously and check it out. But without anything concrete, bothering the sheriff would make Marissa feel foolish.

Inside, she locked the door behind her, something she'd also recently started doing. Getaway had always been the kind of place where residents could feel safe leaving their doors unlocked. For all she knew, it probably still was, but since she couldn't shake that uneasy feeling, she kept everything locked up tight. She'd always been a big believer in following your gut instinct.

Maybe she should get a dog.

Her cat, Roxy, meowed loudly, as if to protest the thought.

"Don't worry, my love," Marissa said, scooping up the feline and cradling her near her shoulder. "I would never do that to you."

Roxy meowed again, her yellow eyes vivid in her dark face, and then jumped down. She walked to the pantry door and sat, staring hard at Marissa, before meowing one more time.

"I didn't forget," Marissa told her pet. "I'm going to feed you right now."

Once she'd filled the cat's bowl with kibble, leaving Roxy

chowing down, she opened the refrigerator to see about getting her own dinner.

As she ate, she thought about Serenity's prediction. With Jared back in town, change was certainly possible, but only if she allowed it. She simply wouldn't. If Jared chose to become one of her clients, that's all he would be. Nothing more, nothing less.

That declaration made her feel better. Like her home/office setup, she'd always been successful at keeping her work life and her personal life separate. Nothing would change. She'd prove Serenity wrong.

That night she went to sleep with a sense of relief.

When she woke the next morning, she sat up in bed and stretched. Next to her, Roxy stretched, too, purring.

"Are you ready to start the day?" Marissa asked, scratching her cat behind the ears. Unlike some of her friends, she never dreaded going into her job. In fact, she looked forward to it.

Work not only kept her busy, but gave her a feeling of accomplishment. She truly enjoyed seeing each patient's progress, and the day she released them with a certificate showing physical therapy was completed, she always held a mini celebration.

Today though, despite her earlier resolution, as the time approached, she felt like a bundle of nerves because of Jared's appointment. Honestly, despite the fact that he had family here in town, she'd never expected to set eyes on the man again.

Once she'd fed Roxy and showered, still trying not to think about Jared, she got dressed, applied a little light makeup, and walked outside and around to the other entrance to begin her day.

Since she had back-to-back bookings, the morning passed in a blur. In addition to working with her clients, she visited with them, catching up on the town gossip. Naturally, all everyone wanted to talk about today was Jared's return. Most people remembered when Marissa and he had been an item.

She bore it all with an insincere smile, feigning indifference when she admitted that yes, she'd be working with him.

Finally, the last of her morning clients left and she turned the sign to closed so she could enjoy her lunch. This time, she made sure to lock the front door before heading back to the kitchen.

She ate her lunch quickly, working on getting a grip on her nerves. Jared had emailed over the paperwork she'd given him, along with his last set of X-rays and his orthopedic surgeon's summary sheet. He'd shattered his knee, messed up his shoulder and undergone knee-replacement surgery. Since she dealt with a lot of rehab from that particular operation, she already knew exactly what regimen to put him on.

He was her first appointment after lunch, which meant she had time to choke down her food, freshen up and give herself a stern talking to before unlocking the door. Despite her resolve to calm herself down, her pulse took a wild leap the instant Jared strode inside. This time, she took note of the slight, almost imperceptible limp.

His larger-than-life presence made the waiting room seem small. Mentally chiding herself for such foolish thoughts, she smiled and welcomed him, trying to ignore the way her heart knocked against her chest.

"I had the chance to go over the paperwork you sent," she said, gesturing toward a chair. "This type of physical therapy is pretty straightforward, with standard exercises.

You'll do some of them here, but I'm also going to ask you to continue them at home."

Lowering himself into a chair and removing his Stetson, he kept his gaze on her and nodded. "I can do that," he replied. "I'm ready to do whatever it takes to get back to full use of my knee."

Assuming he meant so he could return to rodeo, she felt the need to caution him. "This is a slow process," she said, leaning forward. "You can't rush things. You've got to give it time and put in the work."

"I will."

"Perfect." She stood, pleased with how professional she sounded. *This might just work out*, she thought. As long as Jared respected the boundaries she put in place, that is. "Follow me and I'll get you started with some of the exercises."

They went into the actual therapy room. Watching his uneven gait made her remember his former confident stride. She'd get him back to that eventually. In her therapy room, she had a treadmill, a recumbent bicycle and several other pieces of workout equipment. After settling him onto a bench, she had him remove his boots and then stretch out his leg in front of him.

Once he'd started doing the exercises she'd requested, she set the timer and then retreated to the other side of the room, glad she didn't have to keep up the remote, professional attitude for a few minutes.

Having him there alone with her felt…different. No matter how much she might try to deny it, being around him made her come alive. Every cell in her body was electrified, on fire. She could only imagine what would happen if he were to reach out and touch her, even lightly. Somehow, she suspected she might go up in flames.

Ridiculous. Whoa. She needed to put the brakes on. Right now.

Yet even as she acknowledged this, she knew part of it was true. Jared and she still had a connection. Maybe time had been unable to sever it. Perhaps it would always be there. But this time, she was no longer a wide-eyed, green girl believing that love could fix all problems. She knew better than to act on such an elementary and foolish thing. All she'd ever gotten out of acting on wild emotions had been a world of hurt. She had a life plan in motion and none of it included him.

The timer went off. Several quiet pings, enough to remind her that she had a job to do. Hurrying over, she showed him the next movement she wanted him to make, and then the one after that. This time, instead of setting a timer, she had him do twenty-five reps of each. "Then you'll be spending a little bit of time on the treadmill," she said.

He groaned. "I didn't bring running shoes." As she started to speak, he held up his hand. "I know. I read the instruction sheet. I got busy and forgot. From now on, I'll make sure and have a pair in my truck."

Struck speechless, she nodded. Damn. He looked so boyishly handsome, she lost her train of thought. "That's okay," she finally said hastily. "You can do the exercise bike instead."

While he rode the bike, she busied herself by getting on her computer and printing everything she wanted to send home with him.

When his time was over, she handed him the printout of the exercises he'd just completed and several more to do at home. "I'm going to need to see you twice a week for now. Will that work for you?"

"Sure." His easy smile had her clenching her teeth. "Let's go ahead and get them all scheduled."

"Sure thing." So far, so good. She could do this. They were keeping everything professional. She booked him on Tuesdays and Thursdays, changing the time to nine o'clock when he requested being the first appointment of the day.

"That way, I can bring my dad into town with me and let him catch up with his buddies at the Tumbleweed while I do my PT," he said. "He needs to get out of the house more."

"How is your dad?" she asked, and then immediately regretted it. She'd always liked the elder Mr. Miller, but once again this took them into a personal realm, where she didn't want to go.

His smile briefly faltered. She could tell he made a conscious effort to keep it on his face. "He's hanging in there," he replied. "We're taking things one day at a time."

"Hanging in there?" she asked, frowning. "Is he ill?"

"In a manner of speaking," he replied, clearly brushing off her question.

As he went to leave, halfway to the door he stopped and turned. "I need to ask you something." His deep voice had gone serious. "Is there any chance we could be…friends?"

Something of her shock must have shown on her expression because he immediately held up his hand and shook his head. "I guess not," he said, answering his own question. Again, he turned to go and then once more he thought better of it and turned to face her. "It's just that a lot of time has gone by since…you know. We're not kids anymore. We've both moved on with our lives. I always liked you, Marissa, that's all. I guess I don't really understand why we have to be enemies."

"Enemies?" Startled and indignant, she dropped her professional tone. "That's a pretty strong word choice. I thought this all went well. We were civil. Where do you get enemies from that?"

To her mortification, her voice cracked on the last sentence and tears stung the backs of her eyes. She took a step back, needing to collect herself.

Meanwhile, Jared watched her, his gaze intent and sympathetic. As if he knew the tempest of emotions raging inside her. Suddenly, one thing seemed startlingly, achingly clear. She couldn't do this. Just couldn't. They'd only had one session and she was already a complete mess.

"You know what?" she said. "I don't think this arrangement is going to work out. It might be best if you get yourself someone else to do your physical therapy. There are several qualified providers in Midland-Odessa or Lubbock. You could even go to Abilene. I'd be happy to get you a list of recommendations."

"Marissa." The way he said her name, like a caress, made her freeze. And then he crossed the space between them and pulled her into his arms. "Stop," he ordered, cradling her close. She couldn't move, didn't want to move, both longing for him and appalled at how badly she wanted this.

When she didn't resist, he simply held her, exactly the way he used to once upon a time, when she'd been naive and in love and believed they had a future together. Even now, knowing better, she allowed herself to quit fighting for just a moment, and relaxed into his embrace. *Heaven*, she thought, absorbing the achingly still-familiar feel of his strong arms around her, inhaling his scent, still the same combination of leather and soap, and...

What the hell was she doing?

"No." Forcibly, she moved herself away from him. Shaking, she glared at him, her heart pounding and blood roaring in her ears. "How dare you?"

"How dare I what?" He shook his head, disappointment plain on his handsome face. "I offered comfort to someone I consider an old friend. I apologize for being too familiar. And you know what? You're right. I need to find myself another physical therapist. This is never going to work out."

She stood frozen, aching as he strode toward the door and disappeared from view.

Damn. Covering her face with her hands, she tried to get a grip on herself. Ever since Jared had sauntered back into her life, she felt like she'd been riding a roller coaster of emotions.

Still, she'd been wrong.

"I overreacted," she said, talking to herself. Luckily, her next client was late, so she had a little time to pull herself together. Still, it didn't help to realize Jared had spoken the truth. She'd treated him as if they were truly enemies. Whatever she wanted from him—and she wasn't even sure she wanted anything—she didn't want that.

Later, after her last therapy session had been completed and she'd locked the front door before beginning to tidy up, she swallowed her pride and called him. He didn't pick up. She couldn't really blame him. She'd acted like a jerk. Worse, he'd actually been right. Despite her knee-jerk reaction, there wasn't any reason they couldn't be friends. They'd known each other all their lives. The fact that their teenage romance hadn't worked out wasn't a reason to hold a grudge. She knew better. She owed him a heartfelt apology.

Listening as his voice mail picked up, she elected not to leave a message and ended the call. This kind of apology needed to be made in person, anyway. Right then, she decided to drive out to the ranch and eat crow in person.

Once she'd turned out the lights and locked up the clinic, she got into her Tahoe and took off, aware she needed to go now before she lost her nerve.

The drive felt familiar, even though she hadn't been out that way since she'd come home from Dallas. She'd had no reason to since Jared had left town. Turning down the long rutted drive that led to the ranch, she slowed, shocked at her first glimpse of the place where she'd made so many happy memories.

The place looked…different. And not in a good way. The landscaping surrounding the ranch-style main house looked overgrown, though even the ragged shrubs couldn't disguise the peeling paint and occasional rotted boards. She couldn't believe it.

Looking around more, she realized all the outbuildings, including the red two-story barn that had been Mr. Miller's pride and joy, needed repairs and a fresh coat of paint. Some of the fencing had fallen down and the pasture nearest the drive had been allowed to grow tall with weeds. It almost looked abandoned.

This made her incredibly sad.

Clearly, Jared's father hadn't been able to keep up with the place. Though Jared hadn't answered her question earlier, it seemed obvious the older man must have fallen ill. For the first time, she realized Jared must have quite a few things on his plate without her making his life even more difficult.

Parking near the garage, she took several deep breaths, trying to slow her heart rate, before getting out of her SUV. She'd never been a coward and didn't plan to start being one now. She strode up the front steps, across the porch to the door and knocked. The same two rocking chairs and the porch swing she and Jared had spent a lot of time on were still there, covered with spider webs and dirt. Everything needed some cleaning up and some paint.

The door creaked open. "Well, I'll be." Mr. Miller peered out at her, his blue eyes twinkling. "Little Marissa, all grown up." He stepped aside, motioning her to come in.

Once she did, he pulled her in for a quick hug. She couldn't help but notice how much weight the older man had lost.

"How are you?" he asked, showing his yellowing teeth in a wide grin.

"I'm great," she responded. "How about you?"

"Couldn't be better," he crowed. "Especially now that my boy is back home. I imagine that's who you've come to see, isn't it?"

"Yes." Looking around, she saw the condition inside the house matched the exterior. The tattered rug did little to hide the scratched and dusty hardwood floor. Piles of clutter dotted the small room—a stack of newspapers in one corner, a pile of old blankets and towels on the floor in another.

"He's around here somewhere," Mr. Miller continued, his eyes twinkling. "Let me see if I can find him for you."

"No need, Dad." Jared entered the room, his expression hard, unsmiling as he looked from his father to her. "I'm right here. Marissa, what can I do for you?"

He wasn't going to make this easy, she realized. Again, she couldn't blame him. "Do you have a minute to talk?" she asked, then glanced at his father. "In private?"

Hard expression unchanging, he considered. "Sure," he finally answered. "Let's go sit on the front porch."

"You kids have fun," Mr. Miller said, giving them a cheerful wave before wandering off into the kitchen.

Heart in her throat, Marissa watched him go. All of this felt way too familiar and also so very different.

"Come on." Jared held open the door, his gaze shuttered. "After you."

Once outside, she waited to see if he would sit. When he didn't, she decided to remain standing also.

"Why are you here?" he asked, sounding tired.

"I came to apologize." Her voice shaking, she took a deep breath and lifted her chin. She could give a bunch of reasons for the way she'd acted, all of them valid, but she didn't want to make excuses. "I'm sorry for being so rude earlier today."

He jerked his head in a cold nod. "Apology accepted. Is there anything else?"

Holding his gaze, she sighed. Even now, when he was clearly furious, his rugged features were the epitome of masculine beauty. "I'm not going to grovel," she said.

"I didn't ask you to," he responded. This time, the ghost of a smile lifted the corners of his mouth.

Encouraged, she allowed her iron spine to relax a little. "You're not going to make this easy, are you?"

Gaze locked on hers, he slowly shook his head.

"I was wrong," she continued, aware she needed to get it all out. Back in the old days, they'd joked that she was never wrong. She'd been so young and so confident in her ability to see the future in a straight line. "I was wrong and I apologize." Her heart fluttered at the flash of emotion in his eyes. "There," she continued, her voice slightly unsteady. "I said it. I was wrong. You know how much I hate admitting that."

Nodding, he laughed. "I do know. How could I forget? And, Marissa, you were pretty awful. It's all good though. I haven't had time to research other physical therapists, but I'll do that tomorrow."

"Please don't. I'd love for you to continue as my client, if you still want to. And you were right. There's absolutely no reason we can't be friends. The past is all water under the bridge."

Her cliché made him laugh again. Once, they'd spent an entire weekend talking to each other by using as many clichéd expressions as they could think of. It had been hilarious.

Memories. Damn. She imagined quite a few of those would resurface the more time she spent around him. She'd simply have to learn to deal with it.

"I remember that weekend," he said, almost as if he'd read her thoughts. "We always used to have a lot of fun together."

Somehow, she managed to nod. Her throat ached.

Coming closer, he held out his hand. "Friends?"

Sliding her palm into his, she shook. "Friends."

When he released her, she felt momentarily bereft. "Okay, then." She turned to make her way down the steps and back to her Tahoe. "I'll see you Thursday, then."

"Marissa, wait."

Almost to her vehicle, she turned. He still stood on the porch, both hands jammed into his jean pockets. Even now, he looked every inch the cowboy. "We have a lot of catching up to do. Would you like to stay for dinner?"

Panic fluttered in her chest. "Thank you for the invite," she replied politely. "But I have plans. Take care."

Climbing into the SUV, careful not to look at him, she drove away.

WATCHING HER GO, Jared cursed under his breath. Seeing her standing in the living room with his father had really messed with his equilibrium. With a rush of emotion, he realized he wanted her back. Despite the pain of losing her, he suddenly understood the craving would not simply go away. Instead, he knew the more time they spent together, the stronger his desire would grow.

They were like fire and gasoline. The slightest spark would make them ignite.

Once she'd apologized—to his endless relief—he'd told himself he'd go slow. Clearly, even the idea of them becoming friends was a big leap for her to take. All this time, knowing she'd chosen to stay in Getaway over being with him, he'd considered himself the hurt one. He'd assumed she'd had zero regrets. Now he knew she'd been equally shattered by the choices each of them had made.

They'd wanted different things, even though they'd never stopped needing each other. Though young, they'd somehow been wise enough to understand love also meant letting each follow their own path.

He suspected neither had completely understood how big of a loss they'd suffer until it was too late to change.

Shaking his head at his own thoughts, he turned to go in and nearly ran into his father.

"Marissa couldn't stay?" the older man asked, swaying slightly as he peered out toward the driveway.

"Not this time." Jared slung his arm across his dad's shoulders and steered him back toward the house. "Looks like it's just going to be us guys again tonight. How does hamburgers and fries sound?"

Later, after clearing the dishes and getting his father settled in his recliner in front of the TV, Jared headed out to the barn to feed the two horses he'd brought in from the pasture. Neither of them had been too happy to leave the herd, so he made sure both got plenty of exercise each day. Both were geldings, horses he'd trained himself back before he'd hit the road, and he'd hoped they'd remember what he'd taught them despite years of inactivity. He'd only managed to ride them twice, and so far had high hopes.

When he'd first realized the extent of his injuries and realized he'd need to come back to the ranch, he'd imagined feeling restless and bored. He'd likely hate being here and would spend all his days longing for the excitement of the rodeo circuit. With his winnings, this year he'd been close to winning a spot competing at the highest level—the PBR. Only the top fifteen bull riders made it to such a lofty competition. This year, he'd felt it in his bones that he'd be one of them.

Nope. Instead, he found himself back in Getaway, with nothing to show for the year but a healthy savings account.

To his surprise, the bitterness he'd expected to feel had never showed. Instead, seeing how much his father needed him and how much work there was to be done around the ranch, he'd been energized. He'd do his physical therapy, get his body healed and jump right in.

His phone rang, making his heart skip a beat. Marissa? But no, instead he saw one of his rodeo buddy's names on the caller ID. Custer Black, another bull rider who'd been successfully treated by Marissa a few months before Jared had gotten hurt. Jared had first learned about this, and the fact that Marissa had become a physical therapist, when Custer came to visit him in the hospital. Even though aware of Jared and Marissa's past, Custer couldn't stop singing her praises. He'd even been well enough to return to the circuit.

"Hey, man." Custer's ebullient greeting made Jared smile.

"How's it going out there in BFE?"

Their old high school nickname for Getaway made Jared smile. "So far, so good," he replied. "I've gotten settled in, and I've even started physical therapy."

Custer whistled. "You didn't waste any time. Was it awkward seeing Marissa again?"

"Not at all," Jared lied. "It's been a long time and we've both moved on. She was very professional and seemed to know what she was doing. I think it's all going to work out fine."

"Good, good." Clearing his throat, Custer continued. "I don't know if you remember, but I rode in Cheyenne this past weekend."

"How'd you do?" Jared asked. "Cheyenne has always been one of my favorite rodeos."

"Me, too, but this time I couldn't even make the cut." Bitterness rang in the other man's voice. "I got bucked off at six."

Jared winced. "I'm sorry, man. That sucks."

"Yeah, it does. My back locked up again. And I've been doing the physical therapy exercises that Marissa sent home with me. Anyway, I knew you'd understand. Most of the others would just think I'm being a sore loser or looking for an excuse."

"Yeah, maybe." Most of the guys he'd run with considered it bad luck to talk about bad rides. Since he figured Custer knew this, he didn't bother to point it out.

"Anyway, I wanted to caution you. I went into this believing the physical therapy would put me right back like I was before my accident. If that's what you're thinking, I thought you should have a heads-up. Take your time before you return to rodeo."

"Thanks," Jared said, meaning it. "But I'm not coming back. I'm done. I'm going to stay here in town and take over running my family ranch."

Custer went uncharacteristically silent, which meant Jared had shocked him. "Seriously?" he finally asked. "But you were so close to making it to the PBR Championship. I saw your standings. You did well this year."

"Thanks. I had a good run." He paused. "Now I'm done." He didn't tell his friend the rest of it—that he'd been thinking of settling down, starting a family. He didn't want to jinx it. Especially because Marissa was the only woman he could imagine doing that with. Ever.

"Well, you may reconsider," Custer said. "Once you finish your physical therapy and are all fixed up. I know you. You love rodeo too much to stay away for too long."

"We'll see." Jared did love rodeo. But he loved his father and the family farm more. He and Custer chatted a few minutes longer. He ended the conversation by telling Custer to stop by the next time he was in town.

Once he'd fished the call, Jared battled the urge to call Marissa. He just wanted to hear her voice. Not a good thing, especially since she'd turned down his invitation to stay for dinner. The shocked expression on her pretty face had let him know exactly how she'd felt about that.

He knew what he needed to do, even if his body and his emotions might want otherwise. He'd focus exclusively on healing his broken body. Once he'd done that, then maybe he could focus on healing his and Marissa's fractured relationship.

Chapter Three

As she drove away from the Miller Ranch, Marissa's emotions were in turmoil. She felt both a huge sense of relief and an even bigger one of loss.

Jared had invited her to stay for the evening meal. At that exact moment, there hadn't been anything else she wanted more. Except she couldn't. She'd been telling the truth when she'd said she had plans tonight. She and David, the man she'd been seeing for a few months, were going out to dinner.

As the local veterinarian, David worked long hours. He didn't close the clinic until six and often couldn't get out of there until seven, which meant a lot of late dates. Sometimes, they were both too tired to make much of an effort, so they'd scheduled standing Tuesday-night dinners during the week, and tried to see each other at least once on the weekends.

This seemed to work well for both of them.

Marissa liked David. They had similar interests and outlooks on life. But she didn't think she was in love with him, and felt reasonably certain he wasn't in love with her either. When they kissed, instead of sparks, she'd felt...nothing. No electricity, no chemistry, just a kind of friendly peck on the lips. But she'd been lonely, and a male friend with benefits had seemed like a good idea at the time. Not settling, not exactly. They enjoyed each other's company and that would be enough, for now.

Though they'd never discussed this, Marissa believed David felt the same way. That was why she was interested to see his reaction when she told him she'd be treating Jared.

She went home, fed Roxy and changed into a cute sundress and sandals. After touching up her makeup, she used a flat iron on her long blond hair, making it perfectly straight. Finally, she grabbed a pair of her favorite dangly earrings. One final check in the mirror and she turned to head out.

They met at their favorite place, Tres Amigos Mexican Restaurant. As usual, they took separate vehicles to save time. David had arrived before her and had already been seated. As she walked through the crowded festive room, she spotted him at one of the tables near the middle of the room.

Smiling, he stood up as she approached. A handsome man, he kept his prematurely gray hair super short, which gave him a military appearance. With his unusual light blue eyes and craggy features, he drew lots of feminine attention. Now was no different. Several women eyed her as she made her way toward him. Marissa ignored them, greeting David with a hug before taking a seat opposite him.

The waitress brought over chips and salsa and took their drink orders. As usual, David ordered a beer and Marissa a margarita on the rocks, no salt.

They talked while they munched on chips and salsa. David told her about his day—mostly routine, though he'd operated on a kitten someone had brought in after witnessing it being thrown out of a car. The poor thing had a broken jaw and would require a lot of help while he healed, but

David and his staff would do it before finding him a new home. David did this even though he wouldn't be making a dime from the surgery. He simply wanted to help the small creature. This compassion was one of the things Marissa liked about David. He truly cared for his animal patients.

Their drinks arrived. Marissa eyed the large margarita in a festive glass and took a sip. "So good," she murmured. Taking a deep breath, she forged on. "I had a bit of a surprise, too. Yesterday, Jared Miller called me."

"Your old high school boyfriend?" Cocking his head, David appeared interested rather than concerned. "What did he want?"

"He's back in town." She sighed. "He was injured in his last rodeo and came in for physical therapy. I'll be treating him twice a week."

"Wow." David watched her while he took a sip of his beer. "How do you feel about that?"

Another one of his admirable qualities, she thought. He always put her feelings first. With his good looks, compassion and thoughtful personality, he made the perfect boyfriend. If only he ignited the same kind of passion that Jared did.

Damn. Her cheeks heated. Forcing her mind back on track, she shrugged. "I'm not sure. At first, I acted pretty rude toward him after his session today. I even went over to his family ranch to apologize."

One silver brow rose. "You did?" He shook his head. "I can't imagine you being so rude that you felt you had to do that. How'd it go?"

With an effort, she managed not to squirm in her seat. Now she wanted to change the subject. Luckily, the waitress returned to take their order. Though neither had even opened their menus, they both knew what they wanted.

"I'll have the enchilada trio," Marissa said. She loved the combination of one sour cream chicken enchilada, one cheese enchilada and a beef enchilada with red sauce.

David ordered steak fajitas, one of his favorites.

Once the waitress left, Marissa took another drink of her margarita, trying to decide what to say and how to say it.

David simply waited, giving her the opportunity to sort through her thoughts.

"He accepted my apology," she finally admitted. "And he actually held out an olive branch. He wants to be friends." She attempted a smile, feeling slightly foolish.

"That makes sense. Five years is a long time to hold a grudge. If he can get past it, then I bet you can, too."

She almost asked David what he thought Jared could possibly have to get over. After all, he'd been the one who'd left her. Instead, she washed away the words with another drink of her margarita and nodded. "Maybe so."

In retrospect, she had to admit to being slightly disappointed. Part of her had wanted David to be at least slightly jealous. But since they'd never even discussed being exclusive, she guessed he didn't feel he had the right. If the tables had been turned, would she have reacted the same way? Sadly, she suspected that she would.

"Are you okay?" David asked, frowning. "You looked like you were a million miles away."

Since this was something she said to him on a pretty regular basis, she couldn't help but laugh. "Sorry. This entire thing has just thrown me for a loop. Honestly, I never expected to see Jared again. Ever."

David nodded. For a moment, she swore she saw a hint of sadness in his expression.

Their food arrived and they dug in. For the rest of the evening, they talked about other things. Sometimes on Tuesday night, David came back to her place or she stopped over at his. Tonight though, she knew she wasn't up for that. Especially since all she could think of was Jared, and how she'd almost fallen apart when he'd held her in his arms.

When they'd finished eating, David asked her if she wanted dessert. They both loved the sopaipillas, but she shook her head. "I'm too full."

"Same here." He stretched, drawing the gaze of a group of women two tables over. "And to be honest, I'd just like to go home and get some rest. I hope you don't mind."

"I don't." Smiling to take any potential sting from her words, she finished her drink. "Actually, I feel the same way."

When the bill came, they both reached for it.

"My turn," David insisted, snatching it up before she could.

"I'm pretty sure you paid last time," she said. They were supposed to be taking turns paying for their meals, though David often grabbed the check and paid despite her protests.

Tonight, she simply couldn't seem to make the effort to argue, so she let it go.

He walked her to her Tahoe. When he leaned in for a kiss, she met him halfway, hoping against all odds that he could manage to make her think of something else besides Jared.

When their lips met, it felt…nice. Familiar. Cool and friendly, despite the complete absence of heat. Disappointed, she swallowed hard.

Something must have shown in her gaze.

"We'll try harder," he said quietly, grazing her cheek with his finger. "Soon."

Aware they shouldn't even have to try, she nodded. And then she got into her SUV and drove home alone, thinking of Jared the entire way. She realized she would much rather have had dinner with him and his father.

After parking her Tahoe in the garage, she walked quickly toward her house. Tonight, for the first time in a while, she didn't feel as if someone was watching her. A good thing, she thought, letting herself in.

The instant she turned on the light, she realized something was wrong. But what? She checked out her kitchen and then headed for the living room. Glass crunched underfoot. From what?

And where was her cat? "Roxy?" she called, turning on the lights. And that's when she realized her front bay window had been shattered. And a brick with some sort of note wrapped around it sat in the middle of her living room floor.

What the heck? Clearly, someone had thrown this through her window. But why?

She'd check that out later. First, she had to make sure her cat was safe.

"Roxy?" she called again. This time, an answering meow came from her bedroom. When stressed, Roxy often hid under her bed, and sure enough, that's where Marissa found her.

Relieved, Marissa returned to her living room and picked up the brick. She removed the rubber band that kept the note attached and opened it.

Close your stupid business and leave town! Or else.

Reading it again, she shook her head. This made no sense. She had no enemies that she knew of. Why would someone do such a thing? Damaging her property? A window as large as this one wouldn't be cheap.

With a sigh, she pulled out her phone and texted Rayna, asking if she was busy, and if not, if she'd mind stopping by.

Rayna responded by calling her to ask what was going on. Once Marissa filled her in, Rayna promised to be there in a few minutes. "It sounds like it's likely teenagers pulling a prank."

Marissa bit her lip and said nothing.

Once Rayna arrived, Marissa handed her the note. "I'll be honest with you," she said. "Lately, I've felt as if someone has been watching me."

Rayna's gaze sharpened. "What's happened?"

"Nothing really." Marissa shrugged, feeling slightly foolish. "I haven't caught anyone, so I don't have concrete proof. But it's just a feeling I've had. I didn't mention it to anyone, because it seemed paranoid. Until this happened. Now I'm wondering if I was right after all."

"May I keep this?"

"Sure," Marissa answered. "I can keep the pic I took with my phone. I'm a little nervous sleeping here with the window broken."

"I get that. How about I send my husband over with a sheet of plywood and have him nail it up for now? That'll work until you can get someone out to replace the window."

"You know what?" Marissa said, feeling the need to take control of something, no matter how small. "I appreciate the offer, but I have plywood in the garage. I can nail it up myself without bothering Parker."

"Let me help you," Rayna offered.

Together, the two women carried out a large sheet of plywood. Rayna held it while Marissa hammered the nails.

"There." Marissa stepped back. "I feel an incredible sense of accomplishment now."

Rayna laughed "So you should. I'm going to run. Call me if you need anything."

Marissa stood outside until Rayna drove off. Back inside, she double-checked the locks, trying not to feel too uneasy. A sudden urge to call Jared and ask him to come over hit her. Nope. Not going there.

Roxy came out of the bedroom, sidling up to rub against Marissa's legs. She picked her cat up, nuzzling the soft black fur, and felt a little better.

She'd get through this night, and tomorrow would take steps to have her window repaired.

Wednesday morning, she woke up with a sense of purpose and determination. Since her next appointment with Jared wasn't until tomorrow, once she made an appointment to get her window replaced, she had the entire day to get back into the calming routine of her everyday life.

She'd just finished eating breakfast when her phone rang. "Adam!" she exclaimed, answering it. Hearing from her best friend was exactly the kind of pick-me-up she needed right now.

"When were you going to tell me?" he demanded, the pitch of his voice going higher with each word. "I cannot believe you didn't call me as soon as you knew he was here!"

"I'm sorry," she said. "I admit, I wasn't in a really good place. I'm still struggling with how to deal with it."

"It's okay." Adam immediately softened his tone. "So dish. Have you seen him? How does he look?"

She couldn't help but laugh. "Pretty damn hot. As you know, he's always been easy on the eyes, but now…"

Adam whistled. "I have got to get a look at him. But since we weren't exactly friends back in high school, I don't know how."

Adam had chosen to go to cosmetology school when Marissa and Jared had gone off to Texas Tech. He'd done well, and after a brief stint working for the local barber shop, he'd opened his own salon. Now most of the women in Getaway, and even a few of the men, were his devoted clients.

"Offer to cut his hair," she teased.

Her comment made Adam sputter. "Honey, you know he'd never go for that. I bet he has his cut in a buzz cut or something, right?"

"Not even close. You'll see eventually. And you know I was only kidding. I'm sure you'll see him around town at some point. Or you could accidentally be at my studio tomorrow morning at nine a.m. That's when he's coming in for his second physical therapy session."

"Whaaaaaat? You're doing PT with him?"

"I am," she answered. "He got pretty messed up in a rodeo accident. From the way he talks, I think he's planning on sticking around town for a bit."

Silence while Adam considered. "Won't that be a tiny bit obvious?"

"Maybe. Do you really care?"

Adam laughed. "I'm not sure. I think I'd rather try to 'accidentally' run into him around town."

After finishing up her phone conversation with Adam, and telling him about the brick and the weird note attached, Marissa realized she had ten minutes to get herself over to the office, turn everything on and prepare for her first client. Luckily, she thought, still smiling, she had a very short walk instead of an actual commute.

After letting herself out her front door, she used her key to lock it and turned to head around to the business entrance. The back of her neck prickled. Again.

Resisting the urge to spin around, Marissa decided this time to pretend not to notice anything felt wrong. If someone really was stalking her, maybe she could catch sight of them out of the corner of her eye. Even though she hadn't been successful so far, she trusted her instincts. For whatever reason, someone *was* watching her. She just didn't know who, or why.

As she casually scanned the neighborhood, she didn't see anything unusual or out of the ordinary. Since several of the homes in this area also doubled as businesses, there were always a few cars parked at the curb up and down the street. Though she didn't stop and attempt to visually inspect each one, she didn't notice any obvious people sitting inside.

And while many yards had large older trees, if someone hid behind one and watched her, she couldn't tell. Plus, that would be a bit too obvious, she thought.

Nonetheless, the feeling persisted. Maybe from a neighboring building. Or… She glanced up, just in case she'd missed it—a drone. Nothing there. Nothing anywhere that she could tell.

Yet she knew. This was not her imagination. She had a stalker. Possibly the same person who'd thrown the brick through her window.

Marissa had lived her entire life, with the exception of her college years, in this town. She knew just about everyone, had lots of friends and many acquaintances, but couldn't think of one single enemy. Nevertheless, right now she felt exposed, as if someone had trained a rifle on her back. The entire stress-inducing walk around the side of her house made her stomach churn. By the time she inserted her key in the lock of her clinic, her jaw ached from clenching her teeth.

Once stepped quickly inside, she closed the door and exhaled. That had been the worst one yet.

Again she wondered if she should stop by the sheriff's office and talk to Rayna, but without a single shred of evidence, she felt foolish. All she had was her gut instinct. For her, that was enough. All she could do was take extra precautions.

She barely had time to get the coffeepot going when her first client arrived.

Wednesdays were always busy and one of her favorite days. She enjoyed working and chatting with her patients, many of whom felt obliged to catch her up on the latest gossip. She often passed some of what she heard on to Adam, though most times he already knew. Today, several people eyed her and came right out and asked her about Jared.

Luckily, after talking to Adam, she'd been prepared. She told each client the same thing: that she would be providing physical therapy to Jared and she was fine with that. They were both adults and a lot of years had passed since they'd been together.

Her simple explanation seemed to satisfy just about everyone. The sole exception was Mrs. Claverty, a woman who visited Serenity Rune for psychic readings on a monthly basis.

"I'm going to ask Serenity about this," the middle-aged woman declared, patting her teased hair. "It seems to me that I remember hearing her say you two were meant to be together."

Though hearing those words felt like a knife wound to the heart, Marissa managed a casual shrug. "Maybe at the time we were," she said, keeping her voice light. "And now that time is past."

Peering up at Marissa through her cat-shaped eyeglasses, Mrs. Claverty didn't appear convinced. "I'm still going to ask her."

Marissa kept a pleasant expression on her face and got busy doing other things while Mrs. Claverty rode the exercise bike. One thing she knew and admired about Serenity was her refusal to indulge in negative gossip or give readings about other people. She'd likely tell Mrs. Claverty what happened between Marissa and Jared was none of her business.

Marissa called two window-repair companies before getting someone who could actually make an appointment to come out and take a look that afternoon. They'd had a cancellation, though they did inform her that due to the size of her window, it might be a special order and take a few days to arrive.

Finally, after finishing up with Mrs. Claverty, Marissa had an hour off for lunch. Today she'd eat at noon rather than her usual one, due to scheduling. Instead of staying at the clinic like she usually did, she decided to lock up here and go home.

Stepping outside, she casually glanced around. This time, she didn't feel as if someone lurked nearby, watching her. Probably because this wasn't her usual routine. Right then and there, she resolved to try to vary up her schedule a little so she wouldn't be such an easy target.

Both amused and worried at the way her thoughts had

gone, she had her house key in her hand as she walked around the corner toward her front door. The door was open. Just a crack, but since she absolutely knew she'd locked it that morning, there was a distinct possibility that someone was inside her house!

Backing away slowly, heart pounding, she pulled out her phone and called Rayna's office. The sheriff herself answered, which meant her receptionist had stepped out for lunch. As soon as Marissa explained the situation, Rayna ordered her to go back into the clinic and lock the door behind her. "I'm on my way," Rayna said.

"But my cat," Marissa protested, her stomach knotted with worry. "I'm worried Roxy will get out. She's an inside cat and—"

"Go." Interrupting her, Rayna spoke in a sharp voice. "I'll make sure your cat is okay. Right now you need to protect yourself. Now go."

Ending the call, Marissa sprinted back around to her clinic entrance. Hands shaking, she managed to unlock the door, then engage the dead bolt behind her as soon as she stepped inside.

Pacing, she waited for Rayna's arrival, which shouldn't be long since the sheriff's office was only three blocks away. Luckily, she had a large window facing the street, so she had a clear view of Rayna's cruiser when it pulled into her small parking lot.

Though she knew she probably shouldn't, she immediately rushed outside. Though she'd forgotten to check earlier, the plywood she'd nailed up the night before appeared to still be in place.

"No," Rayna barked the instant Marissa appeared. "You go back into your clinic while I secure your home. I've called for backup and one of my deputies will be here any minute."

"But…" Marissa started to protest, only to be cut off by Rayna's choppy hand motion and second order to get inside her clinic. Briefly, she debated arguing, but aware there might be some element of danger, she did as she'd been told and locked herself in the clinic.

The second patrol car pulled up a minute later and parked in the street. The deputy got out and joined Rayna. Then, weapons drawn, the two law enforcement officers went around the corner to enter her house.

Since none of the clinic windows faced that direction, all Marissa could do was pace and worry. Break-ins were virtually nonexistent in Getaway. And since everyone knew Marissa wasn't wealthy, it wasn't like she had a lot of belongings worthy of stealing.

There had to be another reason. She thought of her overwhelming feeling of being watched and her stomach churned. She didn't often have an hour for lunch, so she usually just ate in the clinic. Had this person, this *stalker*, been inside her home before? If so, how had they gotten in? She didn't even keep a spare key hidden outside.

When a knock came on the clinic's door, Marissa nearly jumped out of her skin. Fumbling with the lock, she opened up to find Rayna standing outside. The deputy had apparently already left.

"We didn't find anyone inside," Rayna said. "There's also no sign of forced entry. Oh, and by the way, your cat is perfectly fine. She was asleep under your bed."

Sagging with relief, Marissa exhaled. "What about my stuff? Is anything missing?"

"I don't know." Rayna took her arm. "Come with me and let's go take a look."

Together they walked over to her residence. Rayna opened the door and allowed Marissa to precede her.

Standing in her living room, heart racing, Marissa looked around. "Nothing looks out of place. At all." Slowly, she circled the entire room, headed into the kitchen and then down the hallway to her bedroom. Everything appeared exactly the way it had been when she'd left that morning.

"You couldn't even tell someone was in here," Marissa said, her stomach in knots. "Yet I'm positive I closed and locked the door when I went to work."

Rayna smiled encouragingly. "I believe you." She paused. "Why don't you tell me what you think might have happened?"

With a sigh, Marissa nodded. "For the last several weeks, I've had the feeling someone was watching me. But I could never actually spot them, so at first I chalked it up to an overactive imagination. Lately, it's gotten worse. I'm positive that someone is stalking me, but I have no idea who or why."

"I see." Rayna gestured outside. "Someone just pulled up and parked. Are you expecting a client?"

"Crud." Checking her watch, Marissa grimaced. "My two o'clock is here. I need to get over to the clinic and unlock it."

"Okay, but listen. I think you should consider adding a security system, with camera if possible."

"Good idea," Marissa replied. "I'll make some calls after work tonight."

"Good." Rayna paused. "Get them to come out and set it up as soon as possible. As far as the rest of it, you can put up your own wireless cameras."

Marissa shook her head. "I wouldn't even know where to begin."

"If you want to meet up, I'll be happy to go with you and help you choose the right setup," Rayna offered. "Parker can even help get everything installed." She smiled. "My husband is really good at stuff like that."

Surprised and grateful, Marissa thanked her. "Do you want to grab dinner somewhere while we're out?"

"I'd love that. How about we meet here at five?"

Marissa agreed. Side by side, the two women walked out. After Marissa locked the place up, Rayna made another suggestion. "Either this intruder has a key, or has first rate lock-picking skills. You'll also need to replace the lock. I can show you the most secure type to buy."

"Thank you."

After Rayna drove off, Marissa hurried around to the clinic entrance. Mr. Ransom, clearly unhappy at finding the door locked, had taken a seat on the bench outside. He eyed Marissa through his thick glasses and watched the sheriff drive away.

"Trouble?" he asked, his thick brows drawn down in a frown.

"Not really," Marissa lied, not wanting to involve one of her clients in her personal life. "Rayna and I were just making plans to go shopping together after work."

Unlocking the door, she gestured for him to go in ahead of her.

"You women and your shopping," the elderly man said. "My late wife, Flora, was the same way."

Marissa got him settled and started him on his exercises before heading back to the break room. Her stomach growled, reminding her that she hadn't eaten lunch.

"Miss Marissa?" Mr. Ransom called out, his quavering voice mischievous. "You have a visitor."

For an instant, she froze, thinking of whoever had just broken into her house. Then, she shook off her trepidation, figuring the intruder wouldn't be that bold, and turned to make her way back out to the main part of her clinic.

She turned the corner and stopped dead in her tracks.

Jared stood just inside the door, holding a pizza box from Pizza Perfect. "I'm sorry," he said, the instant he caught sight of her. "I thought this was your lunch time, so I figured I'd surprise you with your favorite pizza."

Aware her mouth might be hanging open, she hurriedly composed herself. "Jared. What a surprise. Why don't you go ahead and take that back into the break room and I'll join you in just a few minutes? I've got to help Mr. Ransom here finish up his session."

Heart pounding, she took deep, even breaths while she watched Jared go. When she turned back to her client, Mr. Ransom grinned up at her. "What's old is new?" he asked, winking.

Checking his chart, she pretended not to understand. "You only have one session remaining," she said. "Once again, I'm going to give you some work to do at home, and then I'll see you back here next week."

He nodded, still smiling. "You didn't answer my question. Everyone in town is talking about Jared Miller being back in town and the possibility that you two have picked up right where you left off. Is that true?"

"Jared and I are friends," she replied, keeping her tone professional. "He is also one of my clients here. Nothing more." She tapped her watch. "Your session is over and my next client will be here shortly." She allowed herself a tiny smile. "Plus, I didn't get a chance to grab lunch, so I'd like to get a slice of that pizza before it gets cold."

Grabbing his cane, Mr. Ransom pushed up. He took the papers from her and made his way toward the exit.

"Enjoy your pizza," he called back over his shoulder as he left.

Waiting until the door closed behind him, she hurried toward the kitchen. She had ten minutes before her next session was due to start. Luckily her client, a teenager who'd been injured playing football, hadn't yet arrived.

Jared stood in the kitchen, hands jammed down into his pockets. He'd placed the pizza on the table. "My apologies," he said. "For some reason, I thought you went to lunch at one."

"I normally do." She went to the cabinet and pulled out a couple of paper plates. "Today I was off schedule. Which turned out to be a good thing. You wouldn't believe what happened. Let's eat and if I have time, I'll tell you all about it."

Opening the box, she swallowed. "Canadian bacon and pineapple," she said. "You remembered."

"Yep." He took one of the plates from her. "That combination is kind of hard to forget."

She ate one slice, struggling not to inhale it. Peeking back into her reception area to make sure it was still empty, she grabbed a second and then, after a second thought, a third.

"You really *were* hungry," Jared commented, smiling. "I'm glad I took a chance and stopped by."

Briefly, she wondered why he had, but put the thought from her mind. "Thank you for bringing this. If you hadn't, I probably wouldn't have had anything to eat."

"You said something happened?" He'd just grabbed a couple more slices, and picked one up to bite into it.

"Let me finish eating first and I'll tell you," she said, stepping to the doorway to check and make sure no one had yet arrived. It was now ten after.

"It's after two," Jared pointed out. "Weren't you expecting another customer?"

"My client is late," she said. "He's a teenager, and not great at being punctual. This time, I'm actually glad."

After she'd polished off her pizza, she debated how much to confide in him. In the end, she went ahead and told him everything, including her feeling of being watched for the last several weeks.

She'd just finished up when she heard the outside door open. "Excuse me," she told Jared. "Let me go get Angelo situated."

Though she felt as if she were escaping, she hurried from the break room.

Angelo, his black curls tucked up under a baseball cap, greeted her. "Sorry I'm late, Ms. Noll. Am I doing the same thing as last time?"

She nodded. "Mostly. At the beginning for sure. Are you ready to get started?"

Pointing to his wireless earbuds, he gave her a thumbs up before taking a seat on the bench and picking up a set of lightweight dumbbells. When they'd first started using them, he'd been incredulous, explaining he lifted weights that were much heavier than this.

She'd pointed out gently that that had been before his injury, and he'd need to work up to bigger weights. After that, he'd understood and generally did whatever she asked him to.

She watched Angelo work out for a minute, then returned to the break room. When she entered, Jared stood. "I've got to go."

"What's wrong?" she asked, stopping in her tracks.

He shook his head. "You're busy and I need to go check on my dad. I'll stop by later tonight, around seven. We'll talk then." With that, he jammed his cowboy hat back on his head and walked out, his limp a little bit less pronounced.

It wasn't until after he'd gone that she realized she'd already made plans to meet Rayna and might be late. She made a mental note to text Jared later.

Chapter Four

Jaw clenched, Jared kept his anger in check—barely—as he left Marissa's clinic. Just thinking that she might be in danger infuriated him, even though it wasn't his place to protect her. He wanted to, damn it, but he didn't have the right. Still, he walked over to her front window and checked on the plywood she'd put up, making sure it was secure. She'd done a good job. This would hold until she had the window replaced.

From a brick with a threatening note to a break-in. And she'd said she felt like she was being watched. Where was her boyfriend in all of this? From what Jared remembered hearing, she was dating the new veterinarian, Dr. Norris. His father had used him, having him out to the ranch to deworm and vaccinate the horses, and proclaimed him a good guy. Jared had doubts about that. He understood the vet stayed busy, but why wasn't he taking steps to protect Marissa?

Maybe the time had come for the two of them to meet. Jared wanted to size him up, make sure the other man would take protecting Marissa seriously.

Even though as far as he knew, she hadn't asked for anyone's protection.

Driving toward the vet clinic, Jared told himself he shouldn't get involved. Marissa's new relationship wasn't any of his business, and she'd be furious once she learned what he had done.

Even as he pulled into the lot and parked, he told himself he could still reconsider. Just back the truck out and go the opposite way. Instead, he turned off the engine and got out. Taking a deep breath, he opened the door, stepped out and headed toward the entrance. Since there were only a couple of other cars in the parking lot, he figured maybe the vet wouldn't be too busy.

A smiling young woman greeted him as he entered. "Good afternoon. How can I help you?"

Removing his hat, Jared smiled politely. "My name is Jared Miller. I'm wondering if I could have a brief word with Dr. Norris. I don't have an appointment and this isn't about a pet. My visit is of a more personal nature."

Eyes wide, she studied him. "Just one moment," she finally said, and hurried off into the back.

While he waited, Jared reminded himself that he'd be cordial, here on a friendly mission to make sure his longtime friend Marissa had the protection she deserved.

When the receptionist returned a moment later, she smiled. "Dr. Norris will be with you in a moment. He asked that I take you to one of our examination rooms so you two can talk privately."

He followed her down a short hallway, then entered the small room and took a seat on the bench. She reiterated that the vet would be with him shortly and left, closing the door behind her.

A few minutes later, a tall man with short gray hair and

piercing blue eyes entered the room. "Hello there," he said, holding out his hand. "I'm David. I've heard a lot about you."

Jared shook his hand, feeling more uncomfortable by the minute. He decided to get directly to the point. "I'm here because of Marissa," he explained.

"Obviously." David's smile widened. He took a seat on the stool near the examination table. "She told me you were having therapy with her."

"I am." Taking a deep breath, he pushed ahead. "But that's not why I'm here. I consider Marissa one of my oldest friends. I really just wanted to make sure you have a plan in place to protect her."

"Protect her?" Rubbing his chin, the veterinarian appeared genuinely puzzled. "From what or whom? You?"

Jared decided to let that slide. He couldn't really blame the other man. If their positions had been reversed, Jared probably wouldn't have been so nice.

Then it dawned on him that David truly had no idea what Jared meant. "Did Marissa mention to you that she's worried she has a stalker?" he asked. "Or that someone broke in to her house today while she was working."

"What? No." Clearly agitated, David got to his feet. "Are you sure?"

"Yes." Jared began to feel a little bit sorry for the other man. "I just left there and drove here."

"I see." With his rugged features, David could have played a doctor on TV. Right now, he appeared to be struggling to regain his admirable self-control.

While Jared knew he could make things easier for the other man, maybe let him know that he wasn't trying to steal Marissa away from him—though that wasn't entirely true—he didn't say anything. Instead, he repeated his earlier question, changing it up slightly. "Okay, now that you know what's going on, I sincerely hope you can put a plan in place to make sure Marissa stays safe."

"I see." Gaze steady, David eyed him. "Does Marissa know you're here?"

Damn it. Jared refused to let the other man see him squirm. "No," he admitted. "I'm just worried about her and I figured since you're her boyfriend..."

Crossing his arms, David eyed him. "And?" he prompted.

Though he found the other man's half smile infuriating, Jared kept a lid on his emotions. "She needs someone to protect her."

David laughed. "Marissa? Are we even talking about the same woman? Look, I know you've been gone for a while, but Marissa can take care of herself. And I do know she wouldn't appreciate you barging in here and trying to orchestrate something that's absolutely none of your business."

The fact that David was right did nothing to endear him to Jared. In fact, Jared realized he disliked Marissa's boyfriend. Not only was the man too damn pretty, but his smug attitude grated on Jared's nerves. Or, he admitted silently, it might just be the fact that David was the one holding Marissa at night instead of Jared.

"I think we're done here," Jared announced. "I apologize for taking up any of your valuable time."

Unbelievably, this comment made David grin. "No need to be like that," he said. "I get where you're coming from, but I honestly don't believe you've thought this through. Imagine how pissed Marissa is going to be when she finds out about this."

"What matters is that she's safe," Jared replied stiffly. "She'll get over being angry. But if someone really is stalking her, I hate the thought of her being in any kind of danger."

"I do, too." David clapped Jared on the shoulder. "But with the two of us looking out for her, I think she'll be fine."

The two of us? Baffled, Jared shook off the other man's hand. "I'll let myself out," he said, and headed toward the exit. David, for whatever reason, not only acted as if he and Jared were a team or something, but didn't seem at all concerned about his girlfriend's safety.

"Wait," David called after him. "Do you mind giving me your number? Just in case I need to get in touch with you for any reason."

Jared considered. David already had his phone out, ready to enter it. He rattled off the numbers and nodded when David sent him a text. There, David had typed. Now you have mine.

Back downtown, Jared pulled into the parking lot of the Tumbleweed Café. He'd taken his father here to meet a couple of his old ranching buddies for lunch. The group was fond of playing dominoes, so after they ate they'd planned to gather in the gaming area and do exactly that. Jared had made his dad promise to wait there for him and not to go anywhere else. Since he hadn't been gone much more than an hour, he felt pretty confident he'd find the men in the middle of a lively game of dominoes.

Stepping inside the café, Jared removed his hat and nodded at the hostess. He immediately caught sight of the group of elderly ranchers, all gathered around one of the big tables with dominoes spread out in front of them.

As he moved closer, he realized he didn't see his father. "Hey, Bob," he said, greeting one of his dad's oldest friends. "Where's my dad?"

"I don't know." Bob shrugged. "He started to play with us, then got frustrated for some reason. He said something about having some shopping to do, and left."

Jared's heart sank. "Did he happen to say where he planned to shop?"

Three of the other ranchers looked up at the question. They all answered at the same time. "Rancher's Supply," they said, naming a popular store on the other side of town.

"That's a mighty long walk," Jared commented. "Unless he got someone to drive him."

No one knew. Bob volunteered that the elder Miller had been a bit grouchy, so they hadn't tried very hard to get him to stay.

"Why don't you just call him?" Bob wanted to know.

Since Jared didn't want to tell them that his father lost his phone on a regular basis, he simply claimed it had been accidentally left in the truck.

"Bummer," Bob said. "He's bound to be around here somewhere."

Jared thanked them and turned away. Since none of the men had mentioned his father acting confused or different, Jared could only hope he hadn't wandered far.

First, Jared double-checked the rest of the café. Then, he stepped outside and headed down the sidewalk, pausing at each business and doing a quick search. Nothing.

He'd made it down one full block and stopped, debating whether to cross the street or continue on the same side, when his phone rang.

Marissa. Aware of why she'd be calling, he almost didn't answer, but he was on the verge of panicking and needed to talk to someone.

The instant he answered, she launched into a rebuke, telling him David had called her and—

"Marissa," he cut her off. "We can discuss that later. My father is missing. I'm downtown looking for him and really worried. Is there any way you can help me?"

"Missing?" she asked. "I don't understand."

Dragging his hand through his short hair, he exhaled. "I left him at the café, where he was supposed to have lunch with his friends and then play dominoes. He promised me he wouldn't go anywhere else and would wait for me to pick him up. But he left. They said he was going to Rancher's Supply."

"I see." She sounded mystified as to why that might be a problem. "Have you looked there?"

"No, because he's on foot and it's clear on the other side of town. There's no way he could have made it that far. He has early-onset dementia." To his embarrassment, his voice broke. "I'm really worried."

She went silent for a moment, clearly digesting this.

"My last client for the day is here," she finally said. "They have ten minutes remaining and then I'll head your way. I'll text you so we can meet up."

He thanked her and ended the call. Across the street, he checked out two places with no luck. The next store was Serenity's shop. While he liked her a lot, he wasn't in the mood for any of her vague metaphysical advice. However, a lot of people truly believed her to be a psychic, so he figured it couldn't hurt to ask her to help him find his dad.

Once he'd stepped inside her shop, the strong odor of incense made him sneeze. He'd actually reconsidered and turned to leave when Serenity herself sailed out from the back, wearing some kind of floaty, fringed shawl.

"Jared!" she exclaimed. "It's good to see you. I imagine you're looking for your father."

Seriously impressed, he nodded. "I am. Have you seen him?"

"I have." She smiled. "He's in back visiting with me and having his tarot cards read. I had a feeling you'd be stopping by to look for him."

Relief nearly took him out at the knees. He gaped at her, then stepped forward and hugged her as tightly as he could before letting her go. "Thank you. I was so worried."

She smiled sweetly. "Come on back. He doesn't realize he did anything wrong, so take a couple deep breaths first."

"I will," he said. His phone pinged, indicating a text. Marissa. He needed to let her know his father had been located.

She'd texted she'd be on her way in five minutes. Quickly, he typed a reply. Found him. No need to come. I'll call later.

Then he took one final deep breath and headed to the back of the store to collect his dad.

The older man looked up when Jared walked into the room and beamed. "There you are, son. You should get Serenity to read her cards for you. It's a hoot!"

"Maybe later," Jared said, keeping his tone light. "Right now, we need to get back to the ranch. Are you ready to go?"

Once he'd gotten his father in the truck with the seat belt buckled, he waited until they'd left downtown Getaway before he spoke. "I went to get you at the Tumbleweed Café earlier. I thought you'd be playing dominoes with your friends. But they told me you'd decided to go to Rancher's Supply. Since that's all the way on the other side of town and you were on foot, I got a little bit worried."

"Rancher's Supply!" The older man slapped his knee. "I love that place. But I don't know why those old coots thought

I'd walk all the way down there." He laughed. "I decided to stretch my legs a little and go visit my old friend Serenity."

"You were supposed to wait for me at the café," Jared pointed out gently. "I was really worried about you."

"No need." His father's gruff voice contained a warning. "I'm not dead yet, you know."

For whatever reason, this statement put an ache in Jared's throat. "I know," he responded, deciding to leave it at that.

AFTER READING JARED'S response to her text message, Marissa found herself blinking away tears. Thank goodness he'd located his father. She couldn't imagine how worried Jared must have been. He certainly had a lot to deal with and she understood how tough that must be, but that didn't excuse the fact that he'd taken it upon himself to pay David a visit.

For whatever reason, David had seemed to find the entire thing amusing. Honestly, his attitude rankled her a little. She would have expected something more. Maybe a tiny bit of jealousy that her former boyfriend had learned about the break-in before he had.

As for the break-in itself, and the fact that she believed she might have a stalker, David hadn't seemed overly concerned about that either. Of course, he had been super busy, like always. He'd promised to discuss that with her as soon as he had time.

And that had been that. Leaving her with the distinct impression that her old high school boyfriend had been more worried about her than her current one.

With the clinic locked up, she hurried around the corner to her house. Though she didn't have the immediate sense of being watched, the knowledge that someone had been inside her home made her feel violated. She made a quick call to one of the local alarm-monitoring servicing companies and scheduled an appointment for tomorrow afternoon. The technician would go over all the options with her then, as well as the cost and the various payment plans.

As for the rest, thank goodness Rayna had offered to help her with choosing cameras and new locks. After everything had been installed, no intruder would be able to remain anonymous or undetected.

After the window repair service came, she had thirty minutes before Rayna was due to arrive, so she fed Roxy and went to her bedroom to change out of the scrubs she normally wore to work. Once she'd put on a pair of jeans and a comfortable shirt, she took her hair out of its ponytail and brushed it.

Rayna arrived promptly at five, decked out in jeans and boots, her wavy red hair swirling around her shoulders. "What do you want to do first?" she asked. "Eat or shop?"

"Shop, if that's okay with you," Marissa answered. "Jared brought pizza and I had a late lunch."

"Jared?" Appearing intrigued, Rayna looked at her with a twinkle in her eyes. "You can tell me all about that at dinner. Let's go get you some cameras and new locks. I'll drive."

To Marissa's surprise, the hardware store on Main Street had everything they needed. She'd thought they might have to go to one of the huge chain stores in one of the larger nearby towns.

"All set," Rayna said happily after loading up Marissa's shopping cart. They'd gotten cameras for both the home and the clinic, as well as new dead bolts and keypad locks for all exterior doors. "I've already talked to Parker and he'll be calling you tomorrow to set up a time to get everything installed."

"Thank you so much." Marissa hugged her.

Laughing, Rayna hugged her back. "No problem. That's what friends are for. I've got your back, girl."

Pleased, Marissa pushed her cart up to the counter. Rayna's words had brought her a rush of warmth. The young, bearded cashier greeted the sheriff, a note of respect in his voice, and then began ringing up Marissa's purchases.

Once she'd paid, trying not to wince at the total, Marissa carried her bags outside. Rayna helped her load everything up in Rayna's vehicle.

"Now we can eat," Rayna said. "What are you in the mood for?" Before Marissa could answer, she heaved a sigh. "Anything but the café. Whenever I go there, I spend so much time talking to various citizens that my food gets cold."

"Since I just ate at Tres Amigos, and just had pizza, I wouldn't mind a good burger," Marissa replied. "I've heard that new place that opened up around the corner from Serenity's has really good ones. Have you ever tried them?"

"Rob's?" Rayna grinned. "Several of my deputies have been raving about them. I just haven't had the chance to eat there. Let's do it."

Since Rob's Burgers hadn't been open more than a few weeks, Marissa hoped it wouldn't be too crowded. No such luck. The parking lot was so full that cars were circling around like vultures, waiting for a spot to open up.

"Maybe this isn't such a good idea," Marissa said. "I bet there's over an hour wait."

"I agree. I'm too hungry for all that. But now I'm really in the mood for a burger." Rayna considered. "Let's go ahead and try the Tumbleweed Café. They have really good burgers, too."

"Are you sure?"

"Why not?" Gesturing at the circling cars, Rayna sighed. "Maybe it won't be too busy there. After all, it appears just about everyone in town is here."

Rayna drove them back downtown. The café didn't appear to be half as busy as the new place, so they parked and went inside.

Violet, the hostess on duty that night, lit up when she saw Rayna. "I'm so glad you came in," she said, smiling ear to ear. "Would you like a booth or a table?"

"One of the back tables, please." Rayna pointed. "Might help cut down on the flow of traffic going past us."

"Right this way." Grabbing two menus, Violet led them to one of the tables in the very back of the restaurant. Anyone else would have to make a deliberate trip over if they wanted to interrupt their meal.

Once seated, Violet promised someone would be with them shortly before strolling back to the front.

The waitress, a teenager named Yolanda Anderson, grinned when she saw Rayna. "I just started working here," she said, a note of pride in her voice. "It's kind of cool earning my own spending money."

Rayna congratulated her and asked about her sister and father, as well as his new wife.

Once Yolanda answered, she asked what they would like to drink. They both handed back the menus and ordered iced tea and burgers. "We're starving," Rayna said.

"I'll have the cook make them extra-large," Yolanda promised, then bustled away to put the order in.

Her comment made Rayna laugh out loud. "I'm glad we came to the café after all."

"You really are popular around here," Marissa observed.

Rayna ducked her head, as though embarrassed, though she smiled. "That's one of the things I absolutely love about this town," she said. "There's a wonderful sense of community here. I can't ever imagine living anywhere else."

"Me neither." Which had been one of the main reasons why Marissa had refused to follow Jared around the rodeo circuit. She'd had plans. And they all included ending up permanently in Getaway. Now Jared had ended up back in town, too. But for how long?

Telling herself that didn't matter, she pushed the thought away. Their drinks arrived and Marissa took a sip of her tea, before leaning across the table to tell Rayna about Jared's impromptu visit to David's vet clinic.

"He did *what?*" Rayna asked, her expression shocked. "Why on earth would he think that was okay?"

"I don't know. But it also bothers me that David doesn't seem to even mind." The admission cost her. She'd never once talked about her relationship with David, not even to her own family. Her parents had been thrilled to learn she was dating a veterinarian. When her mother started planning the wedding, Marissa had straightened her out and then never mentioned David to either of them again.

"How do you feel about the whole thing?" Rayna asked, her expression genuinely curious.

Just then their burgers arrived, giving Marissa time to consider. As the waitress had promised, both burgers were plump and juicy, piled high with toppings and served alongside a generous helping of french fries.

After being assured they didn't need anything else, the

waitress left. Aware Rayna still waited for an answer, Marissa picked up a fry and popped it into her mouth. "Honestly, I'm not sure. I guess I'd sort of hoped David might be a little bit jealous or something. Though our relationship is extremely casual." She shrugged. "I'm not even sure we're exclusive. We've never actually discussed it."

"I see." Gripping her burger with both hands, Rayna took a bite. "Mmm." She rolled her eyes. "So good."

They ate in companionable silence for the next few minutes.

About halfway through their meal, Marissa put her burger down and blotted her mouth with her napkin. "Honestly, I like David a lot, but I don't think he's the one. I kept hoping things might get more…intense as time went on, but they haven't."

"With him being the only vet for all the ranches in this area, as well as people's pets, it's a miracle that poor man even has time to try having any relationship at all," Rayna mused. "I read an article about how the new veterinary school at Tech is trying to get more graduates to practice in rural Texas. I bet David would really welcome the help if another vet were to open a practice anywhere in the county or even one of the surrounding counties."

Surprised, Marissa nodded. "I'll bet you're right. The poor man really doesn't have much time for a personal life."

Rayna finished the last of her burger and almost all of her fries before she spoke again. "Though I know you didn't ask for it, I'm going to give you a word of advice. When you know, you know. If David isn't the one, and honestly, it sounds as if he's not, don't settle. The right guy will come along when you least expect it." She grinned. "Believe me,

I know. That's what happened to me. And I couldn't be happier."

Marissa had seen Rayna's husband, Parker, and judging from the way he looked at his wife, he felt the same way.

A rush of longing filled her. Unexpected, because she'd been focused on her career for so long she hadn't given much thought to anything else. Now she realized she wanted something like what Rayna had for herself.

Someday.

"Are you okay?" Rayna asked. "You look like you got hit by a brick."

The colorful description made Marissa smile. "I'm fine. I just had a bit of an epiphany." Then, since she didn't want the conversation to turn too serious, she changed the subject. "I can't thank you enough for helping me find the right equipment tonight. I've got a regular alarm-monitoring company coming out tomorrow to put in window and door sensors and keypads. Once that's in, plus all these cameras, I'll definitely feel a lot more secure."

"You'll be a lot more secure," Rayna said, grinning. "Proactive is way better than reactive, in my book."

"I've even been thinking about getting a dog," Marissa admitted. "I just don't know how my cat would adjust to that."

"That's where you'd have to get the right dog."

The waitress came over, asking if they wanted anything else.

Marissa shook her head no, but Rayna considered. "I think I'd like some cherry pie," she said. After the waitress went to get it, Rayna turned to Marissa and winked. "I'm eating for two these days."

"What?" Marissa squealed. "Oh my gosh! Congratulations!"

"Shhh." Putting a finger to her lips, Rayna nodded. "Thanks. I want to keep this under wraps for now. Parker and I are telling my daughter and my mother tonight. After that, the whole town can gossip as much as they want."

"I'm honored that you shared your happy news with me," Marissa said. "You must be over the moon."

"I am, but Parker is even more thrilled. He got tears in his eyes when I told him. He can't wait for the baby to be born. I know he's going to make an awesome dad."

Rayna's pie arrived and Marissa sat and watched her friend devour it. "You're actually glowing," she commented. "You look amazing."

"Thanks." Rayna barely looked up from her dessert. She finished it quickly, finally leaning back and patting her still-flat stomach. "I just made it through the first trimester. Parker's been treating me like I'm breakable. I keep telling him I'm healthy and I've done this before. It's all going to be fine."

Marissa smiled. "I'm sure it is," she said. She checked her phone, surprised at the time. Jared had mentioned stopping by around seven and if she didn't leave soon, she'd be late. But since Rayna had driven and was still clearly enjoying her dessert, Marissa didn't want to rush her. If worst came to worst, Jared would have to wait.

Chapter Five

Jared took extra care with his appearance before heading over to Marissa's. Though he wrestled with leaving his father alone and unsupervised, at least on the ranch there was minimal trouble for the older man to get into. After all, he'd been living alone for years and had somehow managed just fine. A few hours here and there should be safe. So far, despite the doctor's warnings, J.J.'s disease appeared to be progressing slowly.

Still, he found himself hovering around the older man, making sure he was settled in his recliner in front of the television, with his dinner in front of him on a TV tray.

"Do you need anything else?" Jared asked, grabbing a lap blanket and settling it over his dad's legs.

"Quit acting like I'm an invalid!" His father glared before picking up his spoon and stirring his soup. "Get out of here and go have fun on your date with pretty Marissa. I'll be fine here. I'm always fine."

"I know." Feeling a rush of tenderness, Jared took a step back, watching as his dad slurped a spoonful of soup. He wished he knew someone he could ask to come stay here while he was gone, though he knew his father would likely get up in arms about that.

"You worry too much," his dad growled without looking up. "Now go. I can't eat with you standing over me like that."

"Promise me you won't leave this house," Jared ordered, crossing his arms.

"You got it. I don't have anywhere to go."

And since Jared had taken all the keys, the older man had no access to any of the vehicles. So far, he didn't seem to mind, which made Jared suspect he knew the time had come for him to give up driving.

"I'll be back in less than an hour," Jared promised, grabbing his favorite Stetson on the way out the door. Once he got in his truck, he told himself to chill. This wasn't a date. Not even close. Marissa no doubt would be angry and light into him for intruding in her personal life.

Truthfully, he couldn't actually blame her. He had no idea what had prompted him to pay David a visit, and after meeting the man, he definitely regretted doing so.

David isn't good enough for Marissa.

The thought came out of nowhere, startling him. It wasn't just jealousy, though he had to admit he felt that, too. Even if Jared took himself out of the equation, he knew deep down inside that Marissa deserved someone who worshipped her the way he wanted to.

Deciding to think on it as he drove, he started his truck and headed toward town. After all, who Marissa dated was none of his business. Where she was concerned, he'd long ago given up any and all rights.

Which, since he still loved her, killed him. Yes, he wanted her. More than he should, but he couldn't seem to help himself. They'd been perfect together once, and he so badly wanted to find out if they still would be now.

He had a ranch to run, his father to take care of and

physical therapy to complete to heal up his body. She had a busy career, an apparently happy relationship with David and hadn't given Jared the slightest indication she'd be interested in him in that way.

By the time he turned onto her street, he'd talked himself off the ledge.

Once he pulled up, he parked in the clinic parking lot, noting one car still remained. Since she'd closed shop well over ninety minutes ago, the vehicle mystified him, but he figured maybe the driver had car trouble or something. Jared didn't see Marissa's Tahoe, but that wasn't unusual since he knew she often parked it in her detached garage.

He walked around to the entrance to her house. About to press the doorbell, a sound from inside made him freeze. Something, glass most likely, had crashed to the floor and shattered. Since she'd had a break-in once already, he immediately suspected someone might be inside.

Which meant Marissa might be in danger.

He froze. While he knew he should call Rayna, he wasn't sure of the situation inside. If Marissa had been hurt, he didn't have the luxury of waiting for law enforcement to arrive.

Or he might be jumping to wrong conclusions. For all he knew, Marissa might have dropped a glass or a plate.

He tried her cell phone, listening to see if he could hear it ringing inside the house. After several unanswered rings, his call went to voice mail.

Just in case, he sent a quick text. I'm outside. Are you home?

A moment later, she texted back. Sorry, I'm out with Rayna. Time got away from me. I'll be home in a few minutes if you want to wait. If not, I'll call you later.

I'll wait, he sent back. Marissa was with the sheriff. Another sound from inside made him freeze. If Marissa wasn't home, then who was making all that noise?

What if he hadn't been there? The thought of her arriving home and walking in on an intruder turned his blood cold.

He continued to listen. Nothing else. Undecided, he clenched his teeth at the sound of something else hitting the floor. It sounded as if someone might be searching Marissa's house and trashing her things.

That settled it. He tried the doorknob first, just in case. Locked. *That's odd*, he thought. *What kind of intruder breaks in and then locks the door after him?*

Still, likely due to the recent break-in, the door felt wobbly, the lock unstable. He leaned his shoulder against it and shoved, hard. Everything held. Not wanting to alert the intruder, he tried again. Still unsuccessful, he went out to his truck and returned with a screwdriver. Wedging this into the gap between the door and frame, he shoved it upward until the lock disengaged. Marissa definitely needed a new dead bolt. He'd take her to get one as soon as possible.

Taking a deep breath, he quietly let himself in.

With no lights on, the interior of Marissa's house felt empty, almost as if what he'd heard had been his imagination. Heart pounding, he moved forward, making as little noise as possible. Jared honestly hoped he'd catch this guy so Marissa would no longer have to worry, and neither would he.

He rounded the corner and saw multiple shards of glass on the ceramic tile floor of the kitchen. A shattered plate. And beyond that, he noticed a broken ceramic coffee cup in two pieces.

Both relieved—he hadn't imagined it—and apprehensive,

he continued into the kitchen. Glass crunched underfoot as he moved through the space.

A sound from behind him had him spinning around. A large black cat, yellow eyes glowing, jumped up on the kitchen counter and hissed at him.

A cat. A thoroughly pissed-off cat. He felt like an idiot.

Backing slowly away, over the shattered glass, he made his way toward the front door and let himself outside. Then he sat down on the steps to wait for Marissa so he could tell her what had happened.

She pulled in about ten minutes later, driving straight to her garage, opening the door with her remote and parking inside.

He stood as she hurried over, carrying numerous shopping bags in both arms. Somehow she managed to close the garage door, too.

"Hi," she said, slightly breathless. "I'm sorry I'm late."

"It's all good," he replied, taking a couple of her bags from her. "Looks like you had a productive shopping trip."

"I did. Rayna helped me pick out wireless cameras and new door locks. Parker is going to come over and get everything installed for me. I've also got an alarm company coming out tomorrow to install window and door sensors. Once I'm done, this place should definitely be secure."

"Speaking of secure..." He told her what had happened. "I was careful not to damage the door. I left it unlocked."

She nodded. "Thanks."

"I didn't even know you had a cat until I ran into it."

"Her name is Roxy," she replied. "And she loves knocking stuff off the kitchen counters. I'm usually more careful not to leave anything out."

"Well, there's glass all over the floor. I can help you clean it up, if you like."

Suddenly her smile faded as she juggled the bags from one arm to the other. "That won't be necessary. Come on inside. We can talk while I clean up Roxy's mess."

Following her, trying not to focus too much on the gentle sway of her hips as she walked, he wondered if he should try to explain why he'd done what he did earlier in the day. In the end, he decided to hear her out first. After all, he couldn't blame her for being angry at his interference.

She flicked on lights as they went, wincing when she saw the mess in the kitchen. "I hope she didn't cut her paws," she said. "Since I don't see any blood, I'm going to assume she's okay. She's likely hiding right now."

Grabbing a broom and a dustpan, she began sweeping up the shards of glass.

"I can vacuum after you're done," he offered, feeling as if he ought to do something to help.

"Thanks." She barely glanced at him. "It's in the hall closet just inside the front door."

Once they'd finished cleaning up, Jared returned the vacuum to the closet and went back to the kitchen. Marissa had her back to him, fussing with something on the counter.

"Okay," he said. "Let me have it. I know you're upset with me for paying your boyfriend a visit and I don't blame you. I shouldn't have done that and I apologize."

Slowly, she turned. Her carefully blank expression told him how hard she was working to keep her emotions under control, which meant she had to be really, really angry. Furious, even. The Marissa he knew had always been expressive. She'd never been afraid to show her feelings. And judging by the way she'd lit into him earlier in her clinic, that hadn't changed.

He swallowed hard, bracing himself.

"Why?" she asked, meeting and holding his gaze. "Why would you think it's okay to do such a thing?" Then, before he could answer, she continued. "Jared, you need to get one thing straight. Yes, we've known each other a long time. And yes, we were high school and part of college sweethearts. But all that is over. You're my patient now. Nothing more. I'd hoped we might even be able to become friends, but with you acting like this, I don't think it's going to work."

All he could do was speak the truth. "I went to talk to David because I wanted to make sure you're protected. I'm worried, Marissa. I don't like the idea of someone stalking you. It terrifies me to think of a possibility where an intruder breaks in when you're home." He took a deep breath, willing himself to steady his voice. "I wanted to protect you. And, as you've pointed out, I don't have the right. That's why I went to the one man who does. David." He didn't have the heart to point out that her boyfriend had appeared supremely unconcerned. He figured she'd find that out for herself.

Her expression softened. "I do appreciate your concern," she said, moving closer. "But I've been taking care of myself for years now. That's why I bought all these cameras and am having a security system installed tomorrow."

Gazing down at her upturned face, trying not to think about how kissable her soft mouth appeared, he found himself at a loss for words.

As if she knew, she took a step closer.

And then, she wound her arms around his back and pulled him down to her. Parting her lips, she raised herself up and met him halfway. Heat arced through him as his mouth covered hers. Hungry, so damn hungry. The feel of her soft body pressed up against him shattered his equilibrium,

Searing, burning, aching need consumed him. Pounding in his blood, his entire body electrified. Marissa. Marissa. All he'd ever wanted, even if he'd been too stupid to realize it.

They broke apart finally, though she continued to hold on to him, her uneven breathing warm against his neck. "I'm sorry," she mumbled. "I shouldn't have done that."

He decided not to tell her he was glad she had. Instead, he relished the way they still fit together, aware she could feel the strength of his arousal pressed against her. He'd do anything for her, he wanted to say. But he knew that would only make her pull away from him, both physically and emotionally. And he knew instinctively that getting close to Marissa was something he'd need to take slow.

With this is mind, he gently disengaged himself from her and turned away. He needed a few moments to get his body under control.

Marissa must have understood this, because she kept her distance and her silence. Part of him couldn't help but hope she'd come up behind him, spin him around and kiss him again. Realistically, he knew that wasn't likely to happen, but he could only dream.

Unfortunately, thinking like that didn't do a damn thing to get his raging hard-on under control. In fact, though he knew walking would be difficult, he figured his best bet would be to leave.

"I've got to go." He swallowed, glancing over his shoulder at her as he made his way awkwardly toward the door.

She looked up and met his gaze. The longing she didn't quite manage to hide nearly stopped him in his tracks.

"Take care," she murmured. "I'll see you at PT tomorrow."

At least she hadn't fired him as her client. Taking comfort in this small blessing, he let himself out.

IT TOOK EVERY ounce of self-control Marissa possessed not to run after Jared. Fists clenched, she didn't even dare to watch him go, though she regained enough self-possession to lock up after he'd left.

Once she'd engaged the dead bolt, she leaned against the back side of the door, trying not to cry.

Damn, she wanted him. Wanted him in a way that David had never been able to inspire in her. She craved him with every beat of her heart, every breath she took, so much so that her insides quivered.

That much had clearly not changed.

Shaking, she battled to get herself under control. It didn't help knowing Jared had to do the exact same thing. Feeling the strength and power of his arousal pressing against her had nearly been her undoing. A rush of desire had overwhelmed her, and all she could think about was how badly she wanted to feel him inside her.

She was in trouble. Big trouble.

Meow. Roxy jumped up on the counter, eyeing her inquisitively. Glad to have something else to focus on, Marissa nearly laughed out loud with relief as she scooped her cat up. "Were you a bad girl today, Rox?" she crooned. "I saw what you did."

In response, her unrepentant cat nuzzled her. Marissa gave her sweet little feline a kiss on the top of her head.

"I'm just glad you knew to hide when that intruder was inside the house. I can replace any of my belongings, but I definitely can't replace you."

Roxy meowed again, sounding her agreement.

Carrying her cat into the living room, Marissa settled down onto the couch and turned on the TV. Maybe some mindless entertainment could help her keep her thoughts from going where they didn't need to go. But despite her best attempt to focus elsewhere, all she could think about was Jared and that earth-shattering kiss.

Before she went to bed, Marissa double-checked her locks and even went so far as to push kitchen chairs under the front and back doors as an extra level of security. She hated feeling fearful in her own home. She wasn't sure what the intruder had been after, since as far as she could tell, absolutely nothing had been taken. This somehow made the break-in feel more ominous. Especially since she knew someone had been watching her. The big question was why.

The next morning when she got up, she felt as if she hadn't gotten any sleep at all. The dark circles under her eyes attested to that truth also. A shower and two cups of strong coffee helped somewhat. When she did her makeup, she had to use her best concealer. Since Jared would be her first client of the day, she wanted to be wide-awake with all her guards up. At least she had his itinerary of exercises already printed out, so he'd require minimal interaction.

Rayna called just as Marissa was about to head over to her clinic. "Parker asked me to call you. He's going to stop by first thing this morning and start installing everything. Will that work for you?"

"Oh, yes," Marissa replied. "The sooner the better. I was

so worried that I put chairs under the doorknobs last night. Needless to say, I didn't sleep well either."

"You poor thing. You'll feel much more secure by tonight."

"I can't thank you enough." Marissa sighed. "I've also got an alarm company coming by this morning to put in the keypad and window and door sensors. Tell Parker to stop by my clinic and I'll give him the keys to the house. I'd rather he start there."

"Will do," Rayna replied.

"How'd it go last night when you shared your news with your mom and daughter?" Marissa asked. "I bet they were thrilled."

"They were!" Rayna's smile came through over the phone. "And I plan to tell my deputies as soon as I get to work. After that, the gossip should be all over town."

Marissa laughed. "I've got to go open up the clinic. I'll talk to you later."

After ending the call, Marissa double-checked to make sure her back door was locked. As she let herself out, she once again had the sense of being watched. She turned slowly, scanning the street. There were a few cars parked at the curb in front of nearby houses, but she wasn't sure which ones belonged to what neighbors. She also couldn't tell if any of them had people inside. She figured at least one of them did.

In order to better document what she saw, she got out her phone, opened her camera and quickly began taking pictures. As soon as she'd finished, she hurried over to the clinic, unlocked the front door and stepped inside.

She flicked on the lights. Everything appeared exactly the same as it had when she'd last left, yet she couldn't shake the feeling that something was out of place. She checked all of the windows, making sure none were unlocked, and found everything secure. Which meant there was no way anyone could have been inside the clinic. Since she had the only key, she figured she was just feeling paranoid.

Pushing these thoughts away, she hurried around getting everything ready. Jared, her first patient of the day, would be there soon and she wanted everything to be as professional as possible. Especially since she couldn't seem to stop thinking about that kiss...

Though she didn't open for another fifteen minutes, someone tried to open the front door. She froze, before gently reminding herself that she usually kept the door unlocked once she'd arrived for work.

Three sharp knocks let her know someone wanted in. Probably Jared, she guessed, though he'd be a bit early. But when she went to open the door, Rayna's husband, Parker, stood on her doorstep.

At first glance, the large tattooed man might seem frightening to those who didn't know him. But Marissa privately called him the gentle giant, and she'd seen firsthand how much he adored his wife and stepdaughter. Well-liked in their small town, Parker ran his own very successful auto-customization shop. He was so talented that people brought their vehicles from all over the country. Rayna beamed with pride whenever one of his creations won an award in an auto show or appeared in a magazine or on television.

"Mornin', Marissa," Parker drawled, pulling her in for a quick hug. "Are you ready to get started?"

Before she could respond, she heard someone clear their throat from behind Parker. Marissa peeked around and saw

Jared standing on the front step, arms crossed and frowning, clearly unsure what to make of the situation.

For whatever reason, she found his expression amusing.

"Jared, you're early," she said, keeping her voice cheerful as she moved around Parker. "Come on in. Have you met Parker Norton?"

Just like that, Jared's frown vanished. "Rayna's husband?" He stuck out his hand. "I'm Jared Miller. Pleased to meet you."

The two men shook.

"Jared, why don't you have a seat and I'll get you started on your therapy in a few minutes?" Marissa said. "I need to show Parker a few things at the house."

"I'm installing video cameras and new door locks," Parker elaborated, grinning. "If you feel up to it once you finish your therapy session, I could always use some help."

Jared grinned right back. "I'll be there as soon as I get done."

After leaving Parker with all the stuff she'd purchased with Rayna's guidance, Marissa returned to the clinic. To her surprise, Jared had gotten started without her.

"I figured I'd at least get warmed up," he explained.

"Good idea." She kept her tone brisk, trying not to focus on his mouth.

"I'm glad to finally meet Rayna's husband," he continued. "I've heard about him, of course. I've even read about him in one of the classic-car magazines. He's pretty famous in those circles."

Trying to keep the conversation on track, she showed him his first few exercises in the progression she wanted him to take. "These are a little different. The first one is designed to loosen up your joint. The others are to work on gradually strengthening it. I want you to take it slow and if you feel pain, don't press through it. Just stop and we'll move on to the next exercise."

Studying the paper, he shrugged. "What if I want to push hard? I'd like to get back to normal as soon as possible."

"Some things can't be rushed. These are exercises you'll work on over and over during the course of your physical therapy. Your goal is improvement, so don't feel you have to be able to do everything right away."

Though he nodded, the stubborn set of his chin told her he actually felt otherwise.

"I'm serious," she said, lightly squeezing his shoulder, just like she would any other client. "While there are some situations in life where you should try to push through the pain, rehab isn't one of them."

When he nodded, she smiled and moved away. "I'll leave you to it. I'll be right over here if you have any questions."

She could swear she felt his gaze burning into her back as she walked off. Probably her imagination, she told herself. That dang kiss had made her jumpy.

Jared spent the next hour diligently focused on performing the exercises she'd given him. Marissa stopped to check on him every ten minutes or so, correcting his range of motion here and there. She had him rest in between, handing him a bottled water and reminding him to take it slow.

Perspiring, he accepted the water and drank. Her gaze followed the movement of his throat and her mouth went dry.

"I'm frustrated that such simple movements are now so difficult," he admitted.

"I noticed." She sat down on a rolling stool next to him. "Most people do get impatient. That's normal."

"Is it?" He gave her a wry smile. "I wouldn't know. All

these movements used to be easy, things I did without even thinking about it. Now…"

"It's a struggle," she finished for him. "But look at what your body has been through. Injury and surgery and now you've got to work a little to get back to the way you were before the injury happened."

As she leaned close, intending to adjust the band he was using, something changed. She'd never been a fanciful person, but she honestly felt as if a spark had passed between them, settling low in her breastbone and smoldering. Heat, now a tangible thing, made her sway toward him. One second, one inch closer, and she'd claim his mouth again, allowing passion to overtake them both, the way it had before.

Chapter Six

Jared inhaled, aware they were about to kiss. He understood the importance of letting her make the first move. He froze, not wanting to spook her, yearning for the crush of her mouth on his with every fiber of his being.

And then, as she drew close enough for him to feel the warmth of her breath tickle his face, she withdrew.

Clearly flustered, she muttered something about ethics with a client and rushed away.

He stared after her, feeling her absence like a punch in the gut. Then, exhaling deeply, he forced himself to go back to the workout, aware his appointment time for today was almost over.

Today had been a day of constant surprises. When he'd first arrived, seeing Marissa all wrapped up in an embrace with the big biker had really rattled him. He'd been shocked by the intensity of the flash of jealousy that had hit him. Then, once he'd learned she'd been hugging Parker Norton, Rayna's husband, he'd felt like an absolute idiot. Luckily, he didn't think Marissa or Parker had realized.

Still, it might have been only his imagination, but the entire time he'd been there, the atmosphere had felt electrified, full of potential.

Keeping his attention on doing the workouts helped keep him from focusing on how badly he wanted her. The incredible moment they'd shared yesterday had proved that what they'd once had hadn't died. If anything...

No. He wouldn't allow his thoughts to go down that path.

When he'd finally finished, he pushed to his feet. Marissa reappeared and handed him some printouts of the exercises he'd just done. Her expression remote, she'd asked him to promise to do them at home in between sessions with her.

Dutifully, he took the papers and said he would.

"Perfect." She flashed a brisk, utterly fake smile. "Your next appointment will be for the same time on Friday. Will that work for you? This Thursday is fully booked."

"Yes, Friday is fine." Matching her smile for smile, he glanced down at the papers, all the while aching to pull her into his arms. Instead, he turned around and forced himself to head for the exit.

Outside, he exhaled, stopping for a moment to get himself together. Then he headed down the sidewalk toward Marissa's house. He found Parker outside near the back door, standing on a ladder, installing a black video camera.

"Hey there," Parker said cheerfully. "You're just in time. She wants these all around the exterior of both the house and the clinic."

"How can I help?" Jared asked.

"Well, since I'm doing the cameras, would you mind putting in the new exterior locks? They're on the kitchen counter in a bag. Rayna picked them out. She says they're the best out there."

"No problem."

"She also sent me over with new screws," Parker continued. "Really long ones. She says that makes it nearly impossible to break in."

"Makes sense." Glad he didn't have to engage in a long, drawn-out conversation, Jared went into the house to gather up what he needed. When he returned, deciding to start with the front door, Parker gave him a thumbs up.

"Marissa put her cat in her bedroom and closed the door," Parker said. "That way she doesn't have to worry about Roxy getting out if we leave any doors open."

Since leaving the front door open while he worked was exactly what Jared intended to do, he appreciated that. He'd hate to have to explain to Marissa that he'd accidentally lost her cat.

With the birds chirping in the trees and a pleasant breeze ruffling his hair, Jared's mood improved greatly.

The two men worked silently, though Parker whistled while he worked. With Marissa's front door open, Jared removed the old lock and dead bolt and got busy putting in the new. He had to admit, the ones Rayna had selected were well made and sturdy.

Parker finished putting up the camera and began running a test. "I've got four more to install," he said. "I figured I'd bring them online one at a time. That way if there's any kind of issue, I know which camera is causing it."

"Good thinking."

Jared finished with the front and back door locks on the house. "Did she want me to do the business now, too?" he asked Parker.

"I'm not sure," Parker replied. "Maybe not, since she has clients. Can you come back after she's finished for the day?"

Jared thought of his father and shook his head. "I can't. Maybe in the morning. I'll check with Marissa and see if I can come by and install them before she opens up at nine tomorrow."

"Sounds good," Parker said. "Hey, do you want to go grab something to eat? It's just about lunchtime and I'm craving Pizza Perfect."

Though he knew he should head home and check on his dad, Jared was tempted. "Sure," he finally said. "Let me call my father and see if he wants me to bring home a pizza for him."

"Or we can swing by your place and pick him up," Parker offered. "I've only met him briefly a few times and he seems like a good guy."

Surprised, Jared stopped and considered. "The ranch is about twenty minutes outside of town. It's a bit out of the way. But I appreciate you thinking of him."

"You're going home next, right?" Parker asked. Something in his expression, maybe the hint of compassion in his eyes, told Jared he likely had an inkling about what was going on.

"I am," Jared answered.

"How about we order ahead, pick up a large supreme to go, and take it out to eat at your place? We can surprise your dad."

Humbled and grateful, Jared eyed the other man. "I'm sure he'd love that," he said. "I should tell you, my father has been diagnosed with early-onset dementia. Right now, he's okay if left alone for short periods of time, but I have to be careful. I don't want anything to happen to him."

"I get that." Parker clapped a hand on Jared's shoulder. "And I've heard a few things about his troubles. Let me get the order in now. By the time we get to Pizza Perfect, it should almost be ready."

While Parker phoned in the order, Jared called his dad. After seven rings, the call went to voice mail. Telling himself not to worry, Jared tried again. Still no answer.

Alarm coiling in the pit of his stomach, Jared shoved his phone back into his pocket.

"Pizza ordered," Parker said. Then, apparently catching sight of Jared's expression, he frowned. "Is everything all right?"

"I'm not sure," Jared replied slowly. "Would you mind just meeting me at the ranch after you pick up the pizza? I can give you the money for my part. I really need to check on my dad."

"Sure, no problem." Parker waved away Jared's attempt to hand him a twenty. "My treat. You can get the next one."

"Thanks. What's your number? I'll text you my address."

Parker read off the digits and Jared set him up as a contact. Then he sent a quick text before sprinting for his truck. He could only hope his father was okay. If the older man had gotten into some kind of trouble, Jared would either have to look into hiring a part-time companion, or taking his dad with him everywhere he went.

He drove as fast as he dared, slowing a bit out of necessity when he hit the gravel road. Still, he had to fight to keep his truck from going sideways as he took a turn too fast. He made it back to the ranch in just over fifteen minutes instead of the usual twenty.

Parking, he ran for the house, hollering for his dad as he went. Nothing but quiet greeted him. The kitchen—empty. Same for the rest of the house, including his father's bedroom.

Breathing fast, heart racing, Jared headed for the barn. Only the horses looked up when he entered, and he saw no sign that anyone else might have visited. Just in case, he called out again.

Nothing.

Calm. He needed to calm down. He inhaled and exhaled, drawing each breath out, telling himself there wasn't too much trouble his father could get into out here on the ranch. When he'd learned of the diagnosis, Jared had hidden all the keys to the ranch equipment and vehicles, so it wasn't like he had to worry about his dad driving around on a tractor or anything. The cattle were in a pasture too far away to present any kind of danger and all of the horses were still in their stalls in the barn.

Which meant his father had to be around here somewhere.

First, he checked the overgrown area that had once been the vegetable garden. Nope. Since he remembered his father had once loved to walk the pastures, checking the fence line, he headed out that way. The midafternoon sun blazed from a cloudless sky. While the true summer heat hadn't yet arrived, he could imagine an older person easily becoming dehydrated.

There. In the stock pond. Squinting into the sun, he jogged closer, trying to make out what he'd seen. The instant he did, panic flashed through him. A cowboy hat floating on the surface of the water. He froze, heart in his throat. "Dad?" he called, trying not to consider the worst. "Dad?"

No response but silence. Then, just as Jared was trying to come to grips with the idea that is father might have drowned, the older man popped up from underneath, spraying water like a young kid, splashing, grinning from ear to ear.

"Hey there!" his dad shouted when he caught sight of

Jared, waving madly. "I went for a swim. The weather's perfect for it. Want to join me?"

"Not right now," Jared called back, trying to slow his pounding heartbeat. "A friend of mine is bringing over a large pizza for lunch. Why don't you come out and dry off so we can eat. And—" he pointed "—get your hat."

"Okay." Standing up, the senior Mr. Miller grabbed the hat before he walked out of the murky water, buck naked and completely unashamed.

Jared looked around, but saw no towel or even clothing, for that matter. "Where are your clothes?" he asked.

"I didn't bring any." His dad chuckled gleefully. "I consider that one of the best parts about living alone in such a remote location. There's no one around to see me."

Checking his watch, Jared shook his head. "Well, there will be in a few minutes. My friend is stopping by with a pizza, remember? Let's get you back to the house and dressed before he gets here, okay?"

Trying not to wince as he watched his father walk across the pasture _____ they made it back inside before Parker arriv___ ___ ___ ared attempted to help the older man dry off, but his dad waved him away. "I can take care of myself," he growled. Then he shut himself inside of his bedroom, hopefully to put on some clothing.

After all that, Jared had the beginnings of a monster headache. His stomach growled, reminding him that he'd had nothing to eat but an energy bar and a cup of coffee.

Luckily, Parker arrived with the pizza. Jared knocked on his father's door. "The food's here," he called, and then went to let his new friend in.

"Nice place," Parker said, following Jared into the kitchen and placing the large pizza box on the table.

"Thanks." Jared knew Parker could see all the things that needed to be fixed. "I've only been back a few weeks, but I plan on getting the place fixed up little by little." He motioned. "Go ahead and have a seat. Let me grab a couple of plates."

Parker pulled out a chair and sat. After placing three paper plates and some bottled water on the table, Jared dropped into a seat across from him, careful not to take his dad's normal place at the head of the table.

He heard his father's bedroom door open and tensed up, hoping the older man had actually put on some clothes. To his relief, when his dad walked into the kitchen, he wore his usually crisp Wranglers and a long-sleeved, snap button Western shirt.

"I know you!" he exclaimed when he caught sight of Parker. "You're married to Rayna and you fix up cars in the shop of yours off Main Street."

"That's right, Mr. Miller." Parker grinned. "You have a really good memory."

Jared hid his surprise, managing to smile and nod as if this was an everyday occurrence.

"Call me J.J.," his father offered, pulling out his chair and sitting. "That pizza smells really good. Even my wife once had to admit she couldn't make pizza as good as Pizza Perfect does."

They all dug in. While he ate, Jared watched his dad devour two slices of pizza. This made him happy. "Do you want another?" he asked.

"Nope." The older man sat back in his chair, hands crossed over his stomach. "I'm full. You boys go ahead and finish it."

Parker and Jared did exactly that, making short work of downing the remaining slices.

"Where's your pretty little girlfriend?" his dad asked, staring at Jared. "Why didn't you invite her to come for lunch?"

Rather than explaining everything again, Jared shrugged. "Some people have to stay at work," he offered. "Today is a weekday after all."

Parker pushed to his feet. "Speaking of work, I need to head back to town. I've enjoyed this. Maybe we can do it again."

"I'd like that," Jared said, following him to the door. "Thanks again for the pizza."

"No problem." Parker shook his hand. "Look, I'm not trying to get up in your business, but I can see you're dealing with a lot here. Let me know if you'd like any help. Just say the word, and me and a couple of my buddies can come out and help you make some repairs."

Stunned, at first Jared wasn't sure how to respond. "Thanks," he managed, hoping Parker couldn't tell how choked up the offer had made him. "I just might do that."

"I'm serious," Parker reiterated, walking toward his truck. "That's what friends are for."

As he watched the other man drive off, Jared exhaled. He'd never been the kind of person who liked asking for help. But maybe Parker was right. Maybe it wouldn't hurt to allow himself to rely on the assistance of his friends once in a while.

SOMEHOW, MARISSA MANAGED to work with her next client, Emma June Hawthorne, although she felt as if she was on autopilot. Ms. Emma felt compelled to tease her about the two handsome studs, as she called them, who she'd seen when she arrived, acting as Marissa's personal handymen. Marissa smiled and laughed, gently getting the elderly woman's focus on the physical therapy, all the while unable to stop thinking about how she'd nearly kissed Jared right there in the middle of his session. Not only did that violate her own ethical rules of conduct, but also the APTA guide for professional conduct. She could lose her license for behavior like that.

Oddly enough, as she reflected on this knowledge, she felt a profound sense of relief. While Jared might tempt her beyond belief, she'd worked hard to get her certification and to open her own business. She wasn't about to throw any of that away for what, a fling with her old high school boyfriend? Not going to happen. So, next time she felt even remotely attracted to *her client*, she'd remember this. She had to.

Feeling settled finally, she showed Ms. Emma out and waited for her third client.

By the time lunchtime had rolled around, Marissa felt as if she'd returned to normal. She wolfed down the sandwich she'd made earlier and went outside to check on Parker and Jared.

Both men were gone, which meant they must have decided to take lunch themselves. Both relieved and disappointed, she checked out the newly installed cameras around her house and the new front door lock. Since Jared had taken the keys with him, she couldn't get inside her house, but then again, she didn't need to right that moment. The alarm company had made an appointment with a window of arrival between three and five, so as long as she had keys by then, all would be well.

She tried to call Adam to fill him in on what had happened, but the call went to voice mail. Instead of leaving a message, she decided she'd try again later.

Back at work, the afternoon passed quickly. Parker stopped by right before three to let her know they were done for the day. "All the exterior cameras outside your home are up and working. And Jared did the locks for the house. He had to get back to the ranch." He handed her the new keys. "I'll come back tomorrow to do the cameras for the clinic, though it will have to be after lunch. I've got a customer coming in with a car in the morning."

"I really appreciate this," she said. "I'll be dealing with door and window sensor installation this afternoon, once the alarm company arrives. By the time all this is done, this place will be as secure as the US Treasury."

Parker laughed. "Good." His expression turned serious. "Jared seems like a real nice guy. He seems very concerned about your safety, too."

Ignoring the implicit question in his statement, she nodded. "We're old high school friends. And, since he got hurt in a rodeo accident, he's now my physical therapy client." The *nothing more* went unsaid, though she felt sure Parker got it.

"Well, either way it's nice to have friends who care and are looking out for you." With a friendly wave, Parker ambled toward his truck.

The alarm company arrived shortly after four. Though Marissa was with a client, she broke off long enough to let them get started on the clinic first. Since there were two technicians, she hoped the process of installing door and window sensors would go quickly.

"Where do you want the keypad?" one of the men asked. Marissa pointed to a spot on the wall just inside the front door.

Needing some fresh air, she walked out to get her mail. Again, she struggled against the feeling of being watched. She looked around, noting nothing out of the ordinary. As usual, there were several vehicles parked at the curb up and down the street. Maybe she needed to start writing those down, so she'd know if any were out of the ordinary. But that seemed a level of paranoia with which she wasn't comfortable, so she discarded that idea. After all, she'd taken steps to ensure her own safety.

To her surprise, she'd just reached the sidewalk when David pulled up. Since it was only a little past six, which was highly unusual for him, she froze for a moment. Then, slightly alarmed, she hurried over to his truck.

"Hi, beautiful," he said, jumping down and pulling her close for a quick kiss.

"Is everything okay?" she asked. "You're usually still working right now."

"I know, right?" He flashed one of his devastatingly handsome grins. "Today was my day of working out in the field, driving to various ranches and taking care of livestock. I was actually able to finish up early for once. I ran home, took a quick shower and changed my clothes before coming here."

"That's amazing." She meant it, though she couldn't help but wish he'd called first. The instant she had that thought, she wondered what the heck was wrong with her? Her handsome boyfriend had gotten off work early and decided to come by and see her. She should be happy, not full of conflicting emotions.

Still…

"Isn't it?" He grinned again and pulled her close for another quick hug. He wore her favorite aftershave—the one that smelled like piney woods. "Now that I'm here, how about we go do something fun?"

Slightly confused, since David was rarely, if ever, spontaneous, she explained she had alarm company technicians working in her house and couldn't leave. "But you're welcome to hang out here if you want," she offered. "I can cook something or we can get takeout. We can still spend time together."

David actually took a step backward. "I'm sorry, but I think I'll pass. I was hoping we could go somewhere and have a beer and maybe catch a movie. I just need to…relax. I guess I should have checked with you first." He took another step toward his truck, looking more and more like a man in desperate need of a quick escape. "Sorry, Marissa. We'll get together another time."

Before she could say another word, he'd gotten back into his pickup, started the engine, waved and quickly driven away.

What the heck? Some boyfriend. Staring after him in disbelief, she realized she'd need to break up with him soon. Clearly, they weren't meant to be together. There didn't seem to be any point in dragging things out too much longer.

A second later, a pickup truck that had been parked across the street pulled out, driving in the same direction as David. Marissa stared at it, trying to see the license plate or even the make and model, but all she got was the first letter of the plate—a *U*. She couldn't tell what kind of truck.

In the end, she wasn't sure it really mattered. The timing had likely been a coincidence, anyway. She'd never been a nervous sort of person, and she hated the way she jumped at every shadow these days. If not for the break-in, it would be so easy to convince herself that this was all in her imagination. But the fact that a stranger had been in her house, her own private oasis, hammered home the point that all of this was far too real.

After grabbing her mail, she went back inside. The alarm company technicians had finished the house install and were running tests on the keypad. They showed her how to use it and then began gathering up their tools.

"I guess we're going over to the office next, right?" she asked.

Both men gave her blank stares. "I'm sorry, what?" one of them asked.

"You still have to do the install on my clinic," she pointed out. "I signed up for both."

"I'm sorry, ma'am," the technician said. "We only do residential. I'm guessing the business installation team will be contacting you to set up a date and time to do that install."

"Is there any way you can just do it now, since you're already here?" she asked.

The man had already started shaking his head before she even finished speaking. "Not only are we not authorized, but we don't actually have the equipment," he said. "You need to contact the sales office in the morning. Unfortunately, they're closed for the day."

Of course they were. Too tired to argue, she thanked the two technicians for their time and escorted them out. Once they were gone, she locked up behind them and sighed. At least, between the newly installed alarm system and the video cameras, her home was secure. While she'd definitely feel better once her clinic was, too, she decided she could rest easy that night.

The doorbell chimed. Frowning, she checked her watch, assuming the technicians had left something behind. Just in case, she checked through the peephole. Instead, she saw Jared standing on her doorstep. He appeared a bit uncertain and vulnerable, which made her heart ache.

Telling herself to cut out the foolishness, she opened the door. "Jared," she said, stepping aside and motioning him in. "What's up?"

"I just wanted to check on you," he said, dragging his hand through his hair. "Sorry, it's been a weird kind of day, but since I never made it back to install those locks for your clinic, I decided to stop by and let you know I'll try to do those in the morning."

"I appreciate that. Parker didn't get the business cameras installed yet either, so he's coming back tomorrow, too." Even now, after so many years apart, she still knew him well enough to know he was unsettled. "What's wrong, Jared?"

"It's my father." And he told her about getting home earlier and being unable to find his dad, finally locating the older man skinny-dipping in the stock pond. "I was terrified," he admitted. "I can't be with him one hundred percent of the time, but what if something happens to him on my watch?"

"Where is he right now?" she asked, frowning.

"He had a big day and it wore him out. Parker came over and brought pizza for lunch, and then he and I worked a little bit out in the barn. He ate a slice of leftover pizza for dinner and then wanted to watch TV. I made him promise to stay put and told him I'd be back in under an hour."

"Do you think he will?"

Jared smiled for the first time since he'd arrived. "When

I left, he'd fallen asleep in his recliner. Hopefully, he'll remain that way at least until I get home."

"What can I do to help?" Marissa asked, her heart going out to him. She forced herself to keep her arms at her sides, though she really ached to wrap them around him and offer comfort.

And more, if she were completely honest. With David's rejection still stinging, the idea that Jared had come to her when he needed someone to talk made her feel warm inside.

"I'm not sure," Jared replied. "But thanks for offering. Between you and Parker, it's nice to feel like I'm not alone in all this."

Startled since the Jared she'd known before had always been surrounded by friends, at first she wasn't sure how to respond. He hadn't really been back in town long enough to reconnect with too many people. But then she also realized after so many years, many of his friends had moved out or moved on. And any new ones he might have made were still likely busy on the rodeo circuit.

He looked so lost that she couldn't help but reach out to him. Instead of an embrace, she settled on placing her hand on his arm. "You're home," she said. "You'll never be alone here in Getaway."

As he gazed down at her, his expression changed. From lost and bewildered to desire. An answering flame leapt to life inside of her.

Trouble, she knew. Yet she couldn't seem to make herself take a step back, away from him.

A loud, plaintive meow from behind her broke the spell. "Roxy!" More grateful than she could express, she turned and scooped up her cat. "I bet you're hungry. I need to feed you."

Roxy meowed again in agreement.

"Let me get that taken care of right now," she said.

When she looked up, she saw Jared eyeing her and Roxy. "She's beautiful," he said, endearing himself to her even more. "The last time I saw her, she was angry and hissed. Do you think she will let me pet her?"

"You can try. She doesn't take well to strangers, especially when she's hungry."

Moving slowly, he approached, keeping his focus on the cat. "Hey there, pretty girl," he said, his voice soft. Roxy watched him, unblinking. To Marissa's surprise, her cat showed no signs of being alarmed. Instead, Roxy remained relaxed. She allowed Jared to pet her, even going so far as to loudly purr.

"She likes you," Marissa said.

Her comment made him laugh. "You sound surprised."

"I am. She hisses any time David tries to come near her."

Jared shook his head. "That's probably because she knows he's her veterinarian and has given her shots before."

Such a generous thing to say. And probably accurate, though she hadn't considered that as a reason before. David hadn't seemed bothered by Roxy's attitude and she'd assumed it was because he dealt with animals all day long.

David. She almost made a face. "I need to feed her," she said. "I appreciate you stopping by."

Luckily, he took the hint. "Right. I'm glad you're okay. I'll see you in the morning when I come by to install the locks."

"Sounds good." She didn't trust herself to look at him as she let him out. Once she'd locked the door behind him, she went to feed Roxy and hopefully spend the rest of the night watching mindless TV.

Her phone rang. Adam.

"Hey, I saw you'd called," he said. "What's up?"

She filled him in on all her latest drama, relieved to have her best friend to share with. He gasped at all the right points in her story and when she'd finished, he told her in a fierce voice that she'd better call him right away if anything like that happened again.

This made her laugh. Adam meant well, but he often said he was a lover, not a fighter. Still, she promised she would, and they ended the call.

Halfway through one of her favorite reality shows, she began to mindlessly scroll social media. A photo of David inside a dark bar stopped her short. He and a slender blonde woman had their arms around each other and were locked in what appeared to be a very passionate kiss. Someone else had posted the pic and tagged him, though not the woman.

Oddly enough, she felt like crying. All along, they hadn't even discussed being exclusive, so she wasn't actually surprised. Still, seeing this stung, especially since he'd earlier rejected spending time with her.

The decision to break up with him appeared to be the right one. Resolutely, she took a screenshot and saved it to her photos. Then she went back to trying to watch her show, all the while itching to call him and end things now, while anger still fueled her.

Chapter Seven

Once he left Marissa's house, Jared drove home slowly, trying to regain his composure. He'd nearly kissed her again. If her cat hadn't meowed and broken the spell, who knew what might have happened?

His body had a pretty good idea. Aroused and aching, he knew he needed to get himself under control before he returned home. Though it seemed likely his father would still be asleep, on the off chance he wasn't, Jared knew the older man's sharp gaze would miss nothing.

By the time he'd reached the ranch, he felt relatively normal.

Inside, with the television blaring, his father still slept, occasionally letting out a raspy snore. Jared stood and watched him for a moment, his heart full of love. Life had not been kind to the older man. He'd worked hard, keeping the ranch going for years, only to be felled early by an illness with no cure. At sixty-four, his father was too young to go through something like this. Jared would give anything to be able to fix it, to ensure his dad could enjoy his later years without complications.

Moving quietly past, Jared went to the kitchen and

grabbed a beer. He took it to his room, intending to watch some television himself before turning in for the night.

Jared made his father come into Getaway with him the next morning. He'd gotten more and more nervous about leaving the older man alone at the ranch, and after he finished installing Marissa's locks, they needed a few things from town.

The instant they hit Main Street, his father pointed. "I want to see Serenity," he said. "I want to ask her if she has any messages from your mother."

Jared glanced sideways, careful not to show his surprise. His father had never been a big believer in mediums or psychics or any of the things Serenity Rune did or sold in her shop. Though she'd been kind enough to detain him the last time he'd wandered away from his friends, Jared wasn't sure if she'd be okay with babysitting the older man once again.

Still, it wouldn't hurt to stop by and say hello. Plus, any visit, no matter how brief, would appease his father.

Pulling into a parking spot right in front of Serenity's shop, Jared jumped out and went around to the passenger side to assist his dad. But the older man frowned and waved him away. "I'm not an invalid," he growled, pushing past Jared to enter Serenity's shop, sending the bells over the door tinkling furiously.

Jared followed, trying not to cough at the heavy smell of incense inside. The scent didn't appear to bother his father, though after the initial charge inside, the older man planted his feet and stood in the middle of the store, glancing from left to right and frowning.

"Serenity!" he bellowed. "It's J.J. Where are you?"

Serenity rushed out from the back, her normally serene expression registering concern. Some of the worry left her face when she spotted Jared, standing a few feet behind his father.

"I'm sorry," Jared mouthed. Hopefully, this wouldn't take too long. Otherwise, he'd need to text Marissa and let her know he was running late. Since he'd planned to park his father in her waiting room, earlier would definitely have been better.

Serenity gave a quick nod before returning all of her attention to his dad. "J.J.! It's so good to see you again. Are you here to shop or just visit?"

"I want you to tell my son's fortune," he replied, jerking his thumb over his shoulder toward Jared. "Or channel his spirit guide or whatever. I think he could use some unbiased advice."

You could have knocked Jared over with a feather. He froze, not sure how to react or how to respond. Hearing his father say such a thing was completely out of character. For as long as he could remember, the senior Miller had claimed mediums and psychics were fake. He'd lumped Serenity in the same category as those he called charlatans and scammers. And now he wanted Serenity to do a reading for his son?

"Dad, I think Serenity only does those by appointment," Jared pointed out gently, gesturing toward a large sign on the wall stating exactly that. "Maybe we can schedule something and come back, okay?" Even though he definitely had no intention of ever doing so.

"No." His father crossed his arms and glared at him, before returning his attention to Serenity. "You're not busy right now, are you? Can you do this now?"

Slowly glancing from Jared to his father, finally Serenity

shrugged. "Only if Jared wants me to. I don't do readings for people against their will."

Putting the ball squarely back in his court. Jared shifted his weight from one foot to the other while both Serenity and his dad eyed him. While he really didn't want a psychic reading, he hated to quash the hope and expectation in his father's face. For whatever reason, the older man appeared really into this idea.

"What harm can it do?" Jared finally said, giving in. "Serenity, if you're sure you have time, let's go ahead and do this."

Serenity spun, almost in slow motion, sending her glittery skirt billowing in a circle around her. Her numerous bracelets made a jangling sound and for one second, Jared almost found himself believing.

Almost.

But in the end, humoring his father was one thing. Taking all this metaphysical nonsense seriously was another.

"You two come with me," Serenity said. "I do my readings in the back, where we can have privacy."

Once they arrived in the back, Serenity gestured at her little table. "Jared, you sit here. J.J., you can take a seat over there. If you want to be present, I will have to ask that you remain completely silent. You cannot interrupt or comment on what comes through to me. Do you understand?"

"Sure," J.J. replied, lowering himself into a chair close to the wall. "This is going to be interesting."

Not sure why his dad was so keen on all this, Jared shrugged and took a seat. Serenity went over to some shelves in one corner and returned with a large, glass ball. She placed this reverently in the middle of the table and then sat down.

A crystal ball. Jared managed to not roll his eyes. While no one had mentioned cost, he'd seen the rate posted on one of Serenity's signs. He figured for that amount of money, she wanted to make sure and put on a good show.

"Place both of your hands, palms down, on the table," she ordered. Once Jared had complied, she stared at him for a moment before giving the crystal ball all of her attention. The longer the silence stretched on, the more Jared found himself leaning forward, trying to see what she found so fascinating in its murky depths.

Finally, after what felt like an eternity, Serenity raised her head. Her silver and multicolored stone earrings swung as she tilted her head from side to side. Something had changed in her, Jared thought. Her dark eyes glittered and for a moment, she seemed much older. Then, her expression settled and she leaned back in her chair, still studying him.

Jared's father could scarcely contain himself. Despite his earlier promise to remain silent, he cleared his throat. "Well?" he demanded. "Tell us what you saw."

Both Serenity and Jared ignored him. "You believe you already know what I'm going to say, don't you?"

Since he saw no point in denial, Jared nodded.

"You're a good man," Serenity said. "And yes, you do have a choice to make, but I see you've already made it. But listen carefully. Someone you love is in danger. This is real, not imagined, and comes from a completely unexpected place. I wasn't shown where, or I would try to reveal that information to you. But your job is to protect and keep safe, without suffocating. Do you think you can do that?"

Was she talking about his father or about Marissa? Though Jared wanted to ask, he couldn't with his dad sitting right there. Maybe he could come back later and request specifics, assuming Serenity would give them.

"Do you think you can do that?" Serenity repeated. "This is very important."

"Yes, of course, I can do that," Jared replied, allowing some of his impatience to show. "But I'll need you to give me a little more information, if you don't mind."

"Choose love, no matter what," she said with a gentle smile. "If you do that, and stay vigilant against the darkness, you will find happiness."

Generic gobbledygook. Exactly as he'd expected. A complete waste of money. Careful to keep his expression neutral, Jared nodded. "Thanks, Serenity." He dug his wallet out of his back pocket and placed fifty dollars on the table. "It's been fun, but now we've got to get going."

"Wait," his father said, pushing up out of the chair. "You didn't actually tell him anything useful."

While Jared agreed with his father completely, he also didn't want to offend Serenity. "Dad, it's okay," he said. "She did the best she could. Come on, let's go."

Jaw set stubbornly, the elder Miller refused to move. "No. Serenity, you can do better. I know you can. Who is in danger and why? If it involves my son, he has a right to know."

Serenity stood, for the first time allowing a flash of exasperation to ripple across her usually implacable face. "I've told him everything I can. It's not like using a search engine on the internet. What I'm given is limited, and specific only to the person who is getting the reading."

"I understand," he said, even though he didn't. "We need to go. I promised Marissa I'd install new locks for her at the clinic."

Serenity's gaze sharpened. "New locks. I see. Then maybe she's the one who's in danger."

He didn't want to fill her in on the break-in, since that wasn't his story to tell, so he nodded instead. "Maybe so. You have a nice day," he said, and then ushered his father out the door.

His dad waited until they were inside the pickup before speaking. "Is Marissa in trouble, son?"

While he didn't want to worry his father, he also wasn't going to lie. "Maybe a little," he admitted. "She's been feeling like someone is watching her. And then her house was broken into. Now she's had an alarm system installed, plus video cameras, and all new locks on her house. I still need to put in the new ones at the clinic."

"Is that where we're going now?"

"Yep," Jared replied. "I promise it won't take too long. I figure you can just sit in her waiting room and read a magazine or something."

"Or I can help you," the older man said. "I do know how to change out locks you know."

"I realize that." Jared kept his tone patient. "But I promised Marissa that I would do this for her, and I'd like to keep my word."

"Ah, I see." His father's expression cleared. "You're still trying to impress her, aren't you?"

"I'm trying to help her. That's all."

They pulled up in front of the clinic. Since they'd arrived later than Jared had hoped, Marissa already had a client. Which should be fine. Jared didn't plan to disturb anyone. He needed to get those locks taken care of and then go finish up running his errands.

Once he'd gotten his father settled in the waiting area

with instructions not to disrupt Marissa's therapy session, Jared started working on the front door. For whatever reason, everything clicked into place and he'd finished within ten minutes.

He'd just started on the back door when his cell phone rang. Caller ID showed it was Jared's friend Custer Black.

"I'm in town," Custer said, after they'd exchanged the usual greetings. "I just got in a few nights ago. Remember I told you that my knee has been acting up? Well, it got so bad I can barely walk. I had to cut the rest of my season short. So I'm back here with the parents, hoping to rest up."

"I'm sorry to hear that," Jared said, meaning it. "But it'll be great to see you. We can catch up on old times."

"Yeah, I'd like that." Custer paused for a moment. "Are you still doing your physical therapy with Marissa?"

"I am. And I'm taking things slow, but keeping up with all the exercises. So far there's a lot less pain."

"Good, good."

"Are you going to start physical therapy for your knee?" Jared asked.

"Maybe. I heard about a guy in Midland who's supposed to be really great. I might try him instead."

Surprised, Jared decided not to comment.

"Actually, you might consider switching, too," Custer continued. "Now that I think about it, I kind of believe that Marissa did more harm than good. I'm worse now than I was before I ever went to see her."

Glancing back at Marissa, who was still working with her client, Jared made a noncommittal sound.

"Maybe it's just me," Custer said, backtracking a little. "I could be the one who messed this up. I wasn't as diligent in doing the home exercises as I could have been."

"It's all good," Jared replied, wanting to get off the phone. "How about we meet up for a beer sometime?"

"Perfect. Does seven tonight at The Rattlesnake work for you?"

Jared glanced at his father, still leafing through a magazine. "I think so. I'll see you then."

After Custer hung up, Jared had to wonder. Did his friend have an ax to grind with Marissa? Was it possible he was behind the brick and the break-in?

But Custer hadn't been in town very long. Marissa had said she'd felt like she was being watched for a few weeks now. Plus, Jared knew Custer. The bronco rider didn't have a malicious bone in his body. No way would he ever have done something like this. It had to be someone else.

But who?

THAT MORNING, NOTHING had gone right for Marissa. Her anger the night before had kept her tossing and turning all night, and she'd forgotten to set her phone alarm, so she'd overslept. When Roxy's hungry meowing had startled her awake, she'd had that heart-pounding sensation of panic, realizing the time.

Rushing around, she'd luckily not only made it to the clinic before her first client arrived, but also before Jared showed up to install the locks.

Unlocking the front door, she saw someone had shoved an envelope into her mail slot. She barely had time to glance at it, carrying it back to her office and dropping it onto her desk before rushing to get a pot of coffee started. Her first client arrived shortly after she'd taken her first sip, and she got busy with work. Then Jared arrived with his father in tow, and the older man watched her like a hawk when he thought she wasn't looking. Which meant she had to keep her gaze away from Jared while he replaced her locks.

What a tangled mess, she thought.

Jared finished the front door. She saw him talking on the phone before he got to work on the back lock.

The glass company called to let her know her new window had come in. They wanted to know if they could install it that afternoon. She agreed, figuring they could work on that at the same time as the alarm company worked on her installation. She'd called them, too, and they'd apologized for the snafu. They were sending someone out to take care of getting her office all set up.

Maybe once all this had been done, she could stop worrying. She didn't know why someone was out to get her, but she didn't like the feeling of being stalked.

Almost all of her clients resided here in Getaway and she'd never had a single complaint about her business. If someone was unhappy, they hadn't come to her about it.

At least she felt as if she was being proactive and doing something to protect herself. Once both alarm systems were in, combined with her new locks and video cameras, she'd definitely feel a lot safer.

When she finally made it back to her office, it was nearly lunchtime. She spotted the envelope on the desk and picked it up. It hadn't come through the mail, since it had no stamp. Probably someone had been going door to door passing out advertisements or other junk mail, especially since her name had been typed neatly across the front.

Opening it, she extracted a single piece of folded paper.

You need to close up shop and leave town. Frauds like you can't fix anyone. All you do is take people's money and entice men with your fake charm. Go away!

What the… She read it a second time, trying to process the words. A disgruntled client? Since she'd never received a single complaint, she had no idea.

Just in case this might have something to do with the brick and the break-in, she took a photo with her phone and texted it to Rayna, along with an explanation. Rayna called her a moment later, asking Marissa to hang on to that note and saying she'd swing by later to pick it up. She'd also said she intended to increase patrols around Marissa's place, just to be on the safe side. Once again, she asked Marissa if she could think of any disgruntled clients or anyone else who might have reason to be threatening her, but Marissa said she couldn't.

The entire day had been so crazy busy that Marissa didn't have time to think about David and the post she'd seen on social media. Though her pride was stung, beyond that she felt more relieved than anything else. She'd been worried David might not take it well when she broke up with him. She no longer needed to be concerned about that.

Jared called just as she'd started locking up for the day.

"Custer Black is in town," he said. "I'm meeting him for a drink at The Rattlesnake and I wondered if you'd like to join us."

"What about your father?" The instant she spoke, she regretted it. How Jared took care of his father wasn't any of her business.

"That's just it. I'm bringing him along." Instead of regretful, he sounded tired. "Custer and I have some catching up to do, but I'd much rather spend time with you."

Just as she tried to figure out what he meant by that, he clarified.

"As friends, obviously," he said. "Plus, Custer said he isn't doing too well, and I think he might benefit from your professional insight."

"What's wrong with Custer?" she asked. "When I released him from therapy, he'd regained most of his mobility and range of motion. As long as he continues with the home exercises, he shouldn't be having any problems."

"Except he is."

"Has he had another rodeo injury?" Marissa couldn't think of anything else that might have made Custer have a setback.

"I don't think so," Jared replied. "But you could ask him yourself if you come and meet us."

Intrigued, she found herself agreeing to meet them. "What about your father? Isn't it going to be difficult to keep him occupied?"

"Not really. I've called a couple of his old buddies who seemed thrilled at the idea of tossing back a beer with him. We'll just need to sit close to them so I can keep my eye on things."

"It definitely sounds as if you've thought of everything," she commented.

"Sheer necessity." He paused. "I'm looking forward to seeing you."

Her heart skipped a beat. She managed to mumble something noncommittal before ending the call.

Feeding Roxy, she tried to decide what to wear. She didn't want to dress up too much, but she wanted to look nice. In the end, she settled on a black denim skirt, ankle boots and a white, cotton, button-down shirt. Checking out her appearance in the mirror, she thought she looked good. Most importantly, she didn't appear to be trying too hard. After all, this wasn't a date.

Before heading out, she made herself a salad and ate it standing up, while scrolling through social media on her phone. Because she was human, she couldn't help but go back and look for the post she'd seen with David in it, but it was gone.

Once in her Tahoe, she backed out of her garage and tried to put herself in the right frame of mind to socialize over drinks with a former client and a current one. That was how she needed to think of Jared from now on—as a client and nothing more.

Still, she couldn't shake an unsettled feeling. Which made no sense. She'd set her new alarms and all her video cameras were operational. No one would be breaking into her house or business from now on.

Sitting in her driveway with the engine running, she glanced up and down the street. At least she didn't have that awful feeling of being watched right now. Hopefully, her stalker had realized with all the cameras and extra security measures Marissa had taken, it would be a lost cause.

Now she just needed to relax and try to enjoy the evening.

Before she could pull out into the street, her phone rang. She glanced at it and cursed under her breath. David. Declining the call, she shook her head. She'd deal with him later. Now would not be the time to have the kind of talk she needed to have with him. And she thought it might be better to have that in person rather than on the phone.

Despite knowing it would be for the best, she took no pleasure in the thought. David was a good man and she felt sure he'd make someone a wonderful husband. Just not her.

With a sigh, she shifted into drive and headed toward Main Street.

Luck seemed to be with her, as every light turned green before she approached. Crossing the train tracks, where she usually got stopped by a train, went smoothly, too. Wow. Maybe tonight would turn out to be better than expected.

She had a green light again when she reached Main Street, where she had to make a right. Slowing, she put her blinker on. Halfway into the turn, a vehicle came out of nowhere and slammed hard into her passenger side with a boom, jolting her hard and sending her Tahoe spinning. Despite her shock and pain—so much pain—Marissa kept hold of the steering wheel, fighting to maintain control.

She hit the telephone pole, anyway. Way too fast, too hard. The sickening scream of metal fighting wood matched her cry of terror. Impact, a thump. The SUV jolted and rocked sideways. She tried, damn she tried, twisting the wheel, but there wasn't anything she could do to stop what came next. It all happened so fast. No control now, nothing she could do but hang on as two wheels met air, and she rolled. Slow motion and also happening too fast. She braced herself, the seatbelt biting into her shoulder, praying she could somehow come out of this alive.

Then everything went black.

Chapter Eight

Sitting at the bar nursing a beer, Jared watched the door. Not only was Custer ten minutes late, but Marissa hadn't arrived yet either. Which was strange. Admittedly, she might have changed over the years, but for as long as he'd known her, Marissa had always been a prompt, arrive at least ten minutes early, kind of person.

He glanced over at his father, sitting with three of his friends, happily engaged in conversation. He'd taken one of the men, a retired cattle rancher named Gus Tomlinson, aside and given him a brief explanation. Then he'd extracted a promise not to let Jared's dad wander off. Gus had solemnly given his word.

One less thing for Jared to worry about. He glanced at his phone again, checking the time. No missed calls, no texts and no sign of either Marissa or Custer.

One of the other men sitting down the bar from him glanced at his phone and shot to his feet. "Bad wreck down the street," he said, telling both Jared and the bartender. "I'm one of the sheriff's deputies. Not on duty, but I'd better go see if I can help." He threw a ten dollar bill on the counter and took off running for the exit.

Jared went back to watching the door. If there'd been an

accident, the resulting traffic tie-up would definitely explain both Marissa and Custer's lateness.

He waited another ten minutes before deciding to try calling. First Marissa, who didn't answer, so he left her a message. Then Custer, who'd apparently turned his phone off as the call went straight to voice mail.

Worry snaked along his spine. Okay, this wasn't good. While he doubted either one of them had been involved in the accident, he had to make sure. Leaving his beer unfinished, Jared got up, paid and walked over to his father's group. Explaining he needed to check on something, he got Gus's phone number from him, promising to call if he ran too late, and headed out to go see. All the way toward the door, he told himself he was likely overreacting. However, it wasn't like Marissa to completely blow him off like this.

Outside, by looking left, he could see the flashing lights several blocks down the street. Not only police cruisers, but a fire truck and an ambulance. Which meant it must be really bad.

For the first time, a feeling of foreboding made the back of his neck tingle. Surely not, he told himself, pushing away the fear.

He had to get down there and check it out in person. Since it looked like they'd closed off Main Street, he decided it would be faster to go on foot. Heart pounding, he took off at a run.

As he approached the intersection, the fire engine parked in the middle of the street blocked his view. About to go around it, he stopped short when Rayna stepped out in front of him.

"Rayna!" Relieved, he tried to catch his breath. "I'm so glad to see you. What's going on here?"

When she met his gaze, her grave expression made his heart catch in his chest. "It's Marissa," she said. "She's been in an accident. It looks like whoever hit her took off."

"What?" He tried to push past her, but she stepped in front of him. "Is she okay?" he asked. And then, before Rayna could answer, he demanded that she let him see for himself.

"Not right now." Voice firm, but gentle, Rayna put her hand on is arm to detain him. "We've got people working to try and get her out of her vehicle. It's on its side. I can't let you interfere with that."

It took a moment for her words to sink in. "Get her out..." His words trailed off. "She drives a Chevy Tahoe. That thing is like a tank. What the hell happened?"

"We don't know for sure. Someone T-boned her and took off. Whatever it was, it was big enough to do a lot of damage. And it likely hit her at a high rate of speed." She took a deep breath. "Luckily, it hit the passenger side. Otherwise..."

His throat closed up. "Is she going to be okay?"

Mouth set, Rayna simply eyed him. Then, she sighed. "I hope so. She has to be. We're doing the best we can to get her out so she can receive the medical care she needs."

"Let me go see her," he demanded. "I'm strong. Maybe I can help." He didn't bother to hide his anguish. "Please."

Finally, Rayna took pity on him and stepped aside. "Stay with me," she ordered. Then, as he started forward, she grabbed his arm. "I mean it. You cannot interfere with the paramedics, no matter how badly you might want to. Understood?"

Resisting the urge to jerk himself away, he moved his head in a nod instead.

The instant Jared caught sight of the Tahoe, crumpled and lying on its side, he froze. Then, his heart pounding, he watched two men, one half-inside the wreckage, working on freeing the trapped occupant. Marissa.

Rayna tightened her grip on his arm.

"Let me go," he implored her. "I can help."

"No. They're trained professionals. You need to give them room to do their job."

Watching them remove a clearly unconscious and bloody Marissa from the crumpled wreck of her vehicle was one of the most difficult things he ever had to do. Fists clenched at his sides, he stood locked in place. Rayna maintained her death grip on his arm.

Only once they'd loaded Marissa up in the ambulance and closed the doors did he remember to breathe. "I'm going to the hospital," he said, remembering his truck was parked at The Rattlesnake Pub.

"You're riding with me," Rayna ordered, and steered him toward her parked sheriff's car. "Come on. If we hurry we can follow the ambulance."

Even with Rayna's lights flashing and siren on, the drive passed in a blur. Jared couldn't stop seeing Marissa's bloody, battered body being pulled from her vehicle. He wasn't normally a praying man, but in the ten minutes it took to reach the hospital, he prayed more fervently than he'd ever prayed for anything in his life.

Rayna dropped him off at the ER entrance. "You go on inside," she said. "I'll be there as soon as I park the car."

Needing no second urging, he jumped out and walked as fast as he could toward the entrance, hating his limp.

Inside, he explained to the triage nurse who he was there for.

"Are you her immediate family?" she asked, after taking his name.

He lied and said yes. The question made him think of her parents, traveling the country in their motor home. At some point, someone would need to call them. Hopefully, Marissa would be well enough soon to fill them in herself.

Pacing the hospital corridor, waiting for word, Jared fought panic. He couldn't imagine a world without Marissa in it. He refused to. No matter what she actually thought of him, he realized he loved her. Loved her with every fiber of his being, with his entire heart and soul.

Suddenly, he remembered he'd left his father sitting in the pub with his buddies. Heart racing, he placed a quick call to Gus. Explaining the situation, he asked if Gus would mind taking his father home when they were done visiting. Gus readily agreed, though he said they didn't plan on finishing up any time soon. Gus then asked if Jared needed him to stay with J.J. until Jared got home. So grateful his throat ached, Jared told the other man he'd really appreciate it if he could.

Rayna came in, looking professional, capable and exhausted all at once. She crossed over to Jared and motioned to a couple of metal chairs in the waiting area. "Sit," she ordered. "I don't know how much longer I can stand on my feet."

Gracefully dropping into one of the chairs, she waited expectantly for Jared to join her. Though he felt way too restless to stay still for long, he sat. "She's still back there," he said. "I know they're being thorough, but no one has come out yet to give any kind of status update."

Rayna placed her hand on his shoulder. "She's going to

be fine, Jared. Once they get her patched up, she'll be good as new."

Rather than listing her potential injuries—who knew what she might have broken or damaged internally—he swallowed hard and nodded. "Any idea who hit her?" he asked, needing something else to think about.

"Not yet. But we're working on it. I've got people going over the accident scene with a fine-tooth comb." She glanced sideways at him, her expression grim. "We will find whoever did this. They can't hide forever. Not in this small town."

He didn't want to, but he had to ask. "Do you think this was connected to all the other stuff she had going on? Her stalker, the break-in and the threatening notes."

"Who knows," Rayna replied. "It's definitely a possibility. Or, this might have just been a horrible accident. One where the other party got scared and left the scene."

"She wouldn't have been there if I hadn't invited her to meet me at the pub," he said. "I still can't believe this happened to her."

"I know, but it's not your fault. Jared, when I talked to Marissa earlier, she couldn't think of a single person who might have a beef with her. No disgruntled clients, no enemies. I know you haven't been back in town long, but you've spent a fair bit of time with her. Do you know of anyone?"

Immediately, he thought of Custer and his complaints. Custer, who also hadn't shown up at the bar tonight. Coincidence? Or something worse? Instinctively, he shied away from even the remote possibility that Custer could have done anything to hurt Marissa. Still, he owed it to her to give Rayna any and all information he had, even if he didn't like it.

He relayed his earlier conversation with Custer to Rayna. "It might be nothing, but he did seem to feel as if his physical therapy with Marissa did more harm than good. And he was supposed to meet me at The Rattlesnake tonight, but he never showed. I tried his phone, but the call went straight to voice mail."

Rayna frowned. "He was meeting you and Marissa?"

"Yes, though he didn't know Marissa was coming. I'm thinking he either got busy and forgot, or maybe he fell asleep. I have no idea."

"Do you know what kind of vehicle he drives?" Rayna asked.

Jared thought for a moment. "I'm not sure, but I'm thinking it's a dually. Ford, maybe."

"Which definitely would be large enough to cause major damage to Marissa's Tahoe."

Shocked, Jared winced. "You're not seriously thinking Custer would have done something like this?" he asked. "I know him well and so does Marissa. We all grew up together. He started rodeo right after I did."

"I'm not thinking anything," Rayna reassured him. "However, it's my job to consider all possibilities. A quick look at his truck will clear things up."

A doctor entered the room, wearing scrubs and an enigmatic expression. Both Jared and Rayna shot to their feet as he approached.

"Marissa is one lucky young woman," he said, smiling. "No broken bones or internal injuries. She has some cuts and scrapes and bruises, but that's about it. We're giving her some fluids and antibiotics, but she'll be able to go home soon. A nurse will let you know when you can see her."

Jared's knees nearly gave out, though he managed to keep

standing. He and Rayna both thanked the doctor, who nodded and walked off.

"She's okay," Jared repeated, finally allowing himself to drop into a chair. Unwilling to let Rayna see the emotion that threatened to overwhelm him, he covered his face with his hands.

Rayna sat down beside him and patted him on the back. "Do you want me to take you to get your truck?" she asked. "If you do, I need to make sure you're okay to drive."

He took another moment to compose himself before lifting his head and meeting her gaze. "That would be great, but I want make sure I'm here when they say we can see her."

"I understand. How about we talk to the nurse and let her know we'll be back in twenty minutes. Knowing hospitals, it'll probably be at least that long before they have her ready to discharge."

Since Jared had been in his share of ERs over the course of his rodeo career, he had to admit she was right. "Okay," he said. "Let's do it."

Rayna kept up a steady stream of chatter on the drive back toward Main Street, saving him from having to make conversation. Grateful, he gave her a quick hug when she'd parked by his truck, and thanked her. After he got out, he unlocked his own doors and climbed up inside. Taking several deep breaths, he started the drive back toward the hospital.

Once again in the waiting room, this time alone, Jared was glad he'd had the time driving to get his act together. Though still shaken, he felt more like himself, centered and ready to help her for whatever she needed. When he finally saw Marissa, he didn't want her to see how badly this had shaken him.

The nurse came out five minutes after his return. "Are you ready to go back?" she asked. Trying not to appear overly eager, he nodded and stood.

"She's definitely ready to go home," the nurse commented as they walked down the hall. "She's told me so several times. Now, I should warn you, she's pretty banged up. But overall, she's a very lucky woman. It could have been so much worse."

When they reached room number eight, the nurse left him. "The doctor has signed off on the discharge papers, so I'm going to get all that together."

He took a deep breath before he walked into the room. Marissa looked up when he entered, her bruised and battered face swollen. "Jared?" She appeared surprised. "I thought Rayna was coming to get me."

"I asked to drive you home," he said gently. "I hope that's all right with you."

"Sure." She looked down at her hands. "Somehow, my phone battery died. I don't have my charger with me. Which is probably a good thing, because I don't want to worry my parents."

Perversely, he thought of her boyfriend. "What about David?" he asked. "Do you want to borrow my phone so you can let him know what happened?"

"No thank you." The lack of emotion in her voice hinted at a story, though he figured now wasn't the best time for her to tell it.

"They did recover my purse, though." She pointed. "With my wallet and all my keys still inside. So at least I don't have to worry about replacing any of that."

He carefully lowered himself onto the bed next to her. "How are you feeling?"

"About as bad as I look," she shot back. "Did they catch whoever hit me?"

"Not yet. I'm sure they will. Like Rayna said, Getaway is a small town. Whoever hit you won't be able to hide a vehicle with that much damage."

"Unless they were only passing through," she pointed out.

The nurse came in with the paperwork just then. She looked at Jared. "Sir, why don't you go get your vehicle and pull it around to the entrance. I'll bring your wife out in a wheelchair in just a minute."

Jared stood, not bothering to correct her. "I'll do that," he answered, and left the room quickly, so he didn't have to hear Marissa update the nurse, insisting he was only a friend.

MARISSA FORCED HERSELF to keep her attention on the discharge papers, rather than watching Jared limp away. She had noticed a small improvement in his gait, likely due to the exercises she'd prescribed him, but it wasn't enough to comment on yet.

"Sign here." Smiling, the nurse pointed. "You must be so ready to go home and let that handsome husband of yours pamper you."

For whatever reason, Marissa didn't correct her. In the scheme of things, it didn't really matter who Jared was or wasn't.

She allowed herself to be helped into the wheelchair. "Is this really necessary?" she asked. "I'm sure I can walk."

"It's a safety protocol," the nurse answered, still smiling. "Once you're at home, you can walk all you want."

When they reached the automatic doors, Marissa's heart skipped a beat at the sight of Jared's pickup. As he rushed around to open the passenger door and the nurse helped her up, she battled a wave of pure panic. Somehow, she managed to get up into the passenger seat and buckle herself in after the nurse closed the door. Yet she felt frozen, unable to move, breaking out into a cold sweat and feeling dizzy.

Jared got in and glanced at her. "Are you okay?"

Jaw clenched, she twisted her hands in her lap. "Not really. I'm having some sort of panic attack. No idea why."

Pulling away from the ER entrance, he parked. "You've just been in a car accident. Cut yourself some slack. We'll sit here until you feel safe enough for me to drive you home."

More grateful than she could express, she turned her face away so he wouldn't notice that her eyes had filled with tears. "Thanks," she managed. "I'll likely need a minute or two."

He sat quietly, giving her all the time she needed. Stiff and sore, her mind as bruised as her body, she tried to convince herself that her unexpected panic was unfounded.

Except that was the thing about panic. It was rarely grounded in reality.

After a few minutes of trying deep breathing exercises, she felt slightly calmer. Maybe she could overcome this. She *would* overcome this.

Jared reached over and squeezed her shoulder, startling her and making her jump. "It's going to be fine, Marissa. Let me get you home so you can get in your own bed and rest. Close your eyes if you need to."

Her heart squeezed. "I don't need to," she said, keeping her gaze locked on his. "You drive. I'm good."

When he pulled out onto the road, she braced herself, almost as if she expected another vehicle to come out of nowhere and hit them. "That's ridiculous," she said out loud, relaying her strange fear to Jared.

"It's PTSD," he replied. "Completely normal."

More relieved than she should have been, she sighed. "Where's your dad?" she asked. "I know you said you'd found a couple of his friends for him to hang out with while you, me and Custer hung out at The Rattlesnake."

"One of his friends offered to take him home and stay with him until I get there," he replied. "And Custer never showed up. I'm not sure why. I haven't been able to get a hold of him."

"That's weird," she said. As they turned onto her street, she realized all her fear had left her and all she felt was the overwhelming heaviness of pure exhaustion.

He pulled up close to her garage and killed the engine. "Let me help you inside," he said, hopping out and coming around to the passenger side. He opened the door for her and then offered her his arm.

Glad to have his strength to rely on, she leaned heavily into him as they made their way inside. Once she'd unlocked the door, her new alarm system beeped, letting her know she needed to disarm it. She punched in the code before turning to face Jared, who waited silently just inside the entryway.

"Do you want me to stay?" he asked, gaze searching her face.

Too tired to hide her relief, she nodded. "Just for a little bit. I know you've got your father to look after."

The anguish that crossed his handsome face made her heart hurt. "Would you help me get over to the sofa?" she asked. Then, as he looped his big arm under hers, she reconsidered. "Actually, I think I'd rather go to bed."

"Which way?" he asked. Once she'd pointed, he helped

her down the hallway and into her bedroom. Held up against his muscular chest, she breathed in the still-familiar scent of him. Leather and pine, she thought, closing her eyes.

"Here?" His voice rumbled under her ear. She opened her eyes just as they reached her bed. He helped her sit on the edge and then, clearly uncomfortable, backed away. His blue eyes blazed, a mixture of desire and some other, warmer emotion.

She hadn't considered the intimacy of having him in her bedroom until that very moment. Even as a tiny spark of need kindled inside her, a wave of exhaustion swamped her, making her dizzy. "Thank you," she murmured, covering a yawn with her hand. "I just need to get some rest."

He nodded. "I can lock up on the way out, but I can't do the dead bolt or the alarm."

"There's a spare key on the dresser," she said, pointing. "If you don't mind taking it and locking up, I've got a remote that I can use to set the alarm."

"I can do that." He grabbed one of the keys. "I'll get this back to you the next time I see you."

"At therapy," she reminded him. "We're still on for Thursday, right?"

Again his gaze swept over her. "Are you sure you'll be up for it?"

"Definitely." She put as much confidence into her smile as she could. "I'll feel a lot better once I get some rest."

He nodded, his gaze still warm. "I'll talk to you later, then."

Listening, she heard the comforting sound of the door closing and immediately, the dead bolt clicking into place. She picked up the remote alarm fob and set the alarm. She plugged in her dead phone and left it charging on her nightstand. Then, and only then, did she allow herself to kick off her clothes and crawl underneath the sheets.

When she woke around midnight, she saw she had two missed calls and five text messages, two from Adam, but most from David. Clearly, he'd heard about her accident and said he was concerned. Not worried enough to make the drive over to her place to check on her, she noted. It didn't really matter, anyway, as she planned to put them both out of their misery soon. Just not right now. She didn't have the energy to deal with him at this particular moment. Maybe not for a while. It's not like it would make any difference in either of their lives, anyway.

After using the restroom, she glanced in the mirror and winced when she caught sight of her face. She staggered back to her bed and pulled the covers up, knowing she needed sleep more than anything else.

The sound of someone ringing her front doorbell woke her. Moving carefully, she got out of bed, grabbed a bathrobe and padded to the door. Peering out the peephole with her less swollen eye, she saw her best friend Adam standing on her doorstep.

"Just a minute," she called out. "I need to disarm the alarm system."

Once that had been done, she unlocked the door and stepped back to allow him in. "I meant to call you back," she began.

He waved her explanation away. "It's okay. I heard." Then he caught sight of her and did a double take. "Oh my God," he said, drawing out the syllables. "You look like you got run over by a freight train."

"Thanks. I know. I'm almost entirely unrecognizable,"

she replied, then attempted a smile. It felt more like a grimace. "You should see the other guy."

"I brought you a latte." He held up a cup. "You look like you could use it."

Accepting it, she took a sip. "Work!" she said, suddenly remembering. "I've got to get ready for work."

"I definitely think you should rethink that," he pointed out gently. "I really think you should take the day off."

"That bad?"

He nodded. "That bad. Come on," taking her elbow, he steered her toward the kitchen. "Give me your client list for today and I'll make all the phone calls. I'm sure they'll understand. By now, everyone has heard about the wreck."

One of the blessings—and curses—of living in a small town. Grateful, she retrieved her laptop and accessed the information. "Tell them I can't reschedule right now, but hopefully they can continue to do the exercises at home until their next scheduled appointment."

Taking the computer from her, Adam waved her away. "Let me handle this. I'm a pro."

Bemused, she sat back and listened while he called every single one of her clients, his chatty good humor not only easing their concern over her health, but alleviating their disappointment over missing physical therapy.

"Most of them said they were expecting this call," Adam told her, once he'd finished. "Now, shall we look at tomorrow's schedule?"

"No," she answered instantly. "I'll rest today, but I've got to get back to it tomorrow. Not only can I not afford to miss too much work, but my patients need their therapy."

Though he frowned, Adam didn't argue the point. Instead, he wagged his finger at her. "Then promise me you'll take it easy."

"I will," she said, meaning it. "My job is mostly supervising, anyways."

"Good." Adam glanced around. "Where's David? I heard Jared was the one who stayed with you at the hospital. I can't imagine your boyfriend is too happy about that."

She snorted. "Some boyfriend." Grabbing her phone, she showed him the screenshot she'd made of David making out with the blonde woman. "This was after he'd stopped by here and turned down my invitation to hang out. Instead, he went to a bar and did his own hanging out with someone else."

Adam used his fingers to enlarge the photo. "Girl, she ain't got nothin' on you." He handed back the phone. "Are you upset?"

"Not really," she admitted. "We were never exclusive and for good reason. I've been thinking about breaking up with him for a while, anyway."

"I see." Adam eyed her. "How much of this has to do with the fact that Jared Miller is back in town?"

"None." Her answer came quickly. Maybe too quickly. "Adam, I could lose my license if I were to get involved with a client. Which means that will not be happening."

Her best friend knew her well enough to read between the lines and hear what she wasn't saying. "And that's the only reason you're keeping him at arm's length, isn't it?"

She sighed. "Not the only reason. One of them. You forget that Jared is the man who chose rodeo over me. That's kind of hard to forget."

"Maybe he's realized the error of his ways. Did you ever think of that?"

"Enough." She swatted at him. "I really don't want to talk about my love life right now. I need to be pampered and coddled."

Adam leaned over and kissed her cheek. "Yes, you do. Unfortunately, I have to go open the salon. I'll check in with you later, okay?"

"Sure." Though she adored her friend, right now all she wanted to do was lie down and sleep. "Just don't be worried if I don't answer right away. I feel like I could sleep for days."

"Sleep will heal your body," he replied. "Toodles for now. Luv ya, girlfriend."

"Luv ya right back." She followed him to the door, a little unsteady on her feet. Once he'd gone, she made sure everything had been locked up, before she climbed back into bed and used the remote to reset her alarm.

She fell asleep moments after her head hit the pillow.

Chapter Nine

After leaving beautiful, battered Marissa, Jared drove straight home. He could have definitely used a stiff drink right about now, but he'd entrusted his father's care to Gus and he didn't want to put anyone else out more than necessary.

When he walked into the house, Gus had gestured toward Jared's sleeping father and gotten up quietly. He walked into the kitchen, motioning for Jared to follow him.

"Is everything okay?" Jared asked.

Gus flashed a wide smile. "I think he had a good time," he said. "He's plumb wore out now. How's Marissa doing?"

"She's home. Though she's pretty banged up, she was really lucky. Her SUV is totaled, but she has no broken bones or serious injuries."

"Thank goodness for air bags," Gus said. He grabbed his cowboy hat off the back of a chair and put it on. "I guess I'll be heading on out now."

"Thank you so much for staying with him. I really appreciate it."

Gus gave the sleeping J.J. a fond look. "No problem. He and I go way back. I hate what's happening to him. If you need any kind of help again, just give me a call. Mildred and I can come over and visit with him anytime."

"That's mighty kind of you." Jared walked the older man to the door. "Drive safely now."

Once Gus had driven away, Jared felt too restless to sit and watch TV. Pacing, he just could not get past the thought that Marissa's accident might have been deliberate. And while he couldn't imagine Custer doing such a thing, the other man still hadn't made a single attempt to call and apologize for standing Jared up.

Marissa might not think she had any enemies, but clearly she must have made at least one. First, she'd said she felt as if someone had been watching her. Then, her home had been broken into. A brick through the window. Threatening notes. And finally, a horrific car accident that could have seriously injured her or worse, ended her life.

If all of these had been caused by the same person, then Marissa didn't just have a stalker, she had a crazed psychopath after her. Rayna needed to figure out who this person was. Because Jared couldn't even imagine what kind of escalation would come after causing a major car accident.

Since it was still fairly early, he dialed Rayna's cell. She picked up on the second ring.

"Don't you think you're getting ahead of yourself?" Rayna asked, once he'd outlined his thoughts. "First off, we don't know for a fact that the accident was even related to all of the other stuff. It might have been a simple, unintentional hit-and-run."

"But why would someone do that?" Jared argued. "They left without checking to make sure Marissa was all right."

"It happens. Most often, the other driver turns out to have

been intoxicated. Or have warrants. They always have a reason for leaving the accident scene."

Jared grimaced, even though Rayna couldn't see it. "Still, you'll investigate it right? Because on the off chance that this is the same person who is stalking Marissa, I hate to think what they might do once they learn she survived the accident with only minor injuries."

"Of course I'll investigate it," Rayna replied. "That's what I do. But right now, you're getting awfully worked up over a theory. We have to stick with facts. If we do learn something that indicates the person who hit Marissa is the same one who broke into her house, then we'll proceed differently. But for now, as a sheriff, I can only work with facts."

"I know," he admitted. "But I really want to make sure Marissa stays safe."

Rayna paused for a moment. When she spoke again, her voice had gone gentle. "You really care for her, don't you?"

"I do." One deep breath, and then he admitted what he hadn't to anyone besides himself. "She's the only woman I want to spend the rest of my life with."

"Does she know this?"

"Not yet," he admitted. "Things are…complicated. But she will, someday."

"May I give you a word of unsolicited advice?" Rayna asked, and then continued before he could decline or agree. "Things are always going to be complicated. I know they were for me and Parker. Life is like that. But when you find the only one you can imagine being with for the rest of your life, you've got to take that chance."

"I agree," Jared answered, quietly. "But I have to be careful not to frighten her away. We have a lot of baggage between us. And she's got a boyfriend right now."

"David?" Rayna made a dismissive sound. "I have a feeling he's not going to be around too much longer. I don't think Marissa is all that into him."

"Really?" For the first time, he felt a spark of hope. "That's good to know."

"You're welcome. In the meantime, I promise to keep you updated if I find out anything else about the accident."

"Sounds good," he said. After ending the call, he pondered what Rayna had said. If she was right, and David was truly going to be out of the picture, that would make his pursuit of Marissa so much easier.

He knew he had to go slow. He understood all too well Marissa's reluctance to get involved again with someone who'd hurt her so badly. He constantly had to battle the urge to bulldoze in, sweep her up into his arms and kiss her senseless. Unfortunately, he knew doing something like that would only piss her off and push her farther away.

One thing at a time, he decided. First and most important, he needed to find out who was after Marissa. Keeping her safe would be his first priority. Only once that had been accomplished, would he allow himself to pursue her romantically.

Proud of his resolve, he finally stopped pacing, and settled onto the couch on the opposite end from his still slumbering father. The nightly news would be on soon. Might as well catch up on what else was going on in the world.

His phone pinged, indicating a text. To his surprise, it was Marissa's boyfriend David.

This is David, the text read. Do you mind if I call you? Which meant he'd likely heard about Marissa's accident.

Not wanting to wake his father, Jared stepped outside onto the back porch before responding. Sure, he typed.

A second later his phone rang. After exchanging brief pleasantries, David got right to the point.

"Have you seen Marissa?" he asked. "She hasn't been returning my phone calls or texts."

"I have seen her," Jared admitted. "In fact, I drove her home from the hospital a little earlier this evening. She's pretty out of it though, so that's probably why you haven't heard from her."

"Maybe," David acknowledged. "But I'm her boyfriend. I should have been the first one she called after the accident."

Though he didn't want to, Jared couldn't help but feel a surge of pity for the other man. "She wasn't exactly in any shape to call anyone. I happened to be down the street and saw the accident. Rayna and I drove to the hospital together."

"I see."

Judging from David's tone, the knowledge that Marissa hadn't actually called Jared didn't make him any happier.

"How is she?" David finally asked. "I mean, I've heard she wasn't seriously injured, just banged up."

Though Jared hated to say what he knew he had to, he also wasn't about to be the go-between for Marissa and her boyfriend. "I think you need to ask her that. Have you even gone to see her?"

"That's the problem," David admitted. "I can't. I'm in the field this morning, driving to various cattle ranches, and I've got back-to-back appointments. I don't have the time."

Though Jared privately thought if their positions were reversed, in a situation like this, he'd *make* time, he said nothing.

David sighed. "Maybe I'll try to stop by after work to-night," he said. "If you see her or happen to talk to her, will you let her know?"

"I'm sorry, but I can't," Jared replied. "She wasn't too happy with me when she learned I'd stopped by your vet clinic and confronted you. I don't want to get involved or in the middle of your relationship." He took a deep breath, forcing himself to say the next words. "You two will need to work out your own problems."

"Understood." David still sounded glum. "Listen, I appreciate you taking the time to talk with me."

What could Jared say to that? He settled on responding with a cordial, "No problem."

After ending the call, he stayed outside for a moment and considered. Rayna thought David and Marissa wouldn't last. And judging by the way Marissa had acted when Jared had asked her if she wanted to call him, Rayna might be right. Only, it didn't seem David knew this. Despite first impressions, tonight on the phone, David had genuinely seemed to care for her. Though not enough to figure out a way to squeeze her into his busy schedule. Unfathomable, but then who was he to judge? He'd also messed up his relationship with Marissa.

Her love life was none of his business, he told himself. Even if he desperately wanted it to be.

WHEN MARISSA WOKE the next morning, everything hurt. She tried to sit up in bed, and groaned. Her entire body felt like she'd had a run in with someone angrily swinging a baseball bat.

Checking her phone, she saw two more voice mails from David, and one text. Just as she was contemplating calling him back, her phone rang. Jared, she saw, feeling relieved.

"How are you this morning?" Jared asked. "I'm hoping you were able to get a lot of rest."

A wave of longing swept through her, so strong she could barely catch her breath. "I'm awake," she managed to say. "And when I move, everything hurts."

"Maybe you should take one more day off."

She heard a beep, indicating another call. Probably David, so she ignored it. "Tempting as that is, I can't. I'll just try to take it easy."

"Are you sure?" he asked.

"Positive."

"Then I'll see you at nine," he replied. "I'll bring you a coffee and a kolache."

"That would be awesome." She glanced at the clock. "Especially since I won't have time to eat breakfast."

After ending the call, she eased out of bed and made her way to the shower. Running the water as hot as she could stand it, she stood and let the heat ease some of the soreness from her muscles.

When she'd finished, she felt slightly better. After carefully toweling off, she winced when she caught sight of herself in the bathroom mirror. Her numerous bruises and cuts still looked angry, but she told herself they were better than they'd been the day before.

After feeding Roxy, Marissa dressed in her most comfortable pair of scrubs, grateful she always wore scrubs to work. Too sore to bother with fixing her hair, she managed to put it in a ponytail before locking up and setting the alarm. She walked slowly as she headed over to her clinic, glad Jared would be her first client of the day.

As she rounded the corner, she saw his truck sitting in the parking lot. When he caught sight of her, he waved and got out, carefully balancing two coffees and a small paper sack. "Breakfast," he said, smiling as he limped over to her.

She waited until he'd reached her and then together they walked slowly to the door.

Once they were inside and she'd flipped on all the lights and deactivated the alarm, she made her way back to the small break room.

They settled at the small table, and he handed her a coffee and the bag containing two kolaches. "They're both yours," he said.

"What about you?" she asked, trying not to salivate at the delicious scent wafting from the bag. "Aren't you going to eat?"

He grinned. "I tried to wait, but I got hungry on the way over. I already ate mine."

Startled, she had to laugh. Then she dug in to her own pastries, making short work of them. "That was lovely," she said. "Thank you." She checked her watch. "And we're still ten minutes early for your session."

"Good. We can visit a little."

"Did you ever hear from Custer?" she asked, eyeing him over her coffee.

"No," he replied. "Which is strange. I'll try him again after therapy today."

She nodded. "Tell me about your knee. Your limp is still pretty pronounced. Have you been doing the band exercises at home?"

"Yes. At least once a day. But there's a lot to be done around the ranch, and my dad isn't able to do very much. That often means I frequently overdo it."

As she started to speak, he held up his hand. "Before you say anything, it's not like I have a choice. It is what it is and I do what has to be done. I'm trying really hard not to stress my knee though."

"I bet you could get some of your buddies to help you," she ventured. "Even maybe some of your father's friends. I know I'd be willing to put in a few hours on the weekends, clearing out weeds or repairing fence, whatever you need."

"That's really kind of you." His smile lit up his blue eyes, making her entire body tingle. "But I really don't think you're in any condition to do work like that."

"Maybe not right now," she conceded. "But once I heal, I can."

Her phone timer pinged, alerting her that five minutes remained before his session was due to start.

She stood, wincing as pain shot through her, so strong she felt dizzy.

Immediately, he came to her side. "What's wrong?"

"Just a bit of dizziness," she managed, holding on to the edge of the table for support. "I probably just tried to move too fast."

He slipped his arm around her. "I've got you."

Allowing herself to lean into him, she briefly closed her eyes. Then, remembering she was his therapist, she straightened and pushed herself away. "Let's get your therapy going now." Somehow, she managed to walk away, into her therapy room. A moment later, he followed.

Once she'd gotten Jared set up with several exercises, she took a seat to watch. The front door opened. Stifling a groan, she managed to stand and headed out to check. Before she made it out of the therapy room, a tall man wearing a black Stetson strolled in. Custer Black, one of her former patients and Jared's old friend.

"Marissa!" he exclaimed, yanking her in for a rough hug. She yelped in pain, startling him. He released her, eyes narrowed. "What's wrong? Did I hurt you or something?"

Tears in her eyes, she nodded, trying to catch her breath enough to answer. When he caught sight of her bruised and battered face, he swore. "What happened to you?"

"She was in a bad accident on Tuesday," Jared said, coming over. "Her SUV was totaled. Don't tell me you didn't hear about that around town?"

Looking from one to the other, Custer frowned. "I haven't been to town. Actually, this is my first time leaving my parents' ranch since Monday."

"Really?" Jared crossed his arms. "Did you forget we were supposed to meet up Tuesday night at The Rattlesnake?"

Custer swore. "I'm sorry, man. I completely forgot."

"Did you get any of the messages or texts I sent you?" Jared asked, his voice hard.

"No." Custer scratched his chin. "I, uh, dropped my phone in the toilet. That's why I'm in town actually. I need to buy a new one."

Marissa looked from one man to the other. The way Jared acted, it almost seemed as if he suspected Custer might have been the one who'd hit her.

Jared's next question confirmed it. "Do you mind if I take a look at your truck?"

"Why?" Then Custer got it. "You're not serious."

"Look, I just want to make sure," Jared replied. "We can walk out there together. Indulge me."

"Okay." Custer spread his hands. "But you'll have to come out to the ranch to see it. I used my dad's pickup today."

Marissa glanced at Jared. If anything, his expression had become even grimmer.

"Why?" Jared asked. Even without him saying the words,

it seemed clear he thought Custer had parked his truck due to damage from an accident. *The* accident.

Custer realized it, too. "I don't have to take this," he said. "Feel free to visit the ranch anytime and see for yourself. I'm out of here." He left, slamming the door behind him.

"Well, that didn't go over well," Marissa commented. "Don't you think you were a little harsh on him?"

Jared shrugged. "I don't know. Depends on if he was the one who hit you."

"What?" Staring at him, she shook her head. "You honestly don't believe that, do you?"

"I don't want to. But several things just aren't adding up with him. His story about forgetting to meet me at The Rattlesnake Pub, dropping his phone in the toilet, and then not driving his truck. Individually, I could believe maybe one. But all of them together... Too much of a coincidence."

"But why?" she asked. "Why do you think Custer would do such a thing?"

"Who knows? It might have been a simple accident. Maybe he was on his way to The Rattlesnake and he ran a red light. Maybe he dropped something and looked down for just a second, at exactly the wrong moment. Or..."

"Or?" she prompted. "Or what?"

He met her gaze. "It's possible Custer has a grudge against you."

"No, he doesn't." Instinctively, she argued. "I've known him as long as you have. If he had a problem with me, I'm sure he'd tell me."

Though Jared didn't reply, she swore she saw something in his expression. "Tell me," she ordered. "What did he say to you?"

For the first time, Jared appeared uncomfortable. "He

might have just been blowing off steam, but he said he thought your physical therapy made him worse. His back kept locking up. He said it was so bad that he had to quit the rodeo after Cheyenne and come home."

"Sometimes that happens," Marissa replied, still confused. "Especially if he hasn't been keeping up with the stretching exercises I gave him. But what I don't understand is why he wouldn't contact me and let me do some work with him."

"I don't know."

Shaking her head, she took a deep breath. "I'll call him at lunch and see if I can straighten things out." She pointed to the exercise band he held loosely in one hand. "Why don't you finish up with that and then we'll go over what I'd like you to do at home? I've got another client coming in soon."

After Jared left, Marissa stayed busy the rest of the day. She sat much more than she normally did, trying to rest as much as possible. She'd just sat down to eat lunch when her mother called.

"Why didn't you tell me?" Sheila demanded. "I had to hear it from Sharon DeAngelo."

"She called you?" Marissa winced. "I haven't told you yet because I slept all day yesterday, and today I'm back at work. I planned to fill you and Dad in tonight."

Her answer appeared to mollify her mother. "I heard nothing was broken. Is that true? Are you really okay?"

"I am. The Tahoe, not so much."

They chatted for a few more minutes. And then her mom asked about Jared. "Sharon told me he's back in town and you've been seeing him. I thought you were dating that nice veterinarian, David."

"I'm not *seeing* Jared. Not that way," Marissa answered. "He's doing his physical therapy with me, nothing more."

"That seems weird," her mom commented. "I know how badly he hurt you. Are you handling that okay?"

"Of course." Marissa laughed, hoping she sounded relaxed. "It's been years since Jared and I were a thing. I got over him a long time ago."

Her words seemed to reassure her mother. They talked a few minutes longer, and Marissa promised to keep her parents updated. "Say hi to Dad for me," she said, right before she ended the call.

Sitting there for a moment, holding her phone, Marissa realized she really missed having her mom and dad around. While she was happy for them getting to live their dream of traveling the country in their luxurious motor home, there were times when she longed for the comfort of her childhood home and her mom's cooking.

Ah well. They'd raised her to be capable and strong, something for which she'd be forever grateful. They'd been there to help her pick up the pieces when Jared had taken off for the rodeo in the middle of college. Without their support, she didn't know how she'd have passed her classes. They encouraged her, let her come home on weekends and cry, and been there for her.

She'd just started to get up when her phone rang again. Jared's name flashed up on the screen, making her catch her breath. It felt almost as if he'd somehow known she'd been thinking about him.

"Hi, Jared," she answered. "What's up?"

"I need your help," he said, worry threaded through his deep voice. "My father fell. Nothing appears to be broken, or even sprained, but once I got him up on the couch, he refuses to move or talk or even acknowledge me. If I come pick you up, will you talk to him? And maybe take a look at him?"

Her heart stuttered in her chest. "Of course. Do you think he needs to go to the hospital?"

"I don't know. He won't respond. Just keeps staring straight ahead." His voice broke. "Marissa, I'm really worried."

That last sentence did it. "If you think he'll be all right while you drive over, come and get me."

"I'm waiting for my neighbor to get here and watch him. Once she arrives, I'll be on my way."

"I'll watch for you," she said. "I really need to see about getting a rental car or something."

Though Marissa had planned to eat something and go straight to the couch and binge-watch one of her favorite shows, her conversation with Jared had her really concerned. Mostly, she hoped Jared's father hadn't hit his head when he'd fallen, though from what Jared had described, it sounded as if he might.

She wasn't sure what she could do to help, but she'd do whatever Jared and his father needed.

Chapter Ten

As soon as Mrs. Perkins from the ranch down the road arrived, Jared took off to go get Marissa. He drove fast, breaking every speed limit. Despite one or two red lights, he managed to make it to Marissa's house in under twenty minutes.

Apparently, she'd been watching for him as she came outside the instant she saw his truck pull up.

He could tell she tried to hurry, but with her still banged up body, she could only manage a slightly faster shuffle. Heart squeezing at the sight of her struggling, Jared got out and came around to help her. She waved him away and pulled herself up into his truck unassisted, the obstinate set of her chin so familiar his heart ached.

Holding the seatbelt, she waited until he'd gotten in before leaning over and brushing a soft kiss on his cheek. "Are you okay?" she murmured, clicking her seatbelt into place.

The swift touch of her mouth on his skin had made him freeze. Even with all the worry and fear over his dad jumbled up inside of him, a wave of fierce longing made him close his eyes. "I'm fine," he lied, his voice raspy. "Though honestly, I'll be a lot better once we figure out what's wrong with my father. Thank you so much for agreeing to come out and help me."

"You're welcome," she responded. "You know I'm here any time you need help."

"Thanks," he said again.

As he put the truck into reverse, she reached over and took his hand, squeezing his fingers. "I know you're worried," she said. "But we'll get it figured out. I promise."

On the drive out of town, Marissa's scent filled the interior of his truck. Body lotion or perfume, he wasn't sure, but she smelled the same as she always had, like a combination of vanilla and exotic fruit.

She caught him glancing at her and smiled reassuringly. "It's all going to be okay. Once we can get your dad checked out, we'll know if he needs more professional medical help."

He nodded. "He's not really that old," he said. "And his early-onset dementia is not far advanced. I don't know what else might be going on with him to make him fall like that."

Back at the ranch, they hurried inside. Mrs. Perkins waited near the door, wringing her hands nervously. "I think you should take him to the hospital," she said. "Poor thing hasn't moved or spoken since I got here."

"We just might do that," Jared replied. "Thank you so much for your help."

"You're welcome."

As soon as she'd gone, Jared took Marissa's arm and led her into the living room. His father still sat exactly where Jared had lifted him, back straight, hands folded in his lap, staring blankly into space. He didn't acknowledge them or act as if he even knew they were there.

"Hi, Mr. Miller," Marissa said brightly, crouching down

in front of him. "Jared told me you fell, so I thought I'd come over and make sure you didn't hurt yourself."

No reaction. His father continued to stare straight ahead, as though he retreated far inside himself.

"Mr. Miller?" She pushed awkwardly back to her feet, using the sofa to maintain her balance. Reaching over, she patted his shoulder. "Mr. Miller, can you hear me?"

Lump in his throat, Jared watched. He felt as if his heart was splitting in two. "Dad?" he tried. "I brought Marissa over to see you. I know last time she was here, you'd said you looked forward to seeing her again."

Nothing.

Jared glanced at Marissa. Blinking back tears, she shook her head. "I don't know," she said, her voice quavering. "Maybe Mrs. Perkins was right. I think he really needs to see a medical professional. If we can get him in your truck, we need to take him to the hospital."

"No." The older man spoke for the first time, his voice thin and sharp. When they both turned to look at him, they realized he'd turned his head to watch them. Life had come back into his faded blue gaze.

"Dad," Jared said. "What happened? I was worried about you."

His father shrugged and frowned, the confusion in his expression breaking Jared's heart. "I'm not sure."

"Do you remember falling?"

Slowly, his dad nodded. "I think so. I don't know why though. I think my legs just gave out."

"When was the last time you had a physical?" Jared asked.

His question made his father's frown deepen. "I don't know. Last year, maybe."

"It might be time for you to have another one. We can tell your doctor what happened and see if he can figure out what's going on."

"He'll just want me to take more medicine," his dad scoffed, his expression growing more and more lucid. "I take enough pills as it is. I don't really want any more."

"But you don't need to be falling," Jared pointed out. "You were lucky this time and didn't break anything. You might not be so fortunate next time."

The older man's gaze drifted past Jared to Marissa. "Speaking of that, what happened to you? Who looks worse, you or the other guy?"

Marissa tried to smile, but the split lip made it difficult. "I was in a car accident. Someone ran a red light and broadsided me."

"Baby girl." J.J. shook his head. "You should be resting up at home. Don't tell me my son dragged you out here to check on me."

"That's entirely what happened," Jared put in, mostly to spare Marissa from having to answer.

Before his father could protest, Marissa moved over to sit down next to him. "Jared was really worried about you," she told him gently. "I was, too. I really think you should let your doctor check you over, just to be safe."

Jared had never loved her more than at this moment. Watching her as she leaned close to his dad, placing her small hand on his shoulder. He noticed his father's hard expression soften, soaking in her genuine concern and sweetness.

"For you," the gruff older man conceded. "I'll call my doctor tomorrow. I promise."

"Thank you." Marissa kissed his cheek. "I think we'll feel better knowing you're getting checked out."

"Are you going to marry my son?" J.J. asked, the loud question coming out of nowhere. Jared froze, both mortified and yet also curious to see how Marissa would handle answering.

Marissa looked down and took a deep breath. When she raised her head, she met Jared's gaze before turning her attention to his father. "Jared and I are good friends," she said softly. "I'm also his physical therapist. I'm helping him rehab after his rodeo accident."

"Which means you can't be in a relationship with him," the older man guessed.

Shocked when Marissa nodded, Jared realized he definitely needed to rethink where he got his PT. "You're not allowed to be involved with your clients?" he asked, just to be certain.

"No. It would be a breach of ethics," she replied. "I could lose my license."

"That explains a lot," he said under his breath, more to himself than anything else. But somehow, Marissa heard him. She shook her head, a half smile playing around her mouth.

Right then and there, he knew he'd be finding another physical therapist. And the sooner the better. If he wanted to have a chance at a relationship with Marissa, he had no choice.

Of course, she was still seeing David. Though he found it interesting—and telling—that she hadn't mentioned her boyfriend just now when explaining to his father why she and Jared weren't dating.

His father yawned, barely managing to cover his mouth

with his hand. "I'm tired," he said. "I think I need to lie down."

Immediately, Jared got up. "Let me help you," he said.

"I'm fine." J.J. waved him away, struggling, yet managing to push himself up from the couch. Moving unsteadily, he held on to the wall as he made his way toward his bedroom. Watching him move like a man twenty years or more older broke Jared's heart.

Just to be safe, Jared stayed a few paces behind him, ready to catch him if the older man stumbled. His dad noticed, glancing once back over his shoulder, but said nothing.

Once they reached the master bedroom, J.J. sank carefully onto the edge of the bed.

"Do you need me to help you get undressed?" Jared asked.

His father grimaced. "I don't know. Maybe. If you could at least help me get my boots off, I'd appreciate it."

Once Jared had done that, he got back to his feet. "Let me get you your pajamas," he said.

"They're in the top dresser drawer."

Jared fetched them, handing them over to his dad. "Do you need help with getting out of those jeans?"

"Hell, no."

Since he'd kind of expected that response, Jared nodded. "Do you want me to bring you a glass of water or anything?"

"Not right now." His father paused. "Son, do you mind if I ask you something?"

Surprised, Jared shrugged. "Go ahead."

"You love her, don't you?" The older man's sharp gaze pierced through any attempt Jared might make at diversion.

Not sure how to respond, Jared settled on going with the truth. "I do."

"Then why are you pretending y'all are just friends? I see the way you look at her." J.J. grimaced. "I recognize that look. I felt that way about your mother."

"It's complicated." Weak, but no way did Jared intend on going into a lengthy explanation. Especially not right now.

"I see." But his expression made it plain he didn't. "Look, Jared. Life is short. You never know when something is going to change, or be gone in an instant." He swallowed hard, and Jared knew he was thinking of his lost wife, Jared's mother. "Do you hear me?"

"I do." Now both his father and Serenity had given him similar advice. "I'm working on it, Dad. I promise you, I am."

This appeared to satisfy his father. "Good." He waved Jared away. "Then go on now. Don't leave your woman waiting out there by herself."

His woman. If only. Jared nodded and let himself out, closing the door behind him.

After Jared walked off to help his father to bed, Marissa got up and went to look out the front window. With her entire body aching, right at that instant she wanted to be home. She hadn't had time to think much about not having her own transportation, but now she realized she either needed to get a rental car or purchase something inexpensive to drive until the insurance settled up. One more thing to do. She needed to contact her agent and file a claim.

Right now, all she wanted to do was go home and crawl into bed. Her most pressing concern at the moment would be trying to figure out how she'd get home. She couldn't really ask Jared to leave his dad, not now, and the ranch was too far away from town to walk.

Her phone rang. David.

She stepped outside onto the back porch to take the call.

"Hey, David." Keeping her tone level, she couldn't help but reveal a little of her exhaustion. Whether he noticed or not, she had no idea. "Sorry, I've been meaning to call you, but it's been kind of crazy."

"I heard about your accident," he said. "I've been worried. Are you all right?"

"Yes. A little beat up, but nothing broken."

"I'm glad," he said, his voice softening. "Listen, can I come see you tonight?"

Though she hadn't planned on actually dealing with their relationship until she felt better, she also knew she couldn't avoid David forever.

"Would you mind picking me up?" she asked, inwardly wincing. "I'm out at the Miller ranch. Jared's father had a spill and I came to check on him."

To his credit, David didn't ask how she'd gotten there. "Is he okay now?" he asked.

"We think so, yes."

"Good." He exhaled. "Sure, I can come get you. I've been out there to treat their cattle before, so I know where the place is. If I leave now, I can be there in under thirty minutes. Will that work for you?"

"Definitely," she replied. "Thanks, David. I really appreciate it."

After ending the call, she remained outside to collect her thoughts. David hadn't seemed at all surprised to learn she was with Jared, or even the slightest bit concerned. Either he didn't view Jared as a threat, or he truly didn't care.

She thought of the screenshot she'd saved of David and the blonde woman and shook her head. None of this mattered. She and David clearly weren't going to take their relationship any deeper. Better to cut ties now rather than prolong things.

The back door opened and Jared stepped outside. "Is everything all right?" he asked, his voice concerned.

"Yes. I just got off the phone with David. He's on his way to pick me up."

Just like that, his expression shut down. "I'm glad," he replied, sounding anything but. "I've been trying to figure out a way to get you home without leaving my dad."

"Well, now you don't have to," she said brightly. "I should go back inside and say goodbye to your father. I don't want him to think I left without saying a word."

"I think he's probably asleep. He was putting on his pajamas when I left him."

"Oh." She blinked, feeling suddenly awkward for no discernible reason. "Then I guess I'll just go inside and wait. It'll be around half an hour before David gets here. I hope that's okay."

"Of course." Jared held the door open. She brushed past him, trying not to touch him, but she overcorrected and almost fell. He reached out to steady her, but somehow she ended up pressed against him, her entire body tingling.

Looking up at him, their gazes locked. She knew he was going to kiss her seconds before he covered her mouth with his. Her heart lurched. She barely had time to take a breath and then...

The touch of his mouth, familiar and electrifying, made her come alive. She'd never realized she'd been a zombie, walking around half-awake. Everything inside of her instantly leapt to life. The heat from his body, his scent, the firm press of his lips on hers.

One delicious shiver. Raising herself on tiptoe, she met him halfway. When he recaptured her mouth, her senses reeled. Her hungry, eager response shocked her. But desire sang a siren song, beckoning. She knew she could have more, if she gave him the okay. She could allow him to give her the thing she'd been missing ever since he'd left. Completion.

A sharp tap on the front door broke them apart. Cheeks flaming, knot in her throat, she tried to blink away the sensual haze.

Jared stared at her a moment, his gaze dark. Then, mouth tightening, he glanced toward the door. "I think you'd better get that," he said. "It's probably David."

David. Emotions swirling around inside of her, she managed to nod. Though she hated to admit it out loud, she needed a moment to compose herself.

"Take all the time you need," Jared said once she told him. "I'll get the door."

She ran for the bathroom, a knot in her throat. Too many feelings, all of them unwelcome. Splashing cold water on her still overheated face, she kept herself from examining them too closely, because she didn't want to know. Not now. Maybe not ever.

Her reflection revealed her inner turmoil. Swollen lips, flushed cheeks and eyes still dark with desire. She wondered if David would even notice. He'd never been the most observant man, at least where she was concerned.

When she finally felt composed enough, she opened the door.

Jared and David stood talking, just inside the foyer. Both men turned as she approached.

"Are you all right?" David asked, frowning as he took in her still disheveled appearance.

"I'm fine," she lied, brushing past him. "Let's go."

"Sorry, man," David said to Jared. "Let me know if there's anything I can do to help in any way."

"I'll do that," Jared's deep voice rumbled. "Take care."

And he closed the door.

When she reached David's truck, she yanked the passenger door open and pulled herself up inside.

Though he glanced at her, David didn't comment. Once he'd pulled out onto the road, he let out a heavy sigh. "Is there something you want to tell me?"

This startled her, though she knew Jared would not have mentioned the kiss. She knew she should bring up the photo, but right now driving home with a man who smelled like hard work and livestock, she didn't have the energy.

"I'm just really tired," she said, dodging the subject. "It's been a rough couple of days."

Her explanation appeared to satisfy him. "I'm sorry." He squeezed her shoulder. "About everything."

"What do you mean?" she asked, wondering if he might be about to confess.

"I know I should have showered first," David replied, grimacing. "And I apologize for the stench. But I've been so worried about you and I didn't want to take the time to go home and shower before picking you up."

"That's okay." And it was. Along with a nearly overpowering sense of relief at being spared having to deal with drama right now, for the first time in a long time, she felt as if she was seeing the real David.

On the drive home, he kept up a running stream of amusing stories about some of the animals he'd seen that day.

Since he'd been in the field, instead of dogs and cats, he'd worked with horses, cattle, pigs and sheep. He'd even seen a few alpaca, he told her.

Glad she didn't have to do much more than listen, she relaxed. She didn't tense up again until he pulled into her driveway.

"Now that I've made sure you're all right, I'm going to head on home," he said.

"We need to talk." There. She'd finally said it. And judging by the swift recoil David made, he knew exactly what she meant.

"Tonight?" he asked, his mouth downturned.

"This won't take long," she began.

"Look," he interrupted, his expression as fierce as his voice. "I think I understand what you're going to say. I've been a terrible boyfriend. We haven't barely seen each other and I've let my job take over my life. Will you please let me try to make it up to you? I promise to change."

Now she should have brought out her phone and showed him the screenshot she'd grabbed with David and a blonde woman all wrapped around each other. But suddenly, a wave of exhaustion swamped her and she realized she was just too tired to deal with all this right now. What difference did it make, anyway?

"Okay, David," she sighed. "I need to get to bed and rest. We can talk another time."

"Thank you." He leaned over and kissed her, aiming for her mouth but catching her on the cheek instead. "I'll try to do better."

Instead of saying something pithy, she settled for a quick nod before sliding out of his truck and heading toward her door. At least he waited to drive away until he'd seen she'd gotten safely inside.

Disarming the alarm, she found herself suddenly blinking back tears. So much for taking control of her life. Of course, judging by what she'd seen on social media, none of this mattered.

Head aching, she went into her kitchen to grab herself a glass of water before heading off to lie down.

Sometime in the night she woke up to Roxy's frantic meowing. She sat up in bed, rubbing her eyes, instinctively reaching out to comfort her cat. "What's wrong, girl?" she asked.

And then she smelled it. Smoke. The heavy, cloying scent of something burning.

Had she left the stove on? No. Clicking on her lamp, she realized her bedroom had begun to fill with smoke.

Quickly, she scooped up Roxy and started for the kitchen. But she barely made it into the hallway before thick smoke stopped her. Ahead, she could see the orange glow of fire.

She needed to get out. Now.

Back in her bedroom, she grabbed her phone and then, keeping a firm hold on her cat, went for the back door. But once again she found her way blocked by fire.

Her only hope of getting out would be climbing out a window.

Back in her bedroom, she closed the door, aware doing so would give her just a little more time.

Roxy hissed and yowled, twisting in fear, trying to escape Marissa's grasp. Since she kept the cat kennel in her closet, Marissa grabbed it and shoved Roxy into it. Then she unlatched the window and, kennel in hand, climbed out.

As soon as she'd gotten outside she saw the full extent

of the fire. Engulfed in flames, her entire office ablaze, the fire had spread to her house.

Quickly, she set the cat carrier down and dialed 911. The instant she gave her address and explained what was going on, the dispatcher told her they'd already received several other calls and that the fire department was on the way.

Not knowing what else to do, she hung up. When she looked around, she realized several of her neighbors had come outside and were standing in a cluster across the street, watching her house burn.

Glancing down at her oversized T-shirt and wishing she had on a bra, she tried to decide whether to walk over and join them, or stay put and wait for the fire truck.

In the end, the approaching sirens convinced her it would be better to wait. Flashing lights accompanied the two engines that pulled up in front of her place.

The uniformed firefighters got to work, using hoses to spray massive amounts of water in an effort to control the flames. Watching this, with Roxy yowling pitifully in the kennel, Marissa blinked back tears. She knew even before the firefighter told her that her clinic would be a total loss.

"And likely the house part as well," he said. "Ma'am, is there anyone I can call for you?"

"I've got this," a voice said from behind her. Grateful, Marissa turned to see Rayna striding across the street toward her.

When she reached Marissa, she pulled her in for a fierce hug. Ignoring her body's instant complaint, Marissa hugged her right back.

Rayna finally released her. "Go sit in my car while I talk to the fire captain. You're definitely welcome to stay with me tonight until you figure out what to do."

Grateful, Marissa did exactly that, bringing the now silent Roxy with her and placing her carrier on the backseat. Then Marissa got out her phone and hesitated. Since it was after two o'clock, she didn't want to wake Jared, but she desperately needed to hear his voice. Without thinking too hard about what this meant, she pressed the button to call him.

"Marissa?" Though sleep made him sound gruff, the slight lilt in his voice told her he was happy to hear from her.

She tried to speak. Instead, she promptly burst into tears.

He tried to soothe her over the phone. "Marissa? Darlin', whatever is going on, it's going to be okay. I promise."

"Is it?" she finally managed, unable to keep the bitterness from her voice. "Someone set my place on fire while I was sleeping. I could have been killed." She took a great gulp of air, trying to catch her breath. "If Roxy hadn't woken me up, I might have died." Despite her best efforts not to, she started to cry again. "My cat saved my life."

"What?" Now Jared sounded fully awake. And furious. "Have you called Rayna?"

Marissa took a moment to get herself back under control before answering. "She's here. I'm sitting in her car while she talks to the fire department captain. And they still haven't gotten the fire under control."

"How bad is it?" he asked gently, though anger still threaded the edge of his voice.

"Honestly?" She swallowed. "It looks like both my house and my clinic are going to be a total loss." She couldn't bear to say the rest of her thoughts—How would she stay in business? Where would she live? What would she do? Not only did she have no vehicle, but now no place to live or to work.

"Have Rayna bring you here," Jared said. "We have a spare bedroom you can have. No strings. And I'm thinking you can set up shop in the old ranch office out in the barn. It hasn't been used in years, so we'll have to clean it out, but it has electricity and air conditioning and heat."

His offer felt both wonderful and surreal. No matter what he said, she knew she'd feel indebted. And there wasn't any way she could make that a good thing.

But then again, what choice did she have?

"Unless you think David would be upset," Jared continued. "I definitely don't want to get in between you two and your relationship."

"I doubt he'd care," she heard herself say. "He seems to really like you." She took a deep breath. "I can't think clearly right now, but maybe it would be better if I try to find someplace in town to temporarily rent."

"Marissa, I'm going to be blunt," Jared said. "You need to go somewhere safe, where you have someone who can protect you. Whether me or David, I'm not sure, but you shouldn't be alone. I believe that someone is trying to kill you."

Rubbing her aching head, she sighed. "Until this fire, I would have said no way. The wreck could have just been a freak accident. But now, I don't know what to think. I guess I'll have to wait and see what the fire investigator says. If this was deliberately set, then I'd have to agree with you."

After that long speech, she felt drained, as if what little energy she had remaining had been siphoned away.

"Have Rayna bring you here," Jared insisted. "You need a place to sleep. I promise, you don't need to make any decisions tonight."

Just then Rayna opened the door and poked her head in. "Hey," she began, before realizing Marissa was on the phone. "Are you talking to Jared? If you are, do you mind if I have a word with him?"

"Sure." Wondering how the sheriff had known, Marissa told Jared that Rayna wanted to talk to him and then handed her cell over.

Taking the phone, Rayna closed the car door before walking away. Did that mean she didn't want Marissa to hear what she wanted to say to Jared? Immediately, Marissa discounted that idea. One thing about Rayna, she never played games. Marissa knew she could count on her to always shoot straight.

In a few minutes, Rayna returned. She slid into the driver's seat and handed the phone back to Marissa. "Jared wants me to bring you to his house," she said. "What are your thoughts on that?"

"I'm not sure," Marissa admitted. "He does have an extra bedroom." She sighed. "I appreciate your offer, too, but I really hate to put anyone out."

"Up to you." Glancing back toward the still raging fire, Rayna grimaced. "They'll have to get the official fire investigator out here from Abilene, but Jud Harris, the captain, says it sure appears as if this fire was set deliberately. As in, someone poured an accelerant around the exterior of your property and then lit it up."

"An accelerant?" Marissa asked. "Like gasoline?"

"Yes. Or lighter fluid. The good thing is, you have those wonderful outdoor cameras. Or had, since they've been pretty much destroyed by the flames. I'm guessing Parker set it so that you could store the camera video feeds in the cloud, right?"

Marissa nodded. "Yes. He showed me how to access

them. My laptop is in there though, which means it's likely a goner. But I definitely can access it on another computer."

"Perfect." Rayna handed over a lightweight laptop. "Use this. Hopefully, you'll have a clear video of whoever did this. Then I can go get them." She slid into the seat next to Marissa and eyed her expectantly.

Since Rayna had already logged in, Marissa went directly to the Web site Parker had given her. She logged in, glad she'd chosen a simple password that she could remember, even though Parker had advised her to change it later.

Once she'd opened her account page, she saw she had several new occurrences, as the site called them.

"Start with the most recent," Rayna advised. "We can go backwards in time from there."

Opening the first file, Marissa found herself holding her breath. Rayna leaned forward, her gaze intent on the screen. "Here we go," she said, as a figure moved past the camera. Due to the lack of light, the footage appeared grainy, but they both could clearly make out a person who appeared to be carrying a gas can and pouring it around the base of the building.

"Come on, turn," Rayna ordered. "Show us your face."

But the arsonist wore a hoodie, the hood obscuring the possibility of them viewing any features.

Marissa clicked on several other videos, all from other cameras, all showing the same individual moving around the outskirts of the building.

"Let's check them all," Rayna said.

Nodding, Marissa accessed every single one. One of them had clearly been activated by a curious lizard moving across the face of the camera. Another had picked up a bird flying past.

Once they'd viewed them all, Marissa returned to the ones with the stranger about to set her home and business on fire. She watched them one at a time, scrutinizing every move, trying to see if she recognized anything at all about the person.

"Slender," Rayna commented. "I'd say average height. Hard to tell, but definitely could be either male or female."

Marissa blinked. "I hadn't thought of that," she said. "But you're right. At least I can tell it's not Custer Black."

Now Rayna turned and eyed her. "Why would you think he'd do something like this? I know at one point we were looking into the possibility—however remote—that Custer might have been involved in your auto accident, but arson? That's on an entirely different level."

"I know," Marissa hurried to respond. "Whoever set this fire is straight up trying to kill me. Custer is not a murderer."

Gaze intent, Rayna nodded. "Tell me the truth, Marissa. Do you have reason to believe Custer would want you dead?"

"No." Marissa didn't even have to think about her answer. "I don't."

"Then who?" Rayna reached over and punched replay on the video they'd just watched. "Who is this person and why are they trying to kill you?"

"That's what I don't know." Miserable, Marissa glanced from the video back at her still blazing house. "I just hope we figure it out soon. My home and my clinic are gone." She struggled not to break down weeping. "I have no idea what I'm going to do."

Rayna squeezed her shoulder before gently taking the laptop out of her hands. "You're alive," she said. "And so is your beautiful little cat. That's what's important. You can rebuild and replace a structure and the contents."

Though Marissa knew what Rayna said was true, the enormity of her loss still crushed her. In the blink of an eye, she'd lost everything. And she didn't have the faintest idea why.

"How about I take you over to Jared's for now," Rayna said. "We can meet again tomorrow after you've gotten some rest."

Too weary to do much more than jerk her head in a nod, Marissa leaned back into the seat and closed her eyes. As the car started forward, Roxy let out a plaintive mew.

Rayna kept up a steady stream of conversation on the way to the Miller ranch. Almost as if she knew Marissa needed a distraction or white noise to keep from breaking down.

Grateful, Marissa kept her eyes closed and simply listened. She felt disconnected somehow, which likely meant shock had set in. When Serenity had told her that her life was about to change, she'd never suspected something on this scale.

Chapter Eleven

Rayna texted to let Jared know she was on the way with Marissa. He sent back a quick thank you before heading into the guest room to make up the bed with clean linens.

Restless, he paced the living room, trying to be quiet so he didn't wake his father. Clearly, he wasn't successful, as he heard the sound of the master bedroom door opening.

"What's going on?" his dad asked, wandering out of the hallway, his mussed hair matching his rumpled pajamas.

Once Jared had filled him in, the older man frowned. "Why would anyone try to hurt Marissa? That just doesn't make any sense."

"I agree."

A moment later, headlights lit up the living room window, indicating Marissa and Rayna's arrival. Jared's heart skipped a beat. Telling his father to wait inside, Jared hurried out to meet them.

By the time he reached the car, Marissa had already gotten out, though she held on to the open door for support. She was wearing only an oversized T-shirt and her feet were bare. She carried a small pet carrier in one hand. With the interior light illuminating her, she blinked at him and attempted a faltering smile. Deep circles under her eyes attested to her exhaustion.

Immediately, he went to her. "Let me help you."

She shook her head. "I'm fine. Really."

Still, when he offered his arm, she took it, leaning heavily on him as they made their way toward the porch. She smelled like smoke.

"I'm going to take off," Rayna said, stifling a yawn with her hand. "I'll be in touch tomorrow."

"Thanks, Rayna," Marissa said, meaning it. "I appreciate everything."

With a wave, Rayna climbed back into her car and backed around, her headlights sweeping over the front of the house.

"Let's get you inside," Jared suggested, keeping his voice gentle. "You look like you're about to fall over."

"Gee, thanks." She gave him a wry, tired smile.

Once inside, with the door closed behind them, he helped her over to the couch. As soon as he'd gotten her seated, with the pet carrier on the cushion next to her, his father appeared, carrying a steaming mug. "Chamomile lavender tea," he explained, handing it carefully to Marissa. "It does wonders for sleep."

Surprised, Jared nodded. He hadn't known his father kept up with herbal teas.

Marissa accepted the mug gratefully. "It's been a day," she said, taking a small sip.

As if in agreement, a loud meow came from the kennel next to her.

"My poor Roxy." She set her mug down on a coaster on the coffee table. "Is it okay if I let her out? She's probably tired of being confined."

"Of course," J.J. said. "I love cats."

Another surprise. Again, Jared refrained from commenting. It seemed he continually learned new things about his father.

"Come on, baby girl," Marissa said. "We're safe now."

As soon as Marissa let her out of the carrier, Roxy jumped down and began checking out the surroundings, her ears alert and her tail high above her back.

"What a beautiful little cat," J.J. said, dropping into his recliner heavily, as if his legs had given out.

Almost as if Roxy understood, she immediately crossed the room to him, jumped up in his lap and began purring. The older man beamed and began petting her.

"Let me put out a bowl of water for her," Jared offered, figuring the cat might be thirsty.

"Thank you. Roxy also needs a litter box, litter and cat food," Marissa said, weaving a little from exhaustion. "Would you mind taking me up to the store?"

He wanted to ask if it could wait until morning, but he figured he could drive to the 24-hour super mart on the outskirts of town if necessary. Judging by Marissa's worried expression, getting the supplies right now would help ease her mind.

"I'll run up to the store and get some," Jared replied. He wanted to ask Marissa what *she* needed, but he figured there'd be plenty of time for that tomorrow. Clearly, she'd lost just about everything in the fire. A shopping trip would definitely be on the agenda soon. Right now, he'd make sure her cat was taken care of.

"No need," his father put in. "I adopted one of the barn cats right after you went off to the rodeo. He was a sickly thing, but he kept me company. After he passed, I kept all of his things in the garage. There's a cat tower, a litter box and a couple tubs of litter. I can bring them in for your little gal."

"What about food?" Marissa asked.

"I don't have any dry kibble, but I still have close to a case of canned cat food. Would that work for now?"

"Definitely. She's already had her dinner much earlier, so I just need something to feed her for breakfast." She stifled a yawn. "I'm sorry. I'm just so tired."

Watching her, more than anything Jared ached to go to her and wrap her up in his arms with a promise that everything would be all right. Since he couldn't, he took a deep breath and offered to show her to her room. "I've put clean sheets and a blanket on the bed," he said. "If you want to go freshen up, I'll get everything set up for Roxy."

"Thank you." She pushed to her feet, the defeated slump of her slender shoulders breaking his heart. "I think I'm going to take a hot shower. I need to get this smoke smell out of my hair." As she turned to make her way down the hallway toward the bathroom, Roxy meowed and jumped down to trot after her.

"Let me help you," his father said, struggling to get up from the chair.

"No need." Jared shook his head. "I've got this. Why don't you go on back to bed and try and get some rest."

"Good idea." The older man gave in gracefully. "Would you mind helping me out of this dang chair?"

After pulling his dad up, Jared headed out to the garage to retrieve the cat stuff. He still couldn't believe he hadn't noticed the cat tree and covered litter box, not to mention several plastic jugs of cat litter. There was also nearly a case of high-end canned cat food.

After carrying everything into the house, he went ahead

and set up the litter box in the guest bedroom, since he figured Roxy would stay in there with Marissa. After filling it with litter, he put the case of cat food on the dresser. Then he retreated, trying to decide if there might be anything he'd missed.

"Jared?" Marissa's voice, from inside the bathroom. "Do you happen to have a T-shirt or something that I can wear to sleep in? This one smells awful and I don't want to put it back on now that I've showered." She paused. "And maybe a long-sleeved flannel shirt that I can use as a robe?"

"Of course." Hurrying into his room, he grabbed one of his softest, clean T-shirts and a red and black flannel shirt. When he tapped on the bathroom door, she opened it just wide enough for him to hand it to her. Once she'd closed it, he stood there for a moment like a fool, unable to keep from imagining her sliding it over her head and down her naked, silky body.

He'd just barely retreated down the hall when the door opened and she emerged, her cat staying close by her side. "Thank you," she told him, her tired smile not quite reaching her eyes.

"Sleep well," he offered, wishing he had the courage—the right—to say more. Instead, he stood there like a lovestruck fool, wishing for what he damn well couldn't have.

For a moment, her gaze met his and held, as if she knew. Then she and Roxy disappeared into the guest bedroom. She closed the door behind her and he was left standing with his heart on his sleeve, glad she hadn't noticed.

Though he turned off all the lights and went back to his own bed, sleep mostly eluded him. He tossed and turned, worrying about Marissa, worrying about his father and trying to make sense of all the random events that had happened since he'd arrived back in town.

Morning came, as mornings do, and he got up out of his bed. Stiff and sore, his knee throbbing, he limped into the kitchen intent on making a pot of strong coffee.

To his surprise, the coffee had already been made. He smelled it before he even turned the corner into the kitchen. Marissa sat at the kitchen table sipping from a cup, his flannel shirt swallowing her up. With her hair mussed and the remnants of sleep still clouding her eyes, she looked more beautiful than ever.

"Mornin'," he managed, feeling self-conscious as he made his way to the cabinet to grab a mug.

"Your knee is bothering you," she observed. "Which I'm going to guess means you haven't done your morning stretches yet."

He poured himself some coffee before turning to answer. "Yes and no. I didn't sleep well last night, so I need a jolt of caffeine before I even think about doing any exercises."

The vulnerability in her gaze nearly stopped him in his tracks. "I'm sorry," she murmured. "I know I woke both you and your dad. I just didn't know what else to do."

Part of him wondered why she hadn't called David, but he didn't really want to know. Maybe she had, and David had been too busy or hadn't answered his phone.

"I'm glad you did," he replied, taking a seat at the table across from her. "You know you can stay here as long as you need."

She nodded. "Thanks. I'm probably going to have to take you up on that. I need to call my parents, but the last time I talked to them, they were on the other side of the country. I know they'd come back if I asked them to, but I'm really not sure me and Roxy would do well living with them in their motor home."

"I don't blame you there. What about your business?"

She held up her phone. "Luckily, I sync my appointment schedule with my calendar. I've got to start calling people and letting them know therapy is cancelled for the foresee-able future. At least until I find a new place to use tempo-rarily." She swallowed. "I know you mentioned something about me using the old ranch office. If you meant that, I'd like to take a look at it, though I'm not sure my clients will be too happy driving this far outside of town for therapy."

"It's better than driving to Abilene or Midland-Odessa," he put in, keeping his tone mild. "Though I don't know what you'd do about equipment."

She grimaced. "I need to see how badly damaged my stuff is. Judging from the size of that fire, I'm going to guess everything is a total loss."

"Do you want me to drive you over there?" he asked.

"Please. We can bring your dad and make an outing out of it." Lifting her chin, she took another swallow of coffee before continuing. "I want to go over to Lou's and see about purchasing an inexpensive used car."

Initially surprised, he realized he didn't blame her. Lou ran a used car lot on the north side of town. He was known for being fair and honest, which is why his business re-mained so successful.

"I've lost everything," she continued. "At least by buy-ing a car, I can start rebuilding my life."

His phone pinged, indicating a text message. "It's Rayna," he said. "She says she didn't want to wake you, but wants me to find out if you can meet her at your place in two hours."

Wincing, she slowly nodded. "I can. If you don't mind driving that is."

"I don't mind at all. And my dad can ride with us. Getting out of the house always does him some good."

As if on cue, his father ambled into the kitchen, still rubbing sleep out of his eyes. "Not until I've had at least two cups of coffee," he grumbled. "And something to eat. Then I'll be good to go."

The warmth of Marissa's smile tugged at Jared's heart.

"We'll get you fixed up, Mr. Miller," she said. "I think we all need coffee and breakfast. We've got enough time to do all that, plus have our showers and get dressed."

Jared's father beamed at her. "You're a delight to have around, young lady."

Marissa blushed and ducked her head, but Jared could tell she was pleased. "I'm cooking breakfast," she announced. "Eggs, bacon and toast. Let me get you a cup of coffee, Mr. Miller, and then I'll start cooking."

"You can call me J.J.," the older man said. "And thank you, very much."

"Do you want any help?" Jared asked.

Immediately, she shook her head. "No, thank you. You both have done so much for me. I'd like to do something, however small, to repay you both for your kindness."

"You could help by fetching Marissa some proper clothes," J.J. added. "And shoes. There should be something of your mother's tucked up in my closet. Won't fit perfect but it'll do a better job than just that shirt."

Jared and Marissa shared a look before she glanced down at herself. "I suppose I could use some pants."

Jared chuckled. "On it," he said, then moseyed off to J.J.'s room. He found some flats, an old blouse and a pair of women's jeans in a storage box, which he set down in the bathroom for her before he returned.

Watching Marissa bustle around the small kitchen as if she belonged there started another kind of ache inside Jared. He could have had this; they'd often discussed what kind of life they'd have together after college. They'd planned to buy a small house with some land, raise a couple of kids, and dogs and cattle.

Instead, midway through college where he'd been working toward a degree in journalism, he'd taken off for the rodeo and she'd gone on with the life she'd planned. Now, he had to do the best he could to earn her trust once again, and hopefully they could manage to get back to that place once again. Jared and Marissa against the world.

"Here you go." Marissa slid a plate of food in front of both him and his father, interrupting his thoughts. She went back and got her own, settling down at the chair in between them to eat.

Once breakfast was over, Jared jumped up and began gathering the dishes. "I'll take care of these," he told Marissa, his tone firm. "Why don't you go get ready?"

"Thanks." Her smile warmed his heart. She jumped up and hurried off to do exactly that. A moment later, he heard the shower start up.

"You sure are moping around like a love-struck fool," his dad observed. "Even I can see that, though Marissa sure appears oblivious."

Jared shrugged and continued taking plates to the sink. He rinsed each one off and placed it into the dishwasher before tackling the frying pans. "As long as she's still dating that David guy, I'm kind of limited as to what I can do."

"Really?" J.J. snorted. "I don't see a ring on her finger.

Nor has her supposed boyfriend been around much at all. If things were serious between them, he'd damn sure be making sure she was being taken care of. And he definitely wouldn't like her staying at her ex-boyfriend's house."

"I'm trying to take things slow," Jared pointed out. "Her life has been nothing but turmoil the last couple of weeks. The last thing she needs is me pushing her into picking up where we left off."

"Agree to disagree." His father pushed up from the table. "You ever think that maybe that might be exactly what she needs?"

He left the room without waiting for an answer. Jared stared after him, wondering if he might be right.

Being in the Miller's ranch house felt comforting. Maybe because the familiarity took her back to a time when things were much simpler and easy. Sometimes when she looked at Jared, she couldn't help but see how things could have been different. She'd never forgotten the plans they'd made or the hope they'd shared. Or, if she were completely honest with herself, how much she'd loved him.

And how awful the pain had been when he'd broken her heart.

For a long time, she'd wondered if she'd ever recover. She'd had no interest in dating anyone else, so instead she'd focused on finishing school and establishing her career.

David had been her first actual attempt at a serious relationship and look how that had turned out.

After showering, she used an old blow-dryer she found under the sink to dry her hair, using her fingers since she didn't have a brush or a comb. Once she'd gotten it reasonably dry, she braided it into one long braid, just to keep it out of her way.

Once she was dressed in the clothing Jared left, she cleared out of the bathroom so Jared could have his turn.

An hour later, they all met in the kitchen again. Though butterflies appeared to have taken up residence in her stomach, she managed what she hoped looked like a genuine smile. "Are y'all ready? Let's do this."

Luckily, Jared's father kept up a steady stream of chatter from the backseat, so she didn't have to talk. Which she knew was a good thing, because there were so many thoughts swirling around inside her head. Anything she said might have come out as gibberish.

"Here's your street," Jared announced. Instantly, his dad went silent.

Marissa gripped the door handle, her knuckles white, and tried to brace herself for what she might see. When she first caught sight of the charred hulk of burned lumber and ashes that had once been her home and business, her throat closed and her eyes filled with tears. She'd worked so hard to get established, spent so much time and money making her home exactly the way she wanted it, not to mention getting top of the line equipment for her clinic.

Now, nothing but soot and rubble remained.

As Jared coasted the truck to a halt at the curb, she turned to see both him and his father staring at the remains of her building.

"At least I have good insurance." She attempted a joke, though her voice cracked midway through. "They're going to love me. First my Tahoe is totaled, and now this is burnt to the ground. Every single thing I own is gone."

By the time she'd gotten the entire last sentence out, tears were streaming down her cheeks. She hated feeling so bereft and helpless, but enough was enough.

"Here." Jared took a paper napkin and began gently blotting at her face. "It's going to be okay, Marissa. You'll see. You've got this."

Swallowing back a sob, she tried to be as strong as he clearly believed her to be. "Thanks," she managed. "This is way harder than I thought it would be."

In the backseat, Jared's dad let out a low whistle. "That must have been some fire. You're dang lucky to have gotten out alive." He shook his head. "You and that pretty little cat of yours. Things can be replaced. Lives cannot."

He was right. She knew this. She also knew she needed to get out of the car, though waiting for Rayna to arrive would give her a little bit of time to compose herself.

Taking several deep breaths, she concentrated on getting her emotions under control.

A moment later, the sheriff's car pulled up. She squared her shoulders and inhaled again, hoping for strength.

Jared got out and came around to the passenger side and opened Marissa's door. "You got this," he repeated, offering his hand. "And I'll be right here with you."

Grateful for his support, she lifted her chin, placed her hand in his and got out.

"Marissa!" Rayna greeted her with a quick hug. "What a mess." She turned to Jared and hugged him next. "Is that your father there in the backseat?" Without waiting for an answer, she waved. J.J. waved back, but remained inside the pickup.

"The fire chief has confirmed what we all knew," Rayna said. "This fire was set deliberately. I've sent the videos from your security camera to a friend of mine who specializes in high tech stuff and he's working on making the images clearer. Once we have that, we'll print off some flyers and post them all around town. Though we don't have a good face shot, maybe something about the person's movements or clothing will jog someone's memory."

Marissa liked that Rayna had a plan.

"Do you want to walk around and take a look, just in case any of your belongings made it through the fire?" Rayna asked.

Skeptical, Marissa hesitated. "I'm not sure anything could survive that."

"You'd be surprised." Rayna took her arm. "I'll go with you. At least take a look."

For whatever reason, Marissa found herself looking at Jared.

"I'll come, too," he said, flanking her other side. "We don't have to take too long."

Grateful, she finally nodded. With Rayna on her left and Jared on her right, she walked across the sidewalk and into her yard.

Her rose bushes—gone. All the carefully cultivated landscaping she'd done to make the entire building look pretty had been lost in the fire. Even her favorite oak tree hadn't emerged unscathed. The flames had clearly spread from the house to its branches, decimating the tree.

She barely had time to mourn that before moving to the husk of what had once been her beautiful home and office. Here had been her physical therapy room. The metal parts of the exercise machines had made it through, the once shiny metal now blackened. Marissa walked past it without stopping, once again blinking back tears.

Only when she reached the part of the building that had

been her home, did she pause. "Ashes," she mused out loud. "Nothing but ashes."

"What's that?" Rayna pointed, before stooping and reaching for something she'd seen. "A picture frame," she said, handing it to Marissa. "But whatever was inside has been burnt away."

Marissa glanced at the frame before dropping it back into the ashes. "I don't want to see any more," she said, managing to keep her voice steady. Blindly, she turned and managed to trip over her own two feet, which made her stumble.

Luckily, Jared caught her. "Steady," he murmured.

Grateful, she looked up at him and nodded.

Back at his truck, she swallowed. "I'm not going to lie. This is really hard. My insurance company will be sending out an adjuster and I'm sure he or she will want to meet with the fire department."

Rayna nodded, the sympathy in her face almost causing Marissa to break down. "Let me know if there's anything I can do to help," the sheriff said. "In the meantime, I'll work on getting some photos printed of the arsonist. We'll get them posted all around town. Someone is bound to recognize something."

"Thanks," Marissa replied. She allowed Rayna to pull her in for a quick hug before turning and climbing back inside Jared's truck. She buckled herself in, staring straight ahead, aware if she allowed herself to look back at her home one more time, she would lose it.

Jared's dad must have sensed her fragile state of mind, because he reached up and squeezed her shoulder. "I'm sorry, Marissa."

A moment later, Jared got in and started the engine. "I know you wanted to go look at used cars, but we can do that later. I have a better idea. Let's go for a little drive," he said. "I know a place about forty-five minutes away that has the best barbecue. They open at noon, but people start lining up around now. Maybe we'll get lucky and be able to get in line before they run out of brisket."

"Great idea," J.J. agreed. "You're talking R.T.'s Barbecue Pit, aren't you? It's worth the wait and I think we'd all enjoy the outing."

Jared glanced at Marissa, as though requiring her approval. She shrugged, then nodded. "Any kind of distraction would be welcome right now," she said. "And I can always eat barbecue."

"And Shiner!" J.J. chimed in from the backseat. "In a frosty glass."

The elation in his voice made Marissa smile. But only for a second. The enormity of her loss turned everything gray.

Jared found a classic country music station on the radio and turned it on low. That, and the repetitive motion of the drive must have put his father to sleep, because quiet snores began to come from the backseat.

The sound had Jared grinning.

"He seems really happy," Marissa offered, keeping her voice low.

"He is." Jared glanced at the rearview mirror. "Right now, he's living in the moment, not as much in the past. I've been told that's likely to change, but I'll take it for as long as I can."

"Speaking of parents, I need to call mine," she said, taking out her phone. "I already told my mom about the wreck."

"Ouch." Jared winced. "I can only imagine how they'll react when they learn about the fire."

"I dread this conversation," she admitted, turning her

phone over and over in her hands. "Maybe I'll put it off until later."

He didn't press her, which she appreciated.

"What about David?" he asked. "Have you let him know yet?"

The instant flash of anger she felt startled her. "What is it with you and David?" she asked, keeping her voice low. "Are you two buddies or something?"

He gave her a startled look. "Whoa. Not hardly. I'm just making conversation. I figured you'd want to let your boyfriend know what happened."

There were several ways she could respond to that. She could tell him that her relationship with David was none of his business. Which would be true, but Jared had been nothing if not kind to her and she didn't want to lash out at him for something that wasn't his fault. Yet, if she answered truthfully, saying she had not contacted David, then Jared would know her relationship wasn't what it seemed. And, since she tended to use that very relationship as a shield in between her and Jared, she definitely didn't want to do that.

Instead, she shook her head and instead of replying, dialed her mother's cell phone, bracing herself for the conversation to come.

To her relief, the call went to voice mail. She left a quick message, letting them know she was fine, but to call her when the opportunity arose.

After ending the call, she let out a big sigh. "I just dodged a bullet," she said. "I really hate upsetting my parents. I almost wish I didn't have to fill them in on what's happened."

"I get that." He glanced sideways at her. "But I'm sure they know how capable you are. Yes, they'll be worried.

That's only natural. I'm thinking they'll figure out pretty quickly that you've got everything under control."

She shot him an incredulous look. "Under control? I'm barely hanging on. I've not only lost everything except for my cat, but I have no place to live and no income stream. Until I get that all figured out..." Letting the words trail off, she shook her head, unwilling to let him see or hear the full extent of her anguished frustration.

After a moment, he nodded. "I get that. Marissa, please understand you've always got me, too. My ear to listen, my shoulder to cry on and all the help I can give. My home is open to you for as long as you want or need it, and if you want to run your business out of the barn office, it's there."

Words that, under any other circumstances, would be enough to make any woman swoon. And not just words, she knew. Jared meant everything he'd said. *At the moment.*

She had to remind herself of this. Because Jared had once promised to love her forever, to always stay by her side. And he hadn't. So she said the one thing she knew would put them back on track, where they needed to be. "Thanks, Jared. I appreciate that." Patting his shoulder, she summoned up a smile. "You're such a good friend."

Chapter Twelve

Startled, Jared barely managed to keep a poker face. With her expressive features, Marissa had never been able to hide her emotions. Now was no exception. Though she knew he was more, she'd designated him a friend, as if that could change the chemistry between them. More than chemistry, actually. They not only shared a past, but he knew deep inside they could forge an awesome future. If she would only let him in past the walls she'd built around her heart.

In the end, what mattered right now was that she understood she could count on him. Words were cheap. Actions mattered. Due to the way he'd let her down once before, he got that she'd be reluctant to believe him. Which was okay. He'd simply have to show her.

At least it appeared Rayna had been right about David. Marissa definitely didn't act like she loved the guy.

His father woke up just as they were pulling into R.T.'s. As expected, a line already snaked around the front of the building, but Jared had seen it way worse.

"Dad, if you want, you can wait in the truck until we get closer to the door," Jared offered.

"I'll stand in line," J.J. replied. "I'm not decrepit."

"I didn't say you were." Jared kept his tone mild. "I just

thought you might welcome not having to stand on your feet for thirty minutes or more."

"That's nothin'," the older man scoffed. "I've waited for brisket for longer than that."

"We've got you." Marissa smiled. Her first genuine smile since leaving the ranch earlier. "If you get tired, you can always sit down on the curb. We'll save your place in line."

This made J.J. guffaw. "I like her," he told Jared. "She's a keeper, so you'd better not let her get away."

"I don't plan on it." Though Jared kept his tone light, he meant every word.

Outside, the air smelled like smoke and deliciousness. For a moment they all stood there, breathing it in.

"Come on," Marissa said, tugging Jared's father's arm. "I've suddenly realized I'm starving."

Jared and his dad exchanged grins. "Come on," Jared said.

They got in line, which appeared to be moving at a steady pace.

It took a while, but they finally made it inside. The strong scent of delicious food made Jared's mouth water.

They got their trays and made their way down the line, each making their selections of meat and then sides. Since they all wanted the brisket, Jared knew they'd have leftovers. J.J. and Marissa went to find a table while Jared paid.

Once Jared joined them, dropping onto the bench next to his dad, they all dug in.

He could get used to this—watching Marissa joke with his father over a heaping platter of brisket that they all shared. The easy camaraderie reminded him that this was the family he should have had. Would have had, if he'd stayed instead of running off to the rodeo.

When he looked up, he realized his father had been watching him. "Stop beating yourself up over what could have been," the older man murmured close to his ear. "Enjoy what you have now. She'll come around eventually."

"What?" One brow raised, Marissa eyed them over a large piece of corn bread she'd been about to take a bite of. "What are you two whispering about over there?"

Jared shook his head, but his dad grinned and replied. "I'm telling him how lucky he is to have you."

A tiny frown line appeared in between her eyebrows. She opened her mouth and then closed it, but Jared heard the unspoken words as surely as if she'd said them. *He doesn't have me.*

Not yet, he silently replied. *But someday. Someday soon.*

After the meal, full and content, they trooped back to Jared's truck for the drive home. As expected, J.J. fell asleep almost immediately. Marissa dozed off a few minutes later, sitting in the passenger side with her head back and her eyes closed.

She woke up when they were ten minutes from the Getaway city limits. "Are we there yet?" she asked, giving him a sideways smile.

"Just about," he replied. "Do you still want to stop and look at cars? We're not that far from Lou's."

"Yes, please. I really need to have my own form of transportation. I've got enough saved to be able to purchase something fairly inexpensive that I can use until my insurance company settles with me on the Tahoe."

"I'm sure Lou can help you out," Jared said. Lou had a reputation for being honest and fair. By now, he'd have heard about Marissa's accident and would no doubt be eager to help her out in any way possible.

When they pulled up to the used car lot, Jared's dad woke. "Are we home?" he asked, sitting up and rubbing his eyes.

"Not yet," Jared responded. "You can go back to sleep. We're making a quick stop at Lou's to see if Marissa can find a car."

J.J. grumbled something unintelligible and went right back to sleep.

Lou himself greeted them as they walked over toward the lot. Though Jared still limped, he honestly thought he'd improved his gait. And Marissa, while she seemed a bit stiff, gave no sign of being in any kind of pain.

"Marissa Noll and Jared Miller!" Lou's eyes lit up when he greeted them. "It's been a long time since I sold you that sweet '69 Camaro."

The memory had Jared grinning. "My first—and last— hot rod. After I wrecked her, you sold me a truck. I've driven trucks ever since."

Lou nodded. "As you should. Any rodeo cowboy in his right mind drives trucks. You and that '69 were never a good fit."

"But I was," Marissa interjected. "I loved that car. The few times Jared let me drive it, I was in heaven. If I could have scraped together enough money, I'd have bought it off him."

"She cried when I wrecked it," Jared admitted. "And not entirely because I managed to escape without being hurt."

Grimacing, Lou clapped Jared on the shoulder before turning to Marissa. "I'm sorry about what happened to your Tahoe," he said. "I'm guessing you're here for a replacement?"

"Yes, please. Nothing too expensive, as whatever I buy will be just temporary until the insurance pays me." She swallowed. "I've got some money saved up, so I can pay cash, but it's going to have to be on a much less expensive vehicle."

"I see. I have an idea. Why go through this twice? Marissa, I've known you for years. Why don't you pick out the kind of car or SUV you want to keep and let me finance it with zero interest?"

"You'd do that for me?" Marissa asked, expression incredulous.

Lou rubbed the top of his shiny, bald head. "I heard about the fire." His expression softened. "You've done a lot to help the people of this town and you've been through enough. Let me do this for you."

"Thank you." Eyes shiny, Marissa nodded. "Then show me what you've got. I'd like another Tahoe or something similar, if you have it. Is there any chance I can purchase one and take it tonight?"

"Of course there is," Lou reassured her. "I have a couple of Tahoes, a Ford Explorer or two, and several others. Let's go take a look."

Jared touched her arm. "Do you want me to hang out with you while you do this? If you don't mind, I'd like to get my dad home."

"Go." Wiping at her eyes, she grinned. "I've got this. I'll see you later."

And then, to his utter surprise, she leaned in and kissed his cheek. He stood there, stunned, watching as she took Lou's arm and they moved away.

Back in the truck, he found his father sitting up, watching Marissa and Lou walk off.

"He's going to take care of her," Jared said, and told his dad what Lou had offered to do.

"Good. We look out for each other here in Getaway," the older man replied. "One of the many reasons I've always loved living in the town."

"I'm beginning to really appreciate small town life as well," Jared commented. "Do you want to come sit up front?"

"Sure." His father climbed out, walked around to the passenger side and got in. Once he'd fastened his seat belt, Jared backed out and pulled away.

"Have you given any thought to what you're going to do in order to make a living?" his dad asked. "Assuming you still plan to stay here, that is."

"Oh, I'm not going anywhere." Jared smiled. "That's for certain."

"Good. I'm hoping I get some grandchildren before I get too old or too sick to enjoy them."

Startled, at first Jared wasn't sure how to react. "That came out of nowhere," he commented, gripping the steering wheel as he continued to drive.

"Did it?" his dad asked, smiling. "Because when I watch you and Marissa, I can see all the signs. You're itching to settle down and start a family. Don't even bother to try and deny it."

"I won't," Jared replied, surprising himself. "Though I admit I haven't started planning that far ahead yet. Right now, it's to start figuring out ways to make this ranch produce an income." He waited, bracing himself in case his father reacted badly.

"I'm listening," J.J. said. "And I have an idea that might work."

"No cattle," Jared interjected. "I know you've had success in the past running a cattle operation, but I just don't have it in me."

"I agree," his dad replied, surprising him once again. A slight smile played around his mouth. "You'd make a lousy cattle rancher."

"Gee, thanks." Instead of being offended, all Jared felt was relief that they were on the same page. "What are you thinking, then?"

"You're good with horses."

The statement made Jared smile. "I am."

"You always have been, ever since you were knee-high. I think that's why you ran off to join the rodeo. I always thought you should have started a cutting horse training business."

"Cutting horse?" Jared asked. "I have zero experience in that area."

His father made a rude sound. "That's not true. You did very well in junior rodeo and you trained your horse yourself."

"Fine. But still. You know as well as I do how competitive the cutting horse business is. People pay lots of money for a well-trained animal. My experience doesn't match up." He swallowed. "I hate to break it to you, but if that's the best plan you can come up with, we'll never be able to keep the ranch afloat."

"Patience, son," J.J. chided. "That's not my idea. I'm getting there." Shaking his head, he chuckled. "But it does involve horses."

"Out with it," Jared demanded. "What's your idea for transforming the ranch?"

"Equine therapy. You provide the horses and hire Marissa to work out the therapy. You could use the old ranch office as a home base. I did a little research and this type of therapy is catching on and in high demand. I bet you could get referrals from hospitals all around West Texas."

Feeling a spark of excitement, Jared stared. Equine therapy. The idea had merit. More than merit, actually. And as an added bonus, something he and Marissa could do together as partners. The only catch would be her. "What if she's not interested?"

His dad shrugged. "You won't know until you ask her. And if she says no, you can see if she'll work on a consulting basis. Or you can hire someone else. There's lots of possibilities and I've been doing some reading. The demand is out there."

"Is it?" Intrigued, Jared drummed his fingers on the steering wheel. "Can you share some of the articles you've read with me? I'm really interested in this."

"I'll email them to you."

Surprised and grateful, Jared realized he might have underestimated his dad. While in the early stages of a serious and debilitating illness, that didn't mean Jared should be counting him out.

AFTER JARED AND his father drove off, Marissa allowed herself to concentrate on choosing her next vehicle. While she'd loved the Tahoe, she wasn't averse to looking at another make and model of SUV.

"I do want relatively new," she told Lou. "Not more than two years old. I need to make sure there's still warranty."

"Can I interest you in extending your vehicle's warranty?" Lou wisecracked, which made her laugh.

He showed her five SUVs, all within the same age range.

In the end, she chose another Chevy Tahoe, the same year as the one she'd just lost, though this one was red.

"Good choice," Lou told her. "This one is really nice and has low mileage."

Signing the paperwork took less than an hour. Lou did the financing himself, with zero interest, exactly as he'd promised. Finally, he handed her the keys and told her to enjoy her new vehicle.

Rayna called just as Marissa was about to drive off.

"Any luck figuring out the arsonist?" Marissa asked.

"Not yet," Rayna replied. "But I'm printing out a bunch of flyers with the photo on it. Once they're done, would you mind picking up a stack and helping me get them put up all over town?"

"Since I just got a new vehicle, I can swing by and pick them up now," Marissa offered.

"You did? Congratulations." Rayna's voice rang with excitement. "The flyers won't be ready until tomorrow at least. But I'm really glad to hear you have your own transportation again. Your car insurance company settled up fast."

"Oh, they haven't cut me a check yet." Marissa told her what Lou had done for her.

"He's good people," Rayna said, once she'd heard. "Yet another reason why I love living here in Getaway."

"I agree. Any progress on the arson investigation? I ask because tomorrow I meet with my insurance adjuster for the homeowner's insurance."

"The fire chief is handling that," Rayna replied. "Though he's promised to keep me in the loop."

"Okay. Then let me know as soon as you find out something. I'll swing by and pick up those flyers tomorrow after I meet with my claims adjuster, if that's all right."

"That should be fine. Unless there's a glitch in the printer, they'll be ready by then."

After finishing the call with Rayna, Marissa drove slowly through town. When she reached Serenity's shop, she almost parked and went in to talk to the older woman, but realized she just couldn't take any more prophecies about changes or whatever. She'd already had more than her share of those.

Instead, she continued on through town and headed out toward the ranch.

When she arrived, she parked next to Jared's truck and shut off her engine. She sat for a moment, trying to catch her breath. She owed Jared and his father a debt she wasn't sure she could ever repay. They'd not only opened their home to her, but gone out of their way to make her feel comfortable.

Back in high school, she'd spent a lot of time at the ranch with Jared. She'd often entertained dreams of one day living there as a young married couple and perhaps raising their own family on the land that had been in Jared's family for generations. How naive she'd been, she thought now. She'd honestly believed she could have everything—her chosen career and the only man she'd ever loved.

Past tense, she reminded herself. Never again would she allow herself to be so vulnerable. Except right now, she kind of was. She'd established a good life on her own, started a successful business from the ground up and now she'd been left with nothing.

Oh, she would rebuild. Because one thing she'd learned about herself was her resilience.

Getting out of her new Tahoe, she walked toward the door and then turned around and took a moment to admire it. She'd never had a red vehicle before. She thought red suited her fine.

Her phone rang right before she reached the front porch. David. She decided to stay outside to take the call.

"I've got exciting news," David said, barely allowing her to get out a hello. "I've got a new vet student coming to be my intern. Once he's trained, having him around will give me a lot more free time."

"Congratulations," she replied.

"Thanks. I think a celebration is in order. Would you like to go out with me?"

Startled, she blinked. "When?"

"Now!" He laughed. "I can swing by and pick you up in thirty minutes and take you out for a nice steak dinner."

"I can't," she said, only mildly regretful. "I went with Jared and his dad and had a huge barbecue lunch. I'm still full. Maybe another time."

For a moment, David went silent. "Are you sure?" he asked, a thread of anger warring with confusion in his voice. "I thought you'd be happy to spend time with me. You know how rare it is that I'm free."

Now, she thought to herself. He'd just given her the perfect opening to end things. "David, I think we both need to take a step back," she began.

Just then the door opened and Jared came out. "Are you okay?" he asked, before realizing she was on the phone.

"I'm fine," she told him, turning away in hopes he'd understand she needed privacy. She definitely didn't want Jared to know if she broke up with David. He'd see that as the perfect opening for him to try and get closer.

But then, would that be a bad thing?

"You don't sound fine," David said, thinking she'd been talking to him. "And if you want to have a relationship talk, I don't think we should do that over the phone. Since I want to celebrate tonight, how about we postpone that until we can have a chat in person?"

Which meant indefinitely. She nearly groaned out loud. "I'm really exhausted, David," she said, more for Jared's benefit than anything else. "You go and have that steak dinner without me. I'll catch you another time."

Something in her voice must have alerted David about how she really felt. "I'll be there in thirty minutes," he said, his no-nonsense tone leaving no room for argument. "I know I haven't been there much for you lately and you've gone through a lot. See you soon."

Before she could decline, he ended the call.

"Great," she muttered, turning around to see Jared was still eyeing her. "David is on his way."

A quick flash of what looked like jealousy crossed his face.

For whatever reason, she felt the need to tell him the truth. "I'm ending it with him," she said quietly, meeting his gaze. "Though I'm thinking we'll still remain friends." Since their relationship had never been truly passionate to begin with, if anything, David's pride would be the only thing she'd hurt.

Gaze still locked on hers, Jared came closer. "Good," he said, imbibing the single word with a wealth of meaning.

The warmth in his husky voice sent a shiver of longing through her. Reminding herself that he was still technically her client, she forced herself to look away and break the spell.

"Let's go inside." Jared took her arm. "You might as well wait for David in the house."

She allowed him to escort her inside, resisting the urge to lean into him. J.J. looked up as they entered the living room, smiling so broadly that she had to wonder if something was up.

"Dad, are you okay?" Jared asked.

"I'm fine. Better than fine," the older man answered, pretending to go back to reading his magazine. "You two kids just act like I'm not here."

Marissa shook her head. "We'd never do that," she answered. "We enjoy your company too much."

J.J. made a tsk-tsk sound, but she could tell he was pleased.

David arrived thirty minutes later. She shot out of her chair the instant she heard the truck tires on gravel, not wanting him to knock on the door or come inside.

He'd just gotten out of his truck when she stepped out onto the front porch. "Hey there," she said as she moved toward him. "How about we go for a drive?"

"Sure." Though he didn't sound too happy about the idea, David at least attempted to crack a smile. "We can do that if you want."

They each got inside the truck. "Any place in particular you want to go?" he asked, starting it and backing out of the driveway.

"How about we park at the place we used to go to watch the sunset?" Back when they'd first started dating and they'd spent a lot of time together, they'd often driven to nowhere in particular and sat in his truck and talked.

"Sure," he replied, expression stricken.

Once they'd pulled into the short rest area, he put the truck in park and turned to face her. "I'm not going to like this, am I?"

"You're not going to hate it either." She kept her tone matter-of-fact. "You know as well as I do that whatever spark we first had between us has long ago fizzled out."

He gave a quick nod, still watching her.

"And I know you are super busy with your job," she continued.

This finally encouraged him to talk.

"It's not easy being the only vet for miles," he said. "Not only do I have my small animal practice, but I've also got to take care of the livestock. I'm stretched really thin. I know it seemed like I never had time for us, but—"

"It's okay." Interrupting him, she placed her hand on his. "I understand. But I can't help but feel you made time for other things."

There. She'd left him the perfect opening to tell her about the other woman—or women—he'd been seeing. Even if the blonde in the bar had been a one-time thing, she felt she deserved to know.

Instead, David shook his head. "Now that I've found some help, I can try to do better," he began.

"I'm not sure I see the point," she said gently. "I think we'd be better off as friends."

David's relieved expression would have been comical in any other situation. "I'd like that," he told her. "I actually really like you, Marissa."

"I like you, too. But you and I both know a romantic relationship needs to be something more."

He gave a slow nod, his silver hair catching the light. "I'm sorry," he began.

"I'm sorry, too," she countered. "I'm sure we'll still talk and maybe catch a bite to eat together now and then."

"I'd like that." Leaning over, he kissed her cheek. "As a matter of fact, I'd still like to have a steak dinner with you.

I know you said you're full, but maybe you could have a salad or something and we could just catch up."

"As friends?" she asked, needing to be sure that he wasn't about to try and make a bid to get her to change her mind.

"Definitely as friends," he replied. "I can't think of anyone else I'd want to celebrate with."

Again tempted to bring up the blonde, she restrained herself. After all, they weren't really together and actually hadn't been for quite some time. "I'd like that," she replied softly.

They had a nice meal in the kind of candlelight normally conducive to romance, except they both clearly felt more at ease now that the air had been cleared. David talked about his new intern and asked a lot of questions about her accident and the fire. For the first time in a long time, the conversation flowed easily.

By the time they'd finished the meal, David eyed her quizzically. "Are you sure you just want to be friends? I've really enjoyed tonight."

She couldn't help but smile. "I have, too. But we do much better as friends, David. Your special someone is out there somewhere."

Slowly, he nodded. "Thanks for that. Friends it is."

After he'd paid the check, they walked back to his truck. "Do you mind if I ask you something?"

"Go ahead." Getting in, she fastened her seatbelt before turning to face him.

"Are you and Jared getting back together?" In the driver's seat, he smiled at her. "Anyone with two eyes can see how crazy he is about you."

Once, she would have immediately shot down the idea.

Now, she merely shrugged. "I don't know," she answered. "And that's the honest truth."

"I think you should consider it," he began.

This made her grimace before lightly punching his upper arm. "I think this is one area where you need to mind your own business," she countered.

Her response made him laugh. "Point taken," he said. "Let's get you home."

Home. The place where her heart was.

Though her first inclination was to shy away from this idea, instead she buried it deep inside her. Truthfully, with her entire life in shambles, she couldn't take the chance of letting her heart be shattered again.

Chapter Thirteen

Though Jared tried not to wait for Marissa to return, he found himself pacing the hallway.

"Will you please stop?" His father looked up from the TV to complain. "She's already told you that she's breaking up with him."

Startled, Jared did a double take. "You heard that? We were outside."

"I had my window open." J.J. chuckled. "You know my bedroom is right by the driveway." He shook out his book. "Why don't you find something constructive to do so you don't wear a path in the hallway with your pacing?"

"I think I will," Jared said. Since the last thing he wanted to do was discuss Marissa with his father, he let himself outside and headed toward the barn.

Letting himself inside, he breathed in the familiar scent of horse and hay and felt some of the tension leave him. He visited with the horses, brushing down one thoroughly before moving on to the other. When he'd finally finished, he felt more like himself. He'd once again allowed his feelings for Marissa tie him up in knots.

Checking the time, he wondered if it was too late to call

Rayna. Figuring she'd let him know if it was, he pulled up her contact info and hit send.

She answered on the second ring. "Hey there, Jared. What's up? I'm about to head home for the day, so I've got about five minutes tops."

"That's all I need," Jared said. "I'm wondering if you've had any luck locating Custer. I've texted and called him a couple times with no response." He thought for a moment. "However, since he said he dropped his phone into the toilet, maybe he has a different number."

"Maybe so. I've been trying to call him also. I even stopped by his family ranch a few days ago," Rayna replied. "His parents say they don't know where he went. And they said he left his phone there, which is unusual for him."

"I wonder if he really ruined it," Jared mused. "Something always seemed fishy about that entire thing. Along with the fact that he wasn't driving his truck... I don't know." He took a deep breath. "Do you believe his parents? It seems weird that he didn't take his phone."

"It does, and for that reason I'm a little skeptical. They don't seem like the kind of people who would lie, even for their son. But they didn't seem worried at all." Rayna sighed. "While Custer does have a history of taking off, him doing so without any way to contact them would be cause for concern, at least with me."

"Unless he got yet another phone. One of those disposable ones."

"That occurred to me also," Rayan admitted. "Which would indicate he's actually done something wrong and is trying to hide. I hope that's not the case."

"Me, too. I've known Custer almost my entire life. I hate thinking he's capable of something like this."

"Honestly, I find it hard to believe. The car wreck might have been exactly that—an unfortunate accident. Except I can't figure out why he'd think he could hide forever."

"Maybe he's just staying away long enough to get his truck fixed," Jared pointed out, though he hated to think that of his friend.

"Possibly, but that kind of thing is pretty easy to find out. Repairs shops keep records. But just in case he shows back up, I've got a guy watching their ranch."

"That's why I was hoping to speak to him, to clear this up once and for all. Have you tried checking with various rodeos?" Jared thought for a moment. "I can look up which of the bigger ones are coming up and check and see if he's entered."

"That would be so helpful." Rayna sounded a little bit stressed. "But I've got to say, after reviewing the videos of whoever set Marissa's house on fire, I have my doubts Custer is involved. He's a totally different body type. Much taller and outweighs that suspect by a good one hundred or more pounds."

"I agree. Plus, Custer would never try to burn someone alive in their own house. I still have my suspicions about the wreck, but I'm thinking it might have been a horrible accident."

"I don't believe Custer was involved with either one," Rayna said, her voice firm. "I have a hunch the same person hit Marissa's SUV and then when that didn't do the trick, set her house on fire."

Stunned, Jared swallowed. "But that would mean someone hates her enough to want her dead." He couldn't fathom that. "Marissa is one of the sweetest, kindest women I know."

Saved by the Texas Cowboy

"I agree." The sympathy in Rayna's agreement warmed Jared's heart. "That's the angle I'm currently working. Who could hate her that much? And why? I don't know, but I'll find out," Rayna promised. "Right now, I need to head on home. I'll talk to you later."

After ending the call, Jared left the barn and closed the large door. He walked over to what had once been the ranch office, an area that had been built on to the exterior of the barn. There were two large windows overlooking the yard, both of which were coated in a thin layer of grime.

He tried the door, unsurprised to find it unlocked. Just inside, he flicked the switch, filling the small room with light. His mother's old desk sat untouched, looking exactly the same as it had when she'd been alive. Moving closer, he traced his finger in the dust. Moving around toward the office chair and the other side of the desk, he saw papers still sat in the inbox, covered with her handwriting.

His father had not been back inside this room since the day his mother had died.

Slowly, Jared walked around the room, trying to envision it cleaned out. Marissa's physical therapy equipment would fit here just fine, once she ordered new ones. He knew a town location would likely work better, but he'd make sure she knew this was an alternative.

Plus, if they ever got the equine therapy operation up and running, this room would be the office.

In the time since his father had suggested the idea, Jared had done quite a bit of reading on the subject. He'd learned that kids with autism did amazingly well with equine therapy, and there was quite a list of other disorders that appeared to benefit. He hadn't brought the idea up yet to Marissa, but depending on her mood tonight, he planned to.

Right now, he went back to the house to grab some cleaning supplies, and spent the next several hours scrubbing the ranch office clean.

Truck headlights coming up the drive alerted him that David had brought Marissa back. They'd been gone a long time, which made Jared wonder if Marissa had changed her mind about breaking up with the other man.

Ignoring the pang of jealousy he felt at the notion, he left the office and headed back toward the house. As he approached, Marissa got out of David's truck, said something too low to make out and closed the door. She gave a friendly wave and stood watching while David drove off.

"Hey there," Jared greeted her. He wanted to ask how everything had gone, but knew it was none of his business.

"Hi," Marissa responded, smiling.

He wasn't sure what he'd expected, exactly. He'd thought maybe she'd be angry, or tired or even hurt. Instead, she appeared relaxed and happy.

Maybe she hadn't broken up with David after all.

While he wanted—needed—to know, he wasn't sure how exactly to ask her. After all, she'd been gone several hours.

"That went better than expected," she said. "David and I have agreed to remain friends."

Relief flooded him.

"We even went out to dinner to celebrate his new hire," she continued. "I think deep inside, David is relieved that he doesn't have to try so hard anymore."

He nodded, unsure what to say. He wanted to tell her that love shouldn't be that difficult, but he figured she'd already realized that. "It's a beautiful night," he said instead. "Do you have a minute? I've been cleaning out the old ranch office and I thought you might like to see it."

"I'd love to," she replied.

Together they walked back toward the barn. Opening the door, he once again flicked on the lights.

"This is a nice space," she said, stepping inside. "And I like that it has a desk for me to do paperwork." She met his gaze. "That was your mom's, wasn't it?"

"It was. And apparently my dad left everything exactly the way it was the last time she used it. I gathered up all her papers and put them in a box."

"Do you think he'll mind that you cleaned it out?" she asked.

"I don't see why he should. It's been years. But I planned to let him have all her old papers so he can decide what to do with them."

He watched her as she began to walk around the room, her long hair swirling softly around her shoulders. He'd always found her beautiful, from the first moment he'd taken a seat next to her in freshman English class.

How he'd managed to leave her, he didn't know. He'd gone chasing after his dreams and left her alone to follow hers. Now that he'd gotten that out of his system, he knew he was lucky that he hadn't lost her.

"This might just work," she finally said, turning and giving him a smile so bright that he couldn't catch his breath. "At least until I can find something in town to rent. I'm thinking it's going to be a long process before my house and clinic are rebuilt."

"Use it however you want to," he told her.

"Shouldn't we ask your dad before we make any final decisions?"

"He's already offered it," he replied. "Actually, he came up with a really great idea for a business partnership."

She blinked. "A partnership with who?"

"You and I. Or you and us. Turns out he's been doing a bit of research and discovered a need for equine therapy. Both physical and to help with psychological disorders."

Her face lit up. "After I got my license, I actually considered doing something like that. But I didn't have a facility to keep horses, along with a riding arena. Not to mention the expense of starting that kind of business." She sighed. "Though there are grants. I was so busy getting my traditional physical therapy business set up that I never really looked too deeply into that."

"We have a couple of horses already," he said. "And the old riding arena can be repaired inexpensively. We can add on more horses as the need arises."

"You're right," she said, her eyes sparkling. Then, to his surprise, she crossed the room and wrapped her arms around him in a hug. "You've got a huge heart, Jared Miller," she said, laughing.

The feel of her, the scent of her hair, nearly brought tears to his eyes. It took every ounce of self-control that he possessed to let her go when she stepped back away from him.

"Let's talk to my dad about it," he said. "He has a lot of information printed out."

Pushing her hair back from her face, she nodded. "We'll do that, just not tonight. It's been a long day. Since I've got to meet the insurance adjuster at the house tomorrow afternoon, I'd like to relax. If you don't mind, I might do a little work in the barn office in the morning."

He slung his arm around her shoulders, deliberately casual. "Of course I don't mind. Would you like any help?"

Briefly leaning her head into him the way she used to do when they'd cruised around in the front bench seat of his old pickup, she shook her head. "Not just yet. Right now, it's something I need to do myself."

This shouldn't have hurt, but it did. He told himself Marissa had always been an independent person, which she had. He'd also never been long on patience, a trait he needed to cultivate, especially now.

"Sounds good." He managed to keep a lighthearted tone. "Just let me know if you change your mind."

"I will," she promised.

Back at the house, she went directly back to her bedroom and greeted her cat before she closed the door. Jared went into the kitchen, aimlessly rubbing his aching hip. He needed to get some physical therapy set up soon. The closest place other than Marissa would be in Abilene, so he'd call and make an appointment.

He went to sleep that night feeling as if life might finally be getting on the right track.

The next morning, after making a cup of coffee, Jared limped into the barn office, where Marissa was hard at work trying to get something set up. He stood in the doorway for a moment watching the way the sun lit up her blond hair. When she looked up, her blue eyes seemed to sparkle. He thought he'd never seen anything so beautiful in his life.

"Hey," Marissa greeted him.

It took him a moment—he had to struggle to find his voice. "I just came by to see how it's going," he said, managing to somehow sound casual.

"Pretty good. I've already ordered some replacement exercise equipment online," she told him, smiling. "I'm just waiting for it to arrive. Two-day shipping, it said."

"That was quick." Heart full, he smiled back at her, wondering if she could see the love he felt for her in his eyes.

If she could, she didn't comment. Instead, she turned away, pointing out where she planned to position everything. "Rebuying this stuff isn't cheap," she said. "That's one of the reasons I was so grateful Lou let me hang on to my savings. That way, I can get my therapy clinic up and running without having to wait for the insurance company. They're taking so long, I'd be out of business by the time they write me a check."

He nodded, the warmth of her smile pulling him closer. He knew she had no idea how she affected him, but he wished he could show her. Sometimes, the ache to reach for her and pull her close felt so overpowering he couldn't think straight.

"Jared?" she asked, eyeing him. "Are you okay?"

Not by a long shot, he wanted to respond. Instead, he nodded again. "I'm fine. I really just wanted to see if there's anything I can do to help." He'd been offering the same thing every day, but so far she'd told him she had everything under control.

Today, instead of sending him away, she cocked her head and studied him.

"You know what? Maybe there is. Do you want to be my first patient?" she asked, her expression serious. "I've had multiple clients contact me and, because they need to have their therapy now, they're driving into Abilene or Midland-Odessa. I'm losing all my customers. I need to get back into the swing of things, and pretty darn quickly."

Somehow, he managed to keep from wincing. For a second, he almost chickened out, but he knew if he wanted to have the slightest hope of a relationship with her, he had to stay firm. "I'm sorry. That stinks." He took a deep breath. "And while I hate to say this, that's actually what I'm going to have to do as well," he said, hoping she'd understand. "I'm sorry, Marissa. I'm going to make an appointment and get started with someone else."

Her face fell. "But we can get back to your therapy right away. You won't have to wait. I might not have all the equipment yet, but I have enough."

Damn. This felt an awful lot like breaking up. Necessary, but still painful. "I appreciate that, but I don't think so."

"I get it," she said, though clearly she didn't. "Why did I even think working out of a barn office would help me keep my business afloat?" The despair in her voice cut deeply.

Crossing the space between them, he took her hand, though he wanted to do more. "That's not why, and I think you know it. Once you're up and running, your clients are all going to return. You're good, Marissa. But as for me, I just don't want to be your patient anymore."

"You don't?" Her expression bewildered, she tried to pull her hand away. But he held on.

"I want to be more," he told her, gazing into her eyes. "You said you can't date clients. So I've decided that I'm not going to be your client. There's too much good between us to ignore it."

"But…" Her mouth fell open.

Gently, he tugged her closer. "I want to kiss you until neither of us can think straight. And if we decide to make love, I don't want anything—or anyone—in between us."

For the first time since he could remember, Marissa appeared struck speechless.

"I know you just got over ending your relationship with David," he continued, figuring he'd already gone this far, so he might as well go all out. "But I also get the feeling it was never all that serious."

Now Marissa wouldn't look at him. Head down, she appeared intent on studying her feet.

"Please look at me," he implored her. He wanted to ask her if he stood a chance, but he figured he already knew the answer to that. Her reaction to his kiss had told him everything they'd once shared still remained. She just had to let down her guard and give him a chance.

Finally, she raised her head and met his gaze. "I don't know what to say." Her voice trembled. "But my life is a complete mess these days. I don't think I can handle anything else right now."

Now he gently pulled her close, ready to release her at the slightest sign of resistance. Instead, she melted into him as if she needed him to hold her as much as he wanted to.

Though he ached to kiss her, he did not. Instead, he simply wrapped his arms around her and held on, breathing in her scent, his heart full.

"I'm afraid," she finally admitted, her voice muffled against his chest. "And I'm not sure I can get past the fear."

"Take your time." He gently kissed the top of her head. "I'm not going anywhere. I promise."

She exhaled. "I can't help but keep thinking you're going to get tired of all this and up and leave."

Which basically was exactly what he'd done before, at least in her eyes.

"I wanted to prove myself," he said. "Make a name in rodeo. Now, I've come to realize what's important. And I have nothing left to prove."

"Good for you." She stiffened and moved away. "Right now, I really need to focus on myself. I'm starting completely over from nothing. That's more than enough to deal with." She paused, shaking her head. "I hope you understand."

His heart went out to her. "I do. That only makes sense. Just realize if you ever want someone to help you shoulder some of the burden, I'm here."

"Thanks," she replied, and moved away. "Now I've got to get busy setting up. If you change your mind about me continuing to do your physical therapy, just let me know."

AFTER SPENDING WHAT felt like a pointless hour talking to her insurance adjuster, a slim, humorless man who refused to make any promises or even give her an estimated timeline, Marissa drove over to the sheriff's office to pick up the flyers.

Rayna came out to greet her the instant she walked in. "You look fantastic," she said, giving Marissa a quick hug.

"Thanks. So do you."

Rayna reached for a large envelope on the reception desk. "Here are ten of the flyers. I've asked one of my deputies to get them put out all up and down Main Street. I'm wondering if you would mind stopping at some of the businesses that are on the outskirts of town. Like David's vet clinic."

"I can do that." Marissa smiled. "Oh, and by the way, David and I finally broke up."

Instantly, Rayna's expression changed. "Honey, I'm so sorry. I'll take the flyers over to his clinic. I don't want you to feel uncomfortable."

"That's okay. I don't mind doing it. David and I agreed to stay friends. It was all very friendly."

This made Rayna shrug. "If you're sure."

"I am."

Rayna studied her for a moment. "I know I'm kind of

poking my nose in your business, but you don't seem too broken up about it."

"I'm not and neither is David." Marissa shrugged. "He and I will work much better as friends."

The phone rang. Rayna sighed. "Two lines at once. I'd better get that. My receptionist called in sick today."

"No problem." Grabbing the envelope, Marissa left.

Once she pulled up to David's veterinary clinic in her new Tahoe, she parked. She sat in her car, wondering if he'd told anyone there that they'd broken up. She definitely didn't want to be the one to tell any of his employees.

Still, as she grabbed one of the flyers, got out and walked toward the entrance, she realized if the opportunity came up, she'd definitely take it. After all, she wanted to make sure there were no misunderstandings. David needed to move on. He'd find his special someone, of that she had no doubt.

And she was actually okay with that.

Entering the clinic, she greeted the receptionist, a young woman named Donna. "Any chance I can speak to David for a minute?" she asked.

Donna checked the schedule. "He's with a patient at the moment, but if you want to wait in one of the exam rooms, I can send him in when he gets done."

"Perfect. This shouldn't take too long," Marissa replied, following the other woman down the short hallway toward waiting room number three.

After the door closed, she took a seat on the wooden bench and looked around. A chart showing how to tell if your pet was overweight decorated one wall. Another contained a giant poster of the various breeds of dogs, grouped into classes. Finally, a cute mash up of various kittens hung on the wall near the sink.

A few minutes later, the door opened and David hurried in.

"Marissa?" Frowning, he eyed her. "Is everything all right? You hardly ever stop by the clinic."

"I'm fine," she said, wondering why he never appeared glad to see her. "I just wanted to ask you to do a small favor."

"Anything," he replied. "What do you need?"

"Do you mind posting this photo for me and Rayna?" she asked. "It's the person who set my house on fire. We're putting them all over town in the hopes that someone can identify them." She slid the glossy eight by ten inch photo over the counter toward him.

When he picked it up and studied it, David's face went ashen. "I believe I recognize that person," he said, his tone as miserable as his expression. "Her name is Taylor. Though I have no idea why she'd do something like this. She doesn't even live here in Getaway."

"She?" Marissa frowned. "You think that's a woman?"

He nodded. "Unfortunately, yes." Swallowing, he looked down at his feet before raising his head to meet her gaze. "I've been seeing someone else."

Immediately she thought of the social media post she'd seen with him and a slender blonde. "I kind of knew," she admitted. "I saw a photo of you two that someone else posted. But why would your girlfriend set my house on fire?"

"She's not my girlfriend," he corrected automatically. "I mean…"

"Stay on track," Marissa ordered. "Why would this woman burn my home and business down?"

"That, I don't know." He studied the photo again. "She's

very…er, passionate. Dramatic, even. But I wouldn't have thought she'd do something so awful."

"How sure are you that it's her?" she asked. "Because we need to let Rayna know so she can be brought in for questioning."

"I'm pretty damn certain." Handing the picture back, he grimaced. "I bought her that hoodie she has on. See the embroidered paw print on the front?"

Squinting, she could just make out a small paw print. "Is the hoodie the only reason you believe this is her?"

"I wish." His glum expression matched his tone. "But this person has the same build."

Remembering the videos on her phone, Marissa pulled one up. "Take a look at this. If you still think it's her, then we need to let Rayna know."

David watched in silence. When he'd finished, he nodded. "It's her. I'm ninety-nine percent positive. Let's call Rayna now. I'll give her the information so she can go pick her up."

Marissa had thought she'd feel a sense of closure, or victory or something when she knew. Instead, she only felt confused.

"I'm really sorry," he continued. "I don't have any idea why Taylor would do something so awful. She's emotional and impulsive, but I didn't realize she was unstable."

Though this technically wasn't David's fault, Marissa realized she couldn't absolve him to assuage his guilt. His connection to her as well as this Taylor woman put him squarely on the hook.

"I should have broken up with you sooner," Marissa said. "I intended to, but so much craziness happened and…"

Instead of appearing surprised, David nodded. "I know.

We were never going to work. I was so busy, too. I had no business trying to have a relationship with you."

"True. Never mind trying to maintain two relationships." She shook her head. "That came out snarkier than I intended, but it's true."

"You're right." He pulled out his phone and dialed Rayna. Marissa listened as he explained what he'd seen when viewing the photo and video. He gave Taylor's full name and address to the sheriff, as well as where she worked, and ended the call. "Rayna's going to head over there now and take her in for questioning."

"Good." Marissa turned to go.

"Wait," David said. "I'm really sorry."

In no mood to hear anything else he had to say, Marissa jerked her head in a nod and sailed on out the door.

Driving home—er, back to Jared's ranch—she felt as if a heavy weight had been lifted off her shoulders. In fact, when she got there, she burst through the door, eager to tell Jared what she'd learned.

Neither he nor his father were in the house, so she headed out back toward the barn. She found them working together, mucking out a stall.

"Hey!" she called out, almost bursting with the news.

"Hey yourself." Jared grinned at her. "What's up?"

Taking a deep breath, she told them what David had said.

"He had another *girlfriend*?" Jared asked, his expression warring between incredulous and furious. "Seriously?"

She shrugged. "I kind of knew. I saw a pic on a social media post where someone had tagged him."

Jared met her gaze. "You didn't mind?"

"Not at all. I was already planning to break things off

with him." She took a deep breath. "I should have done it then. Maybe my house wouldn't have been set on fire."

"Maybe not, but the important question is why?" Jared's father asked, interrupting. "Just because this David guy is a two-timing jerk, why would his other girlfriend attack you?"

"That's what I don't know," Marissa replied. "I'm hoping Rayna can find out when she questions this Taylor woman."

Shaking his head, the older man mumbled something under his breath and left the room.

Both Jared and Marissa stared after him. Then, for no reason, Marissa burst into tears.

Immediately, Jared crossed the room and gathered her in his arms. He held her, not saying anything, simply letting her cry.

Grateful for his strength, she found herself clinging to him. The feel of his powerful body awakened a need that she'd kept buried deeply inside of her. Just once, she wished she could give into her desire without complications.

"Here." He handed her a tissue.

Grateful, she turned away and wiped her eyes before blowing her nose. Dropping the tissue in the trash, she crossed to the kitchen sink and washed her hands.

When she turned around, she found Jared gazing at her, his expression raw.

"Marissa…"

The longing in his voice made her catch her breath.

"I want you," he said. "I always have."

Slowly, she nodded, attempting a smile. "I know."

This made him chuckle. "I also think you want me, too."

She went silent, afraid if she admitted to the near constant desire, she'd be starting something she wasn't sure she could finish. The kind of relationship she'd had with David had been safe, albeit a little boring. But at least she'd known that being with him could never really hurt her.

Unlike Jared. She knew beyond a shadow of doubt if she opened her heart to him and let him in, she'd be giving him the power to destroy her. She'd been through that once. She wasn't sure she could survive it again.

Of course, she said none of this. Because giving him that knowledge would be handing over far too much power. There were some truths she needed to keep to herself.

Chapter Fourteen

Jared had felt Marissa tremble in his arms. He'd heard the quick catch of her breath before she'd moved away. Patient for once, he'd waited, letting her see how badly he wanted her. And then, just when he thought she might reach for him, her expression shut down.

Aching, he took another step toward her. If she wanted promises, he could make them. He'd give her anything, everything, if he could help her understand how much he cared for her.

Then, just when he'd begun to lose hope, she closed the distance between them and kissed him. Not a tentative press of her lips, but a kiss full of demands, of desire. Instantly, his ever-present need roared to life. He slanted his mouth across hers, taking, tasting and giving back as good as he got.

Drowning.

Damn, he'd dreamed of this. For years, it seemed. Ever since he'd made the colossal mistake of choosing rodeo over her.

"You're no longer my patient," she murmured, her lips against his.

"I'm not," he agreed.

She slid her hands under his shirt, lifting it up and off

him. He let her take the lead, knowing he'd go as slow or as fast as she wanted.

But damn, judging by the size of his arousal, he'd have hell keeping himself under control.

Still, he could hardly wait for her to reach for his belt.

Instead, she explored his chest. Not only with her small and soft hands, but with her mouth. He sucked in his breath as she closed her mouth over his nipple.

Hearing, she chuckled and continued her leisurely exploration.

When she finally slipped her hands under his belt, he groaned out loud. His body strained at the tightness of his clothing. As she loosened his belt and his jeans, she looked up at him with heat in her gaze and smiled. "I remember this."

Suddenly, he reconsidered letting her take the lead. He reached for her, intending to remove her clothing, but she swatted his hand away. "Not yet."

He knew he could persuade her. But he also knew that for this, their first time together in over five years, it was imperative that he get this right. Teeth clenched, he dropped his hands, keeping them by his sides.

Then, as she closed her hands around the swollen, hard length of him, he let out his breath in a hiss. "Slow," he managed, not wanting to lose control before they even began. One stroke and he shuddered. "No. Not this way. It's been too long."

Heat flashed in her eyes as she registered his words.

"I want to be inside you," he rasped. "And feel the warm wetness of your body all around me."

"Me, too," she told him, her voice as hoarse with desire as his. With one swift motion, she removed her shirt, and then her sneakers, socks and jeans, finally standing in front of him in a purple bra and matching panties.

"You're gorgeous," he said, meaning it.

"Come here," she replied, opening her arms.

They had no bed, no blanket. Only the desk chair and the desk. For their first time reuniting their bodies, he wished for a soft mattress and satin sheets.

"The desk," she said, correctly interpreting his thoughts.

As she reached for him, he remembered he still kept a condom in his wallet. "Wait," he told her, getting it and fumbling to put it on. She came and helped him, her mouth on his, kissing him until he could hardly think.

When they finally broke apart, they were both breathing heavily.

With a sexy grin, she climbed up onto the desk, tugging him over to her. He stroked her with his fingers to make sure she was ready. The instant he came into contact with her wet, warm center, she arched her back and moaned. "I need you inside me," she gasped. "Now!"

Needing no further urging, he entered her in one swift move. Her liquid warmth sheathed him. The perfect fit of their bodies together felt like coming home.

"Don't move," he rasped, afraid he would shatter into a million pieces. "Not yet. Give me a minute."

Ignoring his plea, she flashed him another sexy grin and lifted her hips, allowing him deeper inside her. Slowly, she rotated her hips, riding him as he stood in front of her.

He hoped his knees didn't buckle. "You feel good," he managed to gasp, using every ounce of willpower he possessed not to let go.

"You, too." They kissed again, tongue to tongue, the taste of her so erotic, so familiar and beloved that his throat ached.

She swiveled her hips, rotating her body around his. Unable to hold back any longer, he went deep and fast and hard, claiming her even as she possessed him.

When her release came, she shuddered around him, clenching with an exquisite tightness that damn near destroyed him. He gave up his tenuous grip on control an instant later, reaching the kind of climax that he'd only ever shared with her.

After, they clung to each other for a moment. He breathed in the scent of her, his heart full. There were a hundred things he wanted to say, and he could speak none of them. So he held on, and in his heart of heart, hoped there would be many more times like this.

Marissa took a deep breath, and then moved away. Scooting around to the other side of the desk, she stood. Avoiding his gaze, she gathered up her clothing. "That was a mistake," she said, her voice flat.

"No, it wasn't." He wasn't sure how he knew, but he understood if he didn't convince her now, he might never be able to. "I can't think of a single reason why we shouldn't be together."

"I can." She lifted her chin and looked at him. The despair in her gaze hit him like a punch in the gut. "How do I know you won't go off chasing another dream and leaving me here alone again?"

"Because I won't." Reaching for her, he stopped himself and shook his head. "I promise."

His words made her freeze. "Don't make empty promises that you can't keep. You forget, I know you, Jared Miller. I've known you for what seems like almost my whole life. Right now, you're back in town, taking care of your father, getting the ranch up and running. But you have a wandering soul, and eventually you'll become restless."

Though he wanted to tell her he'd gotten all that out of his system, he understood that to her, words meant nothing. Actions were what counted. "I'll show you," he said. "No matter how long it takes. We are meant to be together, Marissa. And I'll prove it to you."

She jerked her head in a quick nod. "You do that."

With that, she left the office and headed for the house. Leaving him naked and hopeful for what felt like the first time in a very long time.

Finally, he got dressed and stretched. A hot shower before bed would do the trick. At least tonight, if he dreamed of her, he'd know the reality would far exceed his imagination.

The next morning, he woke with a smile on his face. Heading to the kitchen for coffee, he stopped in the doorway, surprised. Marissa and his father sat together at the kitchen table, steaming cups of coffee in front of them. Heads bent, they poured over a stack of papers. Though Marissa flushed when she saw him, she gave no other indication that their lovemaking the day before had impacted her in any way.

Which was okay, since he didn't want his father to know.

"Good morning," his dad said, taking a sip from his mug. "We're looking over the information I printed out on equine therapy."

"It's fascinating," Marissa agreed happily. "I'm beginning to think this idea just might work."

"Of course it's going to work." The older man poked her shoulder in a playful gesture. "We'll be the only operation like this anywhere near here. Think about how many kids we can help."

"I am." Marissa practically glowed. Jared could hardly tear his gaze away from her. Then, realizing they both were eyeing him as if he'd lost his mind, he forced himself to turn away and make for the coffee pot.

Once he'd gotten his own cup, he took a seat at the table. "Do you mind if I take a look?"

"Not at all." J.J. slid a few papers toward him. "It's really interesting information."

Marissa barely looked up, either too engrossed in her own article to pay much attention to anything else or wanting to avoid him.

Jared began reading. His father had definitely done his research. "This is good stuff," he said, once he'd finished.

Marissa finally met his gaze and nodded. "I agree. I really think we could make this happen." Expression animated, she stood and went to get another cup of coffee. "Not only would it be a dream come true for me, but I believe your ranch could definitely benefit. And there are so many people, especially kids, who could definitely benefit from this kind of therapy."

Watching her, with her eyes sparkling from excitement, Jared felt a glow of happiness. He stood and held out his hand. "Partners, then?"

With only the slightest hesitation, she slid her hand into his. "Partners," she agreed.

At that moment, Jared knew all would be all right with them. Reluctantly, he released her hand and returned to his spot at the table. As he reached for another article, his cell phone rang. He didn't recognize the number, but went ahead and answered it, anyway.

"Jared Miller? This is Cliff Blackstock with the PRCA."

Professional Rodeo Cowboys Association. Interesting.

Over the years, Jared had cultivated a few friendships in the group carefully, to maintain good connections. Still, he had no idea why this man would be calling him.

"What can I do for you, Cliff?" Jared asked, mildly curious.

"We've been reviewing a few of the videos you sent in and we wanted to make you a job offer."

Stunned, for a moment Jared wasn't sure he understood. Yes, he'd made some videos and sent them in, but that had been well over two years ago. Even then, he'd been looking for another job where he could still be around the rodeo but not risk life and limb.

"A job offer?" he asked, when he finally found his voice.

"Yessir. We just so happen to have an opening for a sports broadcaster with the Cowboy Channel and Wrangler Network. You'd be on the road a lot, but about the same as you've been. The job is based out of Colorado, so you'd have to relocate, but I think you'll find the salary more than compensates for that." And then Cliff named a number that made Jared swallow hard.

"I'd like a few days to think this over," Jared replied on autopilot, though he managed to sound steady and unruffled.

"That'll be just fine. You can call me back with your decision on this number."

"I'll do that," Jared agreed. Once he'd ended the call, he looked up to find both his father and Marissa staring at him.

"What was that all about?" his dad asked. Marissa said nothing, but Jared could tell by the tightening of her lips that she had a pretty good idea.

He'd chosen his career over her once. No doubt she figured he'd do the same again.

"Just a job offer," Jared finally replied. "Nothing big."

"Yet you told him you'd have to think about it," Marissa pointed out. "So it must have been somewhat decent. What was it?"

Damn. If he told the truth about the offer, she'd immediately realize he'd just been offered his dream job. She knew him that well. This was the kind of career he'd only dreamed about, even when they'd been together in college. Rodeo had been secondary, another path with an eye toward experience, though the older and wiser he'd become, the more he'd begun to realize he should have stayed in college and gotten that degree in journalism.

He didn't want to tell her. Especially since he hadn't even had a moment to consider or to plan. He knew what she'd believe, even if he tried to tell her otherwise. Worse, he didn't want to see her expression change, the pain replace happiness in her eyes when he gave her the answer.

Yet he'd sworn never to lie to her, and he wouldn't start now.

Waiting, Marissa put her coffee down on the counter and crossed her arms. "Well?" she asked.

"Sports announcer on the Cowboy Channel and Wrangler Network," he answered, trying to sound low-key. "I'm not sure if he was talking radio or television. We didn't actually get into details."

Expressionless, she nodded. Still watching him closely, she appeared to be waiting for him to say something else.

"That's amazing," his father chimed in, oblivious to the undercurrents swirling in the room. "You always wanted to be a rodeo broadcaster, even as a child. How'd your name come to their attention?"

"I sent in some videos a few years ago," he replied,

scratching his head. "Honestly, I never gave them another thought. I can't believe they called me out of the blue."

"And at a time when you've been trying to figure out how to keep the ranch afloat," his dad continued. "I have to say, this sounds like it might be more profitable than running an equine therapy operation."

Jared winced. "They did offer a substantial amount of money," he said. "But money isn't the only consideration that matters for me. Equine therapy would be a way to put my horse skills to work and help others." And he'd be here at home, with his father and with Marissa. "Plus, I really think with Marissa's help, I'd be damn good at it."

"You would," Marissa agreed, her voice as hard as her expression. "As would I. Too bad I doubt you'll ever really give it a shot."

"Why do you say that?" Jared asked, though he knew.

"That kind of job involves a lot of traveling," she replied. "You wouldn't be here long enough to do much of anything else."

With that, she turned on her heel and left the room. A moment later, the front door slammed.

"Is she right about that?" J.J. asked.

Jared nodded.

"And that's why she's so mad?" Then, as the realization dawned on him, J.J. swore. "She thinks you're going to bail on her again, doesn't she?"

Miserable, Jared nodded.

"Well, are you?" his dad demanded. "I'm guessing there's no way you can take this job and still run your equine therapy thing?"

Taking a deep breath, Jared tried to speak past the lump in his throat. It took him a second. "There isn't. If I accepted their offer, I'd have to relocate to Colorado. And there'd be a lot of traveling, following the rodeo circuit, just like Marissa said."

"I see." Now his father watched him intently, his expression revealing nothing of his thoughts. "It doesn't sound like there'd be much time for any kind of family life either. Which is a shame, because I was hoping for a few grandchildren before I get too far gone."

Grandchildren? Jared stared, stunned, which made the older man chuckle.

"It's okay, son," J.J. said, squeezing Jared's shoulder. "You're a grown man and can make your own choices. Just one word of advice from me and that's it." He took a deep breath. "Don't screw this up again." With that, he took off, leaving Jared alone in the kitchen.

DRIVING DOWN THE country roads, Marissa could barely see past her tears. Once again, she'd allowed herself to believe, to have hope, to dream of a future. Jared had claimed he was putting down roots, that he'd be staying in Getaway to take care of his father. He'd even suggested starting an equine therapy place, a dream that she'd long ago relegated to the back of her mind.

It had been then that she'd actually finally allowed herself to begin dreaming of a possible life with him. Ha! Which proved she'd only been fooling herself.

Once more, Jared wasn't the staying kind. And she'd managed to let him break her heart a second time.

Never again, she vowed, wiping at her tears. She might have lost everything, but she'd survive and emerge even stronger. She didn't need Jared to have a successful, and maybe even happy, life.

A pickup truck came down the road, going a little too fast for a pitted gravel road. Marissa pulled as far over to the side as she could, her right wheels digging into the dirt shoulder.

As the other vehicle drew closer, it slowed and instead of passing her, pulled up alongside her. Maybe the driver was lost, Marissa thought, noting the significant front-end damage to the truck. She rolled down her window and the pickup did the same. A woman wearing sunglasses and a baseball cap motioned at the surrounding fields.

"I think I took a wrong turn," she said, confirming Marissa's earlier suspicion. "Can you tell me how to get back to Getaway?"

Then, before Marissa could answer, the woman produced a pistol, aiming it directly at her. "Get out," she ordered. "Or I'll shoot you in the head."

In that instant, Marissa realized who this must be. Taylor, David's other girlfriend. "Taylor?" she asked. "It's you, isn't it?"

"How do you know my name?" Though clearly surprised, the hand holding the gun never wavered.

"David told me. Did you know he and I broke up?" While she spoke, Marissa reached for her phone. She dialed 911 and hoped the other woman wouldn't hear when the operator answered.

"What?" Taylor's mouth tightened. "When? He hasn't said anything to me."

"911. What's your emergency?" a voice said. Luckily, it wasn't too loud.

Instead of answering, Marissa continued speaking to Taylor, directing her own line of questioning. "Why are you doing this, Taylor? I've never done anything to you.

Yet you totaled my other Tahoe and burned my home and office down. Now you're threatening me with a weapon."

"Because you took what's mine," Taylor snarled. "I ought to kill you right now and be done with it."

"And what would that get you?" Marissa asked, keeping her voice gentle. "I've already broken up with David. He's free. And if you murder me, you'll go to prison. David will find someone else."

"You don't know that," Taylor said. "You have no idea how he feels about me."

Deliberately casual, Marissa shrugged. "No. But I still fail to see what you would gain. I'm assuming all these attacks against me were to get me out of David's life. Well, I'm out. You can leave me alone now."

"Ma'am? Are you there?" the 911 dispatcher asked.

"Get Rayna," Marissa muttered, hopefully low enough that Taylor didn't hear. "Taylor?" she prompted, raising her voice. "Just go. Don't do something you're going to regret."

Taylor didn't move nor lower the gun. The sunglasses hid her eyes, which meant Marissa had no idea what she might be thinking.

At that point, Marissa realized she might shoot, anyway, since it appeared increasingly obvious that she wasn't entirely of sound mind. Maybe she felt as if she needed to finish what she'd started.

David definitely wasn't worth this kind of fanatical devotion. If he truly cared about this woman, he wouldn't have kept seeing Marissa on the side. And vice versa.

"You need to die," Taylor declared. "I'm going to have to kill you."

Time to go. Since Marissa had never shifted into park,

she could stomp on the accelerator and take her chances that way. Better than sitting still and remaining an easy target.

Heart pounding, Marissa took a deep breath. *Now or never,* she thought. Slamming her foot down hard, she ducked down as the Tahoe jumped forward.

Though she'd been expecting it, Marissa still jumped when Taylor squeezed off a shot, shattering the back window right behind the driver's side.

Good thing she wasn't a good shot.

"Damn." Still crouched low, but trying to keep her eyes on the road, Marissa kept going.

Several more shots, fired in rapid succession, hit the Tahoe. Her new vehicle. "That insurance company is going to cancel me."

Glancing in the rearview, she realized Taylor had turned her pickup around and was pursuing her.

"Crud." Though Marissa had already reached what she considered an unsafe speed, struggling to keep the Tahoe under control on the gravel, she pushed the accelerator harder. If she wrecked, she knew she'd be as good as dead.

"Marissa?" Rayna's voice came on over the phone. With both hands tight on the steering wheel, Marissa didn't dare reach for her phone.

"Rayna, I can't pick up," Marissa shouted. "I'm on FM 3033, driving north. Taylor shot at me. Right now, she's pursuing me. If I can get to the main road, I should be good. I can outrun her. I hope."

"I'm on the way," Rayna replied.

"Hurry."

Ahead, the road curved. She could go left or she could go right. The ranch, and Jared, were to the right. The main road that led to Getaway was to the left. Since she didn't want to endanger anyone else, she knew which way she'd go.

The Tahoe fishtailed as she took the turn too fast. Easing up slightly on the accelerator, she managed to keep the vehicle under control.

Behind her, Taylor's pickup appeared to be gaining on her. How, she had no idea. Unless Taylor had something heavy in the bed, that truck had to be harder to keep under control on this road than the Tahoe.

"But what do I know," she muttered out loud.

The main road, which was paved, should be coming up soon. She wouldn't dare stop at the stop sign, so she really hoped no other vehicles would be coming. Luckily, she had an unobstructed view of traffic from both directions. And right now, the only thing even remotely close was a large semitruck pulling a trailer. She'd have enough time and distance to pull out before it reached the intersection.

She hoped.

Either way, she doubted Taylor would. Hopefully, the other woman would realize this and abort her pursuit.

Approaching the stop sign, Marissa slowed just enough to make the turn. When she hit the blacktop, her tires grabbed and she shot forward, stepping on the accelerator.

In the rearview, she watched in horror as Taylor made no attempt to slow or stop, even though there was absolutely no way she would be able to clear the tractor trailer.

The semi driver laid on his horn, but Taylor kept going, blowing through the stop sign and skidding sideways onto the highway. With no time to swerve or stop, the large truck plowed right into her, smashing her pickup before sending it rolling over and over into the field.

Shaking, Marissa pulled over to the shoulder. She reached

down and picked up her phone. Her hands trembled so much she could barely hold the phone. Since the call had dropped, once again she dialed 911. "There's been a horrible accident," she told the operator. Then, catching sight of flashing lights from Rayna's cruiser, she swallowed. "The sheriff just arrived. I'm sure she'll call in an ambulance."

Without waiting for a response, Marissa ended the call. She got out of her Tahoe on unsteady legs and met Rayna halfway.

"Go back to your vehicle," Rayna ordered, already on the radio. "This looks like it's going to be bad."

The truck driver, having also pulled over after the crash, came running over. A short, heavyset man wearing a Texas Rangers baseball cap, he was breathing hard. "That pickup pulled right out in front of me," he said, his voice cracking. "I swear, there was nothing I could do to avoid hitting it." He pointed at Marissa. "You saw, didn't you? You're my witness. Tell her."

All Marissa had energy to do was nod. "I saw."

"I've called for an ambulance," Rayna told him, her steady voice professional and in control. "Could you come with me and see if the other driver survived? If so, I'm going to need help getting her out."

"Her?" The man blinked, then shook his head. "Sure. I can help you."

As he walked off with the sheriff toward the wrecked pickup truck, Marissa started to follow them. Rayna glanced at her over her shoulder and shook her head. "Go back to your vehicle, Marissa. Wait there. An ambulance should be here soon and I want you to get checked out."

Marissa stopped and nodded. "Okay," she replied. "I can do that." She didn't want to see what had happened to Taylor, anyway. Stumbling slightly, she turned to make her way back to the Tahoe.

"If you want to call someone, do that," Rayna called back to her. "I'm thinking you should have Jared come and sit with you until the ambulance arrives."

Since Rayna had turned away, Marissa didn't have to tell her that Jared would be the last person she wanted to call right now.

Except she wanted him. Needed him. Only the feel of his strong arms around her would make her feel better. Which would somehow also make her feel worse.

Unable to stop shaking, she figured she was probably in shock. Somehow, she made it back to her truck. She sat, refusing to pull out her phone and dial his number. Tears stung her eyes. Though Taylor had tried to kill her, not once, but three times, Marissa would much rather have seen the other woman arrested and put on trial. She shouldn't have died.

A few minutes later, the ambulance arrived, along with a fire truck and one of Rayna's deputies. Marissa watched as the paramedics rushed over to the wrecked pickup. The deputy used his vehicle, lights flashing, to block off one lane of traffic, as well as put out cones.

Marissa put her head down on the steering wheel and wept.

Chapter Fifteen

Jared's first instinct when his phone rang was not to answer it, figuring it would be Marissa. He hadn't made any attempt to go after her, aware she'd need alone time. They needed to talk, for sure, but he wanted to wait until neither had high emotions running.

Truth be told, while the job offer seemed like the chance of a lifetime, he'd already decided what he wanted. Marissa and the ranch. His father mentioning grandchildren had made him realize he could have it all, and a family of their own, if Marissa was willing.

Luckily, he glanced at the screen. Seeing Rayna's name, he answered immediately.

"There's been a horrible accident," Rayna said, her voice rushed. "I need you to come look after Marissa. She's pretty shook up."

His heart stopped right there in his chest. "Is she all right?" he asked.

"In shock, I think." Clearly distracted, Rayna said something to someone else. "Can't talk now. FM 3033, heading north from your place." And then, before he could ask anything else, she ended the call.

He took off running, jumped in his truck and headed

out. When he saw the flashing lights ahead, he swallowed back a jolt of pure terror. A fire truck and a police cruiser blocked over the other lane of traffic. An ambulance, too, lights still flashing.

Spotting Marissa's Tahoe on the shoulder, he pulled over behind it. He got out and hurried over to the driver's side, where he found Marissa hunched over the steering wheel, her shoulders shaking. She didn't seem to realize she had company.

"Marissa," he called, tapping lightly on the window.

She jumped, lifting her face to him. Her eyes were red and swollen, her face streaked with tears. Trying her door handle, he opened the door and gathered her close. "What happened, honey?" he asked.

Her words tumbled out, running together. "David's other girlfriend Taylor shot at me and then chased me. She ran the stop sign and pulled out right in front of that big truck. I think she's dead."

"You're all right?" he asked, holding her tight. "You weren't hit or anything, were you?"

She shook her head no. "I'm okay," she mumbled.

Beyond the ambulance, he could see the twisted metal of what had once been a pickup. Two paramedics loaded a body, covered with a sheet, into the back of the ambulance and they drove off. A moment later, the fire engine followed.

Meanwhile, Marissa continued to hang on to him for dear life. She'd been through so much, he thought, humbled by her strength. He hated that she'd truly believed he'd leave her.

Rayna and her deputy made their way toward them. Meanwhile, the truck driver climbed back into his truck, though he didn't pull out. Jared wondered what kind of damage he had to his rig and if he'd need a heavy-duty tow truck.

"Marissa?" Rayna called out.

Marissa stiffened, twisting away from Jared before pushing to her feet. "I'm here," she said.

"Did you ask the paramedics to check you out?"

"No." Looking defeated, Marissa shrugged. "I figured they were too busy. And now they've left. I just want to go home, soak in a hot bath and try to rest."

"I think you need to be checked out," Rayna argued. "Maybe Jared can take you by the medical clinic real quick."

"I'm fine," Marissa snapped. "Do I need to give a statement or anything since I'm a witness?"

"Not right now." Rayna glanced over toward the trucker. "I've got his statement and yours from the phone call. He's going to see if his truck is drivable. If not, I'll wait here with him until we can get him taken care of."

"Then I'm going home," Marissa declared.

Jared didn't even think she'd noticed she'd called the ranch home. "I'll follow you," he said. "Are you sure you can drive?"

The look she gave him would have melted metal. Rather than replying, she marched back to her Tahoe, got inside and started the engine.

"You'd better hurry," Rayna pointed out.

Shaking his head, Jared did exactly that. He'd barely climbed into his truck when Marissa pulled out, kicking up gravel. She drove past, heading toward the ranch without a backward glance.

Somehow, he managed to catch up and stay right behind her. When they pulled into the ranch yard, she parked, got out and hurried into the house.

"SOMEONE JUST PULLED into the driveway," his father said, barely looking away from the TV. "I just saw headlights. It's kind of late for a visitor."

Glancing at the vintage clock on the mantel, Jared saw that it was nearly ten o'clock. He shook his head. These days, nothing good came of anyone coming by at night.

"I'll take care of it," he said.

"Don't let them wake Marissa," J.J. warned. "She really needs her sleep."

Jared nodded. "I'll deal with whoever it is outside."

Stepping out onto the front porch, he watched as a large pickup truck pulled in front of the house and parked. Custer Black, he realized, wondering if he should call Rayna.

"Jared, my man." Custer jumped out and strode over, hand outstretched. "It's been a bit. How are you?"

Typical Custer. Acting as if they'd never had a falling out. After shaking hands, Jared motioned for Custer to walk with him toward the barn. "Marissa's asleep," he said. "And my father has threatened my life if I let anyone wake her up."

"Marissa?" Custer whistled. "That was fast. I always knew you two would probably get back together, but it hasn't been more than a couple of weeks and now you're living together?"

Jared stared. "You haven't been home yet, have you?"

"Naw. I'm just now getting back to town. Your place was on the way home, so I thought I'd pop in and catch up."

Jared cursed. "Come with me. I've got a lot to tell you."

Inside the barn, Jared motioned toward a couple of bales of hay. "Have a seat."

Once he'd filled Custer in on everything that had happened, reminding him of the accident the night Custer had stood them up for drinks, then the fire, though he stopped before telling him about earlier in the day.

Custer whistled. "Damn. Poor Marissa. She's been through a lot." As he considered, hurt flashed across his face. "I can't believe y'all really thought I'd run into Marissa and then take off. You know me better than that."

"You're right." Jared spread his arms. "But when I tried to talk to you about it and asked to see your truck, you stormed off. Even after that, you wouldn't answer texts or return phone calls. And you just up and disappeared."

Though normally smiling, Custer looked grave. "That's how I am and what I do. You know that. Heck, right after you practically accused me of causing a hit-and-run on Marissa, I got a call to go check out a horse in Amarillo. I was so mad, I decided not to show you my truck, which wasn't damaged by the way, and I left town. Halfway there, I realized I'd left my new phone, so I stopped and got a temporary one." He shrugged. "I'd just dropped a bundle of money on that new phone, so a temporary one with a different number was the only solution."

Which made sense. But still…

"Why didn't you check in with anyone?" Jared asked.

"Like who?"

"Me. Or your parents." Exasperated and trying not to show it, Jared shrugged. "I'm thinking they might have been worried."

"That's doubtful. They're used to me coming and going. And I was pretty pissed at you. No way did I want to call you." He spread his hands. "You can understand that, can't you? You'd be the same way if the situation was reversed."

"Maybe so," Jared replied. "But you should know Rayna's been wanting to talk to you. I know she stopped by and talked to your folks."

Instead of appearing alarmed, Custer frowned. "Don't tell me you had the sheriff out looking for me because of that accident. I already told you I wasn't involved."

"There were a lot of unanswered questions. Plus, you were talking like you had a serious grudge against Marissa."

"Damn." Custer swallowed. "I was just mad because I wasn't healing the way I thought I should be. But like I said, it wasn't me. I would never do anything like that."

"I'm glad." Jared clapped his friend on the shoulder. "We kind of figured that out."

"I'm glad to hear it. I'm guessing that you caught the guy?"

"Girl." Jared filled him in on what had happened earlier in the day. "Unfortunately, she was killed in that accident. We may never know why she did all this."

"Wait. David's other girlfriend?" Expression astonished, Custer shook his head. "This gets stranger by the minute. I'm guessing that's how you and Marissa ended up together."

"We're not together," Jared explained, allowing his regret to show in his voice. He went ahead and told Custer about the job offer, emphasizing he planned to turn it down and that Marissa didn't believe him.

"Turn it down?" Custer exclaimed. "That's always been your dream job. Why the hell would you want to let something like that go?"

Jared shrugged. "There are a lot of reasons. First and foremost is the fact that I don't want to leave Marissa or Getaway again. And my father needs me."

"That doesn't make sense," Custer scoffed. "You only get one shot like this. I think you should go ahead and take it. If Marissa truly loved you, she'd be willing to go with you wherever you go."

"Thanks, man. But my mind is already made up." To his relief, he still felt absolutely no regret. He was ready for the next chapter of his life, and he intended that to be here at his family ranch with Marissa and his father. "I'm ready for a new beginning."

Custer considered him for a moment, before nodding. "I hope you don't regret it."

"I won't," Jared told his friend.

After Custer left, Jared went back inside and found his father had fallen asleep on the couch. He covered the older man with a blanket and then took himself to bed. He'd call that Cliff guy back tomorrow and turn the job down.

The next morning, Jared had just sat down with his first cup of coffee when Marissa walked into the kitchen, looking straight ahead as if trying to pretend he wasn't there.

He smiled at her, willing her to look at him. When she didn't, keeping her back to him while her coffee brewed, he called her name. A slight stiffening of her shoulders was the only indication she gave that she'd heard.

"Please talk to me," he said.

"What's there to talk about?" she asked, finally turning around.

Any other time, her fierce expression would have made him smile. Right now though, he knew that would be a mistake.

"You had an awful day yesterday. I know there was a lot to process, considering what happened. Maybe we could discuss that."

"Ha." The scorn in her voice made him wince. "Why would I want to share anything with you? You're leaving."

"Please. Come sit."

Reluctance showing in every move she made, she carried her coffee over to the table and took a seat.

"I have no intention of leaving, Marissa."

"Really?" The hardness of her gaze indicated she didn't believe him. "Are you saying you've turned the job down then?"

"No, not yet."

Hearing that, she pushed to her feet. "I see. How about this. You let me know if—and when—you do that. Maybe then, we'll have something to discuss. Until then, I'm going to continue to believe that you won't be sticking around long. Just like before."

With that, she grabbed her coffee mug and sailed out of the room.

Jared didn't follow. Since he had to allow for the time difference in Colorado, it was still too early to call. Once he'd done so, he intended to march right into Marissa's room and tell her. After that, he planned to kiss her until they were both senseless.

"Mornin'." His dad came into the kitchen, still rubbing sleep out of his eyes. He went straight to the coffee maker, made himself a cup of his dark roast and took a sip before coming to take a seat across from Jared at the table.

"Good morning," Jared replied.

"How do you plan to fix things with Marissa?" his father asked, his sharp gaze missing nothing. On days like this, it was easy to forget that J.J. had early onset dementia.

When Jared didn't immediately answer, his dad frowned. "Don't tell me you've decided to take the job after all."

"Of course not. Why does everyone assume I'd just up and leave again?"

"Son." J.J. reached across the table and covered Jared's hand with his own. "I don't want you to do anything just because you think you have to. The regrets will eat you alive."

"I know." Jared squeezed his dad's hand back. "I've been through that once. I know what I want this time. I promise you, I won't have regrets." He took a deep breath. "That said, I have a plan and I need your help to make it work."

Leaning in close and keeping his voice low, he told his father what he wanted to do.

RESTLESS AND NEEDING to get away from Jared and the ranch, Marissa decided to go into town, do a little shopping and maybe have an early lunch at the Tumbleweed Café.

Parking on Main Street in front of Lone Star Western Wear, she got out. Her first stop would be to purchase a new pair of boots, since her beloved old pair had been lost in the fire.

Hester Lindgren's weathered face lit up when Marissa walked inside. "I'm so happy to see you," she exclaimed. She'd been selling Western wear at Lone Star for as long as Marissa could remember.

Marissa told her what she'd come for and Hester invited her to browse. "If you need any help, hon, you just holler."

It didn't take long for Marissa to find the exact pair she wanted. Trying them on, she walked up and down the carpeted aisle and examined them in one of the low mirrors. Then she put her sneakers back on and carried the boots to the back counter.

"Perfect." Hester beamed. "Hey, I heard the news about Jared Miller. Custer Black was in here earlier and spilled the beans."

"News?" Marissa asked, her heart sinking. "You mean about the job offer?"

"Exactly! That boy will make a great rodeo announcer, don't you think?"

Swallowing hard, Marissa somehow managed to hide her dismay. It never ceased to amaze her how quickly gossip traveled in a small town like Getaway. "He sure will," she said, as brightly as she could.

After stowing the boots in her Tahoe, Marissa decided to walk down to Serenity's shop.

"Marissa!" Serenity exclaimed, drifting from the back to greet her. Today, the shop smelled like vanilla and cinnamon, much more pleasant than the heavy incense Serenity used favored. "So good to see you. What can I do for you today?"

Realizing she had no good reason for stopping by, Marissa shrugged. "I just wanted to come and say hello. You were certainly right about change coming to my life."

"And then some." Serenity hugged her, multiple bracelets jingling. "I'm so sorry about the accident and the fire, but I can promise you it will all work out for the best. I foresee great things ahead for you."

This time, Marissa couldn't even summon a smile. "I certainly hope you're right. It's difficult to see a rosy future at this point."

"I can tell you that it will get better. Which is exactly what I said to your former beau when he stopped by this morning."

"David?" Startled, Marissa stared. "He came to see you. That's not like him."

"No, it's not," Serenity agreed. "But he seemed pretty distraught over that woman who died in that horrific wreck with the semi. He said while he wasn't in love with her, he couldn't understand the things she'd done and the way she'd died."

Marissa nodded. "I can relate to that. I think I'll probably have nightmares about that accident for a long time to come."

"That's understandable." Patting Marissa's hand, Serenity offered her a cup of tea.

"Another time, maybe," Marissa said. "I've got a bit more shopping to do. I'm hoping retail therapy can help me clear my mind."

"Retail therapy is the best kind," Serenity replied, grinning. "I hope you'll stop by again."

Marissa promised she would.

After leaving Serenity's, she wandered up and down both sides of Main Street, stopping into more than a few shops, making several purchases and hearing all about Jared's exciting new job opportunity. Most people seemed genuinely happy for him, though she noticed a few eyeing her as if hoping for a dramatic reaction.

She stopped by Adam's hair salon, but he wasn't in.

By the time she finally got back into her vehicle, she had numerous shopping bags to stow in the backseat with her new boots. She sat for a few minutes, trying to decide if she really wanted to stop by the Tumbleweed for lunch and endure another round of gossip. Her stomach growled, letting her know she needed to eat.

Inside the café, she sat at the lunch counter, hoping that having her back to the room would discourage a lot of small talk. She ordered a grilled chicken salad, one of her favorites, and ate it as quickly as she could. She supposed she lucked out, because only two people came up to her and mentioned Jared and his incredible good fortune. Though he'd been gone for five years, he was still a Getaway native, and folks appeared to love him.

Finally, she paid her check and drove back to the ranch. As she carried her bags into the house, she saw no sign of Jared, which she considered a good thing.

J.J. sat in his usual place in the recliner, though he muted the television when she came in.

"Marissa, can I ask you a favor?" Jared's father smiled at her, his smile so reminiscent of Jared's that it made her heart ache.

"Anything," she replied, meaning it. "You've been more than kind to me, letting me stay in your house and eating your food, refusing to allow me to repay you."

"I'd like you to take me to The Rattlesnake Pub tonight," he said, still smiling. "And have a beer with me while we're there. Jared's going to make some sort of announcement."

Her heart sank. It took every bit of self-control she possessed to keep her face expressionless. While she'd do anything for Jared's father, being forced to sit and listen while Jared told the entire town about his new career opportunity would be stretching it. Especially since it appeared everyone already knew.

Nevertheless, she'd straighten her spine and endure experiencing the heartbreak all over again, one last time.

"The entire town has been talking about Jared," she told him, her voice remarkably steady. "Somehow, word leaked out about his fantastic job offer."

"Hmm." J.J. shook his head. "That's not surprising. I think we need to dress up a little, since this is such a special night. Do you think you could get us there around six?"

"I can." Somehow, she managed to smile.

An hour later, she stood in front of her closet, wishing she had something nicer to wear. All of her clothes had been lost in the fire. She'd bought mostly jeans and comfy tops to wear around the ranch and scrubs to wear once she started working again.

She hadn't purchased anything dressier. If she was going to be publicly dumped, she wanted to at least look good. She made a snap decision to drive into town and stop by Three Ladies Boutique, a new women's clothing store that had recently opened. Surely, she could find something cute to wear there.

Two hours later, back at the ranch with two new dresses and a pair of sexy high heels, she felt slightly better. She'd forgotten how helpful retail therapy could be. She'd even purchased a pair of dangly earrings and a bracelet.

"I'm glad you're back," J.J. mumbled from his recliner as she walked into the house carrying her shopping bags. "I got worried you were going to forget about me."

"Forget about you?" She kissed his cheek. "I would never do that. I promised to take you, didn't I?"

He beamed up at her. "Yes, you did. And I need to start figuring out what I'm going to wear."

Startled, she glanced at her watch. Time had flown by. "Me, too," she said. "I bet it's going to take me a bit longer than you."

This made him laugh. "I imagine it will. It's time to start getting ready for our night of celebration."

Celebration. Not hardly. Still, she managed to keep a smile on her face as she walked past him on her way to her room. No matter how much she might hurt inside, she would make sure J.J. never knew. Or Jared, for that matter. She'd keep her head up and a smile on her face, even if it killed her. And she might as well look damn good while she did it.

She applied makeup, flat ironed her hair and then got dressed. When she finally caught sight of herself in the mirror, she stared. She looked like a completely different person. It had been so long since she'd taken the time and effort to fix herself up, she almost didn't recognize the pretty woman she saw.

And then she remembered the reason she'd done all this and the warm glow inside her evaporated.

Checking her watch, she realized it was nearly time to go. Stepping into her heels, she practiced walking in them before she opened the door to the living room.

J.J. looked up at the sound of her entering the room. "Wow!" Grinning, he pushed to his feet. "You clean up well."

"Ha!" She couldn't help but laugh out loud. "So do you."

"I do, don't I?" He wore a brand-new pair of dark blue jeans, shined up cowboy boots, a button-down Western shirt and a bolo tie decorated with turquoise and silver. "Are you ready to go?"

"I am," she replied. "Lead the way."

Once she'd made sure he'd gotten safely into her Tahoe, she took a seat behind the wheel. As she drove, he kept up a steady stream of chatter—unusual for him—for which she felt really grateful, since it kept her from dwelling in the dark place her thoughts kept wanting to go.

As she turned onto Main Street and caught sight of The Rattlesnake Pub, she realized the parking lot had started to fill. "Looks like a lot of people either wanted an early dinner and a beer, or they came to hear Jared's announcement."

Some of her emotion must have leaked through into her

voice because J.J. reached over and squeezed her shoulder. "You've got this," he said.

"Yes," she replied, trying to make herself believe. "I do."

She started to get out, but J.J. motioned her to wait. Then, he hopped down and hurried over to the driver's side, opening the door for her. "Let me be a gentleman," he said, grinning again as he held out his arm. "It's been a long time since I've had the privilege of escorting a beautiful woman."

Taking his arm, she allowed him to lead her into the pub. The place was already half-full. Many of the regulars occupied their usual seats at the bar, but a lot of the tables were already occupied.

"This way," J.J. said, leading the way to the front. "We have a table reserved just for us."

Sure enough, a four-top right on the edge of the dance floor had a placard on top that read *Reserved*. Great. She'd have a ringside seat while the man she loved broke her heart once again.

"Here you go." J.J. pulled out a chair with a flourish.

With no other choice, she took a seat. She managed to wave to several people she knew, praying they wouldn't come over and want to chat. Since she was just barely holding herself together, she didn't think she'd be up for any small talk.

Luckily, no one did.

A waitress came and took their order. J.J. ordered a Shiner Bock for himself, and a glass of champagne for her. "Actually, just bring an entire bottle," he said.

When Marissa started to protest, he touched the back of her hand. "Indulge me this one time, please?"

Naturally, she couldn't say no. She gave a slow nod, dread

coiling in the pit of her stomach, while she waited for Jared to step up onto the band stage and make his announcement.

"He's not here yet," J.J. said, correctly interpreting what she'd thought were covert glances around the increasingly crowded room. "I think he's planning on making a special appearance."

"I see," she replied. Though she didn't. Ever since the incident with Taylor, she'd been too broken inside to allow anyone close.

Not that Jared hadn't tried. She'd brushed off his every attempt to talk with her, aware her capacity for bullshit had become virtually nonexistent. So help her, if he dared to try and make her feel better about him leaving her yet again, she'd definitely throttle him.

Clearly, them being together wasn't meant to be. The fates had intervened and made sure he'd been offered the job of a lifetime. She couldn't blame him for choosing that over a staid life in a small town with his former high school sweetheart.

What made it worse was he'd presented to her the equine therapy idea, which would have been her dream job. It still would be, if J.J. would still allow her to operate it at his ranch.

Except without Jared by her side, the idea lost a lot of its luster.

The waitress brought their drinks. The room continued to fill. It began to appear that almost the entire town had come to The Rattlesnake Pub tonight. Marissa sipped her champagne very slowly, wondering why so many people had come just to hear Jared announce his new job. Not much else going on, she supposed.

More people waved, all smiling. Feeling as if her face

had been frozen into her fake smile, she waved back. The energy level in the bar felt off the charts for some reason. Looking down at her glass, she was tempted to gulp the champagne to help herself relax. But she'd never had much of a head for the bubbly, and didn't want to do anything she might regret.

Especially when Jared told her, in front of everyone, that he'd be leaving her again. She'd been a fool to unlock her heart against him. She'd allowed herself to believe, especially after they'd made love, that this time, he'd stay.

The room looked to be at capacity when she felt a ripple of energy go through the room. She half turned to see Jared had appeared. Instead of his usual jeans, boots and Western shirt, he wore a navy suit and tie. Marissa couldn't help but stare. She'd never seen him like this. He looked so handsome, her heart stuck in her throat and she thought she might cry.

Not now, she told herself sternly. *Not now, not here, not in front of the entire town.* She'd let Jared have his moment in the spotlight, pretend to celebrate his news, and after it was all over, she'd go back to her temporary bedroom at his family ranch and cry into her pillow.

After her first glance at Jared, she turned away, pretending to focus her attention on the menu. As if she could eat.

"You've got this," J.J. murmured from across the table.

Straightening her shoulders, she dipped her chin. "I do," she confirmed.

As Jared made his way through the packed room, he stopped here and there to talk to well-wishers. She tried not to glance back at him, but she felt her gaze pulled again and again. This last time, their gazes met and he smiled.

Then he winked at her—*winked!*—before turning to speak to someone else who'd called his name.

When Jared reached their table, he stopped to greet them. "Thanks, Dad," he said, smiling. Turning his attention to Marissa, the warmth in his gaze confused her. "I'm so glad you could make it."

A curt nod was the best she could do, but she pulled up a fake smile for the benefit of anyone else who might be watching. Jared Miller might have broken her heart, not once, but twice, but damned if she'd allow anyone in this room to know it.

"Here you go, Jared." A beaming waitress handed Jared a drink. Judging by the amber color, Marissa guessed it was whiskey, something Jared rarely drank. He carried the glass up onto the stage where live bands usually performed. A microphone had been set up and Jared made his way to it.

The noise level in the room rose for a moment before quieting.

"Thank you all for coming," Jared said, clearly at ease in front of a roomful of people. "I asked you here today because I have some very special news and I wanted everyone to hear it directly from me."

Marissa nearly snorted. He must have forgotten how quickly news spread in Getaway. Sitting rigid in her chair, her heart thumping in her chest, she struggled fiercely not to cry.

Instead, she took a big gulp of her champagne and nearly choked. Somehow, she managed to swallow and breathe without making a scene.

"I'm sure by now, more than a few of you have heard rumors of what I'm going to announce." Handsome features animated, his brown eyes sparkled as he glanced around the room.

As he shifted his weight from one foot to the other, Marissa realized he was nervous for some reason.

"I was offered a job as a sports broadcaster with the Cowboy Channel and Wrangler Network," he said. "And while such a thing might appear to be something out of a lifelong dream, my dreams don't include leaving Getaway. Therefore, I turned the job offer down."

A murmur swept through the room as people tried to process their confusion. Jared waited a moment before continuing.

"You see, Marissa, my father, and I have decided to start a new business venture. We've researched it and discussed it and feel an equine therapy ranch for disabled children is exactly what this town needs."

He paused, swallowing hard. "But with Marissa, I want more than simply a business partner. Much more."

Stunned, Marissa couldn't tear her gaze away from him. She trembled as he smiled at her. When he left the stage to move toward her table, she caught her breath.

Every eye in the room on him, when he reached her, Jared dropped to one knee. From his suit pocket, he produced a black velvet box and opened it to reveal a stunning, marquise cut diamond ring.

"Marissa Noll, will you do me the honor of becoming my wife?" he asked, his gaze steady and full of love.

Wiping back tears, all Marissa could do was nod.

"You have to say something, honey," J.J. advised, his expression both gleeful and tender. "Give the boy an answer."

Instead, she asked her own question, her gaze locked with Jared's. "Are you sure?"

Eyes full of love, he smiled. "I'm positive. I want to spend the rest of my life here in Getaway, with you by my side."

"Then my answer is yes," she managed, still not quite believing. "Yes, I'll marry you."

He let out a joyful whoop. Taking her hand, he slipped the ring on her finger, before pulling her into his arms to cover her mouth with his and thoroughly kiss her.

The entire room erupted into cheers. Marissa looked up to see her best friend Adam beaming at her, champagne glass raised. He mouthed *congratulations*, before downing the entire glass. Even Custer was there, standing next to Serenity. They both raised glasses in celebration.

"Another Getaway love story," J.J. announced to everyone.

And Jared kissed Marissa again.

* * * * *

COMING SOON!

We really hope you enjoyed reading this book. If you're looking for more romance be sure to head to the shops when new books are available on

Thursday 11th May

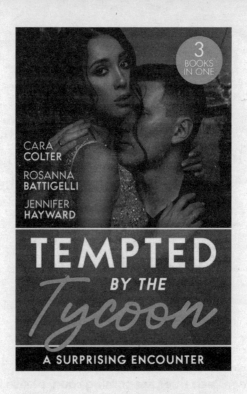

LET'S TALK

Romance

For exclusive extracts, competitions
and special offers, find us online:

- facebook.com/millsandboon
- @MillsandBoon
- @MillsandBoonUK
- @MillsandBoonUK

Get in touch on 01413 063 232

For all the latest titles coming soon, visit
millsandboon.co.uk/nextmonth

MILLS & BOON

THE HEART OF ROMANCE

A ROMANCE FOR EVERY READER

MODERN

Prepare to be swept off your feet by sophisticated, sexy and seductive heroes, in some of the world's most glamourous and romantic locations, where power and passion collide.

HISTORICAL

Escape with historical heroes from time gone by. Whether your passion is for wicked Regency Rakes, muscled Vikings or rugged Highlanders, awaken the romance of the past.

MEDICAL

Set your pulse racing with dedicated, delectable doctors in the high-pressure world of medicine, where emotions run high and passion, comfort and love are the best medicine.

True Love

Celebrate true love with tender stories of heartfelt romance from the rush of falling in love to the joy a new baby can bring, and a focus on the emotional heart of a relationship.

Desire

Indulge in secrets and scandal, intense drama and sizzling hot action with heroes who have it all: wealth, status, good looks…everything but the right woman.

HEROES

The excitement of a gripping thriller, with intense romance at its heart. Resourceful, true-to-life women and strong, fearless men face danger and desire - a killer combination!

To see which titles are coming soon, please visit

millsandboon.co.uk/nextmonth